TRANSCONA LIBRARY
CHILDRE... ...CES
D0456691
WITHDRAWN
...PUBLIC LIBRARY

PRAISE FOR BR...

"*The Farfield Curse* brims with mystery, magic, and fun. Kaleb Nation's wry sense of humor kept me smiling, even while the mystical sparks flew. Get ready for lots of surprises and watch out for gnomes!"

—D. J. MacHale, author of the Pendragon Series

"Whimsy, magic, and suspense collide in this breathtaking tale. *The Farfield Curse* is a story you'll want to pick up, but not put down!"

—Kaza Kingsley, author of the bestselling Erec Rex series

"With characters both silly and serious, Kaleb Nation has crafted a world vastly different from our own where magic sits next to cell phones, and gnomes really do travel. *Bran Hambric: The Farfield Curse* is everything a young adult read should be."

—Kim Harrison, author of Once Dead, Twice Shy

BRAN
HAMBRIC

KALEB NATION

Copyright © 2009 by Kaleb Nation
Cover and internal design © 2009 by Sourcebooks, Inc.
Cover illustration © Brandon Dorman
Cover design by The Book Designers
Bran Hambric title layout and moon logo designed by Kaleb Nation

Sourcebooks and the colophon are registered trademarks of Sourcebooks, Inc.

All rights reserved. No part of this book may be reproduced in any form or by any electronic or mechanical means including information storage and retrieval systems—except in the case of brief quotations embodied in critical articles or reviews—without permission in writing from its publisher, Sourcebooks, Inc.

The characters and events portrayed in this book are fictitious or are used fictitiously. Any similarity to real persons, living or dead, is purely coincidental and not intended by the author.

Published by Sourcebooks Jabberwocky, an imprint of Sourcebooks, Inc.
P.O. Box 4410, Naperville, Illinois 60567-4410
(630) 961-3900
Fax: (630) 961-2168
www.jabberwockykids.com

Library of Congress Cataloging-in-Publication Data

Nation, Kaleb.
Bran Hambric : the Farfield curse / by Kaleb Nation.
p. cm.
Summary: Very strange occurrences have long surrounded fourteen-year-old Bran, who learns of his link to a curse created by his murdered mother and strives to make things right, hindered by the ban on magic in the city of Dunce and pursued by his mother's former masters.
[1. Magic—Fiction. 2. Foster home care—Fiction. 3. Blessing and cursing—Fiction. 4. Fantasy. 5. Youths' writings.] I. Title. II. Title: Farfield curse.
PZ7.N17467Brf 2009
[Fic]—dc22

2009014773

Printed and bound in the United States of America.
BG 10 9 8 7 6 5 4 3 2 1

To Jaden and Brendan and Maddi,
who influenced this book most of all.

CONTENTS

PROLOGUE xiii

PART I

CHAPTER 1
Strange Happenings on Bolton Road 3

CHAPTER 2
Chasing Shadows in the Dark 13

CHAPTER 3
The Creature and His Master 21

CHAPTER 4
The Note in the Grass 30

CHAPTER 5
The Man, the Van, and Dan 44

CHAPTER 6
Secret Letters 57

CHAPTER 7
Sewey Wilomas versus the Oncoming Train 69

CHAPTER 8
The Duncelander Fair 80

CHAPTER 9
The Box in the Bookstore 97

CHAPTER 10
Inside the Hidden Room 115

CHAPTER 11
Another Burglary 124

CHAPTER 12
The Telephone Call 136

PART II

CHAPTER 13
Burglars on Third Street 151

CHAPTER 14
The Man at the Tavern 161

CHAPTER 15
The Name on the Necklace 178

CHAPTER 16
A Path in the Woods 187

CHAPTER 17
Noises in the Kitchen 196

CHAPTER 18
The Man beneath the House 205

CHAPTER 19
The House on Hadnet Lane 217

Chapter 20
The Gnome in the Home 227

Chapter 21
A Room behind the Bookshelf 241

Chapter 22
The Truth 252

Chapter 23
The Face in the Mirrors 260

PART III

Chapter 24
The Girl from the Alley 271

Chapter 25
Lopsis Volgitix 288

Chapter 26
The Good-Bye 300

Chapter 27
The Escape of Rosie Tuttle 312

Chapter 28
The Garage 320

Chapter 29
Inside the Black Van 334

Chapter 30
Fire and Books 343

PART IV

CHAPTER 31
Into the City 359

CHAPTER 32
The Spirit Awakens 373

CHAPTER 33
The Farfield Curse 383

CHAPTER 34
The Battle on Farfield Tower 397

CHAPTER 35
Clarence 409

CHAPTER 36
The Grave of Emry Hambric 419

EPILOGUE 427

Prologue

The night was cold and dead, and so felt Clarence's heart.

He dashed through the darkness, never stopping, always watchful for the men—every passing car making him leap back into the shadows of the trees on the abandoned rural highway. His form was hardly more than a shadow, sweating even in the cold, his face bruised and scarred. With every step, he knew they were gaining on him.

He darted through the mist and onto a deserted side street, lined with thick walls of rock on both sides. His eyes swept the road. He was worn out from a night of running, but he couldn't stop. He had to get to the city before they found him. Or worse, before they found Bran…

Suddenly, there was a burst of light behind him, coming over the hill. He spun, and his eyes flashed, the noise startling him for a second. An engine roared, and he saw the familiar shape of a black van.

"No!" he gasped. He took off in the other direction as the van blasted in pursuit. His shadow was thrown before him, the headlights burning the sweat on his neck. The road cut through the rocks; the rising walls prevented him from going into the woods. He ran faster, panting for breath, his heart pounding in rhythm with his feet slapping against the pavement.

Ahead, there was a flash of motion, a squeal of tires, and a second black van shot out of the shadows. He shouted and turned to run the other way, but the first van tore after him, blocking his escape as the other cornered him. Clarence ran to the wall of rock, desperately digging his fingers into the cracks to climb it, but falling to the pavement when he found he could not.

The vans purred to a stop, standing still and foreboding. The intense headlights trained on his form against the wall, blinding his eyes as he crouched over. He held up his hands to shield his face and heard the doors burst open, two men coming from behind the cover of the windows, their pistols trained on him. He stiffened. Out of the second van came two other men, bald and strong, their faces emotionless and their forms hidden by black coats that swept as far as the ground. Each held in his hand a wand of black metal.

Clarence trembled under their gazes, almost feeling the torturous magic coursing through his body again.

The side door of the first van opened slowly. Clarence whimpered, pressing himself against the rocks. All was quiet as the last man came from the darkness, standing in front of the others. Clarence looked up at him weakly—the man's face was rough, his hair light and to his shoulders, power behind his gaze. His clothes were torn and bloody, as were those of the others. Clarence counted them in the light. There were only five…the police must have caught the rest.

"Running away so soon, are we?" the man said in a soft tone that held poison.

Clarence covered his eyes.

"Wouldn't stick around to help clean up, would you?" the man said louder. "Already tired of the project just because the police break in?"

"Farfield is over..." Clarence managed to hiss, hardly able to breathe. He looked up. "You've already failed, Joris. The police are onto all of you. Baslyn is dead, his spirit is gone...and Emry will hide her son well enough so you'll never bring him back."

"But *you* know where she's taking him," Joris said.

Clarence pulled his head away, refusing to speak. Very slowly, Joris stepped into one of the headlight beams, casting a shadow down upon Clarence.

"You know where he is, don't you?" Joris stated.

Clarence shook his head. No...he wouldn't tell. He would not betray Emry.

"I—I don't know where she's taking him," he stammered, fighting back terror.

Joris narrowed his eyes disbelievingly. "Well then," he said, "we'll just have to...convince you to tell us, won't we?"

"I won't," Clarence choked. "I can't break my promise—the boy is gone. Farfield is over."

Joris gave a dry smile. He leaned down so close his whisper was loud in Clarence's ear.

"Farfield isn't over yet," he hissed. "We're going to find Bran Hambric, and we're going to bring him back."

A freezing wind blew across the alley where Emry Hambric had parked her car. Her windows were down. The cold chilled her face—but not nearly as much as the sudden feeling of dread that crawled across her skin.

"Clarence..." she whispered. Something was desperately wrong. He should have been there by now. She glanced into the backseat: in it was the limp body of a small, six-year-old boy. *My son.*

"I'm sorry," was all she could say. If only the apology could take back years of mistakes, so that maybe she wouldn't be there, running from all she had done...if only she could have lived a few more weeks, she might see herself turn twenty-seven. But she knew in her heart she would not even see the next sunrise. Emry never cried; she was always the strongest—always pretending to be the strongest. But now, as she looked back on her life, and down at the child she loved so much, tears formed in the corners of her eyes. She would never see him again.

"I won't let them get you. I promise."

The moment the whisper left her lips, she felt a start. Her gaze jerked up, out the back window. She had sensed something move—a shadow, or rather the feeling of a shadow, watching her. Someone was coming. And Emry knew who it was.

She's found me.

Emry thought she would be safe in Dunce. No mage would follow her in there, none of the police from outside either. She glanced back at her son. It was too late to run—she'd have to send him elsewhere. There was no more time to waste. She spun around quickly, searching the floor for something to write on. She tried her pockets and finally found an old scrap. Without hesitating she scribbled her note on it.

"This is all I have to give you," she whispered, stuffing it into the little boy's fist and closing his fingers around it. She knew he wouldn't remember anything—her magic was strong enough for that. But at least he would have the note.

She hopped out and threw the back door open, pulling the boy up to her. Much as she longed to, she could not hold him for a second more. The darkness of the alley swept over her as she punched the button on the trunk of the car. The lid swung up, and she pushed her son down into the cramped space.

She reached to her neck, touching the string of a necklace that was hidden under her shirt, but before she could take it out, she heard a scrape far behind her. She jumped forward, slamming the lid shut. Her skin crawled again. Her breath came quickly. She pulled from deep within, drawing on magic. For the magic to work, she needed something that came from the intended destination: a note from a neighbor's house, and he'd materialize there; a shirt, and her son would wake up in a department store. But as every sense within her screamed out in impending danger, her mind drew a blank. In that desperate instant, she flung the magic at the trunk, hoping it would find something to use, anything to send her son from this terrible place.

"*Sideni aywa!*" she gasped out.

She couldn't manage another breath before a hand burst out of the darkness. It caught her by the throat, throwing her backward to the pavement. Her arm scraped against the hard road as she fell.

"You fool."

The woman's voice was harsh. Emry looked up, her back to the ground. She couldn't make out her attacker's form in the dark, but Emry knew who the woman was. Emry heard the click of a gun, but she didn't flinch, didn't speak—she just lay there, bleeding.

"Lock him in the trunk?" the woman said sharply. "You can't hide him from me." She punched the button, and Emry heard the lid pop, sweat forming on her brow.

What if it didn't work? Emry's heart began to beat faster... but then, the woman stopped.

"Where is he?" the woman hissed.

Emry closed her eyes. *He's safe...* She heard the lid slam, and she looked up again.

The woman stood over her. "Where have you sent him?" she hissed.

Emry said nothing.

"You're going to die either way," the woman stated with no emotion. "And we're going to find him either way. It's only a matter of how long it will take."

Emry stared at the end of the pistol. With no traces of magic, the Magic Investigational Police wouldn't even notice the case of a woman's death by bullet, even if they found a way into Dunce.

The woman gave an evil smile. "Who's the powerful one now?"

Emry didn't reply. But slowly, slightly, she forced herself to smile back. And with that, the woman shot.

Emry's body dropped, all strength gone in an instant. Then, with a mocking, vengeful sneer, the woman pulled the trigger again. Another shot rang out, and Emry felt her cheek strike against the pavement.

She slid her fingers on the hard road, struggling to breathe, gripping the black rocks until they stained her fingers. As she lay there, she heard the woman give a small laugh, and saw her legs walking past—leaving her behind to die. The world darkened above Emry, a black cloud drowning out the moonlight like a sheet being pulled over her face. She had known it would end this way.

But at least Bran is safe.

Her eyes started to close as death embraced her. But in that final moment, her gaze fell across the street, and sitting there, hidden in a stack of crates, was a little girl.

The girl's eyes were stained with tears, her face white and trembling.

She had seen it all.

And as the night of April eighteenth passed and the morning came to life, a boy named Bran awoke in the city of Dunce.

Part I

Chapter 1

Strange Happenings on Bolton Road

Eight Years Later

Hanging outside the gates of the city of Dunce was a sign that read:

no gnomes
no mages
etcetera

And if you didn't agree, you had best like jail food. Every other city in the rest of the world allowed gnomes and magic, but for centuries the Duncelanders had proudly stayed the exception. Behind their border wall of brick, the police chief put officers on perpetual watch for any short gnomes wearing tall, conical red hats. Helicopters regularly patrolled the borders, and every good citizen was quick to report anything remotely magic, in case a mage was around. They had orders to report any etceteras as well, if they happened to see one.

Since few people came into Dunce, and even fewer left, rumors about the city grew every year. This notoriety gave birth to streets nearly as infamous—and Bolton Road seemed destined to be the most infamous of them all.

In the thirteenth house on the right side of that street, at eleven o'clock on a Wednesday night, eight-year-old Balder Wilomas dashed into his parents' bedroom, claiming he had heard a burglar struggling with the front door. Sewey Wilomas sent him right back to bed with no more scary movies for a week. Five minutes later, in came Baldretta, Balder's three-year-old sister, having heard someone at the door too. Sewey sent her back as well, with a bag of chocolates to munch until morning. All this was, of course, until *he* heard the noise a minute later and barreled downstairs, revolver in hand, only to find scratches on the door and some dirty tracks.

"Burglars..." he muttered. "And I'm plumb out of Burglar-Be-Gone spray too." He turned to the others, standing at the stairs. Mabel: his wife. Rosie Tuttle: Mabel's cousin, who did the housework and cooking. Balder and Baldretta: his two children. And Bran—the Wilomas' great Accident.

"He'll be coming back," Sewey added. "And being a banker, I learned exactly what to do."

"Call the police?" Bran suggested.

"No scary movies for a week?" Balder mused.

"Mmbbl?" Baldretta managed to say, offering one of the few candies not stuffing her cheeks.

"No!" Sewey spat. "Bran and I are going to *catch* this burglar."

"I think I'd rather catch some sleep," Bran said with a yawn. But inside he felt that watching for a burglar was far better than just another boring evening—one of many he had spent since that fateful morning eight years before.

❋❋❋

The Great and Glorious City Of Dunce, as was its official title, was like an overgrown blot on the map. It covered miles of suburban land so vast that many wondered if it was no longer a city, but rather a small state of its own. If Dunce was a blot on the map, then Bran was a blot on the city of Dunce—the Accident that shouldn't have happened. As if to prove this time and again, there was a driftwood sign tacked next to the front door of the Wilomas' red-brick, two-story house that read:

The Wilomas Family
Sewey
Mabel
Balder
Baldretta

But that was all. After eight years, Bran's name was still nowhere to be found. Eight o'clock on Thursday night found Sewey and Bran on the roof of the house: Sewey with his revolver and Bran with a cigar box of bullets. The air was frigid, and the roof was so steep Bran had to hold to the chimney for balance. Sewey had thoughtfully brought up two pork and mustard sandwiches, in case he got hungry, and had quickly gobbled both down without offering Bran a bite.

One hour passed. Another hour passed. No burglar.

"Keep very quiet," Sewey warned around ten thirty. "I took Burglar Methodology and Tactics in banker school: he'll be coming at precisely ten forty-five!"

Eleven eventually rolled about, and then eleven thirty. Sewey's mood worsened. By midnight, he was so fed up that he climbed down the ladder and returned with a briefcase of paperwork to go over.

"Cold, cold, cold!" Sewey shivered. "Am I the only one in town who cares about this burglar?"

"It's past midnight." Bran yawned. "Maybe the burglar is where *we* should be: *in bed.*"

"Great rot, Bran," Sewey grumbled. "Every scarecrow who's gotten past Basic Burglarology knows they're *never* satisfied with scratching a door and leaving dirty tracks. Mark my words, he's coming back tonight." He shifted. "Now hold that flashlight still; your shivering is making me write crooked."

For the hundredth time that night, Bran sighed and lifted his arm, which was falling asleep without him. To Bran, dirt on the ground and scratches on the door did not spell *burglar.*

"Aha!" Sewey exclaimed, pushing against the chimney.

Sewey hardly ever smiled, and he hardly ever laughed either. More commonly he wore a frown resembling an upside-down banana plastered on his face. His hair and moustache were dark, and though he wasn't fat, he had gained a little weight since he was younger, which perfectly complimented his balding scalp and general grumpiness.

"File this under Evictions," he muttered to Bran. "Old Widow Todilmay won't get past *this* banker!"

Bran set it in the stack marked Evictions without a word. Bran himself wasn't very tall, but he topped Sewey's shoulders at fourteen years old, and had dark brown hair and eyes of the same color. There wasn't much out of the ordinary about him. He was just plain, normal Bran. Except of course, for how he ended up on Bolton Road.

Helping Sewey with his paperwork was a constant, nagging reminder of the Accident, of the whispers Bran often overheard when Sewey called him to the bank for one chore or another: *"There we were, all closed up, the vault locked tight, the next day Sewey gets here early and checks the vault like always… and there he is. A six-year-old boy. Just sitting there in the middle of the floor. Nothing stolen, nothing even moved. And the worst part is the Finders Keepers Law regarding Orphans. That's why Sewey calls it the Accident. According to the Laws of Dunce, because Sewey found the boy, Bran is his 'forever or until the End of Time, whichever comes later…'"*

The strangest part always came after. *"And the note,"* they would whisper. *"It was tight in the boy's hand, and the only thing it said was* 'Bran Hambric, born June 17. To: Clarence'*."*

But no one knew more. Sometimes, in tones so hushed that Bran had to strain his ears, he often heard another word—never shared with Sewey, but offered as the only possible explanation.

"Magic."

"Pay attention!" Sewey snapped, breaking Bran out of his thoughts. Bran counted the papers in Evictions, but when he got to three hundred he decided to give up on the rest. They sat on the chimney beside other piles, some marked Overdue, others Dangerously Overdue, and still others Very Dangerously Overdue.

It wasn't like Bran was the only strange thing that had happened on Bolton Road. Just that Tuesday, a dozen red roses had been delivered to their door, addressed to Rosie Tuttle, with strict instructions addressing them to Rosie and Rosie alone.

The card was signed with an enormous, swirling letter B, and the instant Rosie set eyes on it she tore it to pieces and threw it away, and would say nothing about it to anyone.

Instead of minding his own beeswax, Sewey Wilomas had decided to piece the torn shreds together like a puzzle with staples and sticky tape. When he finally got them in order, he caused such a terrible ruckus with every Bob, Binkey, and Balfred in town that the neighbors had called the police, who carted him off for a day's worth of scrubbing the sewers. Unfortunately for Bran, community service hadn't phased Sewey in the slightest.

"Overdue payment on the Bogwingle's..." Sewey mumbled on, scribbling ONE DAY LATE in bright red.

"Another one for Evictions," he said, passing it to Bran.

"But it's only a day late!" Bran protested.

"Do as you're told!" Sewey snapped back at him.

Bran resisted the temptation to grumble and slid it into the stack, leveling the flashlight and trying to keep himself awake.

Suddenly, a noise brought his head back up. He glanced over his shoulder into the Wilomases' backyard. Everything was still, except for that soft sound—like the rasping breath of someone being strangled.

"You know Bran, I'm some really good banker," Sewey said, stretching. "Always keeping these accounts in line, not to mention raising you after the Accident."

Bran sat frozen, listening, but the hiss faded into silence.

"It takes great skill to be a banker," Sewey went on as he stamped another paper. "But to be a banker *and* run a household? *That* is a miracle in itself—Oh, rot! I stamped the wrong one!" He wiped the ink with his hand, which only smeared the words LATE CHARGE like tire tracks across the page. "Never mind—put it with the others."

Bran hesitated before taking the paper, and then heard the sound again—a rasp that sent a chill through him.

"Bran, stop shivering! You're jarring the light again." Sewey elbowed his leg.

"Hold on, what's that sound?" Bran asked, peering into the backyard.

"What sound?" Sewey demanded. "Come now, there's no use letting your imagination get the best of you. Can't you see it's past midnight? Everyone who has half a brain is in bed by now."

Bran squinted into the darkness. There was a rustling, but it disappeared quickly.

"Bran!" Sewey demanded, louder. "Put this one in Evictions right now, before I evict you off this roof...*headfirst!*"

Bran finally set it in the stack, and the noise was gone. He told himself it was nothing to be afraid of. It could be squirrels, or raccoons, or...anything—there were plenty of sounds in the night. The wind blew the papers into his face again, brushing fear away as he fought them back into the pile. All of a sudden an idea popped into his head. He glanced at Sewey. It looked like the time was right. Sewey yawned deeply.

Perfect, Bran thought, hiding a grin.

"Oh, would you look at this?" he announced abruptly, taking an eviction notice from the stack. Sewey ignored him and went on with his work.

"Old Widow Gray, set to be evicted three days from now," Bran added with a hint of sadness.

Sewey perked up, if only a little; but Bran saw his expression, and knew he was on the right track.

"Remember last year, when you were sick with the Shoebug virus?" Bran asked. "Widow Gray sent a card and even baked you a cake, all to yourself."

Sewey flashed a wry smirk, which he quickly stifled. *Not today,* Bran knew Sewey was thinking. *Won't get the best of me on this one.*

"And she even delivered eighteen rental videos to our door," Bran went on. "I can't believe a nice old lady like her would get evicted."

"Hmmm…" Sewey said in a low, thoughtful voice. "I remember the cake."

"You were sick in bed for three weeks, and who came over to see you every single evening?" Bran went on, shuffling the papers in the air. "Widow Gray, wasn't it?"

Sewey shook his head, but it was no use. The problem was that though his heart was fourteen sizes too small, it was still there, and it greatly got in the way of business when Bran poked it in just the right place.

"Oh, rot, just hand it here then!" Sewey burst, throwing his hand out. Bran had it ready and with one long, angry swipe, Sewey drew an enormous X over the entire page. He rolled it up into a ball and furiously tossed it over the rooftop.

"And look at this: Mr. Brooleybob, eviction set for next week," Bran continued, picking up a paper. "Remember when we all went to the Banker's Banquet in Ellensburg, and you took a wrong turn and we ended up in the desert for three weeks?"

Sewey coughed.

"Which reminds me, remember when we almost got evicted because you spent the house money on Balder's birthday?" Bran leaned a little closer to Sewey with another. "I think it was Mrs. Todilmay who loaned us the money with no interest. Because, of course, she knew that the bank *where you work* would evict us if—"

"Oh, rot, just hand me the whole stack then!" Sewey barked. He snatched the stack with both hands, and with a great heave, ripped every single eviction notice in two. Next came the Overdue, then the Dangerously Overdue, and finally the Very Dangerously Overdue—all torn and over the roof.

"Well then," Sewey growled when he finished. "Since I've just destroyed *all* the work I've done this *entire* night, I might as well sign off on my own resignation." He scowled at Bran. "Now for all the trouble you've caused, just sit over there, *in the dark!*" He grabbed the flashlight and waved the beam across the roof, toward the other edge.

Bran was about to protest but decided against it, sighing as he sat down next to the ladder. Sewey wasn't far off, but the light was dim, and the night was very dark.

What a mess, Bran thought, staring at the torn papers everywhere. *No doubt I'll be the one who has to clean it—*

Bran froze...the strange sound was back, closer than before. He sat up straighter and looked around. Something snarled, hissing and breathing hard, like a seething dog pulling against its chain, choking the air out of itself. But then, just as quickly, the devilish sound faded into the night. Bran could now hear a soft scraping, like feet across metal, getting closer each second.

"Sewey," Bran whispered hurriedly. "Can you hear that?"

"Hear what?" Sewey murmured, oblivious.

"That noise..." he said, looking around with alarm as it got closer.

"What noise?" Sewey asked. "Stop babbling! Can't you see I'm trying to—?"

A flurry of motion next to Bran cut Sewey off in mid-sentence. There was another loud hiss as Bran jumped from the edge—and not a moment too soon, as the most hideous thing he had ever seen leapt onto the roof behind him.

Chapter 2

Chasing Shadows in the Dark

Bran shouted, falling forward and hitting Sewey's briefcase, sending papers into the air. Sewey leapt up at the sight of the creature, jerking back against the chimney with Bran in front of him, the flashlight still in his hands as the monster's feet hit the rooftop.

The creature was crouched over, his hands hovering inches from the shingles—his body the shape of a man, though his face was twisted and his skin rough and mottled with green and brown. The black claw-like fingers were thick and balled into fists, and he hissed and gasped through clenched, jagged teeth—that same sound Bran had heard not a minute before. His eyes shone an empty green, his smell like death and sweat. It made Bran sick all the way through, as if someone was sucking the air from his throat with a vacuum. Sewey pulled Bran back as the creature slid forward, looking from one to the other.

"S-Sewey!" Bran stammered, staring at the monster, hardly able to believe his eyes. Sewey trembled, brandishing the flashlight like a weapon.

"Great Moby..." Sewey breathed, his eyes wide. He struggled to train the flashlight on the monster's face, who cringed and shrieked all of a sudden, covering his eyes.

"Shamblesss!" the creature screamed, turning his head to escape the light, his voice dry and cracking. He gave a horrible, bloodcurdling scream and stumbled back. Suddenly he gave an enraged snarl.

"He's going to jump!" Bran shouted, a moment too late as the creature sprang forward, catching them both. Bran fell to the side but managed to grab hold of the rooftop, scraping his fingers. Sewey scrambled but the creature caught his arm, slamming him against the chimney.

"No, please no!" Sewey shouted, his cheeks white with fear. The creature snarled at him, grabbing the flashlight. Sewey tried to get his revolver up and Bran scrambled to his feet, but they were both too late, as the creature shoved Sewey to the side. Sewey lost his balance and started to roll, and in a second Bran saw him reach the edge and go over with a shout.

"Sewey!" Bran yelled, but the creature spun to face him. The monster's eyes were wild. He threw the flashlight over the edge, crouching again, his gaze trained on Bran.

"Shamblesss..." he hissed, purring almost, stepping forward slowly.

Bran slid back a step. The creature gave a low growl, as if he had cornered a victim and was moving in for the kill. Bran knew he was just steps away from the edge of the roof. He clenched his teeth. "Go away," he whispered. There wasn't any power in his voice, and the creature took another slow step closer, stalking him, waiting for Bran to make the first move. Bran's palms were sweating as the creature's eyes rolled around, watching him closely.

"S-stay back!" Bran commanded, his voice wavering. The creature stepped forward, and Bran held his hands out, ready to defend himself. The creature tilted his head and let out a small hiss.

"Shamblesss..."

Bran swallowed hard. The creature had spoken it again, that word. He stared at Bran; going still, as if waiting for Bran to respond.

"Shambles?" Bran said softly. "Is that your...name?"

It was the first thing that came to him. But in a moment, he thought he saw a glimmer in the green of the creature's eyes—of recognition, of memory, of something that was completely different than what had been there before. It almost seemed that when Bran said it, the creature's muscles relaxed just a bit.

"Yesss," he finally hissed.

There was silence between them, Shambles breathing hard.

"What do you want, Shambles?" Bran asked quickly, stalling for any time he could. Shambles coughed, lurching forward. Bran stepped back hurriedly, but Shambles only fell, trying to breathe. A black bracelet was around his wrist, its green gem catching the light, and something Bran could not see was clutched in his right hand.

"Hambric..." he choked. "Mussst...take Bran Hambric... back..."

Instantly, Bran's muscles tightened. The creature...he knew his name! It made Bran's skin go cold and he jerked his hands up.

"H-how do you know who I am?" Bran gasped, drawing back. Shambles hissed again, looking up, remembering something, like a memory that was surfacing in his mind.

"Emry…" he hissed. "Emry Hambric…wasss your mother…"

Shambles looked into his eyes. "She wanted it…she wantsss you to *come back.*"

Bran was still. "My mother?" he whispered. Shambles's words struck him hard—he had never known her. "I don't have a mother," he finished.

Shambles hissed, trying to breathe, looking over Bran intently as if there was something in Bran he was trying to recognize.

"Her necklace…" Shambles whispered, his eyes moving down. Bran barely caught the words, and he looked at his neck: he wasn't wearing any necklace at all. He looked back, but Shambles was staring at him, almost as if Bran wasn't there and he could see through him.

He's insane, Bran thought with alarm. Shambles closed his eyes, whispering words so low Bran couldn't hear them; and when he looked up again, Bran saw that the color behind Shambles's eyes had gone empty once more. Bran saw something moving in his silhouette—a rope! Shambles held it out, tensing to grab Bran and tighten it around his wrists.

"No!" Bran shouted. There were less than five steps between them. He glanced at his feet, and just as he did, he felt the edge of the roof and almost lost his balance. He was trapped.

"Shamblesss…will take…Bran…back," Shambles hissed.

"Stop, now!" Bran shouted.

Shambles bent over, waiting for the right moment to strike. "Find Bran…bring him back…" he hissed, as if hearing voices in his head.

All of a sudden, Shambles lashed out with his hand, hitting

Bran hard and grabbing hold of his arm. He pulled Bran and spun him around. Bran was faster and jabbed his elbow into the creature's ribs. He heard Shambles gasp with pain.

"Let go!" Bran's voice echoed down the street. He slammed his fist into the creature's skin, but Shambles fought with a strength that was inescapable.

Suddenly, there was a gunshot from below. The bullet hit the chimney and sent shards of brick flying, pieces of it digging into Shambles's exposed arms. He shrieked, grabbing his skin. Bran took his only chance and pushed Shambles hard; there was another gunshot that missed again, and he heard Sewey shouting below. Bran leapt away, but in a rush of motion, Shambles tripped, losing his balance and falling headfirst into a roll, all the way off the edge of the roof.

Sewey gave a shout, and the gun went clattering off. Bran was nearly petrified, but there wasn't a moment to lose, so he rushed down the ladder, not even thinking of what Shambles had said anymore. Just as he dashed around the corner, he was pushed off his feet by Shambles's running the other way. They fell to the ground, but the creature didn't hesitate, his knee catching Bran's chin. Bran shouted in pain, but Shambles leapt up, taking off down the road, and Bran heard Sewey groaning from around the corner.

"Ohhh!" Sewey moaned. "My back! Where is that blasted fiend?"

Sewey was in the grass, searching frantically for his gun, but certainly alive and well, except for a sore back and some very flattened bushes next to the house.

Bran struggled to his feet.

"Sewey, he's gone!" he said as he rushed up.

"Of course he's gone." Sewey snatched his gun out of the grass, and then squinted in the dark.

"Great Moby, what *is* that thing?" he said, and without taking a second to think, he raised the gun and took a crazy shot, the blast sounding through the neighborhood.

Of course the shot missed, and Shambles disappeared into the dark.

"Oh, rot!" Sewey shouted, waving his arms. "Get in the car!"

"You'll never catch him!" Bran protested.

"Just get in," Sewey roared, already running. He wrenched open the rusty door of his old automobile and, finding he had no keys, quickly reached under the car and pulled out his emergency key lockbox hidden above the wheel. The tires squealed as Sewey rocketed out, throwing Bran against the torn cushions in the backseat. Bran managed to sit up as the car flew out of Bolton Road and onto the intersection. He could scarcely see the creature from so far away. Sewey spotted him, though, and punched on the gas, gripping the wheel with both hands. Bran was thrown to the other side of the car as Sewey spun onto Barryless Street, skidding over the curb. Sewey hit eight garbage cans and a row of bushes, uprooting them into the air.

"That burglar thinks he can run fast, eh?" Sewey challenged. "Ha! My old Schweezer can drive faster than anyone."

The Schweezer gave a loud pop in protest. The creature cut through a fence and onto Gnibnobbin Lane. Sewey sped around the corner but then immediately slammed on the brakes. Bran knew why: Officer McMason patrolled that street and wouldn't like at all to see Sewey speeding, *again.* They cruised slowly, Bran's eyes scanning the houses on either side.

There were plenty of hedges and cars that the creature could have darted behind.

"He might have lost us..." Bran said. He moved to the other window and saw no sign of Shambles there either. Sewey went very slowly, watching for any sort of movement and running onto the curb many times. All of a sudden, Bran saw a figure dart out at the end of the road.

"There he is!" Bran shouted, pointing. Sewey slammed on the pedal at Bran's outburst, and they went flying over the curb and onto the sidewalk.

"Where?" Sewey cried, veering into someone's formerly well-tended lawn. He spun the wheel to avoid a tree, spun it again to avoid a bush, and went rocketing off the curb—sailing nearly two feet before they hit the ground with a shattering impact.

"*Behind* us!" Bran pointed in the other direction. The creature lunged down a street, and Bran gripped the sides of the car as Sewey made the turn and they crashed over some railroad tracks.

"Left!" Bran called.

"Right," Sewey agreed. The car skidded on its side, and the instant they made the turn, Sewey slammed on the brakes again, and Bran almost went through the window. The tires squealed, and with a great *whump,* the car fell back, and the engine gave a small spit and died.

"Oh, come on Schweezer," Sewey protested, turning the key. The engine coughed like an old goat."Come on, we're so close," he begged. The engine turned, choking harshly.

"We're gonna lose him," Bran murmured. The engine hacked

and croaked, Sewey pushing the key forward, and it finally gave in and came back to life.

Sewey looked up. "Now where?" he demanded.

Bran shifted his gaze back to the street. The houses were dark, and the streetlamps were dim. They were all alone. Everything was still.

"Well, where is he?" Sewey asked.

It was just then that there came a sudden piercing sound. It wasn't the car, schweezing in protest. Nor was it the burglar ordering Sewey to put his hands in the air. Nor was it the many homeowners whose lawns Sewey had ruined (on more than one occasion). It was, in fact, the most dreaded, feared, and terribly despised sound in the entire world to Sewey Wilomas.

"*Sirens?*" he shrieked with disbelief.

Bran looked out the back window and saw a police car making the same turn they had, lights flashing and sirens blaring through the night.

"Officer McMason," Sewey whined miserably.

The officer was pulling them over. And on top of that, they had lost the burglar.

Chapter 3

The Creature and His Master

Bran hit the side of the car in frustration.

"Not again," Sewey whimpered, and Bran knew exactly what was coming next.

"But maybe I can outrun him," Sewey said, punching on the gas for the first turn he saw.

"Or maybe you *can't,*" Bran said as Sewey turned into a dead-end alley.

"Oh, ROT!" Sewey slammed on the brakes as the flashing lights appeared behind them and the patrol car blocked off all avenues of escape.

"Fourth time this month," Bran observed.

"Third," Sewey snapped back. He stared straight ahead with a stony face, as if he could just disappear if he ignored everyone.

The officer got out of his car and strolled leisurely toward them as if he had done this many times before (which he had).

"Mouth closed, interruptions, none," Sewey growled at Bran between his teeth. "I won't have you laughing like last time when I told him about the ducks spitting rocks at my windshield."

"Or the spider tap-dancing with the giant lizard," Bran added.

"I said interruptions, none!" Sewey ordered. "If there's one peep while the officer is here..." His voice trailed off menacingly.

Having been through the same routine many times before, Bran resolved to let Sewey fend for himself.

"Good evening, Mr. Wilomas," Officer McMason said cordially as he moved for the window. He had a thick black moustache like a fox's tail under his nose. Sewey refused to look at him.

"Haven't you learned yet?" The officer tapped the roof. "This is a car, not a rocket ship."

"I have a perfectly good reason for speeding, thank you," Sewey stated, still staring ahead.

"Don't tell me you were chased by elephants again," Officer McMason said with mock surprise. "I guess I'll have to call Animal Control to round them up."

Sewey went red. "Those elephants were real! And I refuse to speak to you anymore."

"Well then." The officer took a pen out. "I'd say Judge Rhine will be pretty hard—"

"All right, I was chasing a burglar," Sewey interrupted, spinning on him. "Maybe you should be looking for him instead of patrolling for *me.*"

Officer McMason looked confused, but only for a moment. Then he just scratched his moustache and paged through his ticket book. "I'm afraid a different burglar ploy was used five weeks ago, and the one about the runaway bugbears was used two weeks ago—"

"Those bugbears were real," Sewey interrupted.

"Whatever." The officer waved his hand. "I think that means you've run out of excuses."

"But the burglar is real too!" Sewey insisted. "There's a burglar on the loose!"

The officer nodded as if consoling a little child, looking into the air and preparing for another of Sewey's wild stories. He began to write on his pad.

"Wait," Sewey begged madly. "I have a perfectly good excuse for speeding. I was...I was..." He threw his hands in the air. "I was chasing a *gnome!*"

Officer McMason instantly dropped his pen, paper, and jaw, his eyes going wide.

Bran blinked with shock and the patrol car's lights flickered. Even the Schweezer gave a shudder, as if it also was stunned to hear of such conduct.

"A...*gnome?*" the officer asked slowly, blinking at him.

Sewey gulped.

Bran had heard about gnomes, from whispers about the simple indecency of them. He had overheard the news on television once saying that the mayor had declared a day of celebration when the police had caught a gnome who had been sneaking around Givvyng Park. There were three basic rules in Dunce that no one could get past: no gnomes, no mages, and nothing that could even be imagined as an etcetera to the first two.

"Yes, a n-n-gnome," Sewey whispered nervously. They knew what happened to gnomes in Dunce: tossed in jail for life without trial or, more commonly, worse.

"Tell me about this gnome..." the officer said, blinking.

"He was tall and thin and bony, and his skin was dark, and his eyes were green," Sewey described. "He didn't have a hat, but he was definitely a gnome!"

The officer's shoulders dropped. "No hat? A gnome wouldn't be caught dead without a hat."

"But it *was* a gnome," Sewey objected. "I'm sure of it."

"As a matter of science," the officer explained with a shrug, "gnomes are short, have beards, and wear pointy red hats. Sounds pretty much the opposite of your burglar."

"He's not *my burglar,*" Sewey said. "It was a *gnome.*"

The officer picked up his ticket book and began writing.

"It's true!" Sewey whined. He looked left and right, and finding no way to avoid the ticket, promptly punched both hands on the car horn. The alley filled with noise, rising to the sky like a concert of bad tuba players. The officer jumped and started to shout, but Sewey didn't hear him. He just pressed on the horn, eyes closed, and Bran covered his ears.

"Mr. Wilomas!" the officer shouted. "*Mr. Wilomas!*"

He didn't listen. The officer, growing tired of this game, drew his pistol, pointed it toward the sky, and shot. At the sudden explosion, Sewey went as stiff and pale as a whitewashed board.

"Officer?" he croaked. Officer McMason blew on the muzzle of his gun. Sewey trembled.

"I think I've changed my mind about this ticket," the officer said.

"I'm going free?" Sewey said with elation.

"No."

"I'm going to jail?" Sewey whined.

"Worse," the officer said. "I have a better idea to deal with you." He raised a finger. "You hereby have *one week* to convince me there was a gnome—"

"A fortnight, for pity's sake," Sewey begged.

The officer sighed. "A fortnight then. If by that time you haven't caught me this...*gnome,* then..." He blew on the muzzle of his gun again.

Sewey swallowed. "Goodness," he said.

The officer stared hard at Sewey, but gave himself away when he glanced across at Bran—he was hiding a smile. "A fortnight!" he added, louder for effect.

Sewey coughed. The officer tipped his hat and started for his car. Slowly, the flashing lights disappeared, leaving Sewey and Bran all alone in the alley.

After a while of sitting in silence, Sewey rattled the car into gear and pulled out of the alley.

"How long is a fortnight?" he asked.

"Fourteen days, I think," Bran answered.

"Fourteen days?" Sewey moaned. "I'm finished."

And as he pushed on the gas for home, he didn't even notice he was speeding again.

Shambles ran through the gloomy darkness, down alleys and up empty roads, keeping out of sight like a specter. His eyes swept the streets, his ears alert for any noise, keeping him out of view as he crossed bridges and railroad tracks. Twice the lights of a car came close, but he slid into the safety of darkness before anyone could catch more than a glimpse of him.

Following him were voices—playing in his head, distant now, the pain from his arm from the shards of the chimney bricks drowning their words out with burning screams in his brain. But he knew the voices would return, seizing him fully once more, as they always did.

Moving on foot, he crossed the district and came to another: a dirty, unkempt place, with old buildings that had broken windows, houses without lights, and roadways with more holes than gravel. It was quiet, but his ears picked up on cars rushing down the highway far away. Shambles crept to an abandoned building. There were garage doors at the bottom, facing the road. One was open. Shambles moved for it.

"Well, well, well," a voice called out when he came through, and suddenly four blinding headlights were trained on him.

Shambles froze and heard the mechanical sound of the garage door closing behind him. He tried to shield his eyes from the bright beams.

"Bring him here to me," the man ordered. "He can tell us why he's come back alone. Again."

Shambles felt two sets of hands take hold of his shoulders. He didn't fight. He knew them, and he knew they were stronger than he was. They pulled him to a black van, both of them big men with bald heads and long black coats, identical in every way, their muscles taut and their necks thick. They shoved him against the hood of the van, holding him backward against it. He saw two other men, leaning against a second black van a few feet away: Craig had long brown hair and was unshaven, and Marcus's black hair was cut short. Both held pistols.

"Hold him there," the strong voice said, and Shambles saw the man's shoes slide out from under the open door. The man's footsteps scraped against the concrete as he came around the side, until he was standing in front of Shambles. He was tall and strong, his hair a deep blond and down to his shoulders. He stared at Shambles icily.

"I see you've come back alone again," he said in a soft tone. "Where's the boy?"

Shambles only hissed at him with contempt, and the man looked down for a moment.

"I don't ask things twice," he said, stepping forward. He glanced at the two men holding Shambles down, and then back into his eyes. He leaned close to his ear, his lips inches away.

"I can give her a call..." he whispered, holding a silver cell phone in front of Shambles's face.

"She will know of it, and she will not be pleased," the man said. His eyes moved down Shambles's arm to his wrist. Shambles's eyes moved also, to the black bracelet: a thick piece of material, wrapped twice, in which there was a perfectly smooth piece of rock, clear green. It seemed to glow a dark color, and just peering at it made Shambles's heart beat faster. The man looked back to his eyes.

"No..." Shambles whimpered. "Pleassse, tell her nothing of it!" He clenched his teeth, his breath quickening, his arms shaking in the grasp of the men. He could almost feel the sting rushing through his body, like it had so many times before—his screams echoing until it didn't seem to be his voice anymore, only a distant sound in the dark. "Pleassse, Joris, don't tell her. I found the boy, and I saw him." He felt sweat trickling down his back, onto the metal of the van.

The man leaned closer.

"And where," Joris whispered, "did you see him?"

Shambles's eyes rolled around. The room swayed in front of him as he tried to clear his throat.

"Pleassse," he begged them. "Releassse me, and I will tell you."

Joris studied his face. He finally looked satisfied and nodded to the men. They bent Shambles up and held onto his arms loosely.

"I saw him on Bolton Road," Shambles gasped. "Where the addresss leadsss."

"Was it the same as last night?" Joris asked.

Shambles coughed. "Yesss."

"Are you're sure it was the boy?" Joris shot another question at him like a bullet.

"Yesss, I am sure."

"And why did you not bring him to us?"

"I was ssshot at!" Shambles looked up at him with fiery eyes, waving his bloodied arm. "It wasss a man with a car, and I couldn't get to the boy."

All of a sudden, Joris hit the side of the van in fury. Shambles jerked, but Joris seized him by the neck, slamming him back against the metal, his grip tightening like a vice on Shambles's throat.

"Shambles!" Joris shouted in his face. "Who saw you—*tell me who saw you!*"

Shambles choked for air, and Joris squeezed tighter, but then threw him back against the van. Spluttering, he felt his head hit the metal, and Joris spun around, running his hands nervously through his thick hair. Shambles fell to the ground against the side of the van, weak.

"What do we do now?" one of the men asked.

"Shut up, Craig!" Joris shouted, spinning on him with fury.

"We can go to the house and take the boy tonight, if we have to," the other man said.

"Someone might see us!" Joris barked. "The boy should have been brought to us tonight."

He slammed his fist against the hood of the other van and clenched his teeth. "Beat him," he added, pointing to Shambles, his voice echoing in the garage.

"No!" Shambles pleaded, looking from one man to the other.

"Beat him until he tells you everything!" Joris shouted, starting to pace the floor. Neither of the bald men showed any emotion, spinning Shambles around and pushing him against the metal.

"Pleassse!" Shambles begged, sliding out of their grasp. One of the men tried to grab him, but Shambles bit his hand. The man didn't shout or show any reaction at all, only hit Shambles hard across the back, so that he tripped onto the concrete. They bent his arms back, and Craig came forward, tossing his cigarette to the ground and cracking his knuckles. Shambles cried out, fighting them, but Craig laughed cruelly as the men straightened up Shambles against the van for him. He lifted his fist to strike.

"Wait," Joris hissed all of a sudden, stopping them. Shambles fought, but the men held him like two blocks of stone. He looked at Joris with fear, begging him silently for mercy. Joris stared at him, thinking hard. Finally, he shook his head.

"Just put him in the van," he whispered. "There's been a change of plans." He looked at Shambles. "You've got one last chance, or else Clarence will die—" He turned, and under his breath, Shambles heard him finish, "—just like Emry."

Chapter 4

The Note in the Grass

By the time Sewey and Bran got home, it wasn't even that night anymore, but very early Friday morning. Mabel, Rosie, and the children were already downstairs in their pajamas.

"Bran!" Rosie gasped when he came through the door. She rushed forward and hugged him. "Oh, you're back. I was so worried!"

"Of course we're back," Sewey growled, hanging up his coat and getting no hug from anyone. He ordered them back to bed and not another word about it.

Bran lay awake for a long time, thinking about the gnome, or whatever it was, and the things he had said on the roof. He wondered how the creature had found him and what he had meant by that name…*Emry Hambric.* Was the creature making it up? Or was there something true behind it? Had Shambles been trying to tell him something? Questions rolled through Bran's mind. Twice he got out of bed and sat shivering in his room. An attic is a very cold place to sleep, and not simply because of the chill—it kept him clearly away from the rest of the household, as if the others might catch some disease if he slept too close. Years ago, when the Wilomases had finally come to accept the fact that he would not disappear, they had given him the choice of the basement or the attic, and as he had no desire to become further acquainted with roaches and rats, he chose the latter. The way Bran saw it, he had the largest suite in the house.

Since there was so little between him and outside, when it rained he could hear the drops against the hard roof above his head. The place wasn't like most attics because it was walled in and didn't smell so much of wood and insulation. There was a tiny air conditioner unit stuck to the wall on the farthest end. It was a mess since nobody except Bran went up there, and thus everyone felt they could haphazardly toss junk up the hole in the ceiling and let it sort itself out. Bran had scavenged together a lamp, a desk, a bed, and an old, framed cork board on which he pinned various things he drew—not because he particularly liked how they came out, but because when he looked at them, they reminded him of why he had drawn them in the first place.

He did his sketches in pencil, the topmost one on the board depicting a fat, grim-faced turtle with a sling, taking potshots at the Schweezer. It had been inspired by one of Sewey's previous excuses to Officer McMason. Below that was one of a dozen clones of a blank-eyed Sewey, all teetering down the street on old bicycles that were much too small for them. It had come about when Sewey had refused to get Bran a slightly better bike, even though it was so old that it still had Sewey's name carved on the handlebars from *his* school days. Bran snickered at the drawing when the Wilomases put him in a bad humor. The board was covered with sketches like those, and each had a story, but since no one ever came up and Bran had no friends to visit him there, he was the only one in the world who really knew what each of them meant.

To the left of the board of sketches was a small window that was partly over Bran's bed, and as he sat shivering, he looked outside—cautiously, though, for still some part of him remembered the awful creature that had been outside just hours before. He sat there for a long while. When he couldn't take it anymore, he found himself sitting at his desk, like so many times before, the soft light of the moon the only thing he dared let illuminate his face and his work.

He didn't have any drawing paper, but had been lucky enough to snag an old roll of newspaper the printers had thrown out. It was warped on one side and caused jams in the presses, but Bran could easily rip off a clean sheet, though with time the paper had yellowed.

Sliding his pencil across the paper, Bran tried to summon the creature from memory, its rough face, its features, those eyes. His pencil scratched dark lines and sweeping curves on the page, his arm sliding around little pieces of paper that littered his desk, notes and drawings he had left unfinished. Bran had never had drawing lessons; it just seemed to come naturally to him. However, try as he did, he couldn't seem to bring the creature out onto the paper. Usually when drawing, he could feel himself forgetting his troubles. But with every line he drew now, he only seemed to feel worse, until he finally crumpled up the whole page and threw it away. He sat in the darkness yet again, wishing it had all been a bad dream.

Why is this bothering me so much? he asked himself. It was maddening. He could not get his mind off the creature and what he had said.

He finally scavenged underneath the bed for his bag of things. The bag was from Rosie and was lined with tapestry print colored with a mixture of dark greens and browns and mustard yellows. He kept all his things in it that he didn't want the Wilomases getting into, like the torn note with his name they had found in the vault. He took the note out, reading the paper over and over. He ran his fingers along the edge, to where it was jagged and torn at the bottom and where the top corner was bent. He had studied it so many times he had every mark emblazoned in his mind.

Sometimes, as on that night, he liked to wonder about his mother and where she might be, or the reason she had left him in the vault. Had his father made her leave Bran behind? Bran never wondered about his father more than that—he didn't know why, perhaps because his father was simply a person Bran could blame who wasn't there to prove otherwise. Bran wondered if his mother might show up at the door one day, or if she was looking for him at that very moment. He knew he could convince her to take him back, if she would only hear him out. And even though the hope seemed like a thread when set against reality, Bran clung to it each day, to the feeling that he might get to see her face even once.

He had sketched out many things on paper, but the one thing he wished he could draw was his mother—anything that could make him remember her. The oldest memory he had was of waking up in the darkness of the vault, looking up just as Sewey was peering in. It was as if everything that had happened in the first six years of his life was gone: a wall in his mind he could not break through. And the only clue to any of it was the note.

He tried to go to sleep again, but it was little use.

Early the next morning, he got started on his usual routine. There were plenty of chores to do, like shining the shoes, starting the laundry, feeding the cat, and as Bran's name did not end in Wilomas, he was expected to earn his keep by helping Rosie. As it turned out, the most exertion any Wilomas ever did in the morning was a pinky to the snooze button.

Rosie was rushing around the kitchen—frying eggs, cooking sausages, and making a whole lot of racket—when Bran came in to see if she needed anything.

"Good morning," she said cheerfully. "What a noisy evening!"

"What a *long* evening too," Bran said, yawning as he took plates out. "I hardly slept at all."

"Me either," Rosie replied, moving the eggs around and turning the stove up under the sausages. "I heard you two chased a gnome, right here in Dunce."

"Well, we *did* chase him," Bran said. "But we didn't catch him."

"Oh, my!" Rosie said with a gasp. "It's a shame, burglars coming to a nice city like this one."

"But why two nights in a row?" Bran asked.

Rosie just shrugged. She was a small, somewhat chubby woman of thirty-nine years, with brown hair in a bun and a face glowing with a smile most times of the day. For being Mabel's distant cousin, she hardly bore any resemblance. The Wilomases kept her around because they wouldn't dream of doing their own housekeeping, and they used her as a tutor because they didn't trust the Dunce school system. Besides, they enjoyed feeling rich by having a servant and a tutor to boss around—probably the biggest reason of all.

The alarm clock went off upstairs like the Great Bell of Death, and commotion ensued. A furious sound started down the stairs, and that sound did not belong to an angry troll, as one might first expect, but to Mabel Wilomas. The kitchen door blew open.

"EEEK!" Mabel screamed, her voice shaking the very foundations of the house.

Bran winced. Rosie jumped and sent a fried egg flying into the air.

"What *are* you cooking?" Mabel demanded, staring in horror at the stove. Bran caught the egg with a plate a moment before it would have fallen to the floor.

"I'm cooking breakfast, miss," Rosie said quickly. "Like I do every morning."

"Every morning indeed." Mabel swept into the kitchen and dashed to the medicine cabinet.

"Look: eggs, sausage, toast," Rosie said, pointing to each one. "A meal fit for a king!"

"You mean a *queen,*" Mabel corrected, pulling medicines by the armful out of the cabinet and dropping them on the counter. She was only a bit taller than Sewey's shoulders and had black hair with dynamic, burnt red streaks, like fire and smoke, piled in a mess on top of her head. She scrambled for a bottle of drops and started to squeeze it over her eyeballs.

"Make sure"—*drop*—"you cook those eggs"—*drop*—"to a crisp," she said, as she dripped the solution into her eyes. "They've got to be *blackened.* Don't want us getting rispozita poisoning."

When she finished with the drops, she snatched a long pad of paper from across the counter. "Twenty-eight drops of Endgo's root, twelve teaspoons of slippery elm, two grams of crushed fiddlesticks…" She ran her finger down the list, piling dozens of things onto the counter and taking some of each. "…then Ingrid's Elixir, then Snapping Leaf, then Yuletide Extract, then the antibodies, then antiantibodies…"

"And now for the grand finale," Bran said as she came to the last one.

"…and two hundred-forty drops of cloromorophloroso-cillinium!" Mabel finished at the bottom. She took a gigantic rainbow-colored bottle out of the cabinet and began counting drops onto her tongue.

"The way you're acting," Bran said, "one might think you were sick."

"*Toxic!*" she spluttered. "All the toxicity of this city is bound to kill us one of these days. All those people, stepping outside without even taking a dropper full of something! Why, I just read in the *Fitness Witness* magazine—" She slammed an inhaler over her mouth and nose. Her lips went on moving, but Bran couldn't hear it behind the plastic, and she gave the canister three sprays, breathed deeply, and then went into a coughing fit.

"See, see?" she said, hitting her chest. "Toxins! In the air! And it's getting worse!" She rushed to the telephone. "I need an appointment, a consultation, ear candling, I need—"

"A phone book?" Bran offered. She jumped.

"Throw it away!" she commanded. "That ink will make your ears fall off!"

He tossed it onto the table and gave up. "Don't you care at all about the burglar last night?"

"The burglar?" she snapped. "I bet you didn't wash after handling it. Get upstairs and clean your head, shoulders, knees, and toes, then wake up Balder, before he gets a whooping cold."

Rosie knew the drill: she took a sausage out of the pan, wrapped it in a napkin, and handed it to Bran, and he started up the stairs to Balder's room. He made his way through the toys in the dark, flipping the blinds open to let the sunshine in.

"Rise and shine!" Bran said, pushing a few toys aside with his foot.

"Oh, no," Balder whined, throwing the sheets over his head. "Go away!"

"Time to get up," Bran said. "Mother's orders."

"Get out!" Balder demanded. Bran waved the sausage in front of Balder's nose a few times.

"Go aw—" Balder started but interrupted himself when he sniffed the air. Bran waved the sausage a few times, and Balder finally snatched it from him, poking his head out. In a second the sausage was down his throat, all in one stuff. When he finished, he licked his lips and sat up, pouting. "I don't want to get up," he moaned. "I want to stay right here and rot."

"Well, go ahead," Bran said. "And when you're through, you tell me how it feels."

"Blah!" Balder pouted. "I want that new television, the Megamus Maximus! I want it, and I'll run away if I don't get it!"

"Good luck," Bran said. "I heard they're looking for underground mining boys up north."

"I won't be a mining boy, I won't!" Balder said, kicking the sheets off. He had the same dark hair as Sewey, freckles around his nose, and he was as chubby as ever. In all their lives, Sewey and Mabel had never intended to make him the way he was, but it was just a plain and simple fact that he had turned out worse than a whole horde of selfish trolls.

"I want the Megamus Maximus!" he squealed.

"What about the one over there?" Bran pointed to the television dominating the far wall.

"It's old," Balder snapped. "And the new one is twelve hundred times bigger. I want it!" He kicked his piggy bank off the dresser, then pushed a lamp, threw three books, and finally slid out of bed.

"You're not going to watch television?" Bran asked with fake horror.

"The thought!" Balder spluttered. "I'm going for the big one in the living room."

"Baldretta's got that one this week," Bran said, but Balder didn't care.

"I'll just wrestle the bloody remote from her grubby little hands," he sneered.

Bran shrugged and started to pick up Balder's toys, preparing for the worst. It came eight seconds later.

"I don't want to watch *Shink, Nok, and Foops!*" Balder hollered from down the hall.

Bran came to see what was up. Baldretta was in the living room, holding a bag of candy in her hands and sitting on the remote.

"Why does she get the big screen?" Balder demanded, trying to knock her over. Baldretta had flowing brown hair, big brown eyes, and a pretty face that was usually stuffed with some sort of candy. She hadn't yet begun to talk much, and thanks to her perpetual chewing, only the Wilomases could understand her when she did.

"Mbwmbs buwithus," Baldretta smacked.

"But I'm the oldest, you little monster," Balder argued. "I get dibs on the biggest screen!"

"Mbwithis bwathis," Baldretta said, her lips moving in a circle as she chewed.

"I am *not,*" Balder screamed. However, Baldretta seemed quite sure he was. Bran didn't care to interrupt, so he left them there and started out to set the table. He nearly ran into Mabel in the kitchen.

"Keep a distance!" she warned. "I found a trash can you forgot to empty last night."

"I'm sorry, I happened to be on the roof most of the evening," Bran explained.

"Don't be snippy. You had best take it out now before rats come and we all get the Gray Plague and goodness knows what else."

"Maybe leprosy?" Bran suggested.

Mabel went pale. "I'll have to dose up on some neoplytoplismo!" she choked, rushing for her medicine cabinet. Bran tied up the trash bag and started outside to add it to the pile next to the house.

The morning was cool, and the sun hovered just above the horizon, covering the neighborhood with soft light. The grass glimmered with dew. One of the neighbors was driving off for work. Bran saw the Schweezer sitting on the curb, as if nothing at all had happened the night before. Mr. Swinehic was feeding the birds and waved at him.

"Good morning, Bran!" he called, and Bran waved back as he started around the house. Mr. Swinehic threw another handful of seed and started toward him.

"I picked up a lot of trash in my yard this morning," he told Bran as he came forward. "There was a lot in your yard too, so I just bagged it up with the rest."

"What was it?" Bran asked, tossing the trash bag beside the house.

Mr. Swinehic shrugged. "Couldn't tell," he replied. "Looked like a bunch of bank forms: evictions, overdue letters..."

Bran smiled but kept himself from laughing, remembering the night before. "Was it now?"

"Yep," Mr. Swinehic nodded and shrugged. "All of them ripped in half the same. Except for that scrap of paper I found over there."

He pointed toward the side of the house. "Wasn't a bank form and it was all by itself—and it's got your name on it, so I guess it's yours."

"My name?" Bran asked curiously. He hadn't dropped anything outside that he could remember. Mr. Swinehic dug in his pocket.

"I kept it just in case," he said, pulling it out. "It's odd and doesn't make much sense, either."

He produced a single slip of paper, torn at the top and the bottom. It was very plain but wrinkled and dirty, and Bran took it and read what was written there:

Meet me at midnight in Dunce to pick up Bran. Since I cannot save him, you must do it for me; and in return

The rest was torn off. Bran blinked at it and ran his fingers along the edge, very confused.

"See, doesn't make any sense," Mr. Swinehic said. "Looks like it's torn off something." Mr. Swinehic pointed to the edge. "Must go on from there, like part of a letter, but I couldn't find the rest. Sounded important and odd, so I kept it."

"Th-thank you," Bran stammered, unsure of what to say. He turned the page over, but there was nothing on the back except some dirt stains. He looked up to ask more, but Mr. Swinehic had already started back for his house. Bran stood there dumbfounded for a minute, and he turned to look where Mr. Swinehic had said he found the paper.

That's where I ran into the burglar last night... Bran thought, remembering when Shambles had knocked him off his feet. For some reason, the paper made him think of something familiar. He had seen the same style so many times before that in a second he almost felt he recognized it.

"Looks a lot like the paper with my name..." he thought aloud, but he stopped himself and gave a small laugh. *It couldn't be.* There was no way it could have anything to do with something Mr. Swinehic found in the grass—*his* paper was eight years old!

Still, he was very curious, and started back for the house. It would be a wonderful coincidence if the papers matched. He went upstairs and almost to the end of the hall, to the ladder against the side and out of the way. It went straight up toward a hole in the ceiling. Sunlight shone on his face as his head popped through, and he drew the bag out and held his paper up to the sunlight. He looked from it to the one Mr. Swinehic had found, and smiled.

So I was right, he thought. *It* is *the same type of paper!*

He looked from one to the other. The one with his name was written on a torn scrap of yellow notepaper, with soft blue lines for writing on. Some of the lines had been blotted and blurred, but the handwriting was still crisp and black. The one from Mr. Swinehic was the same, and Bran held the two pieces close together, comparing them. The handwriting looked *exactly the same.* His heart began to pound faster, his grin disappearing. "This is incredible..." He shook his head. "Mr. Swinehic found a paper just like—"

Bran froze. He saw something he hadn't noticed before. When he moved the paper with his name to the top of the other, *the edges fit along the tear.*

He held both pieces still, though his hands shook as he studied it. He could do nothing but stare at the edges that fit so perfectly.

"I don't believe it..." he told himself, but it was right before his eyes. Where the blue lines at the bottom of his paper ended, they continued onto the second slip of paper. He read the page:

Bran Hambric, born June 17
To: Clarence
Meet me at midnight in Dunce to pick up Bran. Since I cannot save him, you must do it for me; and in return

The rest was torn off there. Bran shook his head with disbelief. How did the paper get outside their house? He remembered again how Shambles had run into him—*he had dropped it!*

Questions raced through Bran's mind. He told himself over and over it didn't mean anything, but as he looked at the edges of the paper and the handwriting, he knew something strange was happening. He ran his finger along the bottom.

"How did Shambles get this?" he whispered. He wondered if he had gotten it from Clarence, or worse, killed him for it. And where was the last piece, missing from the bottom?

There's more... he thought. *The paper goes on from there!*

All those years of knowing for sure the scrap of paper was the only thing left of his past seemed to vanish in front of him. Now, there was more.

"This note is part of a whole letter," he realized with shock.

Chapter 5

The Man, the Van, and Dan

Bran didn't say a word to anyone about the paper. He just hid it under his bed and went downstairs as the Wilomases gathered for breakfast.

"What's wrong with Bran?" Balder whispered as Rosie handed the plates out.

Mabel gasped. "He handled the trash," she hissed. "He's caught Midhampton's disease!"

She quick-drawed a sprayer of disinfectant from her belt and shot at Bran, but he managed to dodge it. The spray hit Pansy the cat by mistake, who in turn gave a gigantic snarl, but was too fat to attack and settled with dragging herself under the table.

"That fat cat," Mabel said, crossing her arms as the feline disappeared like a worm.

"We need to put her on a diet before we all catch obesity from her," Mabel said gravely. No one listened. Rosie was filling up Baldretta's plate, and Balder was still pouting in his chair, his arms crossed. He began kicking people's legs under the table.

"I don't see why I can't have the Megamus Maximus," he whined. Baldretta sighed and held up two fingers.

"Baldretta's right," Mabel told Balder. "You've only had that new television for two weeks."

"It's an old model!" Balder waved his hand. "I want that new one in the commercial!"

"That one?" she spat. "It's so big, it won't even fit, even if we knocked the roof out!"

"Knock it out then!" Balder screamed. "I want the television, and I want it now! NOW!"

Rosie was next to Balder and shuddered at his scream, which was comparable in decibels to the sound of a jet exploding as a horde of elephants stampeded down a hill with hundreds of roosters on their backs all crowing at once.

"Quiet down, Balder," Sewey mumbled, reading his newspaper and oblivious to the world around him.

"I will not!" Balder retorted. "I WANT THE MEGAMUS MAXIMUS."

Sewey, suddenly aware, reared up like a mad horse. "You aren't getting *any* television, and that's final!"

Balder screamed as if Sewey had struck him with a knife. Then, seeing he was getting nowhere, Balder snapped his mouth shut and sulked. Rosie handed him his food very slowly. He was nearly as interested in food as he was in television, so he instantly forgot his troubles and set to work making a proper hog of himself.

"Hoo hoo, funny article," Sewey started, turning the page of the newspaper. "In the Motivational section," he explained, looking up. "One of those 'You can do anything if you try' pieces of jabber-jobber."

"Since when did you start reading the Motivational section?" Bran asked with shock.

"Thirty seconds ago," Sewey replied, crunching a pickle. "By mistake. The writer blathered a page of hibhiggens about how people have got to dream big or otherwise they'll just be a nobody."

"Jabberbother!" Balder cried.

"Horseradish!" Mabel shrieked.

"Utter nonsense," Sewey agreed. "Dream big—ha! Of course I dream big. *I,* for one, would like to make gobs and gobs of money." He looked about the table. "And *then,* I would want everyone to have a parade for *me,* and bring me crowns and jewels!" He pointed to Mabel. "What about you?"

"Me?" Mabel said, sitting up straighter. A dreamy gleam leapt into her eyes.

"Of all things, I dream of one..." her voice went soft. "To one day, be oh-so-detoxed enough that I can have an entire Spotless Chocomicity Simplicity Divinity Cake to myself! And then, you could crown me *empress,* so I could have everything and everyone obey me like little dogs!"

Pansy snarled. Sewey just shrugged.

"A rational dream," he said, and he turned to Balder. "And you?"

"Pig-out week!" Balder shouted. "An entire week where we eat and eat, and watch more television than the world combined."

"A rational wish," Sewey said. He turned to Baldretta. Her mouth was full, as usual.

"Bwooshi bwishi bwoshbwibluebli bwibliboblo," she said. Sewey's eyes followed her lips.

"Translation please?" Bran said.

Sewey spun on him. "What's your problem? Cotton in your ears? Baldretta has every right to be the world's most famous advanced pyrotechnist in the world if she wants to!"

"Bwamins," Baldretta said.

"Advanced *chemical* pyrotechnist," Sewey corrected. He turned again. "Rosie?"

She glanced down and looked as if she hadn't expected for Sewey to ask her anything.

"I suppose," she said, "one day, I would like to be a world-famous journalist, and go to dangerous scenes and write reports where they pay me a thousand sib per word!" She turned to Bran. "Then, I could pay for Bran's college, and buy you and Mabel and the children all sorts of wonderful things...and even pay off all the overdue bills."

"How irrational!" Sewey replied, moving about in his chair awkwardly. "In fact, I've never heard any more nonsense in my life, paying off all the bills at once." He threw his hands in the air. "You would have to be *wildly* popular to pay off all *our* bills!"

As if to prove his point, his elbow knocked an enormous pile of bills off the table. They continued to spill for some time, like a ceaseless fountain, as he struggled to catch them.

"Look!" he spluttered, waving certain ones in frustration. "This one's for the elephant statue in the basement, unpaid, and late. This one's for eighteen cases of Yinsworth Medicated Tinctures, unpaid, and late. This one's for the pixie exterminator last month, unpaid, and late..."

"And these," Bran said, grabbing a pile, "are twelve speeding tickets, unpaid, and late."

"Give that here!" Sewey said, grabbing them away. He sat on them. The fact was, the Wilomas family simply didn't have the time to deal with paying the bills for the things they bought to make them look richer than the neighbors. They were busy enough buying them.

"Well, cheer up everyone," Bran said, nodding toward Rosie. "One day, she really is going to be a famous writer, and she'll pay each and every one of them off for us!"

All of a sudden, everyone turned their heads to look at Bran, and all along the table, a set of very confused faces stared at him, as if he had just said the most obviously stupid thing in the world.

Sewey blinked, as if for once he couldn't come up with anything more brainless to say. "Look here," he stammered. "This is no time for jokes. We're better off relying on a volcano of gold to erupt in here before *Rosie* of all people gets put in the newspaper—" Sewey glanced at her and added, "—or any paper!"

Rosie forced a smile on her face.

Sewey started to eat again, and then, as if he had abruptly remembered there was another person in the house, he jumped and looked up.

"Great Moby, I almost forgot," he said, tapping the newspaper article. "Bran, what do *you* dream big about?"

Bran had been hoping he had forgotten. However, an idea popped into his mind—it was because of the creature and what he had said on the roof. All of a sudden, Bran felt an urge, but he pushed it away. He knew they'd all laugh if he said it.

"Well?" Sewey pressed. "What *do* you want to do?"

Bran swallowed. "I—I think I..."

"Speak up!" Mabel insisted.

"I think," Bran stammered, "one day, I would like to find out who my family was."

Everyone was silent. And then, two seconds later, Sewey slammed his fists on the table.

"What a ridiculous notion!" he spat. "Insanely out of this world!"

"Indeed!" Mabel agreed. "Why, everyone knows we've looked high and low for your family, and we didn't find them, or else you wouldn't be *here.*"

"This entire town thinks we're a laughingstock because of that Accident," Sewey remarked. "Even the police refused to offer any help. You might as well hang up your hopes of finding your family, because if we couldn't find them after *that* ordeal, nobody can."

Bran resolved to leave it at that, imagining a sketch of Sewey gleefully skipping into a pool of vipers.

Sewey went on grumbling. "Grumpkins, talking like that." He tossed his napkin on the table. "Simply bumblebother!"

"Absolute poppycock!" Mabel said.

"Utter pumpledithers!" Balder squealed.

Sewey gave a cough and reached for his newspaper again. For a while, everything was quiet.

Very soon, though, Sewey began to read another article very intensely. He pulled the paper close to his eyes, as if he couldn't believe what he was reading. He ruffled the pages out, then bent them in, huffing and puffing.

"Is...something wrong?" Rosie asked. Sewey glared at her.

"Something wrong?" he growled. "This morning's wrong. *Everything's* wrong." He slapped the newspaper. "Just to make my morning worse, would you believe this: another gnome, caught, sneaking around Givvyng Park!"

"In our city?!" Mabel gasped, horrified. Baldretta nearly choked on a lozenge.

"Yes!" Sewey said. "Don't the gnomes get it? They *aren't*

allowed. It says so on the sign, and it's carved on the Givvyng Tree: *no gnomes, no mages.*"

"Maybe they just want to go through instead of traveling all the way around," Bran said, giving up on having a peaceful meal.

"I don't see why they can't," Sewey snapped. "After all, they're *gnomes*...not *people.*"

"*Gnomes, not people!*" Balder mimicked, grease from the sausage rolling down his chin.

"My thoughts exactly," Sewey went on, taking a bite. "I see no point in even acknowledging them as a species. How can some wear pointy caps and others leap around on a roof?"

"Maybe," Bran said, beginning to feel a tad irritated, "there is a *slight* chance that the officer was right, and the creature we saw last night...wasn't a gnome."

"Nonsense," Sewey stated. "What are you trying to tell me, I don't know my gnomes?" He fluffed his newspaper. "Can't you remember the film Mayor Demark made?"

"Of course," Bran said. "How could anyone forget the green gnomes with dripping yellow fangs flying in on broomsticks, picking up children, and dropping them in cauldrons?"

"A very accurate depiction!" Sewey declared. "Perhaps if all the other cities were to take up the proud Duncelander flag, and banish gnomes and mages as well, maybe it would keep the children of the world safer, and the Decensitists wouldn't have to be so decent!"

In Dunce, and even in some places outside, there was a group of parents who called themselves Decensitists, which was a name they had made up by butchering the word *decency.* They were very strictly anti-gnome and anti-mage, so severe they would make up stories for their children and tell them such things didn't even exist. They were very careful to erase any mention of them from their lives and warned their friends that if they ever spoke of anything even borderline magic while they were present, they would do something dreadful. Those in Dunce would sometimes go to such ends as to call the city something completely different, just to be safe. Even Sewey and Mabel avoided the group, as did most of the general population.

"At least we've got those black boxes to keep us safe when we're watching television," Sewey said as he fluffed his paper again. The year before, he had come home with a set of black boxes and plugged one into the back of each television in the house. He proclaimed they were for the preservation of the household's decency, so that channel zero, the Mages Entertainment Channel, would be nothing but static.

"Under the rule of the Imperial Countries," Sewey went on, "Dunce has a legal right to make up its own rules, as long as it doesn't go against the orders of the Queen or the Senate, and they haven't made any address making magic or gnomes legal or illegal anywhere." His voice grew louder. "Gnomes are animals like dragons and duggins and ogres. Those all live far away from civilized towns, and gnomes should just as well join them." He slammed his fist on the table yet again, making Baldretta jump. "We've gotten along just fine without them!" he roared, and seized with a sudden fit of anti-gnome zeal, he leapt upon his chair and pointed toward the sky.

"No gnomes!" he shouted. "No mages! And no ETCETERAS!"

"Hear, hear!" Mabel and Balder chanted, raising their glasses of milk, and Baldretta looked at them as if they had all gone mad.

Sewey stood in that position for a whole minute, looking very patriotic, until he looked down and saw Mabel and Balder cheering for him. He bowed, but lost his balance and came crashing to the floor.

Everyone gasped. His head popped from under the table, an envelope stuck in his hair.

"Ahem..." he stammered. "Well then...I'm off to work!"

He stood and stretched, reaching into his coat for his pocket watch. His hand came out empty.

"Hmmm," he said suspiciously. He went on to search through every pocket in his shirt and pants, and then even in his shoes. No pocket watch.

"Rot," Sewey said. "Where's that bloody watch?"

"Maybe a gnome took it," Bran said with a fake gasp. Sewey crossed his arms.

"You're right!" He kicked the pile of bills in fury. "Filthy gnomes! Can't escape them!"

Sewey left his dishes behind and went downstairs, taking his briefcase and coat. He rushed to his car, only to find that his keys were nowhere to be found.

"Rot," he breathed. Then he remembered his emergency key. However, after checking under the car, he found that he had taken it inside with him the night before. "Double rot." But then he remembered he kept *two* emergency keys, and walked to the other side of the car and reached above the wheel. He kissed the key and slid it in. He noticed Mr.

Swinehic outside, tossing birdseed to the pigeons. An etcetera if he'd ever seen one.

"Makes too much money for his own good," Sewey murmured. Then, turning the ignition, he noticed something else: a curious new vehicle parked down the street. "A black van?" he said aloud, wondering who was visiting. He kept tabs on every Bolton Roader's vehicle, because he was nosy and abhorred parties. Any time there was a gathering of new cars at a house, it meant a party. It also meant a courtesy call from Sewey to the police department the moment he heard a peep of their awful party music. However, he shrugged and decided not to let it bother him...yet. He turned his dial to the Radio Dunce morning show as he passed the van and continued on his way.

"*You're listening to Dan the Man on Radio Dunce!*" the announcer said over a jingle that Sewey abhorred. He turned out of the neighborhood and onto the major road, crowded with cars and trucks heading for downtown. He abhorred them too, each and every one.

"*Hello, I am Dan the Man,*" the familiar voice of Sewey's favorite talk show host came on. *"You're just in time for your morning Dash of Dunce news, and this just in: Mr. Parget's cow is loose down on Eggsworth Street!"*

"Oh joy, a cow loose in Dunce," Sewey snorted. "That will *surely* drive up property value."

"*Cows in the city! The idea!*" Dan agreed. "*Here's another news item: Reports of sleezebirds migrating early next month. That means no more firecrackers or sky shooting.*"

"Even *worse* than cows." Sewey sniffed. Every year, the sleezebirds would migrate north over Dunce after fattening themselves to the size of cars on atom rats in the Chubbie Wastelands. Last year, the city had tried firecrackers to scare them off, but then the birds only landed to watch the show, denting the car roofs and snapping the power lines they perched their weight upon.

"Speaking of loud noises," Dan went on. *"Last night, a madman was reportedly shooting on Bolton Road, as heard by twelve witnesses!"*

"Imagine," Sewey said, shocked "That was on *my* street!" He came to a red light but ignored it, sending cars swerving to avoid him, honking their horns. "Quiet down, I'm trying to hear!" he roared, turning the radio up to cover their awful racket.

"*And,*" the radio went on, "*there was reportedly the same madman causing a disturbance in the alley next to Crab, Nab, and Hawkin Law Firm, where he was boxed in by a police officer.*"

"I can't believe it. I was there yesterday!" Sewey scolded himself for not keeping a sharper eye out for the madman. He wished he had been there to catch him and be featured on the news.

"*Since there's nothing going on here...*" A stack of paper was thrown across the room in disgust, "*I might as well go on to international news, and, surprise, surprise: the Activists for Gnome Equality are on the move again with marches in capitol Hildem.*"

"Gnome equality, my foot," Sewey growled. Even though laws outside Dunce allowed gnomes, many outsiders were still vastly prejudiced against them, causing much controversy.

"*They stood outside for hours, waving 'Gnomes are People too' signs. Thankfully, resident senators from Dunce took care of the matter, and promptly set their dogs loose on the picketers."*

"A perfectly sensible idea!" Sewey nodded with satisfaction, proud that his senators were doing such a good job protecting his freedoms.

Dan gave a giant guffaw. "*Looks like the gnomes' beards and pointy caps can't help them this time! I can't believe that creatures so small could cause such big problems!*"

"Small?" Sewey echoed, not sure he had heard Dan correctly. "Pointy caps? Beards? Well, the gnome that came to *my* house was certainly not small." *Dan and the officer must not know their gnomes,* he thought. He was so glad he was one of the smartest men in town, knowing all he did. He decided that there must be two types of gnomes—the tall and the small—and that Dan, the officer, and the rest of the world for that matter, were just confused.

In fact, his wisdom was so distracting, he ran another red light. A car nicked his rear fender, sending the Schweezer soaring into a crosswalk and through oncoming traffic. An old woman leapt to safety, leaving her cane and wig behind; however, at just that moment, a gigantic ice-cream truck hurtled in Sewey's direction.

"Dah!" Sewey yelped, pulling on the wheel. Both vehicles swerved from each other in the nick of time. The truck teetered and rocked, tipping over so far that entire canisters of Vanilla Vonsway and Tattered Da-Chocolate tumbled into the street.

Sewey swerved the Schweezer back onto his side of the road and weaved into the highway, turning Dan up even louder to drown out his overworked engine.

"*And for the top Mage-news story today!*" Dan went on. "*The Mages Council announced they would allow Mr. Tomstone,* *a* gnome, *into the Guild of Historians! Can you believe it? I do—that's what those mages are coming to these days...little, creeping, garden-planting rats!*"

Sewey and Dan both broke out into peals of laughter. Between chortles and chuckles, Sewey managed to glance at his rearview mirror.

Suddenly, he went stiff. He took a second look at what was following him.

"That's odd," he said with a hint of fright. "It looks *just* like the black van I saw earlier!"

Chapter 6

Secret Letters

The black van lurked behind Sewey's car in the flow of traffic, on the side. Its windows were tinted darkly and he couldn't see inside.

He continued to drive, trying to ignore it. However, it appeared to be overtaking his mirror, as if it might run him off the road, chariot-races style. No matter how he weaved through the cars, the black van always seemed to be right behind him. Sewey's first thought was that it might be an undercover police car, so he immediately looked away. But then he figured the driver of the van was probably in league with the gnome on the roof of his house last night.

"The rude pig," Sewey sniffed. "As if ruining my evening wasn't enough!"

His revolver was in his briefcase, so while swerving through traffic with one arm, he used the other to dislodge the gun from one of the pockets, in case it might soon be needed.

"Wait until Adi hears of this!" he snarled as he drove, keeping a cautious eye on the van.

Sewey worked at the Third Bank of Dunce, sometimes simply known as the TBD. It was the only bank nearby, as the First and Second Banks of Dunce had already gone bankrupt. It sat in a row of buildings in the old downtown—one of many large and crumbling establishments, with a plain brick front, a plain wooden door, and a pair of plain columns. The gigantic clock above had been stuck at 3:14 for half a dozen years, but the building was so boring anyway that no one had bothered to fix it, because hardly anyone even noticed.

Luckily, that was just the way Sewey liked it. When he had parked in his usual spot at the NO PARKING: TOW AWAY ZONE sign, he opened the car door very slowly and looked down the street. The very second he did, the black van passed.

"Rot!" he yelped, frantically swinging his door shut again. His eyes followed the van as it passed, going to the end of the street and turning. Sewey clutched his revolver close until the van disappeared.

"Good." He stepped out, examining the passersby warily.

There's probably more disguised gnomes mixed in with the lot of them, he thought bitterly as he went up to the bank.

It was chilly indoors. Adi Copplestone, his secretary, was at her desk.

"Good morning," she greeted him, not looking up from her computer.

"Bad morning!" he retorted loudly.

Adi looked up and jumped. "Mr. Wilomas!" she gasped. "Whatever are you doing with that gun?!"

"Well..." He waved it around and then shoved it into his pocket. "I've only just had the *worst* twenty-four hours of my life, thank you very much."

Adi seemed relieved the gun wasn't intended for its usual

purpose when wielded by a person walking into a bank. She tore her gaze away from him and started to type again.

"Come now, Mr. Wilomas, it's only morning," she said.

"And it's already started off as a bad one," Sewey snorted. "I chased a gnome all the way to Officer McMason last night, and I was chased *by* gnomes all the way to work today!"

Sewey tossed his coat onto a hanger next to the brooms. Adi just nodded. She was used to Sewey's escapades. She had thin glasses on a chain around her neck, shoulder-length, light blond hair, and green eyes, and was in her mid-twenties. She was the type of person who knew practically everyone in town, and no one could ever expect her to do anything wrong simply because she was Adi. To them *Adi* spelled *normal.* But even though she was very popular among the townspeople, to Sewey, she was just his secretary.

"Catch any burglars last night, Soo?" Ben Baggeater asked, coming out of his office with a cup of coffee.

"DO NOT CALL ME SOO!" Sewey roared. "That bloody burglar got away, and hopefully for good—or so I thought, until this morning he chased me to work."

Ben shrugged. Sewey, seeing no one was listening, spun off for his usual inspection of the vault, grumbling curses at Ben as he did. Ever since the Accident, Sewey had been wary of approaching that big, round metal door. Madame Mobicci and the Board of Directors would certainly not be happy if a second orphan was found in there, so Sewey made a point of pressing his ear to the door before opening it, just in case.

Inside was a long, tube-shaped room, the floor and shelves littered with everything from safe deposit boxes to antique furniture dumped by the board members. Most of the money bags were filled with sawdust to throw off would-be burglars, but the trick worked on bank examiners just as well.

Sewey took a glance, then slammed it shut. "Wonderful. The burglars in this town are too busy bothering *me* to even think of the vault."

He started for his office, when his eye narrowly caught a disappearing shape in the front glass.

"There it is again!" Sewey gasped, pointing toward the window. Adi jerked her head up.

"What?" she said. "Where is it?"

"I just saw it pass," Sewey said, rushing to the window. "It was a black van, the same one that chased me to work this morning."

Adi arose from her desk to take a look, and Ben rushed to Sewey's side. But unfortunately, by the time they had all reached the window, the van had already disappeared. Sewey looked both ways, but it only made him appear more like a fool. Adi looked at him strangely.

"Well, it was *right there,*" Sewey insisted. "They're following me, I tell you!"

"What herbs did Mabel give you this morning?" Ben asked with the slightest hint of a snicker.

Sewey, utterly infuriated, threw his hands into the air and went to his office, and refused to speak to either of them for the rest of the day.

Meanwhile, back at the house, Baldretta had finally surrendered the remote to her brother.

"*Welcome to the Bean Bag Show!*" the television speakers boomed into the living room. Bran let his shoulders drop. Balder's eyes were firmly glued to the biggest screen in the house.

"*I'm Manica-bibble Bunnyfluff!*" the man-sized, blue rabbit on the screen laughed. *"And today, we're gonna teach Woody-Goody Wilson a lesson in sharing the carrot cake!"* Manica-bibble looked both ways, as if to make sure the parents weren't listening. The eyes on the rabbit suit rolled in two different directions. "*And,*" he whispered, *"we're also gonna teach him what happens to big fat tattle-tellers too!"*

"Uh-oh," Bran said. "That doesn't sound good..."

"Hush!" Balder demanded.

The *Bean Bag Show* budget must have been cut recently. Manica-bibble's ears were tied above his head due to a split zipper. Some of the other alligators and buzzards were missing eyes, some were on crutches, and others had holes in their suits that revealed the dingy men underneath. It looked more like a hobo show than a *Bean Bag Show*.

Bran just continued to dust the shelves. Friday was cleaning day. Balder had one chore, once a week: wiping a baseboard in his closet. Still, he refused to do it, though Mabel was adamant. In the end, Bran had to take Balder's hand, hold the rag in it, and move his hand for him, with Balder screaming the whole time. The instant his chore was done, Balder shot back in front of the television, like a magnetic pull between them that science had yet to discover.

"Perhaps you could watch it in your room," Bran suggested. "I *am* trying to work in here."

"Silence, serf!" Balder commanded. "*That* one's too small."

"Quiet down, both of you," Mabel hissed, rushing into the room in a new outfit. This time it was a scarlet gown with tight white gloves that were so long, they enveloped her hands, elbows, and shoulders, just like sleeves. She also had a fur hat with a plastic ruby and three feathers poking out so high, they scraped the ceiling when she scurried from one side of the room to the next. She stuffed the end of a nose-spray bottle in one nostril.

"I'm off to get my ears candled, and there's nothing you can do to stop me," she announced, as if anyone would have wanted to. She sprayed once in one nostril and twice in the other before continuing. "My alternative medicine practitioner informed me that this town is full of mites, and the only way to get them out is to have one's ears candled."

She pointed across the room. "And be sure to clean the corners out good. The *Fitness Witness* magazine says that's where spores hide and breed, sometimes to the size of cats."

Pansy looked up. Mabel eyed her suspiciously and opened her mouth to speak again, but was cut off by a loud clicking noise coming from down the hall.

"The spores!" she gasped. "They're coming to eat us!" She leapt behind the sofa.

"No." Bran shook his head. "That's just Rosie, working on another article for the newspaper."

"Oh, oh..." Mabel said, fanning herself with a peacock feather. She broke open a quick-pack of smelling salts under her nose. "You go tell that awful cousin of mine she should be cleaning, not writing! About to drive me into an allergic reaction with all that tapping!"

She went into a sneezing fit and tripped her way toward the medicine cabinet. Bran pushed the rag along some picture frames and thought hard about the paper Mr. Swinehic had found.

It's just a coincidence, he told himself. *Just another paper like mine. There are probably thousands just like it...*

But it was too unusual for him to be entirely convinced it was all by chance. The handwriting matched. It seemed that the piece of paper, the burglar, and the strange things the burglar had said on the roof were all connected, but Bran couldn't put the pieces together in the right order. He heard Rosie go on typing and decided to see what she was up to. The typewriter was rusty and made lots of noise when she typed in bold, like she always did for her articles. She was at her desk next to the door, with glasses on her nose and papers all around. Her room had yellow walls and white trim that looked like sunshine, matching the beams of glowing rays streaming in from the window behind her bed. She looked up when Bran walked in.

"Oh, Bran!" she said excitedly. "You won't believe the wonderful idea I had!"

"What is it?" Bran asked.

She turned a big box of papers in her lap. "After our conversation at breakfast this morning," she said, "I have decided to write an article about the Givvyng Tree and why gnomes aren't allowed." A gleam came into her eyes. "This time, it's going under Rosie Cheeks, my very own pen name!"

"Sounds great," Bran said. "I'm sure it'll make it this time."

"I hope so," Rosie said, getting back to typing some notes from the newspaper clippings.

"Once I've got my toe in the door," Rosie said, typing, "I'm headed off in the right direction for a full job and—" She looked up. "—maybe even *syndication!*"

She laughed and got back to work. She had written about thirty articles for the *Daily Duncelander,* but they hadn't taken any of them, always telling her the same thing: she needed to spice up her stories with rumors and fictitious references to dead witnesses, like they did with their reports, and then her stories might make it somewhere around the crossword puzzles. But Rosie refused to do it. Nothing could stop her when her mind was set, and even after thirty rejections she was still working harder than ever.

"In my research," she said, pulling out a clipping, "gnomes are *always* small, and they *always* wear conical, red hats."

"Nothing like Sewey's burglar," Bran observed.

"Maybe," Rosie said, reading. "It says here that when our founder Droselmeyer Dunce first wrestled this land from barbarians, he stumbled upon the Givvyng Tree at the top of Givvyng Hill, and on it was carved the words 'no gnomes.' Believing it was divine inspiration, he settled the land and made those very words the first law of the city of Dunce."

"So someone had just carved 'no gnomes' on the tree for no reason," Bran said, grinning.

"Actually," she said, scanning the page, "it says here that some claim the words simply read 'hog homes,' but the tops of the h's are worn off, making them *appear* to be letter n's. But most Duncelander historians strongly disagree and hold to Droselmeyer's story."

Bran laughed. Rosie thought it was funny as well. "It also says here that Droselmeyer, according to legend, was murdered by what he suspected to be two gnome mages, and as he lay dying, he crawled all the way to Givvyng Park and carved the words 'no mages' below the words 'no gnomes.'"

Bran thought on that a moment. "He crawled all the way to the park, when he was *dying?*"

"I know, it's very convoluted," Rosie said. "I can't get a clear history of Dunce anywhere."

Bran shook his head. Almost everyone in Dunce believed such nonsense. In Dunce, Bran wasn't even supposed to have an opinion on gnomes or mages until he was eighteen or else he might have to pay a fine, but that still didn't keep him from thinking about it. He had a feeling the real reason Duncelanders didn't like gnomes was because there were plenty who were more successful, more popular, and held higher political offices than they did, outside of Dunce.

"I've kept all the photos and newspaper clippings the Wilomases throw away for years now." Rosie said. She dug her hand in the box and pulled something out.

"Here's one of Sewey's first job." She held it out. In it, a much younger Sewey was dressed up in a white suit and hat. His arms were crossed very grumpily. Not much had changed.

"Before banker school, he stuck the labels that said 'Warning: May contain traces of peanuts' on the peanut butter jars." Rosie said. She reached for a stack of papers on her desk.

"I've got a picture of the last Biannual Wilomas Family Reunion somewhere. Sewey and all the other Wilomases sit at the long table, and me and the rest of the Tuttles sit at the side."

"Why's that?" Bran asked. Rosie just shrugged.

"The Tuttles have served the Wilomases for years and are of no blood relation," she said simply. "That's just the way it's been. It would be scandalous for a Tuttle to attend the reunion at a Wilomas table. After we're through cooking and waiting on them, then we sit down to eat."

Rosie finally found the photo. It showed rows of Wilomases and their relations, in formal attire, sitting at tables on a grassy hill. At the end was Great-Grandmother Wilomas, a faraway speck in the distance. Behind her towered the gigantic Castle Wilomas. There was a hole cut out of the head of the man sitting next to Sewey. Bran knew who it belonged to. It was Sewey's only sibling, his younger brother, Bartley, who Sewey loathed beyond words, refused to see, and whose face he had removed from all photos in the house after Bartley inherited their parents' fortune, and Sewey inherited a jar of dill pickles.

"So you've always been servants?" Bran asked, finally spotting Rosie holding a tray of steaming food in the photo. Rosie thought for a moment.

"For a long time, at least," she finally said. "Mabel was a Hatfield before she married into the Wilomases. By coincidence she was distantly related to me, a Tuttle. When she married Sewey, it tied the Hatfields to the Wilomases, and us Tuttles to both. I've got another picture here—"

She reached for a stack of papers on the end of her desk, but the moment she did there was a sudden pounding on the floor, as Mabel began to beat the ceiling below with a broom.

"Out you spores, all of you!" Mabel commanded.

At her sudden outburst, Rosie jumped, and accidentally sent a whole pile of papers into the air. Bran dove to catch them, but it was too late—all of them flew over the carpet in different directions.

"Oh, bother," Rosie said, bending down to gather them up. "Now they're all out of order!"

"I'll help." Bran reached down to scoop up a stack of the loose sheets.

"Oh, no, Bran, that's much too kind!" Rosie said, but Bran went on gathering them up. "No, I insist!" she added, her hands rushing as she grabbed at the papers on the floor.

Bran blinked and tried to help, but the moment his hand touched a sheet she whisked it out of his grasp. "Are you sure you don't need any help?" he asked.

"No, none at all!" she burst, rushing about. "Why don't you… go dust Baldretta's bedroom?"

"I already did," Bran replied, confused at how she was acting. She didn't say any more but quickly stuffed all the papers into a drawer in her desk, drawing out a small key and locking it. She spun around to put her back to it and opened her mouth as if she was about to speak, but apparently lost what she was going to say. Instead of trying to remember it, she rushed from the room, leaving Bran very puzzled.

He sat there for a moment on the floor. He had never seen her that way in his life. Suddenly, his eye caught on something: an opened envelope that had fallen under the bed and out of view, close to his leg. Every muscle in his body froze at once. He took a glance out Rosie's open door. No one was there.

Very slowly, he reached for it. He felt it touch his fingertips and slid it closer to him, glancing down at it, not even daring to pick it up from the floor.

The envelope had been opened and was empty. However, there was writing in the center of the envelope, but no address—a script, but definitely not Rosie's. It was stronger, bolder, with thin swirls, and it read:

To Rosie Tuttle
From your Beloved B

Bran took a deep breath. The handwriting was exactly the same as what had been on the card with the mysterious roses.

So she does know who it is… he thought with disbelief. *She's getting letters from him!*

He looked toward the door. She was gone. He looked at the envelope one last time, then shoved it far under the bed and left as quickly as he could, hoping he could just forget about it altogether.

Chapter 7

Sewey Wilomas versus the Oncoming Train

By the evening, Sewey forgot all about searching for the gnome, though he did tell everyone what had happened on the road. As usual, he embellished the small details into bigger ones, and because of it no one believed anything he said.

"So a black van chased you to work," Bran said doubtfully, "and then grew wings and flew off into the sunrise?"

"Yes, that's what I said!" Sewey insisted, and Bran didn't bother to press the subject. Sewey's description of the black van amused him though, and later, while cleaning Sewey's office, Bran took a pencil to one of the notepads. Sewey had caught him and was not at all pleased to see the black van again, complete with wings and an evil grin. Mabel wasn't thrilled either, because Bran had taken the liberty of adding a band of spores with gnashing teeth to the back seats, which frightened her so much she spent the rest of the day camped in the closet, moaning horrors.

"You, sir," Sewey scolded, "are lucky to have been caught before you added red caps to those spore-shaped gnomes, or else you'd be hitchhiking to court to pay your indecency fine."

It made Bran feel much better—as if now that he was laughing about it, the burglar wasn't a threat anymore. His thoughts shifted to the envelope in Rosie's room, and he puzzled over every Mr. B. in town, though none of them seemed to fit. In his boredom he sketched out a large letter B, adding sharp flames to its shape as if he could melt away all memory of the man who was writing to Rosie. He knew he would find the rest of the letters soon enough.

Sunday morning rolled about, and the house was abuzz again as everyone rushed to get ready for the Bolton Road Weekly Picnic. They all had to go or else the neighbors would talk about them behind their backs, as if the Wilomases didn't have enough gossip going around already.

"Ohhh," Mabel was moaning. "The Pig-pollens must be high today."

"But the weather's beautiful!" Rosie replied, flipping pancakes. "Go take some nose spray."

"Already did," Mabel sniffled. "A whole super-pack of Christine's Antihistamines." She crossed her arms. "In fact, I took all my medicines, and I still feel the same as I did last night. As if they aren't doing a bloody thing..."

"Maybe the diseases are adapting," Bran said with a fake gasp.

Mabel spun and went pale. "You're right!" she whispered. "They *are* adapting! Help, help!" She clutched her throat. "The spores! The spores! They're coming to get me!"

At that moment, there was a knock at the front door.

"There they are!" Mabel cried, running for the antihistamines. Rosie took the pancakes off the stove and dashed to answer the door, when who should come bounding along but Sewey to answer it himself.

"I've got it," he said, practically tripping over his own legs as he came down the hall.

"I'll get it!" Rosie insisted.

"I said that I've got it!" Sewey said, pushing her aside.

"No, Sewey, don't answer it!" Rosie shouted, pushing him back.

Bran slid to the kitchen door, taken aback at how Rosie was acting. Baldretta, who was sitting on the stairs and munching on a box of chocolates, looked from Rosie to Sewey, her eyes swaying like a pendulum.

"I'm the owner of this house, and I want to answer my door," Sewey snapped, pushing Rosie out of the way, and before she could stop him, he jerked opened the door. Standing there was Bill the milkman, dressed up in his suit with a crate of milk.

"Hello, chap. Hello, Rosie. Just here to deliver a bit o' milk," Bill said.

Sewey eyed Rosie suspiciously, but then stepped forward and left her standing there. "You're late," he growled. "Besides, idiot, you don't deliver on Sundays."

"Sorry," Bill said, his smile not wavering. "Wasn't enough to bring last time. The ice cream company took all we had to make up for a batch lost in a road accident. Company policy."

Sewey took the tray amid grumbles. With a quick tip of his hat to Rosie, Bill turned to leave. Sewey's eyes lit up like strobes when he saw Bill look at her. "Aha!" he said when he shut the door. "No wonder you were acting ridiculous about answering the door! *He's* the secret B from the roses!"

"But I don't even like Bill!" Rosie protested.

"Well, I don't like him either," Sewey said with a snicker. "But that doesn't mean he doesn't like *you.*"

Rosie went red but refused to speak any further on the matter. Half an hour later, they sat down to eat. The pancakes were steaming and had butter smeared across each one. Balder plopped his into an ocean of syrup as Sewey pulled out his day book.

"Today we have the picnic," he proclaimed. "Then we're going to the bookstore."

"Whatever for?" Mabel asked. Sewey was hardly seen touching, much less reading, a book.

"Because I'm not paying for another exterminator who can't even keep regular gnomes away," Sewey said. "So I'm getting a book on pest control."

"Pests!" Mabel shrieked, slinging out her bottle of disinfectant.

"Yes," Sewey nodded. "Gnomes on the roof, in the house, on the streets, at work. *Pests.*"

He started to read the rest of the page in his day book. As they ate, Bran glanced at Rosie. She still seemed to be a little nervous, the same as when she had run to answer the door. It was very unlike her to be that way, and he could tell she was trying to hide it.

Sewey poked another pancake. "I checked the clock in the kitchen," he said. "The picnic doesn't start until eleven, and we've got a good hour and a half till then at least."

At that, Mabel furrowed her brow. Sewey looked at her.

"I just remembered," she said. "I think Mrs. Yankerbank said it started at nine this week..."

All of a sudden, everyone stopped chewing, even Baldretta.

"She what?" Sewey said.

"I think she said they moved the time two hours earlier this week, for some reason..." Mabel said. Realization hit Sewey like an anvil from the sky.

"Oh, rot!" he shouted.

"We're not early," Bran said. "We're half an hour *late!*"

They leapt from their places in horror and left their dishes, stampeding to the stairs.

"How could this happen?" Sewey gasped, fixing his hair in the mirror. Mabel grabbed her purse, and Rosie seized Baldretta so she wouldn't be trampled underfoot. Balder started to scamper back up the stairs, but Sewey caught him like a tiny piglet.

"No time, we've got to go!" he said.

"But I forgot my jelly beans!" Balder squealed as Sewey carried him out the door and Mabel locked it behind them. The streets were abandoned—the neighbors were all at Givvyng Park.

"They're probably talking about us right now!" Mabel gasped.

Sewey ran to the Schweezer and grabbed the door handle, and almost pulled it clean off. The door was locked. And all his emergency keys were inside the house.

Luckily, Mabel had a key of her own. Sewey sped to sixty immediately after turning the ignition. Mabel, who hadn't yet buckled her seat belt, slammed into Balder, nearly crushing him. Rosie sat between Bran and Baldretta's car seat in the back, holding them in as the Schweezer took off like an old rocket. Mabel went pale.

"What is it *now?*" Sewey whined at her.

"I forgot my neoplytoplismo," she whispered. "What if there are lepers at the picnic?"

Baldretta offered a chocolate, but Mabel didn't think it would help. Sewey shoved on the horn to let everyone know he was coming and they had better move. The Schweezer slid around corners, jetting over curb and crosswalk. Bran tried to hold on, but all the movement jostled him back and forth against the seat belt. Luckily, the road ahead of them was clear of cars. However, as Bran distractedly glanced behind them, he saw something.

"Look, Sewey, it's the black van!" he said. Sewey jerked about.

"WHERE?!" he roared. The car screamed from one side of the road to the other.

"Just drive!" Bran shouted, but he had to laugh at Sewey's reaction. "Look, it's only a black van, right there behind us. See?"

Bran pointed. The black van was far, but it was the only other vehicle in sight behind them. Sewey looked at the road, then at the mirror, then the road again, back and forth.

"It's bloody following me *again!*" he hissed.

"No, listen," Bran said. "It's a coincidence. I shouldn't have pointed it out. Now just drive."

Sewey, however, would not, and instead chose to watch the mirror instead of where they were going. They were coming closer to a railroad crossing, and Sewey gunned the engine further, not even watching the road in front of him, or the flashing lights.

"Sewey," Rosie said. "You had better put on your brakes—"

"Hush!" Sewey said. "That black van is actually *gaining* on us!"

"But Sewey," Rosie shouted, "you had *better put on your brakes!*"

"What?" Sewey protested. "Brakes? Great Moby, don't you know that'll slow us down?"

"That's the point!" Bran shouted.

Everyone screamed as the car rocketed up the tracks and the crossing arms came down. Sewey had missed seeing this altogether, and he had even missed the steaming train rapidly approaching around the bend.

"GREAT MOBY!" Sewey shouted, turning the wheel to miss the first guard arm.

"GREAT GOODNESS!" he shouted again, as he swerved and faced the oncoming train.

"GREAT ROT!" he roared, as he slammed on the accelerator and swerved away from the second arm and off the track, just a second before the train crossed. And they were back on the road, as if nothing had happened at all. Baldretta clapped with glee in her eyes and a sucker in her mouth, and they hit a bump.

"Whoopee!" Balder squealed, looking back. "We could have been smashed!"

"Rot," Sewey said, shaking a fist and trying to catch his breath. "I'll have the law on that van *and* that reckless locomotive!"

"Well, it's gone now, Sewey," Bran said, catching his breath. "Look, the black van isn't behind us anymore, either. The train blocked it off."

"That would be the *only* good thing that has happened this morning," Sewey growled. Still, he checked the mirrors. As the train cars rumbled by, he could see the black van waiting behind it, as if staring him down. It was menacing and made Sewey nervous, so he punched on the gas and started off on the shortest shortcut he knew.

***

The rest of the drive was tense and still. Sewey turned on the radio. Unfortunately, he only listened to Radio Dunce, whose music library consisted entirely of dull rock bands like Harmonious Sticky and Glumpius Fiest. It did nothing to alleviate the misery in the air.

"I'm hungry," Balder complained.

"You just ate breakfast, dear," Rosie said. "Now be quiet. Deary daddy is trying to drive."

"*Deary daddy...*" Sewey mimicked in a low, childish voice. "Bah!"

"Bah!" Balder said, and then straightened up to see better. "Look, look! It's Givvyng Park!"

Sewey narrowed his eyes as they drove closer.

"No," he gave a dull laugh. "That's not the park. Our picnic is much more civil than that."

"I do believe that's it..." Rosie said. The park came closer, and the closer it got, the more worried Sewey looked. He punched off the radio.

"What is this?" he murmured.

Bran looked out his window as the park came into view, and it looked so different from their usual picnic spot that even *he* wondered if they had come to the right place. Brightly colored tents and banners dotted acres of the grounds, with flags waving in the wind and animal pens all around. There was a bull in one, nearly twenty pigs in another, and sheep and goats and huge display cages spread about. He couldn't see the whole lot of them, there were so many. It looked almost like a circus, or the mayor's birthday—both of which were very much the same after the kegs of Duncelander Ale had been cracked open.

"Blabl!" Baldretta said frantically, pointing ahead at the road.

"Sewey, a chicken!" Mabel shouted. Sewey swerved off the path to avoid the squawking hen as she crossed the gravel that led up to the park gate. There were hundreds of cars in neat patterns in the parking area, and even more people with balloons and cotton candy running all around. Balder, of course, looked delighted.

"Look, pigs!" he squealed with delight, as if he were finally coming home. Bran sat up straighter to see out. There were lines of people to get in, and even more already inside the gates.

"This can't be the picnic," Bran said. "Where's Old Mrs. Rankle and her doorknob collection? And Crazy Tom with his latest invention?"

"I haven't the slightest idea," Sewey said, his head turning from one direction to the other. "I must have taken a wrong turn back there…maybe this fellow will give me directions." He sped up closer to a college-aged young man in a brown sweater walking in a slow, carefree stride toward the gate. Sewey caught up with him and rolled his window down. "You there! *Stop!*" he ordered.

The man grinned politely as he came forward.

"Yes, sir?" he said, looking down at Sewey through the window. He looked as polished as an antique dresser, with a plain blue shirt under his sweater and orange hair combed just right.

"What are all these chickens and pigs and goats and cows doing at *my* picnic?" Sewey fumed, shaking his hand at each animal as he said their names.

"Dontcha know? It's the Duncelander Fair!" the man replied with glee.

"What?" Sewey exclaimed, very much without glee.

"The...Duncelander...Fair," the man said slowly, enunciating each word.

"Why is it *today!?*" Sewey moaned. "Here! Now! *Why!?*"

"Oh, sir, you see... it rained on Tuesday, which was when we were supposed to hold it. It was Twoo's Day—has been for centuries!"

Twoo's Day was, in fact, nationally held every year on April tenth, which was coincidentally on a Tuesday that year. Twoo himself had been the famous Mezzleheimer Twoo, the first Prime Minister over the Senate in Hildem. He was quite a respected figure, but since it seemed that the mayor could change the date of celebrations because of the rain, it didn't have as much meaning in Dunce and only meant yet another large party and one of the mayor's boring speeches.

"Thank you very much." Sewey rolled the window up. "We're leaving!" he said firmly, shifting gears to plow through the cars behind them.

"Oh, no! Let's stay!" Rosie burst out, so suddenly that Sewey hit the brakes.

"Give me *one* good reason to stay *here,*" he growled.

Rosie looked around the car as if expecting to find an answer on the walls, then down at her feet, then up to the ceiling. "Um...we can listen to the speeches?" she squeaked.

"Well, that's settled," Sewey said, moving the car again. "We're going home and..."

Rosie must have been desperate, because suddenly she thought of the precise thing to say.

"What would the neighbors say?" she said loudly over the engine, and again everyone was thrown in their seats.

"What?" Sewey and Mabel both said at the same time.

"W-what would the neighbors say?" Rosie stammered. Sewey and Mabel just stared at her, and she seemed to melt like a piece of wax in a fiery furnace. Cars started to go around them, drivers waving their fists at Sewey.

"In fact," Rosie added, "they might all just talk about us for the whole Duncelander Fair!"

Mabel gasped. "As if we're not infamous enough!" she turned to Sewey. "That settles it: we're *not* leaving."

"But I don't want to stay," Sewey spat. "I'd rather go home and sit in a rot heap."

"We're not leaving!" Mabel screeched.

Sewey grumbled and growled, but in the end he switched gears.

"All right, have it your way," he said angrily. "Everyone *out!*"

Chapter 8

The Duncelander Fair

Bran closed the door and heard Sewey slam his. He took a deep breath of the fresh air and stretched his legs after being in the cramped car.

"Oh, goody-goody!" Balder squealed with delight as he hopped to the ground.

"Certainly not," Sewey grumbled. Bran gave the menagerie of colorful tents and wooden booths another look. Hundreds of banners waved in the wind, and farmers' trucks drove in and out to drop off even more animals from the farms.

"It's got to be a misery for those farmers driving with *animals* in their trucks," Sewey said.

"Well, it's not much different than driving up with the Wilomases," Bran replied with a shrug.

"Oh, hush!" Sewey said. "The sooner we finish this nonsense, the sooner we can go!"

Sewey started off for the line of people. Everyone else seemed to be having a good time, but Sewey and Mabel walked with frowning, stony faces. Rosie closed her door when she got out on the other side, breathing a sigh of relief. She picked up Baldretta and started to follow.

"We leave at the *first* chance we get," Sewey decreed, looking over his shoulder. "And we are definitely *not* going to listen to one of the mayor's speeches."

"But *I* am going see his wife!" Mabel stated. "I'll see if she has some neoplytoplismo on her."

"You and that sickly friend of yours," Sewey said. "She's the one with all the diseases!"

"She does *not* have a disease," Mabel replied. "She takes double the medicines I do!"

They made their way down the line, coming through into a large open space where everyone was gathered, with roads and paths going in all directions toward rows of booths.

"Bran, do you see those dark clouds?" Sewey pointed to the sky. "Whoopee! It'll rain!"

"You've made up your mind we're not going home, so just try to enjoy yourself." Bran sighed

"Bah! Won't happen *here,*" he spat, but then he jumped. "Look! The van from Radio Dunce!" He started to rush in its direction, but Mabel caught him by the arm.

"You're not going see that vulgar Dan!" she said. "I can't stand the sound of him!"

"But he's Dan *the Man,*" Sewey protested, dusting her hand off his shoulder.

Mabel would hear none of it. Bran looked around at all the people and the booths. Tents were everywhere, some advertising animal performances, others auctions or games for prizes. Bran saw a booth for Performing Cockroaches and another for Visual Tricks Which Do Not Involve Magic. There was a booth for nearly every association in Dunce, including AARS, the Association Against Rabbit Stew, TAZTARD, the Anti-Zofleman's

Tavern Association of Responsible Duncelanders, and DUMB, Duncelanders for Underground Mining Boys. Rosie touched his arm and broke him from his thoughts.

"Come on, they're walking fast," she said softly, and they followed the Wilomases through the jostling crowds. There were so many people that they must have come from all over the city.

"Cotton candy, anyone?" Rosie offered, pointing toward a yellow booth. Baldretta clapped.

"Candy! Gimme some!" Balder squealed.

"No," Sewey said flatly. He kept to the side of the road and was suddenly stopped by a voice.

"Excuse me, sir! SIR!"

"WHAT!" Sewey burst, spinning around to face the woman in the booth. It was painted white with red lines in a rather confusing pattern.

"I'm from the Society to Upgrade People's Intelligent Demeanors, and I was wondering—"

"No!" Sewey stopped her. "My name will not go on your list of donors today!"

"You wish to remain anonymous?" the woman asked, confused.

"I wish to be left alone!" Sewey snapped, pulling everyone away. They stumbled through the crowds again, until Sewey spun about at another one of the booths.

"So why're you wasting *your* time today?" he asked the man behind the counter.

"Me?" the man turned to face Sewey. He wore a ridiculous, purple top hat and grinned at Sewey, then at Balder. In his hand was a waffle cone.

"ICE CREAM!" Balder yelled. "Gimme some! Gimme some!"

"No!" Sewey said, and Balder flipped backward in a screaming fury of whines and squeals.

"WAHHHH!" He hit the ground with his hands and feet and rolled about in the dirt. The crowds around them looked down at Balder, then up at Sewey and Mabel, and hurried away from the scene, whispering about those strange Bolton Roaders.

"Quick, two double scoops!" Sewey ordered, as more people started to look in their direction.

"Triple!" Balder commanded, sitting up with his lip out.

"No!" Sewey said, stomping his foot. "*Double.*"

"Triple!" Balder whined.

"Double!"

The ice cream man was now very confused and looked from Balder to Sewey, and then back again, trying to decide who to listen to. Baldretta pursed her lips—she just wanted *anything.*

"Triple!" Balder screamed.

"No!"

"WAHHHH!" Balder fell to the ground again, picking up dirt and throwing it at everyone. Duncelanders around them dodged the flying clods, huffing and puffing in Sewey's direction about how he should more extensively restrain his offspring.

"Make it two triples, on the double," Sewey hissed, going red under their disdainful glances.

"And make it Tattered Da-Chocolate!" Balder demanded. He dusted his clothes off.

"I'm sorry," the man replied. "There was an unfortunate accident on the road last week, and all the Tattered Da-Chocolate was lost."

"I'll settle for Vanilla Vonsway," Balder pouted.

"That's gone too," the man said, shrugging.

"Blagh!" Balder spat. "Then just give me Honkerbutton Supreme!"

"Now that we *do* have," the man said, and he stacked three scoops into each cone. "Twenty sib, thank you," he told Sewey, handing one to Balder and the other to Baldretta.

"*Twenty?*" Sewey gasped. "Outrageous! Completely absurd!"

"Twenty sib, please," the man insisted, not giving in. Sewey growled, but finally pulled the money out of his wallet with reluctance. The man counted it, grinned, and nodded.

"Come again!" he said. Baldretta giggled as she licked the ice cream.

"This is why I *hate* Duncelander Fairs!" Sewey grumbled. "Twenty sib. Banditry!"

He stormed off, but Rosie caught Bran by the shoulder and held him back.

"Wait." She dug about in her purse. "What kind of ice cream do you want? My treat."

Bran was so surprised that he didn't know what to say.

"Not on your life!" Mabel squealed. "It'll ruin him, all that sugar!"

"But a single scoop won't..." Rosie protested, digging around in her purse for some money.

"No! I say *no!*" And Mabel followed Sewey. Bran shrugged.

"I'll make it up to you later," Rosie said. Balder licked his ice cream and grinned at them, little honkerbuttons sticking to the edges of his mouth.

All of a sudden, there was the sound of horns blasting behind them. They all spun around, and Bran saw a large group of men in white suits carrying trumpets and blasting loud tunes in unison, their faces red and puffed up. Sewey pushed everyone to the side of the path as the trumpeters came by, not even glancing at the people who had begun to cheer in the sidelines.

"Look!" Rosie said. "That must be the mayor coming!"

Indeed it was, but no one could see him. Around the bend came a baby elephant, and on its back was a canopied box. The elephant looked as if it was having a rather hard time carrying the box, and it wobbled to and fro among the acrobats that were doing flips under its feet. The box on its back was covered with thick cloths, all different colors, so no one could see the inside, but so there wasn't any confusion, there was a sign above the box that read:

IN THIS BOX IS THE MAYOR OF DUNCE

AND HIS WIFE.

STAY OUT OF THE WAY AND DO NOT FEED

THE ELEPHANT.

The towering, four-footed beast walked slowly with the parade, and more men in blue suits came behind it, clanging cymbals and banging bells. Bran stood on the tips of his toes to see better as the elephant neared the bend, heading toward a clearing in the distance where the mayor was going to give his speech. The sounds of the parade disappeared into the distance, and soon the conversations started up again among the people.

"Well, now that they're here, I've got to go talk to Mrs. Demark," Mabel said, starting off.

"No!" Sewey said. "I most certainly will *not* stand there and listen to you gab about influenza and Midhampton's disease with the mayor's wife for two hours again!"

"Then *you* can just go off by yourself," Mabel retorted. "And when something terrible happens, you can find us over there at the picnic tables!"

"Fine!" Sewey said, and he started off in the opposite direction.

"I hope you come running back for your life to those picnic tables!" Mabel called after him.

"Nyah!" Sewey stuck his tongue out. Some people looked at them again, whispering more things about those strange Bolton Roaders.

Bran watched Sewey disappear into the crowds. "I've got a feeling he'll be running back in about five minutes," he said, grinning at Rosie.

Sewey grumbled his way through the crowds, jostling everyone aside like a big ape.

What I need is a bunch of trumpeters, he thought. *And an elephant. Then people would move out of my way!*

But he had neither, so he kept pushing. He looked up and down the rows for anything to do. He came to a tent with about eighteen different cakes sitting all in a row on a long table. He tried a bite of each one, and then saw a blue ribbon on the last, awarding it for Best Cake Design.

"Whoops..." he said, still covered with blue icing.

The next tent he came to had a sign strictly prohibiting children to enter.

"Hmmm..." he said curiously, and he looked both ways before going in. It was dimly lit with a small wall set up in the middle. There was a basket of apples to throw at short people running back and forth behind it. The people were dressed up as gnomes, complete with red felt hats and long white beards. Sewey dashed out of the tent, covering his eyes.

"The indecency one finds at these fairs," he gasped. "And they got those gnomes all wrong!"

He moved on to the next tent, and then the next, but there simply wasn't anything to do. He was getting so bored he almost considered going to listen to the mayor's speech. "No, never," he told himself, rushing on. He passed nearly a dozen booths and paused to wipe his forehead, when he was stopped by a hoarse whisper.

"Psst!" It came from his left and between two large tents.

Sewey darted his gaze around. "What do you want?" he growled into the darkness. "You had better not be another charity."

"Come here," the low voice said. Sewey peered into the shadows and saw a man with an unshaven face and a closed umbrella in his hand. The man looked warily about, his uncut, sandy hair so thin it went off in every direction like tiny sprouts. The man was nearly as thin as his hair, his eyes searching the road furtively in case anyone noticed him. Sewey stepped closer.

"Yes?" Sewey asked, his voice filled with irritation.

"You look respectable," the man mumbled. "The name's Rat, Mr. Rat..."

He stepped backward and ushered Sewey deeper into the shadows. Sewey looked around and saw that most of the people were ignoring them, despite their strange position.

"Yes, what is it?" Sewey asked impatiently, crossing his arms.

"It's what's in the umbrella, that's what," Mr. Rat said conspiratorially, patting the umbrella.

"And what's in the umbrella?" Sewey asked, getting tired of the little game being played. The man placed it handle-up on the ground, standing back as he opened it up to reveal...

"Papers," Sewey said, not impressed. "Just plain old papers."

"Not just any normal papers, no siree." Mr. Rat looked around. "*Magic* papers!"

Sewey gasped with shock and his hand came up to cover his mouth. He gulped and looked inside the open umbrella: the sheets were completely blank.

"M-m-magic...?" Sewey's voice was even lower than Mr. Rat's. His heart nearly stopped.

"Yes, *magic,*" Mr. Rat said with a twinkle in his cautious eyes. "Any businessman's got to be interested, but given the, er, circumstances, we've got to keep it quiet around the police. To make it work, you write with a pen here on the page." Mr. Rat proceeded to pull a pen from his shirt pocket, taking up one of the papers and closing the umbrella.

"See, look: I write a five here, and here I write a multiplication sign, then an eight." He wrote on the paper, much to the astonishment of Sewey, who was in too much shock to stop him.

"And now watch—*it changes!*"

And indeed it did. Right before Sewey's eyes, the two numbers and the multiplication sign both wavered and disappeared and were replaced, in clean black ink, by the number forty. It was as shocking as if the man had turned into a rooster.

"See, a calculator, anytime, anywhere. Yours for three sib."

"What?" Sewey squawked. He felt faint.

"Well, it is low, isn't it? But got to take what I can get in Dunce," Mr. Rat said. "I ain't no mage, either, just a simple salesma..."

"NO!" Sewey exploded, screaming even louder than the babbling crowds. "Magic! MAGIC!"

"Shhh! Sir!" the man pleaded. He waved his hands frantically to try and quiet Sewey.

"Magic! Magic!" Sewey screeched like an old woman, running away. "Officer!" he shouted, waving his arms and dashing from the tents. His shouts had already gotten the attention a rotund officer, pushing through the crowds.

After a few gasping words from Sewey, the officer seized the whimpering Mr. Rat, but because he was so thin, Mr. Rat just slipped right out like a weasel.

The officer barely caught hold of him by the hairs of his bushy head. "C'mere!" he officer wheezed, dragging Mr. Rat away and seizing the umbrella. He radioed for two more officers to come quick, and they appeared from either side, attempting to subdue the screaming Mr. Rat. "I need the magecuffs!"

One of the officers yanked the special handcuffs off his belt. They were battery powered and mechanically designed to keep mages from doing magic.

"No!" Mr. Rat protested. "I'm not a mage! Not the *magecuffs!*"

They slapped them on anyway. Sewey clutched at his heart as if it had stopped.

"Will someone stop this madness?" Sewey asked the world around him.

The police shoved Mr. Rat into a car, which rushed off screaming down the road. Sewey did the same, rushing off screaming through the park for Mabel and the picnic tables.

Mabel laughed and laughed and laughed. Sewey barely managed to get his story out with all the noise she was making. Not a single one of them believed it.

"But he *did* try to sell me magic papers!" Sewey insisted, gasping for air.

"Yeah, right," Balder said. Sewey knew better than to try to convince them.

"Why do these things happen to me?" he moaned later to Rosie, Balder, and Bran, all of them sitting at a picnic table. Mabel was with Baldretta and chatting away with Mrs. Demark by another table. The elephant and the trumpeters were gone, but on the stage, Bran saw the mayor signing autographs for a line of people. His wife wore a beekeeper's hat with a net over her head to keep spores from nipping at her eyes.

"Maybe you looked to him like the type of person who would buy magic things," Rosie said, trying to get Sewey to be quiet.

"What?" Sewey demanded. "Magic objects? ME? Preposterous!" He shook his fist at the sky. "I tell you, Rosie Tuttle, there are *six* things that I will *never* do. I will never, ever buy anything magical, and I will never, ever shake hands with a gnome. I will never join the army, or live anywhere near my brother, or help a mage out of jail. And I will never, ever, *ever* become a politician! Is that clear to you, Rosie Tuttle?"

Rosie nodded nervously. They were in a small clearing just below the famous Givvyng Hill, which went very far up above them with a slow slant. On top of the hill was the Givvyng Tree, the same on which were carved the famous words, "no gnomes, no mages." A short distance away, there was a sidewalk that ran alongside the major road; gathering along the sidewalk was a row of booths.

"Blast this crazy Duncelander weather," Sewey moaned. "It's so hot."

"Oh, I give up," Rosie said, exasperated. She stood up and fixed her hat. "I'm going over there to look at the jewelry stand," she said, checking her purse. "I might be able to buy a new pin or something."

"Bah!" Sewey waved his hand, and she started off for the stands close to the road. The table went very quiet when she left.

Bran looked about, bored. A short way off to the west, there was a long brick wall that went for miles north and south, so far that he couldn't see the end. It divided the city of Dunce from the wild and ferocious West Wood. There were tall trees that peeked over the top of the wall, and as Bran peered off into the west, he thought it was darker to that direction in a strange and foreboding way. Balder saw him looking at it.

"Sewey," Balder pointed to the wall. "What's that?"

"What's what?" Sewey said, looking around.

"That wall over there," Balder pointed. Sewey's gaze followed his finger.

"That, Balder," Sewey explained, "is the West Wall. It divides our city from the ferocious West Wood, which is filled with terrible things. Terrible beasts: maybe bugbears, or worse!"

"Bugbears?" Balder sneered. "You're pulling my leg!"

"It's true," Sewey insisted, waving his arms. "No one ever goes in there; not even mages will step foot in them for fear of the beasts. Wish they would though, and never come back! Those woods go all the way up the side of the globe, and no one's ever plotted a map of them, and every airplane that accidentally ventures over never returns." He mopped his brow before going on. "It's best not to even think of the Wall. There are plenty of other, safer things to think of, like banking. And finances. And the stock market..."

"But what's in there?" Bran asked, staring at it.

Sewey wrinkled his brow. "I already said, no one ever goes in," he replied. "So no one knows."

"I bet there are monsters in there, and they'll be getting out soon!" Balder burst with glee.

"Not through *that* wall, they won't." Another voice came from behind them, and Bran turned.

"Hello, Adi," he said.

Sewey spun as she walked up to them, dressed in light green and holding a cup of lemonade. She smiled warmly and nodded toward the wall.

"It's solid brick," she went on. "One door in and one door out, and that's the Greene Gate."

She pointed over Balder's shoulder. Far off, there was a dark green wooden door—thick, bolted, and set into the wall tightly. The hinges were black metal and held it strongly in place. "No one's opened it for years," she added, putting on an air of mystery. "Thirty years ago, when explorers broke down part of the wall to go in, only one of the entire group made it home: Martilla Greene. She was so terrified when she got back, she was mute the rest of her life, spent all her money to build that gate, and never told anyone what was beyond the wall."

Sewey's eyes went wide. He gulped.

"Are there…monsters?" he whispered.

Adi shrugged. "Like I said, no one knows," she said, and she took a sip of her lemonade.

Sewey stared at the wall for a long while, and then finally crossed his arms again. "Well, whatever it is," he said, "it's probably some gnome's fault for causing it! "He turned on Adi. "In fact, after what happened to me Friday, things have only gotten worse!" He began to rant at her about what had happened that morning on the way up.

Bran, having heard it all before, started to watch the people walking by the booths. He spotted one of their neighbors, and across the grass, Rosie at the jewelry stand, looking at something.

For a moment, his gaze was grabbed from her by a man who was wandering down the path. The man didn't look strange at all but for some reason, he didn't seem to be acting right. He kept looking from one person to the next, and finally he saw Rosie, and started to move closer to her.

What's he doing? Bran wondered, watching him closely. Rosie didn't see him, and the man started to move in her direction through the crowd, though he only glanced at her every few steps. A big truck drove by on the road behind them, honking to the people at the fair in greeting, and Rosie laughed at something the booth owner had said.

"And then," Sewey went on beside Bran, "this man named Mr. Rat comes and..."

Sewey's voice seemed to fade into the back of Bran's head, like a distant echo. A strange feeling began to creep over him, something he had not felt before, almost electrifying. He didn't know what it was, but it felt as if his senses were abruptly coming around and he could see and hear a hundred times better than before.

He couldn't tear his eyes from the strange man moving next to Rosie, and he saw her laugh again and start to turn from the booth. And in that split second, something happened.

Suddenly, the man leapt at her, shoving her to the side and into the booth. Bran jumped to his feet, and Rosie screamed, people in the crowds falling over as the man pushed her.

"Rosie!" Bran shouted. The man grabbed for her purse, trying to get it from her. Her arm was caught in the strap, though, and she screamed when he pulled her with it.

Bran leapt off the table and started to run for her, his heart pounding. Sewey and Adi spun, but Bran was already gone, and the man dodged a booth owner and started running toward the road, Rosie struggling to get her arm out as he dragged her behind him.

"Someone help her!" a woman screamed. A police officer ran in her direction, only to trip over a cable holding the tents up. Bran's feet pounded against the grass, and he saw the man give a final jerk on the purse, sending Rosie falling into the middle of the road. The man dashed off, leaving her behind.

"Help!" Rosie screamed, struggling to stand, just as Bran got to the end of the sidewalk.

"Rosie!" he shouted. She was trying to sit up, sobbing. He reached the road and was almost to her when all of a sudden, he saw something rushing in their direction out of the corner of his eye.

He turned his head, and in a moment, it seemed as if time stopped. He could hear the beating of his own heart in his ears. And he saw a freight truck, coming right at them down the road.

No! his mind gasped. He heard the crowd behind him, shouting. He heard Rosie scream, trying to move. And he heard the horn of the truck, the driver unable to stop. It was rushing closer, faster, its horn ringing in his ear, and Bran's eyes widened as it came.

And then, *it happened.*

It was as if something broke free within him. There was a rush, then a quick cold jolt that washed over him as if he had been hit by a tidal wave on a freezing night. He saw the truck coming at them, he saw the grille on the front, closer and closer. He saw the driver, trying to stop, he saw the license plate—all of it at once. And in a sudden motion, he swung his hands out in front of him and Rosie, as if something else was controlling his reflexes, as if he could stop the truck right there. He saw something blue, like a wall in front of him, translucent at his hands, and though he didn't know what was happening, a second later the truck was upon them.

It slammed into him full force and he gritted his teeth together, and all else around him melted away—the sounds, the colors, the people. He heard the smashing of metal, felt heat from the engine. His feet slid on the pavement, but something held him in place. His mind didn't even allow him to consider what he was doing. He held his ground, pushing against the force of the truck—and in front of him, he saw the metal bending and breaking inward, smashing and crumbling.

He shouted, his voice echoing, sweat creeping into his eyes, down his arms, onto his hands. He didn't think—he just pushed against the truck, fighting its force. And in a second that felt like hours, Bran felt the force against him stop, falling back...

There was a sound like a gunshot in Bran's ears. He was thrown backward off his feet, and in an instant everything went black.

Chapter 9

The Box in the Bookstore

Bran heard someone breathing.

It sounded like the birth of new life, as if something dead had awakened and was taking its first breath of air again. It was long and drawn out, and he felt as if it were drawing the air out of his own lungs to feed it. He tried to scream, but no sound would come. He felt someone near him, then above him, reaching out with withered, white hands. Bran couldn't see a face before the figure disappeared like smoke. And as quickly as it had begun—

It stopped.

Bran gasped and found his hands clutching at the grass, his back to the ground and tents towering over each side of him. He was breathing hard and heard shouting nearby. When he sat up, he saw a big freight truck with its front smashed in, sitting far off in the middle of the road. Around it was a crowd of people, helping a woman up. He recognized her in a second: it was Rosie, alive and unhurt.

What happened? he thought wildly, struggling to stand. A thousand questions ran through his head, but every one vanished when he felt a hand grab his shoulder and pull him up.

"Bran!"

When he turned, it was the last person he had expected to see. "Adi?" he said with alarm. He gasped as she clenched his shoulder with a strength he had never imagined her to have. Her eyes flashed with a strange anger.

"Quiet!" she snapped, jerking him into the back of the booths. All of the owners were gone from their stations, and there were boxes of merchandise behind the counters, small partitions dividing the different booths from each other. Through the openings, Bran could see the group of people by Rosie. Adi pulled him out of the sight of the crowd.

"What's happening?" he asked anxiously. "What are you doing?"

"I'm getting you out of sight, Bran," Adi snapped back. "And you might want to be thinking of what you're going to tell those Duncelanders."

"What do you mean? I don't even know what happened!"

"You don't?" Adi said dryly. "You should. Or maybe you don't. That's the way this city is—you don't even know who you are before it happens."

He tried to look back. He didn't know what Adi was talking about at all. She came to the door on the end and pushed through, opening to the clearing by the picnic tables. There was no one around, and Bran could hear the people by the truck in the distance.

"So you don't even know what happened," Adi said, and she spun him around to face her.

He was at a loss for words. He didn't know what to say or do, everything was happening so fast.

"*What* happened?" Bran finally demanded, and all of a sudden, her face softened; the anger wiped away from it in an instant.

"Bran..." she started, but she looked down, and he could see pain in her face.

"Listen, this is very unnatural," she said, but then she shook her head. "No, actually it's not; it's just unnatural for where we live. I mean, in Dunce."

Bran could see she knew something, and it looked as if she was having a very hard time telling him. She stammered for the right words, looking around as if she could pull them out of the air and say the right things.

"I should have known. It's my fault," she said slowly. "Usually things like this are found before now, but since we live in Dunce, there was no way for anyone to find you..."

Her voice trailed off.

"Find me for what?" Bran asked, and she looked up at him again.

"Bran, you're going to have to keep a secret for me," she said slowly, looking him directly in the eye. She gripped his shoulder a little tighter. "If I'm caught, I'll be going to jail," she said. "And if you aren't very careful, you're going there too."

"Why?" he asked, dumbfounded.

She waited for a moment. "Because," she said slowly, "you just did *magic*."

Bran's eyes widened with shock. In an instant, his heart began to beat faster.

"No..." he said in a whisper, not believing it. The world seemed to swirl around him, almost as if everything had disappeared and it was just the two of them there, with Adi gripping his shoulder.

Magic? he thought, and it felt as if he had grown twenty years older in one second. A hundred thoughts flashed through his head the instant she said the word, but in a second every thought vanished and was replaced with one terrifying question: *What's going to happen to me?*

"It can't be true!" he said.

"It is," Adi insisted, shaking his shoulder. "Bran, I *know* what someone's magic awakening looks like, the first time you use it. And it came to save you right when you needed it."

"I don't believe it," Bran said. "The truck stopped; it must have missed us!"

"And smashed its own front in?" Adi asked him. "Bran, if you weren't a mage, both you and Rosie would be dead right now, don't you understand that?" She lowered her voice further. "You did magic, Bran, and you didn't even know it. And I'm sorry, I wish we could have found you sooner—"

"We?" Bran asked with alarm. "There are more mages?"

Adi looked down. "I don't think you realize what's going on here. I'm just one. And luckily, I was here to get you."

She looked around to make sure no one was listening.

"We're here for a reason, Bran," she whispered. "All of us are hiding. And if anyone finds out, it'll be over. Gone. Every one of us will go to jail."

Bran felt the color draining from his face.

"And Bran," Adi went on, and it looked painful to her just to speak. "You must understand—"

"Bran! There you are!" Sewey called out from behind Adi, and she spun around. Sewey was sweating and breathing deep as he ran up, and far behind him was a crowd of people. "There's been a misunderstanding," he gasped. "They think you stopped that truck with your bare hands, and the chairman of the fair wants you to perform the trick again!" Sewey mopped his brow. "He's already started selling tickets. And since you're under eighteen, they want to make *me* do it in your place. We've got to get out of here!"

"There he is!" someone squealed, and the crowd started to run.

"They've seen you!" Sewey said in a rush. "Time to go!"

Before Bran could do anything else, Sewey grabbed his arm and started to pull him away. He tried to protest, but Sewey only pulled harder, and Bran turned to look back at Adi.

She slowly put a finger up to her lips. Bran swallowed hard, feeling afraid and lost, but he nodded to her, as if in a silent promise. And as he was pulled around the corner, he couldn't help noticing that she looked almost as afraid as he was.

Sewey and Bran shot off for the parking lot and dove into the car, where everyone else was already waiting. Rosie was in a heap in the backseat.

"Bran!" she said when Sewey tossed him in. "Oh, you're safe!"

"No time to chat," Sewey said, starting the car and rocketing off as the crowd of people came stampeding out of the park exit. He gunned the engine and made it to the road just in time. Rosie threw her arms around Bran, holding him tightly.

"Oh, Bran," she said, her eyes filling with tears. "You saved my life!"

Bran was so shaken that he couldn't respond. She held him tightly, and he could feel she was trembling.

Sewey waved one hand in the air. "Don't be silly, Rosie," he said. "That truck stopped at least two inches from you. Even the officer agreed with me. There's no way Bran would have been able to stop it otherwise."

"But it threw Bran into the booths!" Rosie said. "Oh, Bran, are you hurt?"

"I'm all right," Bran said, trying to console her, and she held him close.

"Enough of that talk," Sewey said. "He was lucky the grass was there to catch his fall. Luckily, we don't pay Rosie much, or else that purse-snatcher might have made a great steal."

"But my article!" Rosie said. "I had my final draft all typed up and folded inside!"

"Bah," Sewey said. "He'll be so angry with how little money he finds, he'll probably just bring the purse back to our house in disgust."

"We're going home," Rosie said. "I've had enough for one day."

"Home?" Sewey replied. "I think we have one thing left on the list, and that is to get a book."

"But Sewey!" Rosie protested. "Bran and I were almost hit by a truck!"

"Listen, Rosie," Sewey said. "We've already had three pests in this day alone: the van, Mr. Rat, and the purse-snatcher. I can't handle any more." He hit the steering wheel. "We are getting a book, and that is final!"

Baldretta banged a sucker on her seat like a gavel. Thoughts were rushing through Bran's head, and all he could do was look out the window at the cars, every nerve within him raw and electrified. He tried to hide it so no one would notice, but inside he felt sick and scared at the same time. Everything around him had changed, so much that his mind hardly accepted it. He couldn't bring himself to believe what Adi had said, though her words played in his head. They would have been dead. *Could it really have been magic?*

It was only a minute to the library, but when they parked, Sewey realized something.

"Wait a minute," he said. "We can't go to the library. We're not allowed in there!"

"Yes," Mabel said, glaring at Balder. "And we all know why."

Baldretta covered her ears, and Balder took a deep breath.

"*Oh terrible nights of woe and destruction, as I break down and blow up all forms of construction!*" he screamed in delight.

Rosie winced. "Yes, that was what you sang."

"Compliments of Manica-bibble himself," Balder added, satisfied.

"Blast the library," Sewey said. "We're going where we can be as loud as we want and *not* get thrown out!"

"Yay, the zoo!" Balder oinked.

"No," Sewey snorted. "A *bookstore.*"

"Where?" Mabel asked. "We never go to bookstores. I wouldn't know where to look."

"And I don't know any bookstores on this side of town," Rosie said. "I just go to the library."

"Right," Sewey concurred. "Well then, Bran, you go inside the library, since they won't recognize you, and ask the first person you see where the nearest bookstore is."

Bran didn't feel like it, but reluctantly did as he was told.

The place was filled with whispering kids scurrying about, most ignoring the books in favor of the computers. The quiet hum of the air conditioner filled the main room. All the librarians were busy, and as Bran stood there, he realized he didn't want to talk to anyone at all.

As his eyes drifted over the people, he spotted someone watching him from next to a shelf: a tall, middle-aged man with a round beard. He had black hair, and through it was a streak of white, almost as if it had been dyed in a peculiar manner. He looked creepy just standing there watching him, but Bran knew he couldn't just go on staring, so he walked over.

"Excuse me," Bran asked. "Do you know where the nearest bookstore is?"

He felt a little silly asking for a bookstore when he was in a library with hundreds of free books to enjoy. The man looked at him in a way that made Bran very uncomfortable, as if he could look into his eyes and read his mind.

"Yes, I do," the man finally said, his voice smooth. "There's one right down the road." The man pointed, his eyes not leaving Bran's. "It's called Highland's Books."

"Thank you," Bran said, trying to put a finger on what was strange about the man. He just couldn't pick out what made him feel so uneasy.

"You're welcome, Bran," the man said. Bran broke his gaze and turned to walk out, but he stopped when he realized something. He spun back again.

"How do you know my name…" his voice trailed off.

The man was gone, as if he had just vanished into thin air. Bran looked around, but he couldn't see him anywhere, not even behind the shelves of books. It was very odd, but he decided it was best just to leave.

That's great, word's probably gotten around about the

truck already, he thought grimly. He wondered about it all the way to the car.

"WHAT TOOK YOU SO LONG?" Sewey demanded.

"I had to find someone," Bran said.

"Hodgepodge," Sewey muttered. "It's simple: just stand at the door and shout 'DOES ANYONE KNOW WHERE THE NEAREST BOOKSTORE IS?' and then you're done!"

"No wonder you're not allowed in there," Bran said under his breath.

They drove down a way until they saw the sign. Bran had never been there. Sewey really didn't care for books, because average, normal, respectable Duncelanders like him didn't have time to read anything while they were being average, normal, respectable Duncelanders.

"What an odd and unusual notion," Sewey murmured as they drove up. "A store that sells nothing but books…they must get absolutely no business."

"Well, *you* could visit it," Mabel noted. "It's close to where you work. Only a street down!"

"*Too* close, in my opinion," Sewey shuddered. "I'd have to take the alley so no one would see."

When they walked into the store, Bran was flooded with all the different shapes and sizes and colors, books on almost every subject he could think of. Sewey marched inside and stopped, standing in the doorway. He raised his head, cupped his hands around his mouth, and shouted:

"DOES ANYONE KNOW WHERE BOOKS ON PEST CONTROL ARE?"

Everyone in the store looked up at him, some leaning out

from the quiet shelves to see who was making the racket, but no one came over to help him. Sewey, utterly outraged, stomped over to the counter in the center of the store and demanded the clerk tell him where the pest control section was. Rosie headed to the encyclopedias, Balder and Baldretta scurried to the children's section, and Mabel dashed off for the self-help section, because goodness knows she needed some.

That left Bran all alone to think.

He chose a chair against the row of windows in front of the store and sat down. He always liked it when Rosie took him to libraries while she did research, where the rush and noise outside just seemed to slip away and was replaced by quiet and books. The bookstore was just as tranquil. Part of him wished something would distract him, so he could avoid thinking about what happened with the truck, but he couldn't escape it. He had to face it.

So is Adi right? He asked himself bluntly. *Did I really do magic?*

His mind spun. He rested his head in his palm and his elbow on the arm of the chair. He wished that Adi hadn't been forced to leave so soon. Someone had to answer his questions. He had to tell someone who could help him.

Rosie, he thought. *I'll tell her!*

No. His mind echoed back at him. He couldn't. If he told her, it would put her in nearly as much danger as he was. He couldn't bear the thought for a second.

Shambles! Bran remembered. *He has something to do with it!*

It was a sudden reminder—in all that had happened, he had completely forgotten about the burglar! There was just too much coincidence in it. The creature on the roof, the paper beside the house: all of it was connected! In an instant, all the doubt that was in Bran's mind disappeared.

He shook his head and looked down at his hands. There wasn't a scratch on them from the truck. Adi was right. That truck would have killed them; it was going too fast to stop. He remembered feeling it coming upon him, the power rushing out through his hands, shielding them from it. Somehow, he had stopped the truck. He had no choice but to believe her. He had stopped it with magic.

I'm going to figure all this out, he told himself, squeezing his hands together. Everything was starting to connect like a puzzle, and he was going to find all the pieces and put it together.

"Psst!" he heard someone whisper, interrupting his thoughts. He looked up and saw Rosie standing between two shelves a few rows away.

"Bran!" she whispered, beckoning. "Come look at this!"

Bran left his thoughts behind as he went to her. She walked down a few rows of shelves and up a few more.

"This way," she whispered, and he followed her voice. She was ahead of him and slipped through a door, but by the time Bran had caught up to her, it had closed again. Bran pushed it open, but then noticed a sign in bold letters on the door that read:

Employees Only

"Um, Rosie..." he hesitated.

"Hurry up," she whispered, looking back. She smiled, and it reassured him that whatever she was doing was all right. With one last glance at the sign, he stepped through into the dark.

"Close the door," Rosie said. He pulled it slowly, the hinges creaking. Everything was immediately engulfed in darkness. His eyes hadn't adjusted enough to see his way, so he felt around with his hands. He could see his feet, but nothing more.

"It's dark in here," he said, almost tripping over something. "Rosie, is there a light?"

"Just follow me," she said forcibly, as if she were irritated. It was most unlike her, and it made Bran wonder what had happened. He held his hands out in front and felt for the wall, following her voice around a corner. He saw faint movement ahead and followed it. There were shapes of boxes and crates beside him, forming strange pathways. His eyes adjusted a little, and he saw her turn a corner at the end—but when he came to it, she was gone.

"I can't see you anymore," Bran said.

"Just follow my voice," Rosie replied.

"But I can't see anything," Bran said. "I have to go back—"

"No!" Rosie hissed. "Come this way, Bran Hambric."

Bran stopped, his hands frozen against the side of a crate. *Why had she used his full name?* Instantly, his senses were alert.

"Who's there?" he asked, standing up straight and backing into the wall. All was silent around him. His eyes searched the darkness, one way then the next. He looked back but couldn't see the door he had come through between the crates.

Is that really Rosie? he thought with fright. Her voice was the same, but he could feel it—something under his skin warning him away. He started to move slowly, sliding across the pathway, the crates towering over his head like giants holding their arms over him. He came to the corner, and as he looked around the edge, he saw a small light far away.

"Go to the light, Bran." He heard the voice, and he spun

around. It was her again, on the other side of him…but she wasn't there. His heart began to beat faster.

"The light," her voice insisted on the other side, and he spun.

"Where are you?" he demanded. He tripped forward, stumbling down the hall. "Rosie!" he whispered intently.

"The light!" her voice hissed, and he hurriedly felt the edge and came around the corner.

"All right, I'm here," he said, breathing hard. He had come to a large opening where the crates were cleared away into something of a workshop. The glow came from a lamp on a desk, shining onto his face dimly and lighting the dust that was floating in the air. There were books scattered around the desk and boxes lying in disorderly stacks on the floor, piled so high they formed an incomplete wall. Some books were opened, others were pushed around on the floor, torn to pieces. There were spaces between the towers of boxes where Bran could see more light and piles of things, almost as if someone had been collecting these boxes for decades. Beyond the towers he saw the room continue a long way, too far for him to see. The whole place smelled of paper and ink and musty air.

"Rosie, where are you?" he asked, searching the boxes with his eyes but not seeing her.

"I'm over here," she said, but her voice didn't come from any specific direction. "I need you to look in one of the boxes for me."

Bran was still hesitant, but he took a few steps further. "There's a lot. Which do you want?"

"Third box down, on the floor in front of the workbench," she said. "Open it."

He came to the chair, all the while looking around for her. He couldn't see her nor tell where her voice was coming from. He counted as he unstacked them.

"It's taped up," he said into the darkness when he had finished. He set it on the chair.

"The knife is in the bottom drawer on the left side of the desk," Rosie's voice said. "It's underneath the masking tape and the flashlight."

Bran went to the drawer. He set the tape and flashlight on the desk, and below them was the knife, just as Rosie had told him.

"How did you know it was there?" Bran asked. He cut the tape and then lifted the lid. The box was stuffed with paper folders, each tab labeled.

"It's open, Rosie," he said, but he was only met with silence. "Rosie?"

There was no reply. He looked around him. She was nowhere to be found.

"Rosie?" he asked again, but all he heard was his own voice, echoing around him. He was very still. He couldn't hear a sound of anything—no movement, no voice.

He set the knife down on the desk, the click of it touching the surface a thousand times louder in his ears. Everything was silent. His eyes moved from one side to the other, watchful, but nothing moved. His gaze shifted to the box he had just opened.

What did she want this for? He asked himself, slowly reaching toward the files. His fingers lifted one tab, labeled Haartman. He moved to the next, Habmark, then Habmarl, then Habmin.

"They're names," Bran realized. The files were thick and full of papers, some of them ragged and torn. He slid his hand along them, skimming to the far back, and all of a sudden, his eyes fell on a name that grabbed his attention like a lightning bolt across the sky.

"Hambric!" he gasped. It was shoved down and nearly hidden between two others, very thin, but definitely with the name on it. In a flash he pulled it out, and forgot about Rosie altogether.

Written in black marker on the front of the file were the words:

Hambric, Emry
City of Dunce Police Report #H-988

"Emry Hambric..." Bran whispered. That was it, the name Shambles had said on the roof! Bran's heart was beating faster, his hands shaking as he hurriedly unwound the string that held the file closed, and turned it over to dump out...

"Nothing!" Bran said with disbelief. He stuffed his hand into the file and felt all around in every corner, but it was completely empty.

I was just getting somewhere! he thought angrily. He checked it again, to no avail, so he pried the folders apart to stuff it back. However, as he did, there came a sudden, sharp creaking sound from across the room that caused him to freeze in motion, fearful someone was coming.

His eyes swept the room, and they caught movement against the far wall. He saw no one, but as his eyes studied the wall further, he saw that part of it was broken abruptly into the slightly ajar outline of an opening, like a hidden doorway. What was more, the light of the lamp spilled through, so that beyond it, Bran could see there was a hidden room.

He cautiously looked around. No one was there who might have opened it. He told himself the wind probably did it, but as there was no draft he immediately dismissed the thought. Still, a secret room in the back of a bookstore was very odd.

Taking the flashlight he had set on the desk, he carefully stepped around one of the towers of crates and came toward the opening. When he got to it, he peered around the edge, not daring to turn the flashlight on yet. He reached out slowly and his fingers touched against the edge of the opening: it was cold and metal behind the fake paneling that covered it, and as he pushed against the edge, the wall slid to the left with a low rumbling from the rollers hidden above.

"It *is* a door," Bran realized with shock as he slid it open further. He pushed the switch on the flashlight, and its soft glow exposed a simple hallway, about twelve paces deep and lined with shelves. The ones on the left held books, and the ones on the right had boxes labeled with numbers and months. As he shone the beam on the books, their titles glimmered in gold foil, though he could not read their titles from the doorway.

What would they be hiding back here? he wondered. He took a glance behind him again, just to make sure, and when he was certain no one was watching, he slipped through the crack in the doorway, drawing closer to the books and shining the light on them.

The books were very neatly sorted: each the same exact height and depth. There were five rows of shelves, each row holding books whose spines were the same color. He ran the light up and down it: at the bottom, all the books had purple spines, and the shelf above it held red. Next up was green, then blue, and then, on the top shelf, black. The black books on the top shelf were so high he had to step back and shine the light upward to see them, and there were only five, while the other shelves were full to the edges with books of their color.

It was very odd, so Bran drew closer and pulled out one with the green spine that was at eye level, just to see what it was. The book was no more than an inch and a half thick, though it was heavy and tightly bound. He held the light on his shoulder and looked at the cover: it had a heavy front, and in the center was a stamp. The image was of a bird, wings outstretched over its head and forming a circle, with a black oval where they touched and four other ovals formed like gems, two on each of its wings. The two on the right were purple and green, and the two on the left were blue and red. The bird's head was turned with a majestic expression, feathers set with sweeping lines. Inscribed around the top circle's edge were tiny words: *Lite yirou diyestini lidea yuo,* and at the bottom: *adni micagi geuida yirou wiya.*

"What is this?" Bran whispered. Then he noticed more words in a row at the bottom:

ARCHON
- VOLUME 17 -
THE OFFICIAL CATALOG OF MAGIC

The moment he read the last word he jerked backward, dropping the book to the floor, the flashlight falling from his shoulder at his sudden move. They landed with a smack and crash that sounded like a gunshot, the light disappearing and leaving Bran shrouded in darkness.

He stood there, still and breathless, the fear of what he had just read dominating the fear of who might have heard the noise. He stood with his back against the opposite shelf, unmoving.

What have I found? he thought.

Chapter 10

Inside the Hidden Room

When he was sure no one was coming, Bran searched the floor for the flashlight, finding it against the cold concrete and switching it on. He trained it on the book he had dropped on the floor. It lay there, its very presence breaking Dunceland's laws. He let the beam of his light go up the shelves again. That whole room was filled with those books. If the police had stumbled upon this place…

"Who am I fooling," Bran muttered softly. "Me being alive is enough to be arrested."

It was a grim thought, but one that seemed to give him a feeling of power. He couldn't be afraid anymore. Suddenly, knowing he was a mage, one of the things the entire town stood against, he felt oddly free. There was no way to turn back.

He left the book on the floor and came to the opening of the room again, sliding the door closed and leaving it just an inch ajar in case it might lock. Attached to the back of the door was a mirror, and it reflected Bran's flashlight beam across the room. He turned around again and took a deep breath. The books were still there. It felt like this was his moment of truth.

"So," he whispered, stepping forward and slowly picking the book up, "I come to a bookstore and find a file with my mother's name. The same name a burglar used when he attacked me on my roof, just before dropping a note that fits perfectly with one left eight years ago."

He picked up the green book from the floor. "Then, right after discovering I'm a mage, I stumble upon a secret room in the back of a bookstore, filled with books on magic."

He placed the flashlight on his shoulder, sliding down to sit with his back against the shelves, opening the green book. *Magic*...the word stuck out at him. It was still bitter on his tongue, though already the fear of it seemed to have subsided within him, now that he knew he had no choice but to embrace it.

He flipped open the cover, and on the inside of the hard front was a white page, covered with what appeared to be a chart. Again, he immediately recognized the same five colors as he had seen before, on the front symbol and also on the spines of the books: the colors, this time, were set as words in a neat chart, under the title MISSIVS of MAGIC: NETORA the PHYSICAL, on top, in purple, then COMSAR the MENTAL in red. Below it came ARCHON the ELEMENTAL in the same green as the book's cover, then ILLIAN the ILLUSIONAL in blue. Finally, at the bottom, was the last one, in deep, dark black: DRIMRA the MORTAL.

Bran stared at it, and realized that each color must stand for something, and each matched up with the books on the shelves. At the bottom of the inside page was a small quote:

The MISSIV of ARCHON

You are an Elemental mage, master of fire, water, earth, and air. You are drawn to what is natural: to the plants and trees. Your missiv balances the scales of our world's surroundings.

"They must be different types of magic," Bran realized aloud. "Archon mages are Elemental..."

Without hesitating another second, he flipped the pages of the green book open, every nerve on edge as he did. It was almost like an encyclopedia: rows and rows of entries, all numbered, a few with charts and drawings. He read the first his eyes fell upon.

[8601-A] Bright Icy Beam—Winkler
Sends a blinding beam of ice, which is stunning to behold
Open Hand: *Straight beam toward target*
BIMEA GIWLO IECA

Bran couldn't completely understand what it was, and wished he had Adi or someone who could explain it. He figured it was a magic formula of words, so that if he spoke them in a certain way then magic would happen. Perhaps the third line was instructions.

He turned the page and saw that there were rows and rows of similar magics: all organized in the same way and numbered neatly. Each had a title of its own as well, like a nickname. He saw one called Fulton's Fiery Flying Fingers and Muddy Mucktrap, and Windy Snaps just above Caterwauling Cannons of Lightning. Each had something to do with a natural element.

Bran felt as if he were a wanderer and had for the first time in his life found books about his homeland. Sitting against the opposite shelves, he reached across and pulled out one of the books with the purple spine from the bottom.

"Netora," he read, the cover decorated in the same manner as the green one. At the bottom of the inside, the quote read:

The MISSIV of NETORA

You are a mage of the Physical, master of things that can be touched. You are drawn to what can be made melodic by your hands and abilities: to music, architecture, art. Your missiv works in all things that move, and rests in all things that are still.

"The physical," Bran said, paging through that book as well. He was confronted with listings in similar form to the first, except now many of them referred to more dramatic instructions in their lines, such as:

[3601-N] Roran's Rippling Road-Ripper—Roran

Causes a catastrophic, municipal disaster with a satisfying ripple effect. Use only in dire need, as arrests are sure to follow.

Hands Out, Draw Apart: *Gravel stones as a blanket unfurling outward*

BIKREA PIHUSO RIKOCA AYWA

This was followed by many others of similar making, mixed in with magics for teleportation and telekinesis. The question of how the books got there was lost with Bran as he paged through, letting his eyes skim down the markings and the graphs, hardly reading them but rather soaking in the vastness of the knowledge contained within.

It might have only been a few minutes, though it felt like hours before he leaned back against the shelf behind him, closing the book and just staring at the width of its pages bound together. It was then that he caught the boxes behind him out of the corner of his eye, and realized that he had yet to even see what they held.

He set the book down and stood. The boxes were, as he had seen before, labeled in black marker, four numbered boxes for each month: probably a box for each week. He scanned them with his eyes, coming to the one for the second week in April, where the boxes ended. Carefully, he slid it out, the cardboard rustling against the shelf.

Inside was a short, neat stack of papers: large in dimensions, and folded. Bran realized that they were fresh copies of a newspaper. The title at the top read, in bold type:

THE DAILY DUNCELANDER
The Newspaper for Respectable Duncelanders

"Odd," Bran said. He didn't see why those had to be hidden back there, in the same room as books on magic. He peered closer at it, and suddenly, the glare of the flashlight caught something: there was a curious, second edge right where the title of the paper was, as if it was peeling off. This immediately struck Bran as odd, so he reached forward to touch it. It was hardly stuck, and when Bran drew it to the side, it peeled off cleanly and exposed a different title that had been disguised underneath.

THE MAGES PAGES
The Informed Mages' News Source

"A newspaper from the outside…" Bran said with shock. In Dunce, newspapers from the outside were strictly banned, due to high possibility of indecency. No wonder it had been disguised. He stuck his hand down into it: the pile wasn't very thick. But by the size of the box, Bran expected that loads of them had already been delivered…to whom, he didn't know, but there was obviously a sizable amount of people in the city who were curious about the outside.

He carefully removed the one on the top, from which he had uncovered the disguise. It was a single, folded sheet, and almost immediately Bran thought that a great part of the paper must be missing. But any part of an outside paper was enough. He was tired of following and believing what he had been told for so long. It might be his only way of finding anything about others like him: other mages…other criminals. He bent it so that he could see the front page with his light.

But before he could read a word, there came a sound from outside the door. Something slammed shut, echoing in the room outside. Bran immediately jumped from the wall, hearing somebody scratching about. The flashlight was shining through the crack he had left in the door, so he switched it off, about to dive for the door but thinking better of it when he heard someone approaching.

He didn't have any options. He dove as far back in the room as he could, pressing himself against the end bookshelf and hoping the blackness would cover him. He heard the footsteps getting louder and stood petrified in the corner. The sounds outside stopped.

*Don't open the door, please don't...*he thought, clutching the flashlight in one hand and the crumpled newspaper in the other. All was silent. Bran waited.

Then, he heard a low rumbling sound, and right before his eyes he saw the crack in the doorway begin to get larger. Then the door was open all the way, and the light from a lamp pierced the darkness.

Bran pressed back, expecting the person to see him in an instant and shout. The sudden lamplight, though dim, was nearly blinding, so he had to blink to see who had opened the door.

He could just barely make out what she looked like in the soft light behind her: she seemed to be around his age, dressed in ragged, dark clothes. Her hair was a few inches past her shoulders, dark blond and brown, and on her right arm was a thick strip of black cloth, wrapped around her wrist. Bran blinked again as her eyes swept the room, unable to speak because he was sure she would shout for the shopkeeper at any moment.

But something was not right. Her eyes swept straight across him, as if he wasn't even there, down to the two books he had left dropped on the floor. She didn't move from the doorway, staring at them curiously, and then to the box that Bran had left crooked.

"Idiots," she muttered with distaste. "Can't even put them back on the shelf."

She looked like she was about to come in, and then Bran knew he would be caught. But she only shrugged and started to slide the door closed. Bran let out the breath he had been holding.

That was very close, he thought. Then he noticed something in the mirror.

His entire body was gone in thin air: every inch of him completely invisible. It made him jump, and the moment he did his concentration on being unseen must have departed, because the next second he was there in the reflection, all in one piece. Luckily for him, it was in that same second that she finished closing the door, and Bran was immediately engulfed in darkness.

He covered his mouth and tried to catch his breath with as little sound as he could. But immediately he knew why she hadn't seen him: somehow, he had done magic again without knowing it.

Still, he felt that it would be in his best interest to leave that room as quickly as he could. He doubted he could do the magic again if he wanted to, and he was pushing his luck already. He left the books on the floor and was about to set the newspaper back, when he realized that he had already peeled its disguise off, and had not even gotten to read it. So he folded it until it was very small, and jammed it into his pocket, stepping toward the door. The girl had closed it all the way, and it felt locked.

"Great," Bran said. He listened again, but no one was there, so he flipped the flashlight back on. Luckily, he saw a tiny catch that was holding the door closed, attached to a spring that obviously went to a hidden button outside. He felt the latch and lifted it, flipping the light off as he edged the door open slightly. He peered out. No one was there.

He stepped out slowly. He hadn't realized how stuffy and hot it had been in the hidden room, as the air outside was much easier to breathe. He checked again but saw no one, and then closed the door behind him. With quick, quiet motions, he started back the way he had come.

"That was *way* too close," he breathed, coming to the corner. But before he could go around it, someone grabbed him.

Chapter 11

Another Burglary

"Got you!" Bran heard a man yell, and he felt strong arms take hold of him. Bran shouted, but the man held him in a vice-like grip before Bran had fully realized what was happening.

"Shoplifter!" the man yelled.

Bran fought the man's hold and broke free once, but the next instant the man had him again and slammed his face against the wall, pinning his arms behind him. Bran winced in pain and tried to breathe.

"Villain!" the man said, holding Bran's arms. "I've caught you!"

"No, please!" Bran begged, feeling as if his ribs were going to break.

"Astara!" the man shouted, and suddenly, lights burst on all around Bran. He heard footsteps coming up behind him, and saw the girl rushing from between the boxes, now holding a broom.

"I've caught the little thief!" the man said, and Bran was wrenched around to face his captor. He was a tall, strong man, his skin wrinkled a bit and tanned darkly, his face rough and full of anger. He had a dark yellow beard that covered his face, all the way up to the thick hair that was the same color. He looked like a hardened farmer. Bran guessed his age to be about fifty.

"Couldn't find enough books in the front?" the man growled in an angry tone. "So you decided to take my ones from the back?"

"No, please, sir!" Bran said, pointing a shaking finger down the way to the desk, trying to think of any excuse. "If you follow me, I'll show you, I didn't take anything! Just…helping someone find something, that's all."

"Helping someone find something?" the man echoed, not believing him. "There ain't a single soul back here, besides myself and my shopkeeper, Astara."

He waved his hand toward the girl. There was anger in her eyes, a green mixed with blue that almost bored holes into him. But her gaze held no recognition. Bran knew if she hadn't seen him they wouldn't accuse him of being in the secret room, as it wasn't even supposed to exist.

"No, sir, I promise," Bran said quickly, pointing back toward the desk. "Rosie…she came to the door, and unlocked it, and told me to go through the papers back there."

"Papers, eh?" the man said, still not believing him. He tilted Bran's face up close to his.

"Show me what this Rosie's having you get into," he said, "and maybe I'll have me *two* shoplifters before the day's over!"

He let go of one of Bran's arms and had him stand against the wall. Bran walked slowly with the man holding his shoulder and Astara watching from the side.

"These here, sir," Bran said, trying to sound convincing. He gestured to the boxes that Rosie had told him to move, and the man's face seemed to grow harsher as Bran showed him.

"Those, boy," the man said, "are none of anyone's business!"

"Yes, sir," Bran stammered. "But—"

The man didn't let him finish, but he let go of Bran's arm and moved to the desk, and saw the file Bran had left sticking out. Bran heard the man give out a small gasp, but a moment later he covered up his surprise.

"A-and what's your business going around looking at these?" the man asked. "Emry Hambric and all...whoever she is. Don't you know these are official city records?"

Bran looked at his feet and glanced from the man to Astara. The man pointed at the box.

"Why're you looking through these?" he demanded again.

"I..." Bran started, but he couldn't bring it out. He swallowed hard, and felt as if there were a rock in his throat. The man looked at him, cold and unforgiving. "Because I think Emry Hambric was my mother," Bran finally said, looking up at them.

The girl started at this.

"What did you say?" she gasped.

The man slammed the folder down on the desk. "Your mother?" he asked with bewilderment. "What's your name? Who're your parents?"

Bran hesitated. "I—I don't have any parents. I live with Sewey and Mabel Wilomas. My name..." He paused before finishing. "My name is Bran Hambric."

The girl suddenly dropped her broom flat on the floor, and Bran jumped, and when he looked at her he could see she was visibly shaken.

"You are Bran *Hambric?*" the man said, and when Bran looked back at him, he could see that the man was also taken by surprise, which confused Bran very much. Bran nodded.

"And you think that Emry Hambric was your mother?" the man went on.

"Yes," Bran said. "But I don't know for sure."

He looked at Bran deeply. It looked as if he was thinking very hard about something.

"Funny thing is," the man finally said, "that folder's marked to hold a police report in it. Leaves me wondering what your mother's got to do with the police...and an empty folder?"

There was something in the man's voice that caused Bran to feel insult from it, as if the man was accusing his mother of something terrible that Bran knew about, when the truth was he knew even less than before. The man must have seen the expression on Bran's face because he immediately softened his own.

"Well, look. Perhaps it wasn't something that bad: lots of people have police files on them. And she was probably just another Hambric in town, right?" He gently put a hand on his shoulder, and Bran looked up. "And by the looks of you, I guess you aren't really a shoplifter, either," the man said, sounding as if he felt bad for accusing Bran of it. Bran shook his head and the man stepped back, satisfied.

"Just for your information," the man went on, "these papers aren't mine. They belong to the city. I'm just commissioned to store and document them, like a second job." He nodded grimly. "Goodness knows I need the extra money, as very few people in this city read books. And no one is ever allowed to look at these papers except for *me,* though sometimes Astara will help clean th...well, where's she off to?"

Bran turned around and saw that the girl had disappeared, leaving the broom behind on the floor. She had to have slipped off very quietly for him not to notice. The man just shrugged.

"Probably off to clean," he said. He wiped his hands on his pants and held one out to Bran. "My name is Cringan Highland. I'm the owner of this place."

Bran hesitated but then held his hand out, and Mr. Highland shook it in a strong grasp. He had a golden ring around his finger in the shape of a lion's head, and suddenly Bran didn't feel threatened anymore. Mr. Highland let go and turned, putting the empty folder back into the box.

"I know most of these like the back of my hand," he said a little boastfully. "If there's anyone in town you want to know about, I'm the one to come to, because I read them as they come in."

Mr. Highland turned back around and gestured down the hall.

"Just remember," he said, "you're allowed everywhere in my store, *except* the places that have signs telling you to *keep out.* Do you understand?"

His voice was grave. Bran knew why. He held his eyes from glancing at the secret door.

"Yes, sir," he nodded.

"Very good," Mr. Highland said approvingly. "Now come this way, and I'll get you out."

Mr. Highland led him through the towers of crates. Bran, seeing the familiar surroundings, was immediately reminded of the fact that Rosie had, at some time or another, been back there, and it had been she who had started it all. He glanced about for any sign of her, but even when he came to the end he hadn't seen her. When Mr. Highland opened the door at the end, Bran felt as if he was coming out from a dark world, and just beyond the door was a normal bookstore.

"Very well," Mr. Highland said, letting Bran pass. "Off you go, and a very good day to you!"

Bran looked over his shoulder, about to tell him that Rosie might still be in the back room, but Mr. Highland had just finished locking the door tightly and was turning to leave. Bran decided to leave it alone, and he turned around, hoping Rosie had gotten out before, though it would have been very unlike her just to leave him there.

I hope she explains all this... he thought, but since she was Rosie he couldn't bring himself to be angry at her, no matter how unusual she had acted. He walked a little way, back by the window where he had been before, and was just about to sit down.

"Bran!" he heard a familiar voice all of a sudden. He spun quickly, and there was Rosie, standing between two shelves a few rows away, as if she had been waiting for him all the time.

"Come here, quick!" she whispered, beckoning. He blinked, wondering what he should say to her, when she rushed over to him with a book in her hands.

"Look here, Bran!" she said excitedly, waving a book. "*The Complete Encyclopedia on the History of*—whatever's the matter? You look like you've seen a ghost!"

Bran blinked at her and stepped away. He didn't know how to react to her for a few moments.

"Rosie," he asked. "Where'd you go?"

"Go?" she studied his face, blinking. "What do you mean, where did I go?"

"Back there," Bran pointed to the door. "You told me to follow you, and then you left."

"I did what?" Rosie's eyes followed his finger to the door. She peered at it for a few seconds.

"Oh, no, you must be confused," she laughed lightly. "That door has a sign on it that says only employees are allowed. I'm obviously not an employee, so I'm not allowed."

"But Rosie," Bran said, beginning to feel very odd, "you were back there, and you told me to go find the box, and to open it, and—"

"Bran," Rosie broke in. "I can assure you, I never went through that door. In fact, I've been here with the encyclopedias the entire time we've been here!"

Bran blinked, but he could see in her eyes that she was telling the truth. His heartbeat quickened, remembering the voice. It *was* her, he knew it.

Am I going mad? he wondered, just staring at her. Rosie looked at his face for a long time, and she seemed to be just as confused as he was.

"Bran, I—" she began, but she stopped. She didn't seem to know what to say. Then she looked over his shoulder.

"Oh, look, I think it's time to go," she said, trying to force a smile. "They seem to be loading up without us."

Bran couldn't make himself smile, though he tried to hide it from her. Rosie put her arm over his shoulder, and Bran simply took a deep breath and went with her to the car.

❋ ❋ ❋

The Schweezer spluttered and popped all the way back to Bolton Road, and no one said a word the whole time. When they pulled up to the curb and got out, there was a strange feeling crawling up Bran's spine, as if he were being watched by a hundred dark eyes, from the windows of the houses, behind the cars, in the bushes. He couldn't lay his finger on the feeling so he pushed it away as best he could. He had been through enough fright for one day, and he wasn't going to let it get to him any more than it already had.

"Mabel," Sewey said, digging through his pockets. "I can't seem to find my house key."

"I've got one," Mabel said with a huff, leading the troupe to the front door. She stuck the key into the lock and gave it a good wrench around, but it didn't budge. "Funny," she said. "I was sure I locked it before we left."

"I remember that," Sewey said. "Now who's gone and unlocked it this time?"

They began to argue as to who was to blame, and it ended up being Sewey's fault, then Baldretta's fault, then Mr. Rat's fault, and finally landed as Bran's fault.

"Does it really matter?" Bran asked. "I mean, it does look awkward standing here outside our own front door."

"He's right," Sewey said in a rush, looking up and down the street quickly.

"We'd better hurry," Mabel said, flinging the door open. "It'd be the talk of the town!"

"I can see the headlines now: 'Wilomas Family Can't Get through Front Door,'" Sewey said as he flipped the lights on. "It might make it right on top of *Miss Grundy Reports!*"

"Or it might—" Mabel started, but all of a sudden she gave a great scream and fell a few steps backward, her hands going up to her cheeks. Rosie gasped at the horrible sight before their eyes.

Furniture was overturned onto the floor, lamps were knocked down, and papers strewn everywhere. The couches were thrown about and the stairs were littered with their belongings. It looked like a troll had been set loose in the house, and all anyone could do was stand there with their mouths open and their eyes blinking at the horrific scene.

"Goodness!" Rosie squeaked.

"Great Moby!" Sewey burst.

"The burglar!" Balder said what was on everyone's minds.

In a second, everyone was running through the house, shouting at each other from different rooms—all except Bran, who could do nothing but stand frozen in the doorway.

"Oh, my kitchen!" Rosie wailed, moving pots and pans around. Mabel rushed through the house, picking up broken vases and clocks and picture frames. Bran couldn't even think of what monster would have done this—except the creature on the roof.

In an instant, he remembered the look behind Shambles's eyes. He remembered the clawing, searching moves of his hands. He could almost see the creature in his mind, running through the house, tearing it up, searching for something…

"My room!" Bran gasped, and he broke into a run up the stairs, leaving the front door open behind him. He ran as fast as he could and didn't stop until he got to his ladder, climbing up as fast as he could, his hands and feet barely touching the steps.

When he came to his room he stopped, and he looked at it, unable to say a word.

His desk had been turned over on its side, the bulb in his lamp smashed. There were pieces of paper all over the floor and his window was open with the air blowing things all around. Boxes were knocked over, pushed around, some of them ripped open with the things spilling out.

A sudden terrifying thought came to him, and he leapt forward, throwing the sheets off his bed and reaching under it, all the time hoping the creature hadn't found his bag. His hand felt far underneath, all over, but touched nothing. He pushed his head under—the bag was gone!

His eyes searched the room frantically for any trace of it. All of a sudden, he spotted it near some boxes across the room. He dashed over and pulled it into the light: the clasp unlocked and the bag already opened. He pushed the things around with his hand, counting them, making sure everything was there. They slipped through his fingers as he sorted them onto the floor: when he got to the bottom, his hand stopped.

"The papers!" Bran gasped. He dug around in the bag, but the paper with his name was nowhere to be found, as was the scrap Mr. Swinehic had given him. Bran went through the things twice, then a third time. But both were gone.

He slid his hands along the floor, looking for anywhere it might have blown, his mind frantic and his motions quick. His eyes swept across the floor, but came across nothing. He dug through the shreds and the boxes, searching everywhere, all in vain.

He fell against the wall in shock. Not only had he lost the paper from Mr. Swinehic, his only clue from the creature, but he had also lost the paper with his name, the only clue to his past.

"Why?" he asked himself in anger, hitting the hard floor and looking around the room.

"What do you want!?" he called out, as if the creature was there and could hear his words. His hands tightened into fists and his breath became slow and deliberate, unable to solve anything in his head and everything lost to him.

"What do you want with me?" he asked again, his voice lower.

I want you.

Bran gasped, turning at the sound in his head, his breath stopping. His heart pounded. He looked, but there was nothing; he listened, but no sound of movement came.

"W-who's there?" Bran asked; still, silent, alert to the voice. The words had been so quick it was hardly more than a breath in his ear, by something Bran could not see or feel, almost inside of him. His gaze shot all over the room, one place and then the next. He felt the eyes again, watching him from all directions at once. He blinked but didn't move.

He saw a rush of motion sliding to the side and turned, pressing against the wall. It was such a fleeting movement it was hardly more than a shadow of something black, going behind a pile of boxes. Bran spun, grabbing for something to defend himself. His hand came across a piece of wood from a broken crate, and he held it in front of him, nails sticking out at all angles.

"Where are you?" Bran said quickly, his throat dry and his forehead becoming warm with alarm. All was motionless. He stepped toward the box he had seen the figure dart behind, his hands shaking. There was a black cloth hanging over some crates, and for a second it seemed to rustle, almost as if someone was behind it. Slowly, Bran came forward, reaching for the cloth.

"I know you're there," Bran hissed, and in a sudden motion, he swept the material away, holding the board out, ready for anything...

But he was met with his own reflection.

He jumped. For a moment he was startled but a second later, he recognized his face. It was an old mirror, leaning against the boxes. But there was no one else.

Chapter 12

The Telephone Call

Sewey called them together ten minutes later.

"There's no getting around it," he said. "We've been robbed."

"But nothing's missing!" Rosie said. Bran had kept quiet about the missing papers.

"We've been robbed nonetheless," Sewey said. "By what?" He nodded matter-of-factly. "By *gnomes.*"

Balder and Mabel gasped, and Baldretta hiccupped.

"What gnome?" Sewey asked aloud, raising a finger. "The gnome from the roof. This—" He gestured around at all the mess. "—is definitely a *gnome mess.*"

"And no witnesses," Rosie realized grimly. "All the neighbors were gone for the picnic!"

"Right!" Sewey said.

"The perfect time to break in!" Mabel said with a gasp. Sewey nodded with a glum frown.

"Goodness! Let's call the police right away, then!" Rosie said.

"Can't," Sewey told her. "The Law clearly states if a gnome enters one's house, the homeowner is just as guilty as the gnome; because after all, he *was* harboring a criminal!"

"Goodness!" Rosie said. Baldretta crossed her arms with disgust.

"Maybe he found what he wanted and now he'll just go away," Mabel said.

"Don't be so sure," Sewey warned. "Mark my words, that gnome is somewhere out there—and if my name is Sewey Wilomas, he'll be back for more."

The conversation was beginning to wear on Bran's nerves, so he started for the door to go outside. He couldn't stand being in the house anyway: it felt as if every inch of what he had deemed a safe haven had been invaded.

"Where are you going?" Sewey asked him sourly.

"Outside," Bran said.

"Where?"

"Just outside," Bran murmured, pushing past and shoving the front door closed behind him. Sewey was too upset or bewildered to follow. The family had hardly ever seen Bran angry before, but Bran didn't care. He just wanted to be away from them and the house and everything else.

He paced the little bit of lawn they had. He knew if he started to concentrate, his thoughts would end up back on what had happened at the park and the bookstore and then in his room. He didn't want to think about any of it anymore.

But eventually, he found that he had wandered beside the house, to the spot where Mr. Swinehic had found the paper that the creature had dropped. The grass was still slightly messy from where Shambles had scratched up the dirt in his haste to get away. Bran pushed it around with his foot, wandering aimlessly until his eyes caught the ladder, still sitting against the house.

"Now *that* will probably stay there until it rusts," he muttered. Sewey was awful about getting things out of his shed and leaving them lying about. But the ladder gave Bran an idea, so he moved for it, and started up. He got to the top and climbed to the roof, the same place he had been just a few nights earlier, when the creature had appeared. He went to the chimney and sat against it, just breathing the cool air that was moist with the approaching storm clouds. Everything was gray and blue. But up there, Bran felt safe.

He gazed around at all the houses. He could see far, even though clouds were drowning out most of the sunlight. He knew it wasn't a good idea to be there with the storm coming, but right then, he didn't really care.

He let himself mull over all that had happened: the bookstore, the secret room, his mother's note. Then he thought about the strange man at the library: the one who had acted so odd, pointing him right to Highland's Books for apparently no reason. But Bran was finished with believing in coincidences. He felt as if there was some great puppet-master twisting the strings above him, tweaking him so that these things would happen. But what was it all for?

He felt the folded newspaper in his pocket, and it gave him a start immediately. He had made it from the bookstore without it being discovered. He drew the sheet out. It felt odd having it in the open, even though no one could see it from the ground. It was a welcome distraction, so he smoothed out the creases and peered at the front page headline:

CITY OF WINDALE MAGES STRIKE:
TROUBLE FOR THE FLOATING CITY?

Below the headline was a photograph of a city on the edge of a cliff, with a sharp drop-off into the sea, waves crashing against the rocks and throwing foam into the air. There was, however, one strange feature. At what appeared to be a few hundred feet away from the top of the cliff, hovering over the water, was a second city, its buildings poking into the clouds and an airplane just flying in. There was simply nothing underneath it at all.

He skimmed the report: apparently, the two cities had been one on the seaside coast, before a terrible crumbling of the rock underneath nearly spelled the demise of half the population into the ocean. They were narrowly saved by a large, around-the-clock group of Netora mages who kept the doomed city aloft telekinetically. It seemed that the group, after nearly a century of work, had begun to tire of the long hours and were ready to drop it, much to the understandable disagreement of the Windalers.

There were other articles on each side, one a review of a book called *Kitchen Magic* by Barbara Smithens and the other detailing a disagreement between a group of archmages and the Primirus, which the article alluded to as the head of the Mages Council. Bran pulled the pages apart but inside there were no other plies of paper: a simple, one-sheet newspaper. It seemed quite odd to Bran, even as he ran his eyes over the articles, detailing the news and what was going on outside: disagreements, the death of a famous mage, statistics of mages in political office. It was all very eye-opening that so much went on outside Dunce. The city walls had severed off an entirely different world.

While he was glancing down the page, Bran's finger absently

brushed against a large black box printed in the bottom corner. Suddenly, the paragraph that Bran had been reading fizzled and disappeared. It caused him to jump, but just as quickly as it had disappeared, a new article was in its place. In a second, all the letters and photographs had changed, as if the paper had scanned forward automatically.

"So *that's* how you turn the pages," Bran realized, touching the black box in the corner. Again, the words fizzled away, and were replaced by the next set. It held him in awe simply watching the words change like the switching of a channel, the whole newspaper held in less than a millimeter of paper.

As he jumped through the pages with a newfound interest, he saw lists of things beyond his imagination, so simple to the outside world that they were casually placed in a newspaper. He saw coupons for vials of dirt from various places in the world for Netora mages to use to teleport, and discounts on magic stamps that sent letters gliding to their destinations. There were advertisements for books similar to those Bran had seen in the back of the bookstore—different editions with tear-out cards for ordering—and promotions for a new computer program called Magebinder, which promised to cut any mage's research time in half. It was another world to Bran, so strange and different from what he knew inside of Dunce. It was the same feeling as in the back of the bookstore: as if he had been living abroad and the paper was speaking of the homeland he had been away from for years.

He finally looked up, almost dizzy from all he had read. His eyes went wandering over the edge of the roof, and inadvertently happened to rest on a vehicle parked at the end of the street. It was a black van, the same type he had seen earlier, behind them on the way to the park.

It seemed to be just sitting there for no reason, which was odd, because he hadn't noticed a van there before, and he knew the neighbors didn't own it. Such a creepy feeling passed over him that he momentarily forgot about the newspaper in his hands. He could see nothing, but it felt like there were people behind the dark windows, watching him.

All of a sudden he heard the front door burst open below him.

"Bran!" came the voice of Sewey. "Where are you? Telephone!"

"The phone?" Bran said, breaking his gaze from the van and hurrying to his feet. He never got calls. He folded the newspaper up and hid it again as he climbed down. Sewey was standing at the door. The wire on the handset stretched all the way back to the kitchen.

"Where the rot were you?" Sewey hissed, holding the receiver against his shoulder.

"On the roof," Bran said.

"The roof?" Sewey snorted. "How foolish. Well, it's for you."

Bran hesitated. "Is it Great-Aunt Cornelia?"

"No, she's in the asylum now," he said. "It's some girl."

"Odd," Bran said. He held the phone against him to drown out the noise as he hurried to the kitchen, and then he placed it to his ear.

"Hello," he said.

There was silence, so long that he thought whoever it was had hung up. But then he heard someone take a deep breath, almost as if they were as surprised as he was.

"Bran," a girl's voice said, "are you by yourself?"

He didn't recognize her as anyone he knew, but deep inside he felt he had heard the voice before, somewhere. He hesitated at her strange question, glancing at the kitchen door where Sewey was pretending to dust things with his hand.

"Somewhat," he replied hesitantly. "Who's this?"

"You don't know who I am," the girl said. "What's important is that I know who *you* are."

He thought she sounded a little nervous. It instantly put him on his guard, and thinking it might just be a prank call, he smiled slightly and decided to play along with her game.

"Just knowing my name isn't going to get my attention," he replied. "I'm sure everyone in town knows it by now."

"But everyone else doesn't know," she hissed, "that you're a *mage.*"

In an instant, Bran's smile disappeared. His heart almost stopped at those words. He glanced in Sewey's direction to see if he had heard, but he was gone, and Bran lowered his voice.

"What did you say?" he whispered, hoping he had heard her wrong.

"I know who you are, Bran," she said. "If I was out to get you, all I'd have to do is call the police right now and tell them everything."

"I'm listening," Bran said quickly, and he really was. He pressed the phone harder to his ear.

"Bran, you're in a lot of danger right now—danger you don't even know of," the girl said, her voice filled with a strange edge of fear. "Your magic is just a part of it."

"How did you see me do it?" Bran asked, keeping his voice low. "Were you at the park?"

"I didn't see you do anything," she said. "I *know* you can. I know who you really are."

The words seemed to resonate inside of him, making his heart beat faster. *Who he really was?* Did she really know the answers?

"I can't say it over the phone," she said. "I need you to meet me, tonight."

"Tonight?" Bran said with alarm. "I can't get away from here, they'd know I was gone."

"Can't you get out through a window?" she asked.

"I live in an attic," Bran said. "If I go through that window, I'll fall two stories."

She let out a breath, and he could tell she was thinking hard. He was at a loss as to why she was so desperate to talk to him that night, but after what she had said, every nerve within him was on edge. Somehow, *someone* had found out his secret; if she knew, who else did?

"Where can you meet me?" she asked, almost desperately. "What about at your house—when will everyone be gone?"

"I can't tell you that!" Bran hissed, instantly wary. "What do you mean, when will they be gone? I don't know who you are."

"Bran, they're going to get you!" she burst. At this, every trace of anger disappeared in him. There was a strong desperation in her voice that couldn't have been faked. She was afraid of something, he could feel it.

"You have to meet me somewhere," the girl pleaded. "Can you make it to the bank where Sewey works?"

Bran blinked. "How do you know Sewey works there?"

In a second, he was alert again. This girl, how did she know all this about him? Why was she trying so hard to get him to come away in the middle of the night? Bran was struck with a thought—what if she was from the burglar and trying to lure him somewhere? It sent a warning through his flesh, and the words she had said were wiped away.

"Listen, whoever you are," he said angrily, before she could reply. "I'm not going anywhere tonight. If you want to come here, you can, but it'll be during the day and they'll all be here."

"Never mind," she broke in. "Just be ready tonight. Go down the alley across the street; turn right, and then left, then down to the first door on the right."

"What?" Bran asked, blinking. "What do you mean by that?"

"You'll want to remember it," she assured him. "I'll see you tonight."

"Wait a minute!" Bran said, but he heard a click on the other side, and the line went dead.

"What?" he said, louder. "Hello? Are you there?"

His words were met with silence. She was gone, and he slammed the phone down, and didn't believe her for another minute.

Adi stayed at the park for a few more hours, trying not to appear as shaken as she really was. The instant she had a chance to leave, she rushed to her car and drove off with her thoughts whirling around her like a tornado. If she had been anywhere other than

Dunce, things would have been so much easier, but if *anyone* found out about Bran, there was no telling what they'd do. What if he told on her? Then it would be over for everyone hidden in Dunce. There were so many loose ends, so many people who knew—*too many* people who knew she was a mage.

She turned, driving nowhere in particular, and looked up to the clouds, which promised rain. She sighed; she didn't know anything about Bran. *No one* knew anything about Bran.

That means I can't meet his real parents...she thought grimly. *But maybe there was another mage related to him.* She decided she would have to look his name up in the Mages Database on her computer, and took a quick glance in the backseat. Her laptop bag was still there.

She parked in the deserted lot of the library. Inside was quiet, with very few people among the shelves. A librarian waved as she came in. Everyone probably thought she was coming in for some volunteer work, but Adi was on a mission and hurried upstairs to the study area. She swept the room with her eyes to make sure no one was watching, and started her computer up. Swiftly, she reached into a hidden pocket in her bag and pulled out a single disc, pushing it in.

It took her a few minutes to pull up the database, with two different passwords for safety, but finally she was in. She scrolled down the names. The program was simple and updated annually, listing nearly each and every mage's name and record, living or dead. The database wasn't released to the public, but she had pulled some strings to get permissions from the Mages Council—and even then, only because she was in the Special Services and Operations Division.

She set the records to sort by alphabetical listing and started down the list. The screen lit up her face as her fingers moved across the keyboard, scrolling all the way to H-A-M-B:

"Hambart, Trisha." She slid her finger down the list. "Hambort, Dr. Jay. Hambribe, Minny."

She came to the next one: Hambric, Emry. Her finger stopped. The record stood out on the screen because it was in red, and she had never seen a name in the records in that color before. She didn't know what it meant, but it certainly made it look important.

That's strange, she thought. If this woman was related to Bran, he would be very surprised to know that there was, or had been, someone in the world who shared his last name.

When she clicked, it seemed to take quite a while to load. Adi wondered what could be holding it up, but then a window popped up in front of everything that read:

Restricted Access

Please enter your special access ID to view record

"Hmmm," Adi said, but she put in another password anyway, confused as she was. She had never had that happen to her before with the database. She didn't know what could possibly make it so encrypted.

Her thoughts were left hanging, though, because the moment the record appeared on the screen, she saw something she had never, ever expected to read.

Her eyes darted down the screen rapidly, her heartbeat quickening as she read the words. All the suspicions she had about Bran were destroyed in an instant—and were replaced with raw fear.

"It can't be..." she said, her voice dropping to a whisper. She brought her hand up to her forehead, her face going pale.

"The Farfield Curse..." she gasped, and cold, icy fear took a grip on her heart.

Part II

Chapter 13

Burglars on Third Street

Bran opened his eyes, but he was not in his room anymore. He was falling through the sky like a stone, but around him, there was only darkness.

There was nothing under his feet, nothing over his head, and no walls around him. It was a dark, icy prison, his body racing downward and upward and in all directions at once. Fear crawled through him. He felt eyes upon him, coming from all directions. The motion began to slow, then speed up, then slow again, confusing him; he had no track of time before he felt his back touch with something solid and his fall came to a stop.

He stared up into the blackness, unable to move, unable to do anything. His breath echoed around him as if he were in a large, metal box. He heard something: a terrible, evil laugh.

I can see you, Bran Hambric.

The voice echoed from a man: from somewhere, from nowhere, from everywhere. Swirling black shapes danced around Bran, moving like a whirlpool of watery, smoky shadows.

You will bring me to life.

Bran was so paralyzed he couldn't shout, and the shapes began to slow. As their pace went down they seemed to fade into the background. And suddenly, he saw the face.

The face was of a man, standing above him: milky white and smooth, with black circles framing piercing, dark blue eyes. It was sickening, the man looking as if he had just come out of his grave, his skin tight against his skull. What little hair he did have was mostly hidden by the black cowl.

"Who are you, Bran?" the man asked. "*Who are you?*"

His shout echoed like in a long, dark hall, the force of it slinging Bran backward, as if the words had sent a blast of wind at him. It threw him off his feet like a thousand pounds of water against his chest, like the truck from the park, throwing him across the street. Bran hit the ground on his back and slid, falling with a shout, the marble surface breaking underneath him.

And the voice came again, now in a whisper:

I can see you...

The words echoed, though the man was gone.

Bran Hambric, you will bring me to life.

Bran pulled away, wrenching within the powers that held him like webs, spinning themselves, tightening.

"Who are you, Bran?" the voice echoed. Bran shouted wordlessly, fighting the bonds to break free—and all of a sudden he rolled over, and found himself back in his bed, in his room.

He bolted up, his eyes wide with fright and his forehead damp with sweat. He gasped for breath, terror still in his heart, his fearful gaze flying over the room, along the boxes, the crates, the old furniture. He thought he saw a movement behind a box, then another, and his eyes darted to the other end of the room, but nothing was there. He wiped his forehead with the back of his hand as the dream cleared itself from his head like the last echoes of a dying man's voice. He fell back against the wall and glanced at the clock: 2:14 a.m.

So much for catching up on lost sleep, he thought terribly. Everything flooded back all of a sudden—Adi, the bookstore, the telephone call. It was as if he had never even slept at all. He listened hard to the wind whistling through the hole in his window and tried to calm himself.

However, just when he was about to settle down again, an awful, nerve-wrenching noise erupted from downstairs. He sat up in bed with a start.

"What now?" he asked with exasperation. It came a second time, like a bell choir getting into a fight, bells and all. By the third time, he knew what it was.

"The telephone," he shook his head, throwing the sheets off his legs.

Who would be calling at this time of the night? he wondered as he came down the ladder and hurried across the hall. However, just as he reached the top of the stairs, he heard a door slam, and Sewey came running out, tripping over his own feet again.

"Great Moby, what's going on?" Sewey blew angrily as he pushed Bran aside on his way down the stairs, grabbing the phone.

"Hello, Wewey Silomas here…ah, Swilly Swollymoo…WHAT DO YOU WANT?"

Bran stood at the top of the stairs, listening.

"Yes, officer, what, who, where, how—" Sewey asked. "The bank? Ah, yes, no, it was locked up…definitely not, yes, sir, no, sir, three fuzzy sheep, sir, two, sir, how, sir, silent alarm, sir? Oh, sir! I'll be right there, sir. Good-bye, sir."

Sewey hung up the phone and spun to face Bran.

"You, get my cigar box of bullets!" he commanded. "We've got a very dangerous emergency on our hands! The TBD's being robbed!"

"Being?" Bran said as Sewey bounded up the stairs. "Don't you mean it's *been* robbed?"

"No, *being!*" Sewey called. "The burglars don't know we've caught on because it was a silent alarm. Mr. Brewer's on his way, and so are the police, and so are you and I. We're going to catch that thief *red-handed!*"

Bran instantly didn't believe it was as bad as it appeared. He wasn't about to get excited over a frog or snail setting off the alarm, which had happened many times as the windows in Sewey's office were commonly forgotten and left open. And besides that, the alarm was only wired to half of the windows, so the burglar probably would have had to arm it himself just to get it to go off.

Bran was dressed and waiting at the front door before Sewey was even ready himself. Sewey went on running around upstairs, this way and that, then back this way, then back that way again.

"Hurry, hurry, hurry!" Sewey shouted throughout the house. "Burglars! Burglars!"

Sewey skidded to a stop and thought for a few seconds. "*GNOME* burglars! That's it!" he shouted, clapping his hands. "Why didn't I think of it before? Wake up everyone: there's a GNOME BURGLAR!"

"Gnome burglar?" Rosie yawned, coming out of her room. "Who's got a gnome burglar?"

"I've just about!" Sewey said, starting down the stairs on the tips of his slippers. "Hurry!" he told Bran. "You're going to make me miss them!"

"Them?" Bran asked. "Now the gnome is two gnomes?"

"Maybe three or four, or a hundred!" Sewey said, waving his hands. "Who knows?"

Bran leaned against the wall next to the door as Sewey dashed to the kitchen, stuffing some muffins from the fridge into a paper sack, then running to get something from the pantry.

"But then watch us get there," Sewey said as an afterthought, "and it's just some kid throwing rocks at our window."

With those words, a sudden thought erupted in Bran's mind that made him stand up straight as if he had been electrified. In a moment, he realized exactly what was going on.

The girl from the telephone! he remembered with dismay. *All of this is her doing!*

It all fit together so perfectly he was astonished at how smartly she had pulled it off. All of a sudden, he was nearly petrified with how things had fallen into place. And there he was, going just where she had wanted him all along. His heart began to race. Why was she going through so much trouble just to get him there?

"Hurry up!" Sewey said, rushing for the door and still in his slippers. Bran had to shake his thoughts away and rush out to follow him. They shot off into the night, over corner and curb, through rosebush and hedge, with Sewey Wilomas at the helm. Before Bran even had a chance to try and sort anything out, they were swerving onto Third Street. The bank was guarded by two police cars, lights flashing on the buildings around them, but there weren't any burglars that Bran could spot. The glass on one window and on the front door of the bank was broken.

Across the street...Bran remembered what the girl had said, looking across from the bank. There was a restaurant there, but it was closed, and he saw an alley between it and another shop.

She probably wants me to meet her there, he thought. The alley looked very dark from where he was. He began to get a creepy feeling about it all, meeting her in the alley at night when he didn't even know who she was.

"See some gnomes in the alley?" Sewey whispered, and Bran turned forward again.

"Er, no gnomes there," Bran said. "I suppose they must have gotten far away."

"Invisible gnomes!" Sewey said, hitting the dash. "Or sneaky ones, at least."

"There's Mr. Brewer," Bran said, pointing at Sewey's coworker.

Sewey shrugged.

"And there's Officer McMason," Bran said. Sewey frowned. The officer was examining the door and spotted Sewey as he drove up, and gave him a little wave.

"Oh, rot, why'd *he* have to come?" Sewey lamented. They pulled next to Mr. Brewer's car and walked toward an officer. Sewey opened his mouth to speak, but before he could, she moved for the bank with a fingerprint duster, and Sewey was left with his mouth open.

"Sewey!" came the voice of Officer McMason as he started for them. Sewey shriveled up.

"Not him!" he growled. Sewey began to look into the sky, as if he wasn't there at all.

"Hello, Sewey!" the officer said. "Up so late?"

"Up so *early,*" Sewey corrected none-too-goodheartedly. "It's the *morning.*"

"Oh, yes, of course," Officer McMason chuckled. "How's the hunt going along?"

"I've still got a few days," Sewey murmured. "Now to business. Please explain all this."

"I suppose it was just a bunch of kids," the officer said, sipping a coffee and watching the action as the officers searched the building for evidence.

"Kids?" Sewey asked with disbelief. "Then where are the gnomes?"

"No gnomes," the officer chuckled uncomfortably. "Just a vandal or two, breaking windows. We haven't found any tracks or fingerprints yet, only a few rocks."

"Rocks?" Sewey said, confused. "Did the gnomes turn into rocks?"

The officer shook his head. "Nope, no gnomes at all."

"No gnomes, hmmm..." Sewey said. He drifted toward the bank doors, so Bran followed him. He saw Mr. Brewer standing inside, watching the officers as they lifted papers, pushed things aside, and made a big mess. Bran felt bad because he was the only one who knew the girl hadn't come to take anything, but he knew he couldn't say a word without sounding guilty himself.

"Vile villains," Sewey declared as he entered.

The lobby wasn't damaged much, just some broken glass.

The officers didn't look too happy, and Bran guessed they were still clueless.

Mr. Brewer led Sewey down the hall toward the vault, and Bran was left alone in the lobby. He tried to kick a few things around and act like he was searching for evidence, but it wasn't very convincing because he knew there wasn't anything to find. His eyes kept drifting toward the door, as if a magnet were pulling him toward the alley. He knew she was waiting.

Calm down, think about it first, he told himself. But he wanted so much to know the truth. For years he had dreamed of knowing his past, and for years he had gotten nowhere. It seemed to seize control of his mind—the words she had spoken, the tone of her voice that told him she wasn't lying. Now might be his only chance. Thoughts went through his mind, telling him his life depended on going across that street, as if he was about to discover something terrible but he had to know what it was. He had gotten that far, and he wasn't turning back. With one final glance to make sure no one was watching, he started for the door.

I hope this is worth it, he thought. He crossed the street, and when he got to the other end, he stopped. Everything was dark between the buildings. He could see a turn at the other end where another alley crossed, and there was trash littering the ground all the way.

"Couldn't remember to bring a flashlight, now could I?" Bran said aloud with a hint of wryness. He started into the dark, biting back any fear that still held on. The shadows of the high buildings covered him in a deep darkness like a blanket over his head, and he could just faintly see his feet and hands in front of him. There were a few broken windows on the sides, which reflected the moon, and some thick, closed doors, all of them dark and dirty. There came a few squeaks from a mouse, and he saw it shoot off from some boxes, sending empty crates tumbling down. He didn't let it perturb him as he came to the end, where it split in both directions.

"Down the alley," Bran remembered. "Turn right, then left, then the first door on the right."

He found it amusing how she had been right—she had told him he'd want to remember it. It seemed to only make him grimmer inside as he continued on. He walked with his hands out, brushing the Dumpsters as he passed. When he came around the final corner, he saw two doors: one on the right and the other on the left. The end of the alley faced Fourth Street.

"The door on the right," Bran said, moving for it. He stepped around some bags stacked against the wall and came toward the door, stopping in front of it—scratched, torn, and metal, with dents and graffiti all over. He looked toward the top and was surprised at the words he saw.

"Highland's Books?" he exclaimed, stepping back to look at it better. The words were in thick black letters with a number over the top, and he looked down the alley on the other side and saw the other door had letters over it too.

This is the alley behind the stores, Bran realized. He guessed they got deliveries back there, but he was still very confused as to why he had been led back to the bookstore. He didn't like the looks of it either. He took a deep breath and reached for the handle: it was cold, smashed on one side, and to his surprise, the door creaked open, unlocked for him. He peered into the darkness that was beyond.

The back of the bookstore was the same as he had seen the day before. Piles of boxes and crates were all around, tarps over some so that they formed a long row that almost looked like a hallway. It was empty and quiet. A rat scampered off at the sudden moonlight, and Bran stepped through, closing the door halfway behind him.

"Hello?" he asked into the darkness, his eyes searching between each tower. There were too many shadows...too many places for someone to hide. He felt as if he was entering an ambush.

I've got to find her, he thought. *I can't turn back now.*

He took a step forward, his shadow blocking the moonlight so that it shone softly on both sides of him. The room was as abandoned as a sunken ship, still and haunting like a prison cell. Three small windows sat high on the ceiling with bars over them, and the light they let in was like straight beams of white steel that cut through the dust floating in the air. His breath echoed around the room as he searched the walls, until he came to a corner and stopped.

Where is she? Bran wondered, looking around.

However, the moment he thought it, there was a scrape behind him.

"Be quiet," a girl's voice whispered, and Bran jumped.

Chapter 14

The Man at the Tavern

In a split second, Bran jerked around, raising his hand, and in that same moment, he felt something burst inside of him, erupting from his palm toward the girl. He didn't have a moment to think before it happened. He felt a burst of power shoot down his arm, and as if he had struck her with a giant rush of wind, she was picked up off her feet and slammed backward into a stack of crates.

Bran gasped and instantly the power disappeared.

The girl coughed, and two crates fell to the side from the top of the stack. She didn't stop for a second and pushed her hand out, and all of a sudden, Bran was pulled off his feet and slammed to the ground. He didn't have a moment to catch his breath before the back of his head hit the hard floor.

He shouted with pain and pushed himself away, jumping to his feet and against a stack of crates in the darkness, breathing hard and putting his hands in front of him.

"What are you doing?" he shouted.

"Be quiet!" the girl hissed. The back of his head throbbed, and he winced when he touched it.

"A mage!" he said with anger in his voice.

"As if you're any different," the girl spat back. They were

silent for a few moments, watching each other, trying to catch their breath. He was unable to make out any of her features in the dark. In a moment, his anger fell away, and he unclenched his fists.

"Either way, I wish you wouldn't do that to me in the dark," he said. "You've got police crawling all over this place now."

"I had to get you here somehow," she hissed. Before Bran could speak, she shifted from the shadows. A beam of moonlight crossed her face, and suddenly, he recognized who she was.

"You!" he shouted. "You're the girl who was here yesterday!"

"Shhh!" she said, but there was no doubt in his mind. It was Astara, the girl with the broom.

"Why did you do this?" he demanded, his voice echoing. "What's going on with this shop?"

"Be quiet!" she said harshly, putting a finger to her lips and looking around. "You know more about this shop than you should: leaving books all over the floor in the room. I'm not stupid."

"I want some answers, now, or I'm not listening to you at all," Bran said. "I want to know who you are, how you found me, and why there's a hidden room full of—"

"That's enough about the room," Astara cut him off. "Don't talk about it."

"What is it?" he demanded.

She hesitated, as if she didn't want to say, but she finally gave in.

"If you really need to know," she whispered, "Mr. Highland works with the Mages Underground here in Dunce. He's a distributor of the outside newspaper—not just to mages, but to others as well, people sympathetic to the cause."

"The books," Bran pressed. "There's enough for a hundred jail sentences in that room."

"Those are for the mages hiding in town," Astara said. "We distribute them as well. There are code words they say at the counter, and then Mr. Highland brings them up."

"And I suppose you just looked Sewey up," Bran said bitterly, "found out he worked at the bank, and knew if something happened I'd know to come along."

Astara nodded. Bran shook his head.

"I don't know how you pulled it off, but you're good at it."

She said nothing, but even then Bran knew she was pleased. He looked about the room.

"Well, you've got me here," he said. "I'll listen. But only for five minutes."

"You can't begin to understand it all in five minutes," she said, and something in her voice signaled urgency. "You're the one who's filling in the missing pieces. There's so much you don't know about your mother or why she left you."

"Please tell me," Bran said, forcing himself not to flinch at her mention of his mother. "I don't know anything about my past, and even if I can't believe you, it's more than what I've got now."

Astara glanced down for a moment. When she looked up again there was a strange light in her eyes, as if there was a story behind them, written with pain and sorrow. Just looking at her seemed to read volumes of it to Bran.

"Your mother's name was Emry Hambric," she said slowly. "I know you've heard it before."

There it was again, that name. Bran clenched his fingers together.

"Yes, I've heard it," he replied with a hint of frustration in his voice. He felt as if her gaze could pierce into his soul, and she could see all the pain and loneliness he had felt for years, never knowing his parents.

"Bran," she said slowly. "I know it hurts you, never knowing her. It has to. But even though you never knew her, the things she did are still left behind."

Astara lowered her voice. "Your mother was murdered, because they were searching for *you,* and she wouldn't tell them where she had left you. So they killed her."

Bran was completely taken aback. *Murdered because she wouldn't tell them?* How could Astara possibly know this—more about his own mother than he did?

"Who was searching for me?" he blurted out. "Why?"

"People your mother knew," Astara said. "The others who helped her create the Farfield Curse."

Something ominous in Astara's words seemed to catch in Bran's mind, echoing with a flare of evil in it. *The Farfield Curse.* He had never heard it before, and yet it seemed as if it were something familiar: darkly recognizable, like the name of an infamous serial killer.

"What is that?" Bran asked, his voice instinctively lowering.

"Your mother created a curse, Bran," Astara said, her voice going to a whisper. "The Farfield Curse is what they called it. It's a secret not even most mages know about, something so terrible I can't even find out what it was. But your mother was a part of it: a great criminal plot that was being worked years before either of us was even born."

"My mother was a magic criminal?" Bran said, hardly believing it, even as his words echoed what Astara had said. She nodded slowly.

"It's all secret," she said. "The plans, the plotting. It went on for years. You won't find a mention of what she did anywhere, at least not in any records we have access to."

Bran was left in a stupor, unable to comprehend the words she was speaking, as if a wall in his mind was instinctively blocking them out. His mother a criminal? The two words didn't even seem to fit in the same sentence together, and when he thought them, all of a sudden his face felt hot and his fingers curled into fists. It wasn't true. It couldn't be.

"I—I can't believe it," Bran said. "Please, this has got to be a joke."

"Does it sound like I'm joking?" Astara said with disbelief. "Do you think anyone would joke about this, bringing the police here just to talk to you? Why would I go through all that trouble?" She shook her head. "Bran, your mother died while trying to save *you.* And even though she stalled them, they will search for you until every corner of the world has been checked."

Her words were dark and shattering; they were nothing that Bran wanted to hear or believe. They wrecked everything he had ever clung to about his mother. *She was dead?* He had told himself for years that somehow his mother might be alive somewhere. He had imagined it so many times that he had come to believe it without question, so that when Astara told him it wasn't true, her words were a knife, striking down his mother right before him.

"You didn't know her at all," Bran said, feeling anger rising inside of him. "She might be alive, and out there looking for me right now. She might not have been able to take care of me years ago, that's all. You probably didn't see her once. You're making it all up!"

Astara motioned for him to be quieter. "Everyone is going to hear you!" she hissed through clenched teeth.

"I don't care if they hear," Bran said. "You brought me here and lied—my mother is *not* a criminal."

"I didn't lie," Astara said. "You just don't want to believe the truth."

Her words came at him like a slap to his face. Why were her words upsetting? He knew better than to believe her.

"You're making it up," Bran said again. "You can't even tell me how you know my mother."

Astara opened her mouth to speak, but suddenly, there came a piercing sound from the windows, and Bran heard the horn of the Schweezer going off, and Sewey shouting his name.

"Sorry, my time's up," Bran turned away from her toward the door, feeling relief that he had been distracted from listening to more.

"Wait!" Astara said quickly. "You don't understand."

"Maybe I don't *want* to understand," Bran said. "Just leave me alone."

He heard her scribbling on something with a pen, and he looked over his shoulder and saw her rip a piece of paper off a clipboard on one of the crates. She shoved it at him.

"Here," she said. "*This* is how I know your mother."

Bran hesitated but finally took the paper, pushing it into his pocket without reading.

"I think after that you'll believe me," she said. "If you don't, at least I've kept my word."

She reached into her pocket and pulled out a small, white envelope.

"This too," she said. "Believe me or don't: I made a promise to give you this."

He met her gaze, unsure of what she was saying, but took the envelope as well.

"Don't open it until you get home," she whispered. "You'll be glad you waited."

Bran looked at it but promised nothing, still frozen in the doorway at the strangeness of her actions. He didn't know what to say in return.

"Meet me back here in two days," she said, stepping from him slowly. "I'll tell you everything that happened."

"I won't be there," Bran said, shaking his head as he turned for the door.

"You will," she replied, in a way so certain Bran began to feel uneasy. *What could she do that would change my mind so much?* At the moment, he didn't really care.

"BRANNN!" He heard Sewey's voice again. "I'M LEAVING!"

He stuffed the envelope into his other pocket and hurried back the way he had come. Just as he shot out of the alley toward the bank, there was a flash of headlights, and behind them, the angry eyes of Sewey Wilomas. When Sewey saw him, he honked the horn.

"Bran!" he shouted. "This is no time to be wandering across the street in alleyways!"

Bran hopped in, and Sewey huffed and puffed like he was going to blow the bank down.

"Couldn't find a filthy gnome anywhere," he said. "And not a filthy clue either!"

They rocketed out onto the road and were quiet for a while, until Sewey spoke up.

"What the rot were you doing in that alley?" he demanded grumpily.

Bran wasn't ready for Sewey to ask that, and he started stammering for an answer. "I...um..."

"Stop it!" Sewey burst. "If you don't have a sensible thing to say, then just be quiet!"

Bran didn't feel like talking anyway. There were few cars on the road at that time and even fewer businesses with their lights on. Sewey careened over a crosswalk and passed a stop sign without pause, and nearly hit an early-morning newspaper truck. He slammed on the brakes.

"Rot!" he roared. The car screeched to a halt, though the truck passed unscathed. "Look, the trucks are already out. It's so early, why am I even going home?" he asked aloud. "I'd never get to sleep this way, and I'd just lie in bed like a sick old crab and feel miserable."

"I think I'd rather get twelve minutes of sleep than none at all." Bran said, irritated.

"Then you can be a sick old crab and sleep in the backseat," Sewey said, "while I go off to the pub and cool my nerves."

"Are you sure the pub's the best place for that?" Bran said.

"Who do you think you are: my father?" Sewey roared. "I'm an adult, I can do what I want!"

Bran knew Sewey hardly ever went to a pub except when he was at the Biannual Wilomas Family Reunion with his relatives, and they visited the one owned by his great-grand-uncle Groshnus. However, Sewey seemed set in what he wanted to do, and he turned the car around, looking for a good pub to stop at. He couldn't seem to find just the right one, and they eyeballed almost every pub all the way from Seventh to Eighty-Seventh Streets.

"What's wrong with this town?" Sewey asked. "Where have all the good pubs gone? They—"

He was about to say more, but suddenly, there was a flash of motion in front of the car. Someone leapt from the side of the road in front of them, as if he had appeared from nowhere.

"Sewey, look out!" Bran shouted, and Sewey slammed on the brakes.

"What the devil!" he roared. Bran was slung back and forth, the brakes squealing all around them, the car skidding down the road and swerving.

"What's going on?" Sewey roared.

"A man jumped out!" Bran said, looking all around. "He was right in front of us!"

"What?" Sewey's head rolled about. "I see no man!"

Bran looked again, but suddenly there was no one there at all. He rolled his window down quickly and looked down the street.

"I'm sure someone was there!" he said. He knew for certain he had seen the man.

"Close the window!" Sewey ordered. "It's very late, and early, and I don't have time for this."

"But we almost hit him!" Bran objected.

"Not a word!" Sewey said. "There's no one there, and that's final!"

Bran fell back into his seat. Sewey was just about to start driving again when he realized where they were.

"Oh!" he exclaimed. "Here we are!"

He raised his arm, and Bran looked at where he was pointing. It was a large, wooden building with lights on inside and a sign showing OPEN on the front door.

"It's the Flob Hopkin's!" Sewey said with a chuckle, pulling forward to park on the side of the road. "I haven't been here in ages! Practically the last of the good pubs, I'd say!"

Eying the pub suspiciously, Bran saw through the windows that there were still some people in it and not too many ruffians, and the place was well lit. It had been kept well on the outside at least, a large wooden sign hanging over the door with a picture of a pint of Duncelander Ale spilling over, and the words Flob Hopkin's Tavern and Inn painted beside it.

"Come on," Sewey said, and Bran followed him through the door. The wooden ceiling was very high, and the walls were made of dark bricks on which hung many animal heads and trophies from great hunts. There were round tables set out in rows in the middle of the floor, with booths against the walls and a few men about, most of them hanging to the corners. The air smelled of smoke and beer, but it was mostly a quiet place. A heavy, black raven sat on one of the fans in the ceiling, going around slowly and watching the people below. When Bran stepped in, the bird gave a loud screech and flew off. Sewey leaned to Bran's ear.

"Watch out," he warned. "There are adventurers at places like this, maybe Wild Westmen, or even hardened criminals! Tell me if you see one, and I'll report him to the authorities."

"What do hardened criminals happen to look like?" Bran whispered back.

Sewey paused, looking around the room. "Hmmm...like that man *there.*" He pointed at a man sitting in the far corner of the tavern. The man was leaning over with his eyes closed, sitting across from two other men whose faces Bran could not see. He was in dark clothes and had thick, blond hair; he was quietly listening to the other men and circling a silver cell phone in his fingers on the table. He didn't look like any Duncelander Bran had ever seen.

"They look like *him,*" Sewey went on. "Always find their type, looking for treasure, looking for love, or looking for their lost father—but always looking for trouble. I'll keep an eye on him. Maybe I can get him thrown in jail for something before morning breaks."

Sewey started toward the man but stopped just one booth short, sliding into the seat to face him. Bran had to sit down with his back to the men, but none of them noticed him or Sewey at all, even when Sewey went on clearing his throat for quite some time.

"May I assist you?" an old woman stepped forward with a tray under her arm and a pitcher in her hand. She had silver hair tied in a tight bun and two cigarettes in her mouth.

"I, er..." Sewey stammered. "I'll take a water for Bran, and some Duncelander Ale for me."

"Sorry chapperoo," she growled, burying the end of one of her cigarettes into the table. "Intoxicating beverages ended five minutes ago. Have to get water if you're thirsty."

Sewey was about to protest, but the woman just shrugged.

"Or motor oil," she sneered. "It's on special today."

Sewey gulped and settled with the clearer of liquids. She lit up another cigarette and went for the kitchen. The three men behind Bran started to talk in soft whispers, but he couldn't hear what they were saying because Sewey kept scratching himself. They waited for a long while, and Sewey started to fidget with the salt shaker and ended up spilling it all over the table. He started to draw in it with his finger.

"I wish they'd hurry up!" he said. "What could possibly be taking so long?"

"Maybe you should go check?" Bran said.

Sewey brushed the salt to the floor with disgust. "Maybe I shall," he retorted, and he started for the counter, kicking the pile of salt with his slippers as he passed. Bran was left alone—and for that, he was grateful. He rubbed his forehead. Getting up early and sleeping hardly any hours were beginning to take its toll on him.

He remembered what Astara had told him, as much as he tried to forget it. Her words were like a foul taste in the back of his mouth. He didn't even know why he had been fooled into going there in the first place. It only made him feel doubtful, and he wasn't going to let himself believe any of the nonsense she had made up.

Still, he looked around to make sure no one was watching, and slowly drew out the white envelope she had given him. It was worn and dirty and old. He studied it closely, running his fingers along the torn edges and turning it over, taped in half so it formed a square package. There was something hard and bulky inside. He couldn't tell what it was because it was a very odd shape. She had obviously gone through a lot of trouble to give it to him.

*Don't open this until you get home...*he remembered her words. Why couldn't he? He didn't have any idea why she would say that. He held it to the light and tried to see through, but couldn't make out what it was, so he shrugged and set it back on the table between his hands.

He listened to the sounds of the people around him and to the fans, trying to distract his mind from Astara. He fell into a half sleep leaning against the wall. The whispers of the men behind him gradually grew clearer, until he could faintly make out their words. He didn't have anything else to do, so he concentrated on listening.

"Aye, that's right," one of the men whispered, and his scratchy voice sounded like it came from the stouter one. "You've got no business going about town looking for him: 'tis not safe."

"Take it from a local," the thin man said, and his voice half-drunk. "Best if you leave, Joris, and give up while you can, before somebody tries to toss you into the jails."

"It's the boy I want, not the runaround you're giving me," Bran heard another man's voice, and it was filled with a commanding air about it.

"I want to know anything and everything either of you can

tell me about him," he said. "Cooperate with me on this now, or both of you will turn up dead before next week."

Bran gasped softly, and he heard the two men shift uncomfortably. The strong whisper that the man had used felt like a knife, as if he could kill them right there in the tavern.

"Aye, sir, you don't needin' be threatening us now," the stout man said. "What me and Larry's got to know is why you've been movin' about in these parts, lookin' for him here?"

Bran was very still because he was listening hard. His breath had slowed down until he could barely hear it going in and out of him, and the man's voice lowered even further.

"I hunt the boy Bran Hambric," he said. "That is all you need to know."

Bran froze in the chair. For a moment, he didn't believe he had heard right.

"Aye," the stout man said. "We've heard some of Bran before."

"What do you know?" the man asked. They were quiet for a while, debating on telling him.

"Heard he was living in town," the stout man finally said, "with the Wilomas family of Bolton Road. Ain't his real parents: found him, in a vault, couldn't leave 'im after that. Still keeps the name Hambric, I think, 'cause of the paper they found with him."

The man sipped from his drink. Bran was listening so intently, all the sounds of the tavern faded away—but then he heard something above him and shifted his gaze up. It was the black raven, perched on the light, its head turned down to watch him. It gave a loud sound again, and Bran sank lower into the booth, fearful the men might hear the noise and turn around.

"There was that truck too," the stout man was continuing. "People say he was at the park on Sunday and stopped a truck with his bare hands."

"Doesn't go to school either," Larry said. "They've got some cousin teaching him with textbooks. No one sees much of him."

The bird rocked back and forth, looking down at Bran intently. It opened its beak and flapped its wings, as if catching its balance, tilting its head at him.

"No..." Bran hissed through his teeth, though he didn't dare let his voice be heard. The bird cawed again. Bran heard one of the men slurp something from his cup. The bird rocked forward, as if he was about to jump and take flight.

"No, don't!" Bran whispered strongly. The bird gave a loud sound and leapt off the light, but instead of flying off, it gave a sudden dive in Bran's direction.

Bran heard its wings flapping down; it landed on the table next to his arm. Bran froze and the bird tilted its head, looking at Bran closely. It had a thin line of feathers down its back that were bleached white in a strange manner. It tilted its head at the envelope, almost as if it wanted it.

"Shhh..." Bran tried to quiet it, being very still so he didn't draw attention, but in the next second, the raven moved.

With an enormous shriek, it leapt into the air in a sudden flurry, diving at Bran with its sharp beak. Bran shouted as he felt it dig into his shoulder, driving like a nail into his arm and screeching wildly in his ear. He slung his hand around and caught the raven once, but it only slid across the table and leapt up again, diving at his face and knocking him backward.

Bran fell out of the booth, hitting the floor and hearing the wings of the bird in his ear.

He rolled over and caught the bird with the back of his hand, sending it under a table. He leapt to his feet, and the bird fluttered about, shooting toward him again. Bran held his hands up to block his face, and the raven slammed into his arm, scratching at him with his claws and screaming into his ear. Bran swung his fist into the bird once more. It fell again and was still.

Bran gasped for breath and held the side of his arm, looking at the raven; and it was then that he realized that the entire tavern had gone completely silent. Slowly, he looked up, and saw that everyone was staring at him with wide eyes. The waitress was standing in the doorway of the kitchen, her face filled with shock.

"Th-the bird, it dove at my face," Bran said, shakily pointing down toward its body on the floor. The waitress looked where he was pointing.

"What bird?" she asked, disbelievingly.

"The bird, right there," Bran said, looking back to where it was laying. Then he stopped. It was gone. The raven had disappeared into nothing, as if it had never been there at all.

"No, really," Bran said, looking back up at her quickly. "It attacked me!"

The men at the tables slowly turned back to their conversations. The waitress shook her head.

"A raven of all things, in the Flob Hopkin's!" she hissed. "Should take a strap to you!"

Bran blinked and he looked back under the table, where the bird's body had been.

"But I'm sure it was there..." Bran insisted, and he reached up to wipe the blood from his arm. His fingers stopped, and he looked at his arm.

"The cut..." he said with disbelief. The gash that had been on his arm had completely disappeared as well, as if it had never been there at all.

"It's gone!" he whispered, not believing what his own eyes told him. There wasn't even a trace of blood on his fingers. It was as if he had imagined everything that had happened.

"But it did," Bran told himself. He could only shake his head, as not even he could see any evidence of the bird. He began to turn around back to the table, when all of a sudden a shadow fell over him, and he was face to face with Joris.

Chapter 15

The Name on the Necklace

Bran gasped and stepped backward. Joris didn't move.

"What's a boy doing at a place like this?" he said, his words like fire.

"I-I'm here with somebody," Bran stammered, unable to break his gaze.

"Oh?" Joris said with disbelief. He lifted his hand, and Bran almost jumped. "Here," Bran heard him say, and he reached out with something. "I think you dropped this."

Joris held out his hand, and in it was the envelope from Astara.

Bran hesitated, but slowly reached forward to take it from Joris.

"Thank you," Bran said slowly, and Joris watched his movements, almost as if he could recognize something. Then, his gaze lifted up, scanning the room once, before shifting back.

"Harley, Larry," the man finally said. "I'll talk to both of you tomorrow."

His eyes did not leave Bran's as he spoke, until he stepped forward and passed Bran for the door. Bran was still and felt the man's shadow as he passed. The two men who had been with him rose unsteadily from the booth, mumbling among themselves, and Bran hid his face as they passed, though they were too drunk to notice him anyway.

"Joris." He said the name to himself. He tightened his hand around the envelope, remembering the way he had looked at him. It was as if Joris had recognized him as the boy he was looking for: but for some reason, he had done nothing.

Bran turned to look at the table where the men had been sitting, and suddenly, his eyes locked on something out of place. It was on the edge, sitting alone, softly reflecting the light of the lamp: *Joris's silver cell phone.* Bran froze when he saw it. Joris had forgotten it on the table.

That'll have the answers I need, Bran thought instantly. He hesitated: what if someone saw him, or Joris came back looking for it? He didn't want to be seen touching the phone, but on second thought, it might hold the only clues he could work with to find out who this man was. He checked the door: Joris was gone. Quickly, Bran stepped to the table, sweeping his hand across and sliding the phone out of view, slipping it into his pocket before anyone could see.

"*Don't ring,*" he hissed, his fingers clutching it so tightly his palms became hot against the metal. He felt in an instant that everyone in the tavern could see it burning through his pocket, telling the world that he had it, and he knew he couldn't even take a glance at it until he got home for fear someone might see. His heart beat quicker as he realized what he had done.

All of a sudden, he heard loud shoes coming up behind him, and some things crashing in the kitchen. He spun around, and there was Sewey, his slippers flopping on the floor, and over his clothes was a white apron, as if he worked at the tavern.

"Forget the blasted drinks!" he said, tearing the apron off. "We're leaving!"

He tossed the apron into the booth, grabbed Bran's arm, and started to pull him to the door.

"Stop gawking like that," Sewey ordered. "What a waste of time this whole trip was! I wish you never would have suggested the pub in the first place!"

Sewey pushed through the doors. As Bran stepped out, he glanced down the street to make sure the man wasn't watching for him. What he saw almost made him stop: a black van, driving toward the end of the road, the same as had followed them on Sunday, and the same as had been sitting at the end of Bolton Road the day before.

Bran's eyes didn't leave its form, even as it reached the corner. His grip on the cell phone tightened as he watched the van disappear down the street.

When Sewey and Bran got home, everyone else was asleep. Bran started up the stairs, and when he got up to his room he didn't dare turn on a light for fear that Sewey would see it and get suspicious. He moved for his bed and drew the cell phone out of his pocket. It took hold of the moonlight from his window and reflected it like a mirror, the surface polished and smooth, now showing fingerprints from where Bran had been gripping it.

"Let's see what you can tell me," he whispered to it, lying back on his bed. He held it in front of his eyes, all the while feeling his heartbeat beginning to quicken. It felt strange to be holding something that not half an hour before had been in the hands of a man who was hunting him.

He flipped it open. The inside was arranged like most phones, with shiny black buttons like glass and a color screen playing light across Bran's face. It seemed to be a sleek and expensive model, every detail sharp and crisp, and the front screen showed the time and date. Bran pressed a button at the top of the keypad and pulled up the menu. There was a list of options on the screen, and he began to navigate through them, down to one labeled Recent Calls.

I wonder who's been calling Joris, he thought, selecting it. A list of numbers popped up, going down the screen. Bran looked at the top: it was marked in large letters PRIVATE NUMBER, and next to it was the date from the day before. Bran scrolled to the next one, and it read the same, but dated one day earlier. Bran continued to scroll down, but each call Joris had received seemed to be from the same person, calling almost every evening at the same time.

This is odd, Bran thought, but as he scrolled, the name changed. There was a different record on the screen, labeled simply with a single letter: T. The letter was all alone, as if a name should have followed it, but there was nothing next to it but a date, *April ninth.*

Two days before we heard Shambles at the door, Bran thought. It struck him as very odd. He paused, his fingers poised over the buttons, and finally navigated the phone back to the main screen and tried for the address book. He clicked it, but suddenly, before it showed the records, a red screen popped up: ENTER PASSWORD.

"No," Bran hissed. He punched in J-O-R-I-S, but of course he wasn't stupid enough just to use his name. Bran tried

S-H-A-M-B-L-E-S, and even H-A-M-B-R-I-C, but none of them even made the red screen waver. He punched all the keys at once out of frustration.

"And I was just getting somewhere," he said. He had risked so much for that phone, and now it hardly gave him anything in return. Bran found the volume and turned the ringer to vibrate; he certainly couldn't answer it. If Joris knew he had it, he'd come for Bran in an instant to get it back. As long as he didn't know where it was, it might deter his plans just a little.

Bran felt there wasn't much more to be done with the phone, and so he started to change clothes. He folded up his jeans out of sheer habit, and wasn't even thinking as he went through the motions of getting ready for bed again. His mind was on other things and bitter at having been let down with the cell phone. He began to set his jeans into the drawer when something fell out of the pocket: the envelope Astara had given him, and the paper she had written on. The envelope slid across the floor and under his bed, and at the sudden sound Bran froze. In getting wrapped up in the cell phone, he had completely forgotten about Astara.

For a moment, he stared across the room at the envelope. He looked down at the paper at his feet. He hadn't believed her enough to read what was on it. Now he wasn't so sure of himself. Very slowly, he bent down for the paper, and he read what was written there:

Helter Lane and Jackston Road
Go down the path.

—Astara

"More directions," Bran said with slight disappointment. He had at least expected something more—now she was just sending him somewhere else for the answers. He slowly came to his bed and slid his hand under for the envelope.

Best not get my hopes up, he thought. But already his senses were jarred by what he had heard at the tavern. Suddenly, he felt as if his mind was beginning to listen to the words Astara had said, though he fought hard against them. He sat on his bed slowly so it wouldn't creak and reached for the edge of the envelope to tear it open. It was taped shut and had dirt under the edges.

He heard a noise across the room. His hand froze over the edge, his gaze looking up.

All was still. His eyes shifted to the other corner. Nothing. A strange, eerie feeling began to creep up, but he brushed it away and looked back to the envelope, reaching to tear the edge.

There was another sudden sound, on the other side, and Bran jerked his head up again. A small shoebox fell off the top of a stack and hit the floor: a small sound, but it made him jump.

"Who's there?" he said quickly. He sat frozen on his bed, listening for any movement, any voice that might come from the darkness. His eye caught a movement, in the mirror leaning against the wall, like someone rushing past. He turned his head, but all was still again.

He watched for a minute, but then looked back to the envelope and ripped the end of it quickly, glancing up again but seeing no one. The light from the moon streamed in from the window as he pulled the paper apart and turned it over, dumping its contents into his hand.

Something metal touched his palm. It was small, and as he held it up close to his face, he saw that it was a silver, moon-shaped pendant on a thick black string.

He turned it over—so smooth and polished that it seemed a silvery white. It was curved exquisitely and reflected his face on the smooth side, the points sharp. It seemed so perfect he could almost feel power radiating from beneath its surface, like he was holding something terrible and great at the same time; he could almost feel something moving inside and rushing to break free, but held tight within its silvery shell. Only his mind could perceive it, and even then it was very faint. All he could do was stare in wonderment.

What is this? he asked himself, turning it over in his hand. He turned back to the envelope and saw a slip of paper stuck at the bottom. He drew it out and read:

Your mother told me to give this to you, and wanted you to wear it.

—Astara

Bran blinked at the paper. *His mother?* He reminded himself not to believe anything from Astara. But instantly, his heartbeat quickened, and he looked back to the necklace. He was very mystified, and slid his fingers over its surface. How could this girl have possibly gotten something from his mother—the same mother he had never met?

It can't be true, he thought. Still, he felt around the edges of the string again, lifting it up to his eyes. Then he noticed something: there appeared to be light blue markings underneath the glassy surface of one side, though they were dark and he could not make out what they said. He lifted it into the moonlight to see better, and as he did, something happened.

The blue markings suddenly flashed forward in white, blinding Bran with their light for a moment and then fading the next second so he could see again. It happened so fast that he didn't have a chance to react; and then, as his vision cleared, he saw that the glow had settled into the surface of the necklace like white drops of light, moving in thin lines across the necklace's surface and filling the blue markings like water into tiny cracks. He could not move his hands, his gaze riveted on the motion of the lines, his breath quickening as he saw them fill the shapes along the bottom curve, forming letters which spelled the name *Hambric.*

He moved his hand to cover it quickly, looking up toward the ladder in case someone had seen the light; and when he heard no one coming, he slowly slid his hand away from the necklace, and saw that the glow had disappeared, leaving behind only the faint blue letters nearly invisible in the dark... though still spelling his last name.

"It's the moonlight," he realized, lifting it again toward the window. The instant the beam struck it, the letters flashed again like thin white fire, and when he saw them, he pulled it back into the darkness, and the words faded once more.

"Where did she get this?" he wondered with amazement. He was sure it was magic. He looked back to the paper—his mother wanted him to have it?

He pulled the necklace up by the string. It was something very strange to him, and he almost found himself wanting to believe what Astara had said. But how could his mother have given her something to give to him? But as he read what Astara had written, he decided it wouldn't hurt to do what she said, so he lifted it up, and put it on.

The moment he did, it was as if the world around him exploded at once.

Instantly, there was a burst of white light that hit him full force, electrifying and washing through every nerve he had. Bran fell, losing control of his muscles, and the moment his hands touched the ground, he was somewhere else.

It was a cold, white room bathed in light, everything around him blurred as if there were a sun ray in his eyes. The walls were empty, the room was blank, and in the middle of the space was a bed which rose out of the floor—and it held a body.

The body was white and deathly, shrouded in black robes… motionless. Bran recognized the face, even in the suddenness of seeing it—the same man from his dream! His eyes were closed, hands by his side, but then, the body gave a jerk, as if a tremor had been felt.

There was a sharp intake of breath, choking once for air. In a flash, the eyes of the body flew open, staring toward the ceiling in terror and pain; and then, the next second, the body fell again, and Bran felt his back hit the floor. And in that same second, he was back on Bolton Road again, and he heard the necklace clatter to the floor beside him.

Chapter 16

A Path in the Woods

Pass the sausages, Rosie," Sewey said at the breakfast table later that morning, gobbling down heaps of food. He gave Bran a curious glance, waving his hands in front of Bran's blank eyes.

"Well, what's the matter with you *now?*" Sewey demanded. "You've hardly touched your food. Don't tell me it's that burglary last night!"

"N-nothing," Bran stammered. He grabbed his fork and tried to eat some sausage. Even that didn't taste good. The cell phone was hidden in his room, but he could feel the necklace in his pocket, constantly reminding him of the name that was on it—of the girl, the magic, the creature…and the man he had seen the night before. But mostly what he thought about were the directions Astara had given him on the paper. Now he *knew* he had to follow them.

Sewey shrugged and absently reached for the pile of bills beside him, accidentally knocking it over. It sounded like a miniature avalanche.

"*There's* my day book!" he said, spying the black leather book that had been underneath. "Ah yes, nothing important today, and nothing important…"

He squinted. "Well, there's *something* tomorrow, but I can't tell what it is. Someone scribbled in my book."

He crossed his arms at Bran. "And who here likes to make ridiculous markings on paper?"

"That's just your handwriting," Bran said, pointing. "It says Formal Dinner Night."

"What?" Sewey said, bewildered. "Formal Dinner Night? Is that code?"

"Fool," Mabel snapped at him. "It means we clean the house and dress up for dinner."

"For *whatever* reason?" Sewey squealed.

"It's the healthiest thing," she protested. "The *Fitness Witness* told me so!"

"Bah!" Sewey waved his hand. "I'll have no part in formal dinner whatevers!"

He started to strike it out, but Mabel slapped his hand with the business end of a fork.

"Youch!" Sewey cried. Formal Dinner Night stayed.

Sewey left for work, and Bran left to start on the dishes, his mind elsewhere. Not long afterward, Rosie came into the kitchen and started to put a hat on in the reflection of the mirror. She was dressed up more than normal.

"Where are you off to?" Bran asked, setting a few dishes back in the cabinet.

"To the market," she replied, putting a small daisy in her hat. She dropped her voice. "I'm also stopping by the newspaper to drop off a new article!"

"That's wonderful!" Bran said. "Maybe it'll make it this time."

She looked happy, but then something passed over her face,

some thought she didn't like. She stood there for a moment, watching him do the dishes, and finally sighed and moved for the sink.

"Come on, move aside and let me wash!" she commanded, rolling up her sleeves. "I was born a dishwasher like every other Tuttle, and I can't sit and watch someone else do it without me!"

Bran grinned and stepped to the side, and she started to wash, passing them to him to dry. The room was quiet all except for the clanking of the glass, and Bran could feel that there was something on Rosie's mind.

"That's my dream," she finally said. "Get into a big paper, have everyone read it. It's not like the old days, when we had heroes running around to write about—defeating evils, fighting fires, rescuing children. Now all newspapers want to hear about is weather, wars, and old politicians."

She shook her head. "Heroes have practically disappeared these days."

"Maybe they've just gone into hiding since then," Bran mused. Rosie handed him a dish but didn't put her hands back into the water. She looked out the window and thought.

"Maybe you're right," she said. "When I think of a hero, I think of someone who goes to the greatest lengths to bring happiness to others, even at great danger and cost to themselves." She nodded. "*That* is a hero."

She handed him a cup. He rubbed the towel across it, and warm water ran down his fingers.

"Bran, maybe you're a hero in secret too," Rosie said thoughtfully. "*Then* I could write an article on you!"

Bran laughed a bit. "Not me! All I do is spend my nights on a roof, watching for burglars, and in a car, chasing burglars, and at the breakfast table, talking about burglars." He took another dish. "Just wait until I *become* a burglar—then write an article on me."

Rosie laughed as she handed him a set of forks. "But what type of person *are* you going to be, Bran? Are you going to be ordinary like everyone else?"

She shifted the dishes around, the sound of her fingers raking through the water catching against the stillness her words left over the room.

"Will you just give up when things get hard?" she went on. "Let them force you to forget who you are? Or will you find the courage to make the choice—"

She looked up at him. "—and be a hero?"

Bran looked at her for a long time, and she stared back, unrelenting. Her words stuck him as very odd, as if there was something on her mind causing her to say them so abruptly. It wasn't like her to be so serious all of a sudden. She lifted her eyebrows, finally letting a little smile cross her face before she turned back to the dishes.

"Like you said: maybe they're all just hiding," Rosie said. "Maybe you *are* one, and you don't know who you really are."

Rosie's final words were meant well, but they immediately jerked Bran's mind back to what Astara had told him: *You don't know who you really are.* He tried to hide what he was feeling from showing on his face, and Rosie winked and splashed some of the water at him. He jumped out of the way, and she grinned, grabbing a towel to dry her hands, and he used it as a distraction so she wouldn't notice what he was thinking.

"Well, anyhow, you've still got your textbooks to do work in," Rosie said. "I've marked some pages down on that list on the table for—"

"Hurry up, you slug, and bring Baldretta along!" Mabel shouted from outside. Rosie sighed.

"I'll figure it out," Bran said, and Rosie reluctantly scuffled off. Bran had been used to teaching himself from textbooks for years, as the Wilomases held great distrust of the Dunce school system after a book of shapes had been used that included tall red isosceles triangles, far too reminiscent of gnome hats. They had pulled Balder and Bran out immediately. Not that Bran actually cared that much: most of the other Duncelanders his age were spoiled bullies.

He was only able to work for a little while, just long enough to make sure that Mabel wouldn't turn the car around and come back early. When he was certain they were really gone for the day, he went to the kitchen drawer and took out some spare house keys.

"Time to solve all this," he said, taking the necklace from his pocket. It barely glinted in the light from the windows, though he could still read the blue letters on the side that told him it had been real. He didn't dare put it over his head again for fear of what enchantment it might have, but instead took out the paper that Astara had given him the night before.

Helter Lane and Jackston Road
Go down the path.

—Astara

I'm going to follow it, he told himself. His mind was made up. It was time to end all the mystery and questions. He wanted answers, and he was going to get them. He checked the map and started outside.

It was warm that day, and not many people were out. Bran got his bike from the side of the house and glanced down the street. The black van was gone.

Probably wasn't anything after all, he told himself.

Or else they followed Mabel thinking I was with them, he thought next. It was grim, so he tried to forget it. He took a turn right where he usually went left for the bank, and started off.

He rode for what felt like an hour, checking his bearings every few minutes. There were some sharp turns, and he almost crashed when his bike went into a pothole. Crossing a bridge, he found himself in a more rural part of Dunce, where the trees overshadowed the roads with their branches, and he came to Helter Lane very quickly.

After a few minutes, the pavement ended, and the wheels of his bike crunched against a light, dirty road with rocks all over. He went on a little further and was just about to stop for a rest when he saw an old and weathered street sign up ahead, almost covered by the branches of an overgrown tree. The place was very quiet and deserted as he pulled up.

"Jackston Road," Bran read the sign, wiping his forehead. He looked down the street and saw that it went a long way out of sight, up and down hills; the road behind him seemed to swirl in his gaze as the sun beat down on his back.

"Is this it?" he asked aloud, though there wasn't a soul

around to hear him. Wind rustled through the grass. He took the paper out again.

"Go down the path," he said. He looked through the trees on both sides of the road and spotted some cleared space. He started for it, and as he came closer, he saw that it was indeed a path that went deep into the woods and out of sight. His curiosity leapt.

"She's been right so far," Bran told himself, almost with disbelief. Everything she had said was turning out to be true. He knew he couldn't get carried away. Not yet. But he had to go on. He wasn't going to turn back then, not knowing the truth. The brush was thick at the beginning of the path, but got thinner the deeper he went. It was cooler in the shade of the woods than it had been on the road, the smells of the grass and trees surrounding him. He didn't quite know what to expect as he went deeper, and he scratched his arms a few times on the branches because he was so busy looking around.

I probably should have told someone where I was going, he thought. He looked back the way he had come. He could just barely see the faded colors of his bike at the edge.

Too late now, he thought, and all of a sudden, while he wasn't looking where he was going, he tripped over something hard which threw him forward off his feet. His head hit a branch, and he fell to the ground with a gasp of pain.

He winced at the sting on his head and rolled onto his back, staring up into the trees. They seemed to spin around him as his forehead throbbed, and he blinked to clear his eyes. He sat up slowly and saw that he had run right into a large piece of granite sticking out of the ground.

"Great," he said angrily, pushing to his feet. He rubbed the front of his head again, looking all around. He saw that the trees were farther apart where he was, and they let the sunlight in so he could see the leaves and the dead branches that had fallen to the ground. It was a very serene place, and a curious spot to have a piece of granite just sitting there.

As he looked closer at it, though, he noticed it wasn't a plain piece of granite at all—there were soft markings inset into its surface, covered with dust. It struck him as odd, but he knelt anyway to rub the dust off the stone. It was strangely smooth on the front, and as he brushed it off, his heart began to beat a little faster, because he was beginning to see words.

This thing's not just a rock; it's a headstone for a grave! he realized. He hurried now, brushing off the top row of letters with his fingers, the throbbing pain on his forehead forgotten.

"To be remembered, from this day forth," he read the stiff, straight letters on the headstone, brushing off more with his hand. "This headstone was placed to mark the grave of…"

His hand stopped at the bottom. The rest of the headstone was buried under the grass. His heart began to beat faster as he dug roughly with his hands and pushed the leaves and grass out of his way. There was dirt smeared all over the front, and he started to wipe it off with his hands.

"There's an E," he said with anticipation, "an M…"

His hand stopped. *No.* It couldn't be.

"It says Emry Hambric!" he gasped quickly, and with another handful, all the dirt was gone, and there were the letters, right in front of him.

"To be remembered, from this day forth," he said softly. "This headstone was placed to mark the grave of Emry Hambric."

He stared at it, struck motionless at what was before him. He read the words again, hardly believing his own eyes. It was that name again. The name Shambles had spoken. The name the girl had said. The name he knew inside belonged to his mother. And there it was…on her grave.

Looking at the words made tears came to his eyes, angry tears that stung his face. The name was there, no matter what he did, no matter what he said; it was etched in stone before his eyes. That was all that was left of his mother, and somehow, Astara had known about it.

He looked toward the road, blurry through his teary eyes, and in anger he tore the grass with his hands. He read the words until he was so sick he had to lean his back against the stone with his head to his knees, alone, not wanting to face the stone ever again. She was dead.

He pulled the slip of paper out of his pocket and read the directions again. Astara had led him right to the grave. He ripped the paper to pieces and threw them into the grass. She had been right about everything now. His mother was dead? He knew it was true. She had been a criminal? That had to be true also. Astara had no reason to lie about it now. She had been right all along.

Chapter 17

Noises in the Kitchen

It felt as if no time passed between leaving the grave and arriving back on Bolton Road, Bran's mind so far elsewhere that he was hardly watching where he was going. Mabel's car was still gone. He went up to the attic and stayed there, staring at the wall across the room and thinking to himself, angry and bitter at the same time. The house was so empty it seemed to quell his feelings, and he just sat there alone, as had always been.

Out of habit he pulled at the roll of blank newspaper that was leaning against his desk, ripping off a sheet and putting his pencil against it. At first he couldn't make his arm move, but the second he started, his motions became furious, almost as if his anger and confusion were fueling his fingers. He almost didn't know what he was drawing, line after line seeming to form something his mind kept a secret from him, until he stopped and looked at what he had done.

The page was darkened from his motions, but the marks held true to what he had seen in his mind all along. It showed the strong, dark trees, shadows cast all about the woods, just as he had seen not an hour before. There was a dirty path that stopped where a tall stone stood out of the ground, a beam of sunlight from a hole in the trees dashed across the page, shining straight upon the headstone. But there was one thing missing. On the headstone, there were no words.

Bran stared at the blank stone, empty of the markings that had pained him so much. He couldn't bring himself to write them, couldn't make his arm move the pencil to it again to etch the words that proved his mother really was dead.

Usually when he drew, he would feel better. But this time, he did not, even as he took a deep breath and quietly pinned the paper next to the others on the board. He didn't look at it or any of the others, because he knew inside none of them would make him happy. But slowly, he reached into his pocket and pulled the necklace out. His fingers clutched it tightly; and as they did, something within the necklace almost seemed to make his pain fade away.

He turned it over, tracing it with his thumb. He took a deep breath and looked around the room: he was alone. But was he really? He could still feel eyes on him, always watching, from every darkened corner. He remembered what had happened the night before, the last time he had tried to put the necklace on. He knew there was something important about it. Every time he touched it, something seemed to happen.

I'm going to try it again, he thought. He slid his fingers through the black string and lifted the necklace, not even looking as he did, his eyes on the room. Very slowly, he lifted the necklace and brought it over his head, still hesitant. When nothing happened, he began to lower it, until he felt the string touch his neck. Still nothing.

"What's going on?" he asked himself, running his fingers down the string. It was almost as if he had expected it to happen so much, he was even more shocked when it didn't. He slipped it under his shirt to hide it, and then suddenly, he heard something.

It was a soft buzz coming from the top of his dresser. Immediately, he turned his head, though he didn't move from the chair. He could see the light of the screen on Joris's phone reflecting off the wall, bright colors, as the phone buzzed with a call coming in. Bran was motionless, as if the person calling might hear him if he moved.

He didn't know if he should look to see who was calling or not touch it at all in case it might accidentally pick up: he chose the latter. A few seconds later, the call ended unanswered. Bran took a deep breath, his fingers nearly trembling with fright.

But then, suddenly, there was something else. It was so soft he might not have noticed if he hadn't been so quiet. It came from below his feet, as if someone were moving about hastily in the kitchen, and immediately it made Bran alert, for no one else should have been in the house yet.

He froze, as the sounds ceased, and then he heard them again: the refrigerator opening, and closing, something being softly set on the counter.

The burglar? It was Bran's first thought.

He wasn't exactly sure what to do, but he slowly turned in his chair to face the hole that went down to the house, listening intently. As he did, however, his elbow accidentally brushed his roll of newspaper, and before he could catch it, it fell to the side and slammed into the floor.

He winced, and immediately heard whoever was downstairs shuffling about quickly. He heard nothing for a few seconds, and then there was a slam, like one of the kitchen cabinets had been closed. Bran leapt into motion, dashing down the ladder for the kitchen. He rushed downstairs, but the kitchen door was closed, and he shoved through it.

"Who's there?" he demanded before it was even open, but he was greeted with an empty room. He rushed to look behind the door, but there was no one there either. His eyes ran across the room, from the small table on the side to the pantry door, to the refrigerator and the counters. His eyes stopped, for on the counter was a plate, and on the plate was bread, ready to be made into a sandwich.

Before Bran could even react to seeing it, there came another sound: a soft squeak from the dumbwaiter cabinet on the far wall. Bran dashed toward it, pulling the cabinet door open, just in time to see the empty dumbwaiter shelf stop at the kitchen level.

He stared, sure of what he had just seen though hardly believing it. The dumbwaiter was old and very large, and even though it went from the basement to the kitchen and up to the dining room, the Wilomases never used it and preferred to see Rosie and Bran carrying plates of food up and down like a small row of servants. He looked around the room again. No one was there, and he was the only person in the house—or so he had thought.

Part of him still said it was his imagination, all the burglaries making everything sound to him like another intruder. But another side told him that he was sure of what he had seen; something in the air that told him someone had just been in that room moments before.

A very odd idea came to him when he looked back to the dumbwaiter, one that seemed so far-fetched that at first he discounted it. He was not usually afraid of much, but the unfortunate fact was that he was abysmally claustrophobic, and just thinking of any intruder cramming themselves into that tiny dumbwaiter shelf nearly made his knees start to shake.

Another idea immediately followed it.

No, Bran told himself. *I'm not doing it.*

But inside he knew he didn't have time to be afraid, and if he didn't do something then whatever had been creeping in the kitchen might escape—or even if it was his imagination, he would live in fear for the rest of the evening that someone would leap out at him. There were doors from the basement out through Sewey's shed in the backyard, and though they were locked on the outside, Bran knew a determined burglar might be able to break through. So, biting back his fear, he grabbed one of the chairs and set it against the cabinet to climb in.

On second thought, he realized that it might actually be the burglar again, and since he didn't have anything else he grabbed one of the short knives from a drawer. He shoved himself into the dumbwaiter and set the knife next to him.

It was quite a large dumbwaiter, but a small space when stuffed with a person—especially when that person was afraid enough just looking into tight spaces. He had to bend over in an odd fashion to fit, the wood creaking as he shifted. The compartment was much like a shelf with a ceiling, with two ropes going through to make the dumbwaiter go up and down.

It's just an elevator, Bran told himself. *A very small, extremely tight elevator…that could very well break at any second, sending me plummeting to my death.*

He reached for the ropes, taking one last glance into the kitchen. He felt dizzy already. But he pulled on the ropes before he could let his fear get the best of him, and started down. He tried to keep as quiet as he could, hoping he might catch the intruder by surprise. The dumbwaiter squeaked dreadfully once, and then in a second Bran's eyes cleared the kitchen level, so that he was immediately engulfed in darkness. It did nothing to alleviate his phobia.

Had to go through the dumbwaiter, didn't you, he scolded himself, feeling sweat on the back of his neck. *Just had to get into the tightest space in the house.*

He kept his hands on the rope, slowly wheeling his way down. He hoped it had all been his imagination and no one was there. It might have been a mouse in the kitchen and the ice maker in the freezer making the sounds, and the sandwich was probably forgotten there by Rosie before she left. Still, the dumbwaiter continued on. In the last few seconds of his downward journey, he noticed that there was a soft light coming from below, so that when he finally touched the bottom, there was a golden glow on his face through a crack in the cabinet doors.

Sewey sometimes forgot a lamp on down there so Bran didn't let it bother him at first, though he took a cautious glance around as he pushed one of the doors open. The basement was very large, bigger than the whole length of the house. Before the Great Fire, the house had covered the entire basement, but after half the house burned down, the doors going down were left in Sewey's shed, and the Wilomases were left to purchase the house for a very much reduced price. The basement still had remains from the old house and even a working bathroom, though the Wilomases knew exactly what to do with a gigantic space: *fill it.*

And to the brim. Everything from boxes to crates to wine to cheese to old furniture: the entire basement was rows and rows of the Wilomas' things. There were old rocking horses, tables and chairs, hanging meats and onions, decorations, pictures, and all sorts of junk, many of which the Wilomases had bought only to toss down the steps. Bran didn't wonder at all where all the unpaid bills were coming from. The family was sitting right on top of them.

There was a small lamp plugged into the wall and sitting on a stack of crates a way off from where he was. It lit the floor softly, and he hesitated a few moments before he stuck his head out farther. It was very quiet and still, and all the columns that held the ceiling up cast long, dark shadows. Bran couldn't see anyone, so he slid to the floor, taking the knife with him just in case.

He moved toward the lamp and stepped over the piles of mess. There was a stack of crates that went up to the ceiling filled with giant rolls of cheese and covered with labels that read, "These are Sewey's" and "Don't touch" and "ALL MICE KEEP OUT!" in Sewey's squiggly handwriting. Bran stepped around them until he came to the lamp. No one was there.

"Wonderful," he said. "Just my imagination."

Then he noticed something on the floor a few feet from where he was standing. It was a huge, busted box, big enough for a refrigerator and reinforced on the edges. Bran stepped closer. He had been in the basement many times before and didn't remember it, or even remember seeing Sewey bring it home. Normally he wouldn't notice it, but it was so very large it seemed odd. Besides, Mabel thought cardboard boxes carried omniprotoids, and usually had them incinerated.

When he came closer, he saw that a large hole had been cut out of it, but at the top there was still an address sticker, along with markings all over warning that it was FRAGILE. Bran glanced at the address label, and yet again, it was addressed to Rosie. As so many times before, where the writer had spelled the word Bolton, there was large, swirling letter B. In an instant, Bran recognized it—from the same Mr. B. that everything else had been coming from.

He was about to study it further when he saw something else, lying on the floor next to the box. It was one of their old sleeping bags, unfurled and messy, with a pillow at its head. It looked as if someone had slept in it very recently.

"That's it. I'm calling the police," Bran whispered, spinning for the dumbwaiter. But before he could, there was a sudden scratch of motion.

"No!" a man's voice shouted, and there was a rush.

Bran stiffened at the sudden noise, then fell to the side and crashed into a stack of pots, sending them flying through the air and filling the basement with noise. He caught himself and had the knife up in a flash.

"Who's there?!" he demanded, and he saw someone dart from behind the dumbwaiter shaft.

"Listen, I can explain all this!" the voice said, coming around with his hands out.

"Don't come any closer!" Bran demanded, holding the knife out with both hands. He saw the shape of a man, but his face was blocked as he rushed to the other side. Bran turned the knife.

"I'm not getting any closer to that knife," the man said. "In fact, I might get farther away."

A bit of the lamplight crossed the man's face, and in an instant, he became familiar. In fact, he was so familiar, Bran nearly dropped the knife altogether.

"Wait a minute," Bran said. "You're..."

"Bartley Wilomas," the man finished for him, with a slight bow. "At your service."

Chapter 18

The Man beneath the House

If the man in the basement whose name began with B had been standing at a distance, Bran might have thought he was a younger version of Sewey: thinner, with browner hair, his face missing the marks left from years upon years of ceaseless frowning. As Bartley's head had been so painstakingly removed from every photograph in the house by Sewey, and Bran could not remember ever seeing him in person, it was hard at first to believe it was actually him. Bartley didn't look like a swindling, inheritance-stealing deadbeat. But Bran didn't make it a habit to trust men whose name began with the letter B and who happened to be hiding in the basement.

"Please," Bartley said, holding his hands out. "We can discuss this rationally, Bran, without calling the police, who we both know will probably call Sewey."

"That might actually be a good idea," Bran said, sliding to get farther from Bartley.

"No, it wouldn't." Bartley shuddered. "Not for me. Unless he's tossed his revolver for good."

"He hasn't," Bran said. "He's still got it, and if you don't start explaining all those letters, and you being here in our basement, I'm going to go back up and call him."

Bran knew that if Bartley really wanted to keep him from getting away, he certainly could. The basement doors were locked from the outside, and scrambling into the dumbwaiter was not quite the easiest nor fastest maneuver. But he kept his face stern. Bartley dropped his hands.

"All right, I'll tell you," he stammered. "Rosie knows all about it. The box was her idea."

"What's the box got to do with it?" Bran said, not letting the knife fall but a few inches.

"That's how I got here," Bartley said, wringing his hands. "I've been living in Rowhaven, a bit northeast of Dunce, and I knew if I went through the gates and got a visitor permit, they'd all know another Wilomas was in town, and somehow it might get back to Sewey."

"Go on," Bran said.

"So," Bartley nodded, "I loaded myself into a box with provisions and had myself shipped into the city. The plan was to be delivered while you were all gone to the picnic on Sunday."

"No wonder Rosie wanted us all to be gone," Bran said.

Bartley nodded again. "Overnighting a fragile package is not cheap, nor a courier that delivers Sundays," he went on with a shrug. "But it worked. I was delivered to the door, and as no one was around, I just cut myself out and used the key under the duck sculpture to get in. Then, I just went through the back door, down into Sewey's shed, and have been down here with my box ever since."

"And then you came up to the kitchen," Bran accused. "Just five minutes ago, I heard you."

Bartley scowled slightly. "Rosie's been sending me meals with the dumbwaiter since Sunday," he said. "Except today she was gone for lunchtime, and I got rather famished. And, as I didn't hear anybody up there, I went up to fix myself a sandwich. Then, I hear someone coming, and I think it's Mabel. So I did what everyone does when they think Mabel is coming, and that is run for their lives." He shrugged. "Fortunately, it was you. Unfortunately, you are holding a very sharp knife."

Bran looked at it, then back to Bartley.

"All right," Bran said, and he set the knife onto the crate beside him.

Bartley relaxed. "Whew, thank you," he said. "I promise, sincerely, I meant no harm. All this was Rosie's idea, in order to get me here so I could rescue her."

"Rescue her?" Bran said. "From what?"

"From Sewey and Mabel," Bartley said. "See, they would never, ever let her leave here, and poor Rosie would never make it out the front door without turning back—no chance. So the scheme was for me to show up, rescue her, and then we escape together."

Something in what he had said caused Bran to stand up straighter with a slight alarm.

"Escape?" Bran stammered. "Why? Where to?"

Bartley pressed his lips together and turned his gaze away. He looked nervous.

"She didn't tell you?" Bartley said. Bran shook his head.

"Well," Bartley said lowly, "Rosie and I...are getting married."

Bran opened his mouth to object, but he was so taken aback

it felt as if his heart had just stopped. But all the pieces suddenly fit together to tell him that Bartley's words were true.

Then, before he could do anything, there came a sudden noise above them, like feet faintly over their heads. It made both of them look up.

"They're home," Bartley said, listening.

Bran's mouth was still open, unable to say anything back to Bartley…to this man who had unexpectedly appeared in their basement—only to say he was stealing Rosie away, the one real friend Bran had in the world. With all the strange events that had been happening for so long, he was an idiot not to have seen it: that Rosie really had been planning it all along, behind his back.

He turned quickly without another word, and started for the dumbwaiter.

"Wait—" Bartley started for him.

"No," Bran said. "I'm going up to talk to Rosie."

"Wait, please Bran," Bartley pleaded. "Don't tell the Wilomases."

Bran stopped, his hand on the dumbwaiter opening.

"I said I'm going up to talk to Rosie," Bran said. "She's not a Wilomas. Yet."

And he lifted himself into the dumbwaiter and started to wheel himself up toward the kitchen. His teeth were tightened together, feeling angry and betrayed and lied to at the same time. How could Rosie keep it a secret from him for so long? Why hadn't she at least told him? Did she plan to just run off and disappear? As he neared the top, he heard voices in the kitchen.

"Mess, mess, mess!" Mabel was complaining. "Don't you know yenzimes practically breed in food left out on the counter?"

"Sorry, miss," Rosie said. "Perhaps Bran left it out or something."

"And that too," Mabel sniffed. "He had better not be in town spreading rumors about us."

"I'm sure he isn't, miss," Rosie consoled her. Bran stopped in line with the cabinet doors. They were split in the middle so a thin shaft of light went in on his face, and he could slightly see into the kitchen, where Rosie was nervously standing nearby while Mabel rushed about.

"Where are my fiddlesticks?" Mabel said, knocking things aside. "I saw a man at the store today, and I'm certain he was a harlowpath. And I probably caught it. I'll probably die tonight."

"I'm sure you won't, miss," Rosie said.

Mabel finally found her fiddlesticks and crunched some into a cup of water, drinking it down hurriedly while holding her left ear. "I'm off to watch soap operas," she said. "Make Sewey dinner while you're cleaning that mess. He's working late, and there's no use in him coming home and making a mess here when there's a janitor like Trolan who can clean it up at the office. When Bran shows up, send him to deliver it." She scanned the room with her eyes. "And if you see a yenzime, douse it with mayonnaise."

"Yes, miss," Rosie said. Mabel finally started out the door. The moment the sound of her footsteps disappeared, Rosie breathed a sigh of relief, starting for the dumbwaiter.

"Lunch, lunch for Bartley," she whispered, looking like she felt very bad for forgetting it. She reached for the dumbwaiter doors.

"Don't worry, it's halfway finished on the counter," Bran

said when the doors swung apart, and Rosie gave a shriek and fell back against the counter. Bran leapt out quickly. "I'm sorry, Rosie," he said, hurrying to her side and regretting giving her a scare. She had immediately gone as pale as paper, and was clutching at the counter for support.

"Y-y-you..." she stammered. Then the kitchen door blew open.

"Did you catch a yenzime?" Mabel shrieked. Rosie and Bran both turned to face her, and Bran realized the dumbwaiter doors were still open. Mabel's eyes were wide, and she looked ready to attack, her gaze leveled on them, and then shifting to the counter, then the dumbwaiter.

"Nope, no yenzimes," Bran said quickly. "None at all. Rosie just slipped."

"Sheesh," Mabel said. She turned to leave, and Rosie nearly collapsed to the floor.

"Bran, what were you..." she said, shaking her head, trying to catch her breath. "I mean, the dumbwaiter, the basement..."

She looked up at him quickly. "Bartley—?"

"I know about it," Bran said, stopping her.

She stared into his eyes, looking sadder and more ashamed than he had ever seen her before. Bran didn't need to say anything else. Rosie knew that he found out her secret, and now, it was her turn to tell the rest.

"I—I know I should have told you sooner." Rosie looked dejected. "I should have, really. But I was afraid...afraid of hurting you, of making you think I was just going to go along and leave."

"You could have just told me," Bran said, nodding, though

not angry at her anymore. He could see that she felt very guilty for what she had done, keeping it from him for so long.

"I know," Rosie finally said, looking away and putting her hand up on the refrigerator. "I just...didn't know what you would do. Think I betrayed you? Hate me?"

"It would take a lot more than that for me to hate you," Bran said, and he gave a slight smile that he hoped would put her fears to rest.

Rosie saw it but looked away, leaning against the wall. "I should have anyway," she said. "As if you wouldn't have found out on your own eventually. Sewey was too busy chasing all the Mr. B.'s in town to think of his own brother, right underneath his own nose."

"And, at the moment," Bran said, "right underneath his own house."

The sadness on Rosie's face broke slightly, and she looked back up at him, as if trying to decide something. Then she reached into her pocket and brought out an engagement ring.

"See?" Rosie said, looking at it. "He gave it to me months ago."

The diamond caught light from the window, and just looking at it seemed to mesmerize Rosie's eyes. Bran looked from it to her and then back again. The ring was simple, though the diamond was pure and dazzling.

"So you really do love him enough?" Bran whispered. Rosie looked up and met his eyes, and he could see in them that it was true.

"Well then," Bran said, "there's not a moment to lose. Your future husband is starving in the basement, and we'd better finish his sandwich."

Rosie's face finally brightened. "Both of us will do it, faster that way."

Bran got the cheese and ham from the refrigerator, and as the bread was already out Rosie started to lay out pieces. Bran returned for the mayonnaise.

"I've heard it's good for yenzimes," Bran joked, and Rosie punched him in the arm. She spread the mayo over four pieces of bread and had the sandwiches finished in a flash, and the room took a much lighter air as they made them. She bagged one up for Bran to take to Sewey, but kept changing Bartley's sandwich, as if something just wasn't right, until she seemed to discover the problem, and took a knife to remove the crusts. Then she cut the sandwich into the shape of a heart, separating the pieces. She smiled, her face aglow as she went to the dumbwaiter, and Bran left her behind to send down Bartley's dinner.

The sky had become cloudy outside. Bran didn't mind bringing Sewey his food, especially when it was in the evening. The sun wasn't far from the horizon, and for a few moments, he felt free and alive as he sped down the street.

He rode on, steering his bike for a detour, and not much later he saw Givvyng Park coming up in front of him. All the tents and streamers were gone, and the place was deserted. He could see the same spot where the booths had been, and the dirty parking lot on the other side, and the strip of road where he had stopped the truck. The huge form of the Givvyng Tree towered above the park, its branches hanging out like a giant canopy. It was so big around, it was larger than the width of the Wilomas' living room, like a giant watching over the city of Dunce day and night.

As he passed through the park, he thought about Rosie and Bartley. Bran knew Rosie wasn't the type to rush into a decision like that. She would have to think about it, and once she made up her mind, it was right. Bran knew that if Rosie trusted Bartley, then he would trust him too; and if Rosie loved Bartley, then he would too.

But just thinking it and doing it were two entirely different things. Part of him wished that someone would just tell him what to do and how to act, but no one was there to do it for him, so it was all up to him to figure it out. He let his thoughts release for the rest of the way, and he hurriedly parked his bike in the alley beside the bank. Inside, Adi was at her desk.

"Good evening," she said, staring at her computer.

"Hello, Adi," Bran said, closing the door behind him. Adi immediately looked up.

"Oh, Bran," she said. "I wasn't expecting you this evening."

"I wasn't expecting to come here either," Bran said. "It's one of those rare days when Sewey's working late. How is he, anyway?"

"Awful!" Sewey burst, exiting his office. "Simply *awful!* Where's my dinner?"

Bran set it on Adi's desk. Adi smiled, but there was something behind it, and he noticed that she looked him over for a few seconds before going back to her keyboard. Sewey, however, was obviously in a rotten mood, and he dropped a stack of paperwork onto Adi's desk.

"This is misery," Sewey snorted. "I'm through with working anyhow. I'm eating at home!"

"Then why did I come all the way here?" Bran objected.

"Enough from you!" Sewey burst, grabbing his coat. "I'm leaving, and that's the end of it!"

With that, Sewey was out the door. Bran dashed behind him but only managed to get outside just as Sewey leapt into the car and pulled off, without even giving him a second thought.

The car was halfway down the road when it stopped, switched gears, and started backward, stopping in front of the bank again.

"I guess he's going to take me home after all," Bran muttered to himself, very much taken aback. Sewey rolled his window down and furiously waved at Bran to come.

"Here, Bran," Sewey said, shuffling around in his briefcase. "I need you to stick these on the front door of the bank."

Sewey picked something out from the papers and shoved it into his hand. Bran looked down and saw that it was a rectangular sticker, typed with words in bold lettering:

ABSOLUTELY
NO SOLICITORS

"Put it where everyone can see," Sewey said. "I want them to know the TBD's strict policy on politics."

"Politics?" Bran said. "I'm wondering how banning the sale of items by peddlers will show anyone your political views."

"What, what?" Sewey said. "Oh, no, I'm afraid you're dreadfully mistaken. A *solicitor* is someone who is pro-gnome. And we don't allow them at all."

"It's not a peddler?" Bran asked.

"No, it's not. Not anymore, at least," Sewey said, shaking his head. "The mayor suggested we stick it on all doors of every business that's properly anti-gnome. You *do* need to keep up to date with the changing definitions of things."

With that, Sewey pushed on the pedal, without even giving Bran a chance to get his feet out of the way. Bran shuffled backward quickly, just in time to hear Sewey shout:

"Go get sticking!"

And he was gone, leaving Bran in a cloud of dust. Bran looked down at the sticker in his hand and shook his head, pressing it onto the door of the bank as he went in.

"Now I've got to bike all the way home," he said, closing the door behind him.

"Wait a moment," Adi stopped him. "I'm off too. Do you want a ride home?"

Bran hesitated, but found he really was too tired to bike. And, any chance to talk with Adi in a place no one would hear them was certainly welcome. He nodded.

"My car is in the back, this way," she said, starting to clean up her desk.

Bran's bike wouldn't fit in her trunk, so luckily she had some cords to tie the lid down and just left the tire sticking out. Her car was navy blue and had leather seats, not schweezing even once as they pulled from the parking lot behind the bank.

They were silent for a while. The air was tense, and Bran kept trying to make himself say something, but every time he opened his mouth no words would come. It seemed that for days he had had so many questions he wanted to ask, but suddenly they were all gone.

"All right, Bran, I've got to get right to it," Adi began without warning. "I don't know what to do with you." She glanced at him. "You and me: we're both in a grave situation—a very grave situation."

It's worse than even you *know,* Bran thought, mulling over what he had learned from Astara.

"But Bran...you're different than the rest of us." Adi went on. "What you have could..." She looked back at the road and let out a deep breath. "It could really make things difficult."

"What do you mean?" Bran asked.

She started to say something but decided against it, and looked back to the road. He felt as if she were a wall, and she kept laying up more bricks to make herself stronger. There were so many questions in his mind, so many he didn't know the answers to.

"And I hope you don't hate me for this," Adi said, and she glanced at him. There was a deep sadness in her eyes, almost like she had been betrayed by him, when Bran had done nothing at all. They sat in stony silence for a long while, not saying a single word, but pages being written between them as she drove on.

"There's the turn for Bolton Road," Bran said, seeing it coming close. He said it just as she passed it up. "You passed it..." he said, pointing back over the seat.

"We're not going to Bolton Road," she said, and the tone of her voice caused fear to creep under his skin.

Chapter 19

The House on Hadnet Lane

There was nothing Bran could do. He looked at Adi, but her face was set with determination. She turned onto another road, the sign reading Hadnet Lane.

"Where are you taking me?" he stammered.

She didn't answer, and her silence seemed to press on him like a weight.

The car slowed about halfway down the street. The house they had come to was small and had a white stone front, with a miniature yard that was enclosed by a black metal fence. The gate on the front was against the sidewalk and had the number 108 twisted into the metal. All the houses on the street were pressed close together with similar fences and sequential numbers. It was a cozy street and unimposing, though to Bran it seemed ominous.

"Time to get out now," Adi said, taking her keys. "Just be quiet and come with me."

"What do you think you're doing?" Bran demanded with anger.

She turned to him.

"I thought you were trying to help me," he said, feeling betrayed. Adi let a deep breath out, but she didn't reach to grab hold of him, like he had expected. She just sat there, and her eyes became filled with sadness.

"Bran, if you want to leave, you can go right now," she said suddenly. "You can run off, forget everything that happened. You want to go to the police and get us thrown in jail? You can do that too. I can't make you stay."

She looked deep into his eyes, and in them Bran saw the weight of thousands of secrets, all kept inside. He avoided her gaze.

"Go now, if you want," she said to him. "But if you want to come with me, and if you want to know the truth, and if you've got the will and the courage in you to make the right decision, then you make it; and whatever you choose, I won't stop you."

In Adi's voice, Bran did not hear anything of ill intent. He felt that she cared about what happened to him, and she was his friend. Slowly, he slid away from the door and back into his seat, and he looked out the front window, feeling bitter again. She reached and grasped his hand.

"I thought so," she said.

"Adi, I just don't know what to do," he said, and her grip on his hand tightened. "I don't know what's going to happen to me, now that I know I'm a mage."

"Don't ever be afraid to face the truth, Bran," Adi said, squeezing his hand. "If we can't face the truth, then we're living a lie."

"But what *is* going to happen to me?" he asked.

She met his gaze, but then looked away, as if there was something that she had wanted to say but couldn't bring herself to do it. She squeezed his hand again, then let it go and stepped out of the car. Bran followed her up to the house, the skies dark and cloudy from the approaching storm. Adi slipped a key into the lock, then reached for another and unlocked the second. Beyond, the house was dim, and Adi gestured for Bran to go in first. With a moment of hesitation, he passed her, and she locked the door behind them.

It was dark inside. The thick curtains and drapes over all the windows only allowed the faintest glow from the stormy grayness outside. Bran squinted and saw that he was in a long hallway with a light-colored stone floor, and that there was a sitting room to his left and another hallway to the right. It seemed much like any normal home, except that nearly every wall was lined with shelves, and every shelf filled with books. Shadows fell down the rows as Bran peered into the room, the titles too far away to read, though the spines of them tempting him to come take a look.

"The house is a bit too big, if you were to ask me," Adi broke the silence. "But more room for more books, that's what I keep telling myself."

"You've practically got a whole library in here," Bran said, looking up and down the hallway as they passed. Even in there, the entire right wall had bookshelves built in, covered with novels and old papers and reference books.

"Well, you can't exactly blame me," she said with a small laugh. "Most Illians are that way by nature."

Bran looked up at her, though he bit his tongue to keep from saying anything. He had heard that word before: *Illian.* It had been in one of the volumes in the back of the bookstore. Bran didn't know how Adi would react if she knew he had been there, so he kept quiet.

"I've lived here for a while," Adi went on. "When I came to Dunce to be a part of the Mages Underground, the Special Services and Operations Division of the Mages Council bought this house for me. They even let me pick it out, and a car too—any car I wanted, all paid for."

Bran was lagging behind and glanced at the other wall. It was covered with pictures in ornate frames, paintings unlike any he had ever seen. They were on canvas with colors that seemed so vibrant and glowing, they almost immediately made all other paintings he had ever seen appear dull and boring. They were of farmhouses and dirt roads and sunsets and all sorts of beautiful things that were so alive, he wanted to touch them. He had never seen any quite like them before.

"I've got to keep my records straight, though," Adi went on from ahead. "The house is paid for, but I've still got to work at the bank so no one gets suspicious."

She noticed that he wasn't listening, and stopped and glanced at him.

"Oh, you've noticed the paintings," she said.

"They look so real," he replied.

She nodded. "That's the best thing about gnome art. It seems to capture the best of everything."

"A gnome did this?" Bran asked, looking over his shoulder. She nodded again.

"You like drawing too, don't you?"

"Well, it's nothing like this," Bran replied, still looking at it. "Mine are just pencil sketches."

"It sure makes our paintings seem so harsh, doesn't it?" Adi asked, sighing a bit. "Well, go on, you can touch it if you'd like."

At her prompting, Bran reached forward to touch the surface of one, a slowly moving stream next to a cottage with a wide, sweeping roof. However, the second that his fingertips touched the surface of the painting, they sunk into it, and suddenly something chilled the ends of his fingers. He drew back in fright, and little drops of liquid flew behind him like he had splashed wet paint.

"I'm sorry!" he said, shaking his hand. "I think I put a hole in it!"

It was then that he noticed that Adi was laughing.

"What's funny?" he asked, baffled.

"No, Bran, I'm sorry," Adi said. "I should have warned you. Gnome art is *different.*"

She touched the painting, and just as Bran's had, her fingers sank in through the canvas as well, and from the stream in the picture a smooth trickle of water began to rush down Adi's hand, dripping into a puddle on the floor.

"See?" she said, drawing back. "That's the magic in it."

She slid her fingers into the grassy area, where they were dried. It left the grass in the painting matted and dewy, though nothing underneath the surface seemed to have moved.

"Well, come along," she said. "We've got a lot to do."

She turned and left Bran standing there, his eyes wide. He reached forward to feel the grass, and it felt just as if it was there before him. He curiously touched the bright sun in the picture, but immediately jerked his hand away, because it almost scalded his fingers.

All the walls going up the staircase and the balcony were filled with more pictures of oceans and forests and waterfalls, some so vivid and inviting that if Adi hadn't been walking so fast, Bran might have spent hours touching them and feeling inside. Adi led him down a hall from the balcony, which was lined on both sides with more bookshelves. There was a small slap of thunder outside, and both of them glanced through the glass.

"Looks like rain is coming," Bran said, but Adi didn't reply. She came to a door and pushed it open. It revealed a large and wide room with dark wood floors and a high ceiling with thick trim around the edges. There was a massive fireplace in the center of the opposite wall, and yet again, more stuffed bookshelves going all the way around. A gigantic chair was in front of the fireplace with its back to Bran, and there was a fire crackling beyond it and a soft lamp in the corner, though in this room the windows were uncovered and let in gray light.

"Go ahead and look through those books while I'm checking on things," Adi said. "And say hello if he wakes up: he might find you something interesting."

"Who's *he?*" Bran asked, but Adi had already disappeared through a door on the side. Bran stood very still, and instantly the room seemed frighteningly empty. He leaned forward to look through the doorway Adi had passed through, but she was gone. There was a crash of thunder outside the windows. Bran took a deep breath, looking back to the bookshelves.

"Look through the books," Bran repeated. "He might find you something interesting."

Bran wondered who the *he* was and if *he* was even around. Bran looked through the room, but there wasn't anyone else there. He shrugged. He would have preferred going back down the hall to look at the paintings, but he decided to follow Adi's instructions. He started to read the titles on one of the shelves.

Most of them were novels, like *Harriet Travels to Wumpidun* by Tracey Titus or *Mayonnaise Goes with Everything* by Sylvia Splinindad. He even saw a couple of Rosie's favorites by Christine Rocco—but, he noticed, absolutely none on magic.

He knew that Adi probably wouldn't have kept them out in the open, though he was a bit let down that there wasn't much interesting in that room to look at. He turned, and all of a sudden his eye caught something in the chair in front of the fireplace. It gave him a start. It appeared to be a pile of blankets spread out on the chair, covering something small and lumpy underneath. The blankets went up the thick back of the chair, like a small tent, and at the top, something pointed poked out by an inch.

It was very odd, to say the least, so Bran started to shift nervously in its direction. He thought it might be a cat or some other pet, hiding under the blankets, as he saw no feet poking out the bottom to signify there was a person there. As he got closer to it, though, something else across the room gave a loud thump, and immediately shifted his attention upward.

"Hello?" Bran whispered.

No one answered. Bran tried to get a better look in the direction he had heard the sound. At first, he saw nothing; then he saw a shadow move on the wall. Bran started and jumped backward. But no one was there.

"I can't see you," Bran said. Still, the shadow moved, as if there was a tall, invisible person casting it, though the light was obviously not from the lamp or the window.

As Bran stared at it, he noticed that the feet of the shadow were not touching the floor, and in fact, the shadow seemed to be pointing to a huge nail tacked to the wall, where the shape of its foot was, almost as if the nail was holding it there. It gestured furiously in the nail's direction.

"You're stuck?" Bran said, trying to make himself speak. The shadow nodded profusely. Bran gulped. The shadow moved its hands up to its head, as if running its hands through its hair.

"I see," Bran stammered. "You want me…to help you…take the nail off."

The shadow nodded. Bran looked over his shoulder, hoping Adi might appear. She was gone. There came a tapping noise as the shadow tried to get Bran's attention by drumming the wall.

"All right then," Bran said, stepping forward hesitantly. Where his own shadow brushed with that of the one on the wall, instead of being dark, the part where they crossed went light. He was cautious nearing the shadow, unsure exactly of what he was doing. The hand pointed at the nail.

"I'll get it," Bran said. The nail was sticking out considerably, but it wouldn't budge.

"It's stuck," Bran said.

The shadow pointed again. There was a hammer on one of the shelves, just out of its reach. Bran grabbed it, and started to bend the nail out.

"Funny how you'd get stuck here," Bran remarked, feeling a bit silly. The shadow nodded remorsefully. Bran bent the nail head, wiggling it out. "But then again, it's even stranger that—"

But before he could finish, the nail was loose. Suddenly, the shadow's foot flew forward, launching the nail right at Bran's face and kicking him to the floor with a crash.

"NO!" a shout exploded from next to Bran, but it was already too late. Quick as a flash, the shadow leapt through the air, dashing across the room toward the door.

"Catch him, quick!" the new voice screamed, and there was a flash of motion, so quick Bran hadn't a chance to see it, and something leapt from where the blankets on the chair had been, jumping at the door and slamming it closed a second before the shadow reached it.

"Don't just stand there! Stop the cotch!" the voice said. Bran leapt toward the shadow, but it scaled the ceiling, tripping over the blades of the ceiling fan. It fell, tumbling across the bookshelf and sending books crashing as it whizzed across the room again, toppling the chair.

"GRAB him!" the voice roared, and Bran jumped, falling on top of a shadowy foot just as it was about to reach the window. The shadow toppled over, knocking against the wall.

"The nail! The nail!" the voice said. Luckily, the nail had fallen right next to Bran, so while holding the struggling shadow down he got the nail and started to pound it furiously with the hammer. The shadow struggled but was already stuck to the floor.

"Oh, oh, almost got away, we were *so* close to our dooms," the voice next to Bran said, and he was breathing just as hard. Bran, finally realizing that there was someone else in the room, looked at who was next to him, and nearly jumped through the roof.

The thing that had been sitting covered under the blankets had not been a cat, but was in fact a man with a bushy white beard and scruffy clothes. However, he was not exactly a man, for he was only about two feet tall, and on the top of his head he wore a long, red, felt conical hat.

It was a gnome. *He* was a gnome.

Chapter 20

The Gnome in the Home

Bran gasped and fell backward, pushing away from the little man; the gnome did the exact same, until they were staring at each other from across the room, each with wide eyes. Then, after staring at Bran for a second, the gnome crossed his arms angrily.

"You idiot!" the gnome said, now unafraid. "Coming in here while I was trying to sleep, releasing the cotch it took me *hours* to apprehend from his dubious thievery."

The gnome pointed an accusing finger at the cotch, who only crossed his arms in return.

"I don't have a clue what you're talking about," Bran stammered, inching farther away.

"Of course you don't," the gnome said. "You just barge on in here, pulling nails out of the walls. Look at all this junk!"

The gnome kicked a box out from under the chair in which he had previously been napping. It rattled with bunches of metal items.

"I'm the one having to sort through all this mess," the gnome said, shuffling its contents about. "Keys and pens and jewelry and pocket watches—"

"Hey," Bran said, stepping forward. "I've seen that watch before! And those keys!"

It was Sewey's pocket watch, still as shiny as when Sewey had lost it, and bunches of house and car keys with key rings Bran recognized.

"Good for you," the gnome snorted, kicking the box back under the chair. "There's probably hundreds of things from that old cotch cache we dug up over on Hodsbury Street. This little villain's been plaguing the town for weeks." The gnome sniffed. He had skin that was all wrinkled and light. His eyebrows were bushy and thick, just like his beard. He turned to face Bran. "I'm guessing you're the Hambric Adi's been telling me about. I was expecting her to bring you sometime. Call me Polland."

The gnome did not offer his hand, but only scuttled around the chair to hop back onto it, pushing the blankets around to make an enormous cushion. Bran could only stare as Polland moved about, as if everything was normal with a gnome in a house. Polland looked up and opened his eyes really wide to show that Bran was staring at him.

"Something wrong?" he grumbled. "You do know how to make one uncomfortable."

"I'm sorry," Bran said. "It's just I've never seen a real live gnome before."

"A real live gnome?" Polland echoed. "Maybe we should start a zoo and put me in it, then."

"No, not like that," Bran said, but Polland cut him off.

"I will have you know, young fellow," he said, "that there are garden gnomes, house gnomes, clock gnomes, kitchen gnomes, factory gnomes, Western gnomes, Southern gnomes, birdhouse gnomes, Husky gnomes, and all sorts of gnomes. We are a very proud race."

"I can see that," Bran said.

Polland huffed indignantly. "I," he proclaimed, "am an *Eastern Ridwell gnome.*"

"Well, I'd say it's nice to meet you," Bran replied.

Polland twisted his face up a bit, and looked a little embarrassed that he was so grumpy to his guest. He finally waved his hand. "Go make yourself useful," he said. "Open those drapes some more so I can see the rain, and maybe it'll make some of my grump disappear."

Bran was still taken aback, so he did as he said. The room filled with a flash of lightning from outside. When he turned back, Polland had removed the cover from the food tray on the small table beside him. Underneath, there was a plate with some cheese, bread, butter, and a knife resting beside it.

"Oh well," Polland said, taking off his glasses. "I can't say I blame you, being in these parts. All those ideas being put into your head. It's a sad thing I can't even step foot outside." Polland nodded grimly. "See, it isn't *you* I'm mad at, just makes me grumpy with these laws where I can't enjoy a good rain on a decent park bench."

"You have to stay here and never come out?" Bran asked.

"Yes, sadly," Polland replied.

"Then why don't you move?" Bran asked. "Go someplace where you're free?"

"I can't," Polland said, staring into the fireplace sadly. "Adi needs someone here who can speak Gnomish to those poor fellows we break out of the jails, and I'm the only gnome who's missing enough good sense to do it."

"So that's why you're both here," Bran realized. "You're the ones who help them escape!"

"So we are," Polland said. "It's such a sad thing: our sacred land, owned by Duncelanders."

"Is that why gnomes keep coming through?" Bran said. Polland nodded again.

"It's the Sevvenyears," he explained. "An old, honored religious custom. This place used to be our land, before Droselmeyer Dunce ran us off. Every seventh year in our lives, we journey from far and wide to the sacred Givvyng Tree. Now, we've got to sneak about in the dark."

"That sounds awfully brave of all of you," Bran observed. "Dangerous too."

"Ah, but Bran," Polland said wistfully. "If you could only sit at the top of the Givvyng Tree—they say it's magic that makes it grow so big, magic that draws us to it. But perhaps it isn't magic at all, but echoes of the faith of thousands of gnomes who have journeyed there for centuries." He shook his head. "It's every bit worth the danger."

"You can't just take off your hat then?" Bran said, gesturing to it. "That might make you a bit more inconspicuous."

"Now, Bran," Polland crossed his arms. "It's just not proper for a gnome to go about stark hatless, showing his bald head like a heathen."

"You wear it because you're bald?" Bran said. "What about the women? Do they go bald?"

"Silly idea!" Polland said. "Of course they don't. But if you were a gnome, and it was your tradition, I think you might put up more of a fight than just giving it up, even if it's just a hat." He sighed. "The day we let them take our hats is the day we cease to be free."

Bran and Polland were silent for a long while, and the fireplace crackled between them, and Bran felt very quiet inside, as if he hadn't just met a gnome, but another person. Despite the things everyone in town had told him about gnomes not being people, he felt just like Polland *was* a person, so that all his former thoughts about gnomes left him.

Polland straightened his hat.

"Oh, well, enough misery-talk for a while, eh?" he said. "If Adi brought you here, then that means you're counted as one of my friends. And that means you get a Friendship Gift."

Bran was stunned for a moment. "For me?"

"Of course!" Polland said. "It's a tradition. And I know just the thing for you." He chuckled. "But I've got to make it first, and then you'll get to see it."

Bran really didn't know what to say. Polland seemed so friendly that any last traces of Bran's fear vanished like a blown-out candle.

"Bread and butter?" Polland asked.

Bran shook his head.

"Some for me, though," Polland said, waving his hand in the air. For a moment, nothing seemed to happen. Then Bran saw something behind Polland begin to move. It was the flowerpot—or rather, what was *in* the flowerpot. The leaves on the plant leapt forward, weaving around the plate and seizing it like small hands. Then the plate, cradled in the leaves, was thrust into Polland's lap, while a thick root came out of the dirt and tightened itself around the knife on the table, spreading a thin layer of butter on the bread. Then, as instantly as it had come to life, the plant sprang back to its former position. Polland hardly batted an eyelash.

"Are you sure you don't want any?" Polland asked, taking a bite.

Bran shook his head again quickly, still staring at the plant. "H-how did you do that?" he stammered.

"What?" Polland looked up. "Oh, you mean the pot?" He crossed his arms. "Well, while I'm up for jail time for being a gnome, I might as well be a mage while I'm at it, hmm?"

Polland chuckled at Bran's expression, turning in the chair. It was almost as big as a small couch to him, so he put his legs up onto the arm and looked very comfortable.

"Yes, always good to keep a flowerpot handy for the miniature tasks," he said. "That is of course if you're a mage from *my* missiv."

"Your what?" Bran asked. He leaned forward instinctively: *another word from the secret books.*

"My *missiv,*" Polland said, looking up. "My order of mages: the Missiv of Archon." He took a bite. "I'm an Elemental mage: fire, water, earth, air. My powers are in those."

Bran remembered the green books. The various forms of magic had all revolved around the elements. But he couldn't remember any of them then, nor the names of the others.

"There are more?" Bran prodded, hoping Polland would go on.

"Of course!" Polland burst, looking up with surprise. "In fact, there are five altogether."

He brushed his hands off. "There are the Comsar, the Mental, whose powers revolve around the things of the mind: speaking languages, mind control, computers. Then you've got the Netora, the Physical: telekinetics who can lift objects and teleport by having an object from their destination. And you have Illian mages like Adi, the Illusional, who can make conjurations. And finally, there are the Archon mages, the Elemental, like myself."

Polland took a sip from his teacup.

"That's only four..." Bran said, counting in his head. Polland stopped.

"How...perceptive of you," he said. He glanced across the room, and the cotch was still there, nailed to the floor, though his head was down, and by the shadow, he appeared to be asleep.

"The fifth missiv is the rarest of all," Polland said. "The Drimra: mages of the Mortal."

There was a hushed tone in his voice. Bran remembered those books: few, and on the highest shelf in the secret room. They had been the ones with black covers.

"The Drimra are the easiest to sway to the darker magics," Polland said lowly. "Their magic is hardest to control: powers that deal with the very being in each of us, what makes us mortals."

Polland shook his head. "Many a good person has fallen prey to his own self as a Drimra. Their powers are too great. The ability to breathe existence, to create monsters, to bring spirits from the dead and call forth the gift given to each of us..." He looked up at Bran. "*Life.*"

A hush seemed to fall over the room at the weight of his words.

"Besides those powers, knife stabs and bullet wounds are of hardly any lasting effect to a Drimra," Polland continued. "What else can the authorities do, burn them at the stake?" There was dryness to his words, but he shrugged. "They're not *all* evil. Some Drimra choose the path of healers and doctors, so it wouldn't be right to say that *every* Drimra has gone wrong; though to this day, I have never known of one to be completely free of himself."

"But if I'm a mage," Bran said, "which missiv would I be in?"

Polland shrugged. "Plenty of ways to find that out."

He clapped his hands once and called, "*Minnie Roga's, please!*"

Bran didn't know what it meant, but before he could blink an eye, there was a scratch on the bookshelves, and one book slid out from the rest, all on its own. Polland gestured, and Bran hesitantly grabbed the volume, passing it to him.

"Wait, it's the wrong book," Bran pointed out. "That's—"

"*Off to Mount Em,*" Polland read. "A novel by Henry Mayes, on the outside. But..."

Polland cracked the cover open, and inside Bran saw the title page for the book on the cover. However, in the bottom corner was a printed black box, just like in the Mages Pages newspaper. When Polland pressed his thumb to it, the title text changed, so that instead it now read:

The Properties of Missiv Personalities
Dr. Minnie Roga

Polland flipped through the pages, ignoring Bran's shocked expression.

"Here we are," he said. "The list of missivs!"

Polland pointed to it.

Bran had seen that list before, at the bookstore: *Netora, Comsar, Archon, Illian, Drimra.* They still sounded so strange to him.

"And these," Polland pointed to the next page, "are their official properties."

Bran had seen these as well, or at least two of them, from the books he had pried into. Like for Netora and Archon, which he had read, these also followed the same arrangement, and Polland's finger had stopped over Illian.

The MISSIV of ILLIAN

You are a mage of the Illusional, master of things seen and unseen. You are drawn to that which brings knowledge: books, journals, and writings. Your missiv uncovers the wonders disguised, and disguises those which should be unseen.

"That fits with Adi, to be sure," Bran said, looking about at all the books in the room again.

"She follows with her missiv quite well." Polland chuckled. "Though, of course, it doesn't *always* follow: as witnessed by my art hanging about on all the walls, when I am no Netora."

"Well, which am I then?" Bran wondered aloud.

Polland turned a few pages in the book. "Well, do you like gardening?" He sounded hopeful.

Bran shook his head. "I pretty much murder plants," he admitted.

"Cross off Archon, then" Polland said, turning pages. "What about writing or books?"

"I read," Bran replied, "but not as much as Adi."

"Hmm," Polland said. "You *could* still be an Illian. What about pets: any cats, dogs…chinchillas?"

Bran shook his head.

"Cross off Comsar too, then," Polland turned more pages.

"I like to draw," Bran tried. "Does that mean anything?"

"Some of the greatest artists are Netora," Polland said. "It comes in mighty handy if you can use magic as an extra hand when painting or making music, as many are drawn toward."

"I don't think I'd mind that," Bran said, seeing visions of pencils flying about his room, shading papers and then sticking them on the board without him ever having to lift a finger. Polland nodded. Bran noticed that he had, probably intentionally, left Drimra out.

Polland opened his mouth to speak again, but suddenly there came an awful shriek from behind Bran. Polland jumped to his feet in a flash, standing on the chair.

"Look out!" he shouted, and Bran, unable to react in time, was hit in the head by something. He fell to the side, grabbing the back of his head, and he heard another shriek. Something black dove through the air, and Polland, with a look of terror, began to change. It happened in a second: he shrunk down to nearly half his size and petrified into what looked like a miniature gnome statue. It all happened so fast Bran didn't have a moment to do anything, and then the black flying shape slammed into Polland, knocking him off the chair and to the floor.

"Polland!" Bran shouted, diving for him, but Bran was too late. Polland collided with the floor, and little pieces of him smashed against the wood, breaking off. In a flash, Polland transformed back to himself.

"Help!" he moaned, and Bran rushed to his side. The black shape disappeared from sight.

"I'm here!" Bran said, unsure of what to do as Polland rolled over. Bran saw that, thankfully, none of his face had smashed: though he saw in an instant that all the fingers on Polland's left hand had been broken off, and were still made of a crusty stone.

"Oh, Polland!" Adi's voice came from the doorway.

"He's been hurt!" Bran said.

Polland was seething. "That stupid bird of yours!" he roared. "Did it again! Right at my face this time!"

"Quick, the first-aid kit," Adi said, motioning for Bran to go for one of the cabinets. Bran hurried over, found a white plastic box, and carried it back.

"Can you fix it?" Bran asked, horrified. Polland was breathing heavily. It was then that Bran noticed there was no blood on the severed ends of Polland's fingers.

"Don't worry," Adi opened up the box. "Gnomes are creatures of earth. It'll be fixed."

"Not as if this hasn't happened before," Polland hissed. "All because of *that bird!*"

"I'm sorry, it was an accident, I opened the door," Adi said, flipping open the lid on the kit. Inside, there were no bandages or medicines or in fact anything Bran had expected. There were simply tiny bottles of water and bags of different colors of dirt.

"Wrong box," Bran said, about to snatch it and hurry to the shelves again.

"No, it's right," Adi stopped him. She quickly took a small silver bowl from the box, and then poured some of the dirt and the water into it. She smeared it around with two of her fingers until it was mud. She dipped two of her fingers in and then smeared it onto the end of Polland's broken finger, and then onto Polland's knuckle. Then she stuck the two muddy ends together, and just as they touched, the clay finger transformed and connected, and Polland moved it. Bran managed to break free from his stupor and help with one.

"Apologies, profusely," Polland said, breathing hard as they worked. "It's a natural instinct. Comes from running from the Dep Krokus in my homeland."

"You just turn to stone?" Bran said. "If you get broken, isn't that dangerous?"

"Not as dangerous as a flying, five-nosed, bloodsucking Dep Krokus," Polland said fearfully. "They've hunted gnomes for centuries—eat us alive if they catch us. But they're totally blind. So by turning to stone, they can't smell our blood anymore." Poland sniffed. "Even in Dunce, away from them, I'm still so skittish I just petrify right off."

"Good thing you weren't smashed to bits," Bran said. "I doubt we'd get all the pieces right."

"You'd have to load my pieces into a jar and take me to the Gnimbler," Polland said, wiggling another finger. "She's the only one who's got the skill when something drastic happens."

Bran smeared the mud over the broken knuckles, and Adi pressed the fingers back into place. As each one touched, it grew from being petrified into fingers, and Polland wriggled them.

"Much better," he said.

"Wait," Bran noticed. "You're missing one: your ring finger."

He was about to search for it, but Polland stopped him. "No point in looking for that one now, look, it's here where it belongs."

He pulled a thin, white string from around his neck, and hanging on the end was a clay finger from the knuckle down, a hole through it for the string.

"What's your finger doing there?" Bran asked. Polland coughed loudly. Suddenly, the black shape dove from where it had been perched at the top of the bookshelves, and Polland held onto both ends of his hat.

"Ginolde!" Adi scolded, and the bird, as if pulled by a string, changed course and flew toward her. It perched on Adi's shoulder, cawing into her ear.

"Oh, the menace," Polland said, scooting back.

Ginolde was a very large crow with sleek black wings that had tints of purple. However, there was one very unusual feature to her.

"Her beak looks like it's made of gold," Bran said with amazement.

"That's because it is," Adi replied, rising from the floor. "I usually keep her locked in my office and let her out through the window. She escaped when I was coming back from upstairs."

"Upstairs?" Bran noticed. He thought they were already there.

Adi gave a small smile."I'll show you up," she said, turning for the side doorway. Bran started to follow her, and Polland was right next to him, still holding onto his hat and watching the bird closely. They passed through into another room, very similar to the first, though stuffed to the walls with more furniture. Because of all the bookshelves dominating each wall and the piles of papers and unsorted novels on the floor and desk, Adi's office appeared to be a bit stuffed. To the left, there was a very large window with the curtains drawn back, showing the falling rain outside.

"Very nice office," Bran observed. "I thought—"

"We're not there quite yet," Adi cut him off. She continued

to the bookshelf at the far end, as if she was about to take a book down, and slid her hand along the edges until her fingers stopped behind the trim. She turned her wrist, and Bran heard a creak from the bookshelf. She pulled back, and an entire section of the shelf swung out in front of his eyes.

Bran was speechless. There was a tiny set of red, carpeted stairs going off to the left of the room behind the wall. When Adi saw the surprise on his face, she smiled with pride.

"And here, Bran," she said, "is yet another secret of my house."

"Stairs!" Bran said. "Where do they go to?"

A mysterious gleam came into her eyes.

"To my private office," she said, and she turned around and started up the steps.

Chapter 21

A Room behind the Bookshelf

Cold air came from behind the door. Bran was only a bit hesitant when he came to the entrance, and he looked into the small space. It had barely enough room to walk standing straight, and looked almost like a stairway in a large dollhouse. Bran was not one for tight spaces, but he forced himself to start upward.

"This is incredible!" he breathed out softly.

"The owners before me had it put in this way," Adi said, pushing open the door ahead of him. "The instant they showed it to me, I knew I had to have this house."

"I wish I had a secret room," Bran said.

Adi opened the door to reveal a very large room, the entire attic of the house all in one place, with the roof as the ceiling and the edges sloping into tight corners as the boards met the floor. It was quite the opposite of the Wilomas' attic: hardly any junk around, save for a few spare boxes in one corner and a rack off to the side with clothes hanging on it. Straight ahead, there was another thick, wooden desk with a lamp, computer, and telephone on it, and a small bookshelf behind. Three small couches were around a short coffee table in the middle of the room, and two dark windows with closed blinds were behind the desk. The floor had the same red carpet as in the stairway, and around the walls, going across the entire perimeter of the room, was a thin line of cobalt blue tape.

"Mind clearing the way?" Polland coughed.

Bran stepped forward quickly. When Adi reached the desk, she turned back to him.

"This, Bran," she said, "is my *real* office."

She pointed to the television.

"That's how I keep up with the news," she said. "I watch Channel Zero, the Mages Entertainment Channel."

She pointed to a black box next to her computer.

"That's my modem," she said. "It connects my computer to the Mages Network. On the table there," she said, pointing to a strange, gun-like object, "is a wittscounter, for measuring your witts."

"Witts are a way of measuring magic power," Polland explained, "There are all sorts of laws about how many witts you can use and where you can use them."

"There are strict laws regarding magic, even outside of Dunce," Adi explained. "You can't use any magic that'll go above two hundred in urban areas. The more witts, the more power, and the bigger magic."

"So it's like a speed limit," Bran thought out loud.

"Yes," Adi said, nodding. "On the scale of witts, you're bright or dim: if you've got a lot of power in you, people might say that you're with the brightwitts."

"And those with hardly any or none at all," Polland commented, "are known as *dimwitts.*"

"So most people like me should be somewhere in the middle, right?" Bran asked.

Very quickly, something passed over Adi's face: a strange shadow that seemed to darken her features, and Bran saw a sadness pass into her eyes, a hurt look that he didn't understand.

What did I say? he wondered. He remembered when Adi had looked the same way, in the car, when he had been talking to her. He didn't know what the matter was, but she just turned toward her computer. Bran decided not to press the subject and started to walk around the room.

"What's the line of blue tape on the wall for?" Bran asked Polland, speaking quietly so he wouldn't interrupt Adi.

"That means the room is warded," Polland explained. "A powerful magic has been put on it, so any magic done here cannot escape the room. The Magic Investigational Police use it in mage prisons, so people who get caught abusing magic can't do any more harm. For the worst of magic abuses, though, some people are turned into *faylen,* trapped in the form of an animal, like a rat or a snake, for years...sometimes for the rest of their lives."

"Are they locked up like that?" Bran said.

"Well, they can't do much harm in that condition, can they?" Polland replied. "No, they usually roam the world, scratching for their own food, though you can be sure they come back the day their sentence is up so they can be freed...if they aren't roadkill by then."

It was quite a thought, and one that didn't sit well with Bran, especially thinking about magic criminals. He began to inspect the attic again to distract himself. As he looked around the room, he spotted a strange thing sitting in the corner, all alone and very still...like a small birdcage with a black blanket over it, so he couldn't see anything inside. He stepped toward it, but the blanket was thick, and he wasn't able to see through. He reached out to touch the cloth, just to lift it up a bit.

He lifted the corner slightly, but accidentally brushed it too hard, and before he could react, the cage teetered toward him and toppled over. It hit him and fell to the floor with a crash. He gasped and jumped against the wall, and Adi gasped also, leaping up from her chair. The base and the lid of the cage fell apart into two pieces.

"Sorry!" Bran said quickly, his hands frozen in front of him. But then, a very strange thing happened, as something slipped out of the cage; a hive of floating flashes of light, rushing onto the floor like ants, taking flight and moving into the air. Bran slid away as they started swarming and swirling in circles. They just seemed to be floating wisps of light. Some of them shot toward him in the air, and he tried to brush them off.

Bran heard Adi laughing, and he looked up at her with surprise, and she smiled at his reaction.

"What's this?" he asked her, looking down at the open cage. They hovered lazily in the air, coming toward him and Adi and different places in the room.

"Just let them move around you, Bran," she said. "Look, they don't hurt; they're all over me."

They were hovering on her face and going down her neck. Bran hesitated but finally stopped brushing them off, and they drifted toward him as if he were a magnet gently pulling them closer. The only thing he felt was cold air all over him, and when he reached to touch one, it slipped through his fingers. They made ripples through Adi's hair, and when Bran looked at Polland, he saw there were many around him too, and he was trying to swat them with his hand.

"What are these?" Bran asked.

"They're Winx," Adi said, looking at him.

"A whole stinking drove of them," Polland grumbled. "An entire *forty* Winx."

"I've got to have forty," Adi told Polland. "If I have more or less, they'll all die."

Polland blew one off of his nose.

"Why are they going around us like that?" Bran asked.

"They feed off magical auras," she said softly. "They go to the strongest sources of magic in a room and stay there."

"Like a moth, to a bright light," Bran said.

"Right," Adi said. She reached to her desk and picked something up. It was a long and slender rod and looked to be only a few inches more than a foot, made of shiny, polished silver that gleamed in the light when she moved it, reflecting onto his face and around the room. It almost seemed to narrow at the far end, on which was a blunted, golden tip; the gold wasn't shiny and reflective, but dull and misty. The light glinted off it like a sword's blade, and on the end facing her wrist, Bran saw a small, clear diamond embedded in the handle, where only a bit was sticking out for him to see. There were deep designs on it and small, sweeping molds that seemed to point toward the tip of it. If anything, it looked like a very expensive treasure.

"This," Adi said, "is the most useful, most precious tool of a mage. It is a weapon, a shield, a work of art, but most of all, the wand is the symbol of a mage."

Already, some of the Winx were hovering toward it, as if its very presence held magic. Ginolde swooped by and cawed, perching on the top of Adi's computer monitor.

"What do you do with it?" Bran asked. Adi swayed her arm, and the Winx followed the motion of the wand, almost as if it was leaving a glowing blur behind.

"Plenty of things," Adi said. "For enchantments, if I want to do an Elemental magic, and I'm an Illian, I can get Polland to charge an Archon magic into my wand for me, in case I need it. Or, you can use a wand to focus your magic, to make is stronger and targeted."

She waved it. "A wand is very dangerous in the hands of someone who isn't well trained. It might be years before you receive one, but by then, you will be ready. Watch me."

Adi took a deep breath, and then stepped backward. However, as she did, it was almost as if she hadn't moved. A duplicate of her was still standing where she had been a moment before, looking ahead just as she had been, so that when Adi stepped from behind her, Bran could not tell which was real and which was the illusion. He was left speechless.

The Winx, though, shot toward one of the Adis like flies, some even moving away from him to go to her. As they flew toward her, their color changed, fading to the same blue as that of the color for Illian in the books.

"See?" one of the Adis said regretfully. "The Winx give the real me away."

They were hovering only around the Adi on the left, and seemed to be ignoring the other.

"No hiding which one is really you when they're about,"

Polland said with a grin. Adi gave a small laugh and then, turning to her duplicate, she shifted her wand, and the other Adi hardened and turned to a dust. The particles fell to the floor but disappeared before they even hit. The Winx stayed around Adi, though not as tightly as before.

"A simple illusion," Adi said. "But, you saw what the Winx do to magic." She moved for the shelf behind her desk, as the Winx continued to float away from her.

"Here, Bran," Adi said, setting the thick book where he could see. It had a hard, leathery cover, and was hundreds of pages long. The front had been pressed with an intricate design along the edges, and in the center was a single word: *Magic.* Below it, far at the bottom, was a name: *Wencias Gnarl.*

"This," Adi explained, "is the most used book by mages in the world. It contains histories, knowledge, tips, and magic from the greatest mage of our time, Wencias Gnarl, a recluse whose whereabouts are secret to all save for his publishers."

She opened the book and let the pages flutter by, so that Bran could see all the words.

"Unlike the others, which have magics for specific missivs, this book seeks not to separate, but to bring them together. It is a compendium of sorts." She nodded toward it. "Take a look. I want you to pick a magic to try yourself."

Adi pulled her hands away, encouraging him to page through it. Like he had seen in the bookstore, it was filled with magics, intermingled with sketches and notes. Every page was thin and seemed easy to tear, but the book appeared to be in perfect condition, though it felt as though something so filled with knowledge should be ancient and withered.

The book was divided into parts, and each cover page was completely black, and in its center was a round stamp of a bird, with its wings forming a circle above its head, just like he had seen on the ones at the bookstore. He saw the strange words again: *Lite yirou diyestini lidea yuo,* and around the bottom: *adni micagi geuida yirou wiya.*

"See those words?" Adi said, following his gaze. "It is written in Alvondir, the ancient language used for all spoken magic: different from magics just done with your mind. It reads '*Let your destiny lead you, and magic guide your way.*'"

"It is part of a poem by Wencias Gnarl himself," Polland said. "It was chosen as the official code of the Mages Council."

"There are so many things in there," Bran said. "I don't know how I will ever learn it all if I'm going to be a mage. It seems like so much."

"Becoming a mage isn't like going to school," Adi told him. "It is like an extra muscle that you have been gifted with, something you must exercise, and work at, to become strong in it. Every exercise you learn is your choice. The knowledge of two mages are never alike."

Bran let his eyes skim down the pages as he soaked it all in. He could have gone on reading it for hours if he had the chance, awash in the newness of it all and enraptured by the doors that it opened before him. He stopped on one at random, because it appeared to be simpler than the rest.

[6116-A] Electric Fingers—Smeefe

Pulses electricity on one's fingers or where directed, power dependant on witts. Does not affect the caster, though potentially dangerous to others. Use cautiously.

Fingers on Hand Up or Out: *Curling electric arch around fingers*

ECLECTRI FIRINGE

"This looks good," Bran pointed. "Though I don't have a clue what any of it means."

"Let me explain." Adi ran her finger on it. "First comes the Official Catalog Number, from the Association of Magic Cataloging. That letter A after the dash means this is an Archon magic. Next comes the title, and then the last name of its creator."

Bran really felt he should have chosen a Netora magic, for it fit his personality better, and he was certain if he tried Archon it would not work for him. However, Adi didn't even seem to notice, sliding her finger below the description.

"That is the action you must be doing: in this case, holding your hand with your fingers up or out. Next to it is what you must be thinking as you do the magic."

"Don't overlook that part," Polland said importantly. "Your mind is the main factor."

Adi nodded in agreement. "And the last ones, in bold, are the words you need in Alvondir."

"That's not too complicated," Bran said, though inside he wasn't nearly as sure of himself as he appeared. He brushed a Winx out of his face again.

"It may be different than what you did with the truck. Consciously this time," Adi said, and he could almost hear a strange eagerness in her voice, "I want you to reach deep in you, deeper than you ever have, and feel the magic. Pull it out, wrap it around your fingers."

Bran took a deep breath but did what she said, lifting his fingers together as the book had dictated. He felt inside with his mind. He thought he perceived something, a strange power. It was different from anything he had felt before, making him eager to feel the magic against his mind again, as if visiting with someone he had met once before.

"When you think you've got it, say the words," Adi's voice came. Bran hardly heard her.

"*Eclectri firinge,*" he whispered. But nothing happened. He opened his eyes, and none of the Winx had moved, and some even started to drift away, as if bored by just being near him.

"Reach deeper, Bran," Adi said, not reproachful. "Close your eyes if you must. Pull the magic out like a string, *ignite* it with the words, and set it all aflame. *Think* of energy on your fingers."

Eclectri firinge, Bran repeated in his mind, burning the words into his memory. He tried it again, pulling the power, and it slipped away. He held it stronger, tightening his will around it like a rope that was pulling at his fingers. It felt as if it were slipping from his grasp, but he wrenched it around again.

"*Eclectri firinge!*" he said with determination, and it happened. He felt it, even though his eyes were closed, even though his mind was confused, his heart was racing, and his nerves were on edge. He felt it rush out of him, to his hand, going a thousand miles per hour through his body.

He opened his eyes, and there it was, curling across like a living thing: a great, glowing blueness of energy, rushing on the tips of his fingers like lightening crackling between them.

And all of a sudden, there was a great rush in the room from all over, like a stick being slung in a circle through the wind.

Bran heard it and looked up, but before he could react, every single Winx in the room leapt upon him like a giant, glowing beast, and slammed him against the wall.

Chapter 22

The Truth

Bran's back hit the wall, knocking the wind out of his lungs so hard he lost all grip on the magic. The power vanished, but the Winx crawled over his skin, chilling him as they fed off him, up his arms and his neck. They felt so cold that goose bumps rose on his flesh. Their intense glow was like a spotlight in a room of mirrors.

"Adi!" he said, not sure what he had done. There wasn't a spot of Winx on her skin, not a wisp left around her or Polland. But what frightened him more was her face, stricken with panic.

"What are they doing?" he asked.

Adi did not reply, but moved for the cage, setting it back again and putting something inside. Slowly, the Winx started toward it, and she closed the door behind them.

"Like I said, Bran," she said in the deathly silence. "They feed off the most powerful source of magic in the room."

"What in the world does that mean, then?" Bran demanded, still shaken.

She looked at him. "It means that you are different," she said, setting her hand on the top of the cage. "And it also means you really are the Hambric I feared you were."

"What Hambric?" Bran asked.

Adi shook her head. "Bran, you need to sit down. I have a lot to tell you."

She draped the cloth over the cage, and Bran could see her mind was far from that room. She was thinking of terrible things, he could see it by her face. She slowly sat behind the desk but was quiet, staring off and thinking.

"Did you see the color of the Winx when they were around me?" she began. Bran hesitated at her strange question, but slowly brought himself to answer.

"Blue..."

"And the color when they came to you?"

"White," he replied. Adi looked down, and then at Polland.

"Tell him," Polland said.

"I'm lucky enough to own the Winx: most people can't get them," Adi said. "The way we know for sure which missiv a mage is from is by the color of the Winx. Each missiv has one."

Polland drew the book out again, pointing to the circles on the insignia. "Purple for Netora, green for Archon," his fingers moved to the left side, "blue for Illian, and red for Comsar."

He touched the black one at the top. "All joined to the black, the one for Drimra."

His last sentence had a serious, jagged sound to it—something he was saying without words. Bran studied the circle, and noticed with a start that there wasn't a white marking anywhere on it.

"Then what about white?" Bran asked, a tinge of fear in his voice for what they would say. Adi glanced at Polland.

"Tell him," Polland whispered.

Bran could sense there was a tension in the air, and it only drove his alarm deeper. What were they trying to say that was so hard to get out?

"To be honest with you," Adi said, "you're the only living mage to have Winx go white."

He was silent. *The only one?* There was more to it; he could see it in her eyes.

"What does that mean?" he asked. Adi took a deep breath.

"I believe it's time I told you the truth about your mother, your past…and the Farfield Curse."

The last part of her words caused him to sit up straighter, though thankfully she had turned to her computer and did not notice. *The Farfield Curse*…Adi knew about his mother? Immediately, Bran felt uneasy. He had heard those words before, from Astara. A bad feeling crept over him.

"Have you ever heard of it?" Adi asked.

"No, never," Bran lied, speaking before he even thought about it.

"That's good," Polland said in a low voice. "Everything's still kept quiet."

"What is it?" Bran asked quickly.

"Farfield is a big city up north, not too far from here," Adi said. "It's wonderful, filled with skyscrapers. There's a museum with records and displays for hundreds of landmarks in the history of mages. It's just an ordinary city, to most people."

She turned to her computer. "But years ago, something was happening in Farfield that was nothing but evil." She typed a few things in, bringing up a record. She had to type multiple passwords.

"Inside that city," she went on, "was a secret group of mages: *dark* mages. These people were far opposite of me or any of the others under the Mages Council, and they had terrible, hidden plans behind everyone's backs. It was all secret, and no one knows about it all, even today."

"How do you know, then?" Bran asked. Astara had said the same thing to him—about how secret the Curse had been—and suddenly Adi knew of it as well.

"My work, here," she stammered. "And because of my involvement in the SSOD and the Mages Underground. What I mean to say, Bran, is that what I tell you now is a secret. If anyone ever finds out, no matter if it's another mage, I might even be expelled by the Council."

Bran nodded slowly. "But why is it so secret?"

"Because it's so terrible," she replied. "In that city, there was a group of dark mages, led by a man named Baslyn, a very powerful Drimra who had been leading them in secret for years. The dark mage cult was illegal, and still is, in every civilized city and country there is."

Adi looked down before going on. "Baslyn's group created something so evil, it was the duty of the Council to destroy it. So terrible, if word got out, the world might rise up against us, go into chaos, and try to kill every mage across the world to save themselves from the danger."

Bran felt his heartbeat quickening at her words.

"We came very close," Adi said. "If we had missed them, it would have been a disaster. And I'm sorry...but I don't even feel safe telling you the details. You'll just have to trust me."

There was a long silence between them all. Adi looked back at her computer and turned the screen so he could see the picture as it loaded.

"This," she said, "is a picture of Baslyn."

He moved to see better, and the moment the image appeared, something leapt within him.

It was the man from his dream.

Bran recognized the face in an instant…the same he had seen in his dream that night, the same man looking up from the bed in the white room. It sent a jolt through his skin, and he felt the blood drain away from his face.

"T-then what does all this have to do with me?" he asked slowly, trying to hide his fear. There was something going on, and he didn't like it. Something that involved him with this strange man. Both Adi and Polland were quiet. The silence bore upon Bran, and he looked from the screen, and saw that they both had dire looks on their faces.

"Also in Farfield was a woman," Polland said. "She was what we can only call a magic phenomenon."

"Meaning," Adi said, "her powers and witts highly surpassed those of every other mage, so much that it went unnoticed by everyone and she was able to hide it."

Adi looked down. "Her power was of a missiv never known to any mage besides in that of legends—*all the missivs together.*"

"The power of *Dormaysan,*" Polland said. "Scourged, by her own magic."

"Scourged?" Bran said. "Why would it be bad to be in all the missivs at once?"

Adi shook her head again. "It is not as it appears, Bran."

She went silent. Bran looked from her to Polland.

"All the missivs," Polland said lowly, "but the only magics she could use…were those for *evil:* the powerful, evil magic she needed to create the Farfield Curse."

Bran was frozen, unable to speak, unable to move as their words sank in and he realized exactly what they were saying—and who the woman was of which they spoke. Bran wanted to deny it, wanted to say something to tell her that she was wrong, it wasn't true…but hearing it from Astara, and seeing the grave of his mother: it was slowly becoming so that he could not deny what he struggled so hard not to believe.

"Somehow, she gave up her ability for good, and replaced it with evil," Polland went on.

"We came very close to missing them," Adi said. "But, we got an anonymous tip, and the police rounded up the group, though some of them got away. The police locked Baslyn's body into a secured morgue, but days later, his body was stolen, though he was dead. Thus the plot of the Farfield Curse was over, locked away, and marked confidential."

Bran could hardly hear what she was saying. Each sound felt like a sting on his face.

"We never found the woman," Adi said slowly. "No one knew…she had a son."

"It was me," Bran said, and though his voice was a whisper, it caused them to shift.

"How did you know?" Adi pressed.

But Bran was not listening.

"Emry Hambric…" he said aloud, unable to control what he was saying as everything came together, and he realized exactly what they were saying. He shook his head weakly. "Why tell me this now?" he said, leaning forward on his hand, unable to sort through feelings of anger and betrayal and fear within him. "Why ruin everything that I have?"

Adi looked to be torn to pieces before him, seeing how it hurt him so much.

"Because..." she started, but then took a breath. "Because you *had* to know. Because every power, every ability your mother had in her being...has been passed on to you, Bran."

It hit him like an icy wind as he heard her.

"No," he said, trying to deny it.

"The Winx showed the truth," Adi said with sadness. "The powers of all the missivs lie inside you: but, even though your mother was a Dormaysan, *you* are free."

Bran looked up at her, his eyes becoming glassy.

"Free?" he whispered.

"Yes," she said softly. "Your mother was a slave to dark magic, but you are free from the bondage—to use any magic from any missiv, with powers no mage has ever possessed." She stopped. "Free to follow the ways of good...or the ways of evil."

The words echoed in his head, haunting him, pounding through him like a gong in his ears. *No...it was too much.* He heard the rumble of thunder outside.

"Bran...please." Adi sounded concerned. *No...he had to get away.* His mind screamed within him, driving him mad with her words. The thunder crashed outside, and he leapt out of his chair.

Adi and Polland shot up, staring at him fearfully. Lightning flashed over his face, his eyes wide. He stumbled, tripping over the chair to get away from them.

"Bran!" Adi said, but he dashed for the door. He ran out, his hands shaking and his mind a blur. *He had to get away.* She was close behind on the stairs, but he was already dashing into the pouring rain. Adi called after him again, but he ignored her. He didn't care. *She can keep her magic, her secrets.* He felt as if everything he had ever imagined of his mother was a lie. He grabbed his bike from her car; tears sprang into his eyes, no matter how much he tried to hold them back.

"Wait!" Adi pleaded, running after him, but he didn't look back.

Rain beat against his face, and he could hardly see his own hands in front of him. Lightning lit up the sky, and deafening thunder nearly threw him off his bike as he swerved across the street. He was soaking wet, unable to tell the difference between the rain and the tears that streamed down his face.

He wiped his eyes with his hand and felt sick and dizzy, but the bike kept moving, and he kept pedaling on into the dark, until he couldn't hear Adi anymore, and her voice was just an echo in his mind.

He slid around a curb and nearly fell over, splashing water everywhere. He tried to follow the path Adi had taken, but in his bitterness, he became lost in the winding roads. He couldn't get his sense of direction but started off again, only to find he was going the wrong way. He just kept turning and turning in the rain, until he no longer had any idea where he was.

Chapter 23

The Face in the Mirrors

In the dark it was impossible to find his bearings to get home. Bran thought he saw a familiar street and started moving again, but when he ended up at Givvyng Park he knew he was too tired to continue on.

There was a tall brick building that served as rest rooms for the picnickers at the park, and as it had covering, Bran pulled his bike up to it. He hugged his knees for warmth and sat on the edge of the concrete, watching lightning flash across the sky and water gush from the corners of the roof. The storm was violent, but he hardly seemed to care anymore. He was much too far across town to start biking all the way back home in this weather; he knew he would just get lost again. His clothes were soaked and they clung to him, and he finally got up and went into the building, listening to the storm echo through the walls.

The bathrooms were abandoned, and he checked the place quickly for anybody who might be hiding. It was very dark and lit only by a single fluorescent bulb that flickered intermittently. There were five mirrors on the left wall, each above a sink, and dull, moist concrete floors. The place was not welcoming, but Bran had no choice but to stay.

He slowly gathered himself up and went to the sink, splashing cold water into his face. It helped to clear his senses but not the pain that still throbbed throughout him. Adi's words were like one final blow from the mother he never knew—that not only would he carry on as her son, but also wield the same powers that had started everything and had led to her death.

He dried his face with the towel and then looked into the mirror above the sink. He could see his face clearly though the room was dim. He looked tired. Every inch of him seemed so tortured, as if with everything that had happened, he had grown into a different person.

As he stared at his own reflection, he looked deep into his own eyes, trying to read them and make sense of all that he knew. Did he even want to be a mage? Was it worth risking all that he would face the rest of his life, the powers that his mother had cursed him with?

I've still got a choice, he told himself strongly, and in the mirror he saw his jaw tighten together, a determination that surprised even him as he thought of it. But what were his odds? He knew now that people were already searching the town for him, waiting to take him, probably afraid to make a move, he realized, because they knew his powers, waiting for the first time he slipped up and fell into their hands. Bran didn't even know why they wanted him—would they force him to finish what his mother had begun?

He saw the edge of the black string of the necklace poking out from under his shirt, so he pulled it and took the necklace off. There was no moonlight so the letters remained plain, dull blue. He stared at the name on it again, the name he shared with his mother. Was it one he could be proud of anymore?

He looked back to the mirror, and his eyes locked with his reflection. It was at that moment he heard a sound, like the faintest of whispers, more like the wind going through the building than anything else, though he could hear it clearly over the rain outside. He didn't move, his hands still clutching the edges of the sink, but he swept the room with his eyes. Nothing had moved. Not even a shadow.

Still, it was like a faint voice in the back of his head, speaking unintelligible words, whispering things he could not make out over his shoulder, first in one ear, then passing into the next. Bran clutched the edges tighter and stared at himself in the mirror, not daring to turn.

"Is someone there?" he said lowly, though the mirror revealed no one. He could almost feel breath on his neck, as if someone were standing right over his shoulder. He turned his head to the side, but the coldness shifted past. He looked back to the glass.

He suddenly noticed that there was something odd about his reflection. He could not tell what it was, but something was different. His face was paler; the features were the same, but his face appeared to be more sinister. Bran looked closer, and instantly his grip on the countertop tightened—for the reflection in the mirror had smiled.

It wasn't a smile of happiness. It was one that had never before crossed Bran's face, one that held such darkness and evil that it caused Bran's eyes to go wide.

"Who are you, Bran?" the reflection asked. Bran had not moved.

"Who are you?" the lips said again, the eyes on the face narrowing on him, trying to provoke an answer, the words echoing around him from all directions.

"I don't know," Bran said, involuntarily. He jerked from the mirror, going to the next sink to avoid what he was sure was his imagination.

"You know who you are," the reflection assured him, following him to the next mirror. "You are Emry Hambric's son. Heir to her powers. Heir to finish what she had begun."

"No," Bran hissed, drawing away to the third mirror in the row. "Go away. I don't want to hear you!"

"You cannot fight me for the rest of your life," his reflection said, meeting him there again. Bran gripped the edges of the sink, looking down, away from the haunting face. Slowly, it was as if the room around him started to fade, the light turning to a deep blackness.

"No, go away!" Bran seethed through his teeth, looking back up to the mirror only to see the face there yet again, not following his motions. He tried to turn, to pull away, but his hands were hardened to the sink.

"You cannot fight me," his face said again. "My very being is part of who you are."

"I don't even know you," Bran said, struggling to break free.

"Though perhaps you do," the voice echoed, the tone never rising. "I've been closer to you than anyone else for most of your life. Bran Hambric, *you will bring me to life.*"

It instilled terror into his heart. *Those words.* He remembered them. The words from his dream, the same man in the white bed, the same man from Adi's computer screen...

"Who are you?" Bran hissed, nearly out of breath, as the echoes of the voices began to grow stronger, beating him from the sides like gusts of wind. "Tell me who you are!"

The face in the mirror gave a laugh, horrible and chilling, and then the face began to change. It made Bran sick to see it, the skin stretching and contorting, his hair withering and falling out. It gave a shudder, and there was a great upheaval of magic in the room, so strong that a flash of light erupted from the mirror, blinding Bran, filling the air with intense whiteness. He tried to cover his face, but he couldn't move his hands, the light surrounding him until he saw something new.

Suddenly in front of Bran was the man he'd seen before—in a black robe that covered his head and made him look dressed for burial. His face was solid white, his eyes the most striking against the skin: vivid and dark, like blue crystals that made him seem both old and young at the same time. He looked like someone who had not completely died, but was between life and death. The man smiled, and Bran was stricken with fear.

"No!" Bran gasped. "You're dead!"

"My body, yes," the face of Baslyn said. "Though my spirit?" Baslyn smiled. "It lives on."

The echo of Baslyn's words seemed to spin Bran around in the blinding whiteness, flowing from the mirror like walls around him, blocking all sight of the room. Bran fought the sounds, torturous magic coursing through him so that he gritted his teeth in pain.

"I'm imagining you!" Bran said, calling out though his words did nothing to spite Baslyn, who only laughed again and spread his arms.

"Am I not real before you?" Baslyn said. "Have you not seen me, leading you through the town, revealing to you secrets you should never have known?" He lifted his head. "You know because I have led you to see it. I see and feel all."

"No!" Bran shouted, but his voice seemed weak and stifled in the echoes and the rising noise around him. He struggled to break free, feeling wind against his face from the mirror.

"You have no choice, Bran Hambric," the image shouted. "You cannot resist what has been placed inside of you. What I have hidden within your own self."

Bran fought the hold on his hands, shouting as he did, closing his eyes. The room ceased to exist around him in the blinding light.

"What do you want from me?!" Bran hissed, trying to fight, to grasp anything to free himself.

"Bran Hambric: *you will bring me to life,*" Baslyn's voice said again, and it surrounded Bran with the deepest of echoes, pushing him from one side to the other.

"No!" Bran shouted, and in an instant, as if the powers were breaking, one of his hands came free. It was in that same moment that Baslyn's face became filled with a maddening rage, and he came toward Bran out of the glass.

"You have no choice!" the voice roared again, but Bran threw all his strength forward, slamming his hand toward the mirror. There came a great flash, crackling and filling the room, and all of a sudden Bran was thrown backward off his feet, the white exploding around him.

His back hit with the opposite wall, and suddenly, he was in the building again, and he heard glass falling and shattering on the floor. He rolled over, dazed, but threw his hand out with a force of the first magic that came to him.

"*Eclectri firinge!*" he said, the words coming out of him automatically and without thought, the same he had used in Adi's house. Lancing from his fingers with the force of his unrestrained powers came a crackling burst of blue energy, slamming into the glass of the mirrors and shattering the remaining four at once. He immediately jerked his hand back, terrified of what might happen if he lost control of it, and the magic vanished, jagged shards of glass scattering across the concrete as he shielded his face.

The room went still.

He opened his eyes and saw he was clutching something tightly: in his fist was the necklace. In the darkness it did not glimmer, but somehow it seemed as if behind its surface, Bran could feel a power still pulsating, like a creature breathing hard with him after a fight.

"What do you want from me, Baslyn?" Bran seethed, wiping his forehead and looking back to the broken mirror shards that were spread across the floor. Where the mirrors had once been was plain concrete, a dark, heavy wall—and Baslyn was gone.

It was then that he heard someone calling his name from far outside the building.

"Rosie?" he said, jumping to his feet and hurrying to the entrance. When he stepped out, he saw the Schweezer parked a way off on the road, headlights slicing through the heavy rain. He could see Rosie in a red raincoat, holding a lantern and rushing toward where his bike was.

"Bran!" she gave a cry and dashed across the grass, the lantern lighting up her face.

"Oh, Bran, I was so worried!" she cried out, seizing him and pulling him close. He was all wet, but she didn't care because she was soaked as well. She held him for a minute, not caring about the rain, not caring who might be watching; he held her as well, and she was warm.

"When you never got home, we looked everywhere, and then I saw your bike," she gasped. "I thought all sorts of things might have gotten you!"

He could feel that she was trembling with fright. Even under the raincoat her hair was damp, and he knew that she had been out looking for him for a long time.

"I—I got lost," he managed to stammer, not knowing what to say. He gestured toward the building, then toward the road, but nothing more would come out.

"You got *very* lost!" she said. "Bran, we've been all over this side of town, on every street..."

"Come on, you two!" the voice of Sewey erupted from the driver's side window. "Get in, before we get washed away by this rainy rot!"

"Sewey came too?" Bran said. Rosie nodded quickly.

"All of them are in there," she said. "Nobody knew where you were..." Her voice trailed off, and she clutched him tightly. "I was just so worried," she said. "But now I've found you, and everything will be all right."

Water dripped from Bran's hair, and she smiled at him reassuringly, but even as they walked toward the car, Bran was not sure how anything could ever be all right again.

Part III

Chapter 24

The Girl from the Alley

Nightmares struck Bran all night, one after the other, and when he woke from each he was sweating and curled up in fear in his bed. One image permeated each nightmare: it was his own face, every time, mocking him, saying what Adi had told him before, repeating her words and telling him he wielded the same powers his mother had used to create the Farfield Curse. Then in the dream, his face would change to Baslyn's, and the echoing voices would shatter the ground beneath him, and he fell into a blackness. Each time, he would wake up.

He awoke a final time early the next morning, and the house was so quiet that the echoes of his dream seemed to fade against the walls. There was a hint of morning light coming from the window. It was golden and bright, so much different than all had been the night before.

He got up and dressed, and when he passed his desk he saw the paper on which he had drawn the single letter B. Suddenly it seemed all alone and obvious, now that he knew what it stood for, and so he took his pencil again and finished the rest of Bartley's name. It was a grim motion, almost a distraction from where he was headed that day.

There are only a few more pieces to this puzzle, Bran thought. He had to meet Astara again; it was the only chance he had of finding out the truth.

He came down from the attic and crossed the hall, and he heard the television already on in the living room. Sewey and Mabel were up, and Bran heard Rosie in the kitchen, flipping up pancakes. The news was on, so Bran paused in the door.

"*...the rioters were protesting the admittance of Mr. Tomstone the gnome into the Mages Council Guild of Historians,*" the announcer said, giving a helicopter view of a spacious piece of property in the mountains and a rather large house—or at least what had been a house. It was now mostly a burning pile of rubble. Legions of police were like little ants moving about. In the top corner of the screen, next to the logo for Dunce News Channel 12, was a picture of a tall red triangle with a circle and a line through it, which was known to mean No Gnomes just as a circle with a line over a cigarette meant No Smoking. Next to it was a blue circle with a line through it, much like a No Smoking sign except with stars instead of smoke and a mage's wand instead of a cigarette—it meant No Mages.

"*They formed very early this morning at his mansion in the Wishywashy Hills. The police were called, and the protesters became violent until, as witnesses report, there was a loud boom, and the Tomstone residence exploded into a hailstorm of shrapnel.*"

Bran watched the screen with total attention, his eyes surveying the damage.

"*The explosion took the life of Mr. Tomstone and set the house afire. In the terrible riot that broke out afterward, the lives of three others were also taken. Mrs. Tomstone and the baby Tomstone twins were barely rescued from the house and brought to safety by the police.*"

The footage switched down to the ground, where police were leading off some rough-looking men in handcuffs, and then a row of gnomes too, their hands cuffed as well. The Dunce News station pixilated the gnomes so that no one could see more than their outlines.

"There was also some action from the militant anti-gnome group Grechin as protestors and parts of the Tomstone security were arrested for questioning, as seen here..."

Abruptly, from the side of the screen, large men in black jackets with folded red cloths covering part of their faces shot out of the police barrier, knocking the gnomes aside. The police officers struggled to fight off the men, but it became a frenzy as clubs were drawn and the Grechins started to hit at the gnomes, who could do nothing with their hands cuffed behind their backs. Bran cringed as he saw the police being shoved aside and the gnomes rolling on the pavement, trying to avoid being hit or trampled.

"Balder, turn it off," Sewey said from the couch. Balder didn't listen, and one of the gnomes on the screen shouted in pain. People leapt upon them, a frenzy of those trying to help and others trying to beat them as well. It became a sea of madness—the Grechin were notorious for violence, and while even Duncelanders couldn't bring themselves to voice support of the group, they could hardly condemn them outright, though the sight on the television was startling enough to rattle Sewey.

"Balder, *turn it off,*" Sewey demanded, but Balder's eyes were wide and riveted on the screen. Sewey finally fumbled for the remote, slamming down on the button. The screen immediately switched to the Bean Bag Show.

"I don't want you watching all that violence on the news," Sewey ordered Balder, throwing him the remote. "Keep it to these kids' shows."

"*Hey kids, let's have fun with chain saws and grenades!*" Manica-bibble was shouting. Sewey wasn't paying attention—he still looked uncomfortable from the news. He noticed Bran standing in the doorway.

"What are you doing?" he asked Bran.

"I—I forgot to thank you for coming to look for me last night," Bran stammered.

Sewey grunted. "No point in thanking us," he grumbled. "It was Rosie who was worried about you. I was worried about my car. She wasn't going to drive it alone, no sirree."

But Bran could feel a hint of untruth behind Sewey's voice, because he fumbled around on the couch and tried to ignore Bran even being there.

"I've got to go out this morning," Bran said, trying to slide it in quickly.

"Where to?" Sewey demanded, pretending to watch the television.

"Just out," Bran replied. "Around Third Street. Just to get some fresh air."

"Got plenty last night. Don't see why you need any more," Sewey said, but Bran was already starting for the stairs. Rosie was in the kitchen and saw him going for the front door.

"Out so early?" she said, pressing the toaster button. He could hear in her voice that she was still concerned over the night before, though he had assured her many times he was all right.

"Don't worry," he replied. "I just want to go ride my bike around for a bit."

He left before she could say anything else. Everything outside was wet and glistening from the rain, but Bran hardly paid it any notice. As he cut through the neighborhood on his bike, the echoes of Baslyn's voice had strangely quieted, as if for some reason his presence was stifled.

Once, he thought he saw the reflection of a black van coming around a corner, but when he turned it was gone. He checked the streets warily as he rode, and by the time he got back to Third Street, there were cars all about. The bank was open, most likely Ben or Adi inside. But he wasn't headed for the bank. There was something more important.

He left his bike in the alley and headed toward the back door for Highland's Books. It was before opening time, just as he had hoped. The door was unlocked.

"I guess she's still expecting me," he muttered, remembering how he had told her he wasn't coming back. He stepped into the back room, the door resonating behind him when he shut it.

His steps echoed as he walked, remembering the way. Thin rays of sunlight flowed in through the glass above, and Bran could see his way better than the first night. There were a few doors that were closed on both sides, some of them with small, square panes of glass.

"So you came back," a sudden voice came from behind him, and he straightened up quickly.

"I'm here," he said, recognizing her voice.

Astara was standing at the corner, leaning against a pillar of crates. Her arms were crossed, and she looked at him with a smile that said she had proved him wrong. He had come back, and she had known all along he would.

"I thought you weren't coming," she said, and Bran smiled just a bit and shook his head.

"I think I changed my mind," he said. He pulled the necklace out from under his shirt. "I want to know everything," he said, holding it where she could see.

She looked at him strongly but was silent, thoughts going through her eyes that Bran couldn't grasp. "There's a lot," she finally said.

"That's why I'm here," Bran replied. "I came back, now it's your turn."

She nodded slowly, then shrugged. "Follow me, and I'll tell you everything that happened."

She started between the boxes. They went down a row and turned the corner, and then up to a door that was out of the way.

"First," she said, "that file you found on your mother wasn't supposed to be empty. Mr. Highland and I burned it, because we didn't want anyone to get involved."

Her face went grim. "But now it's too late for that."

Astara said nothing more, but pushed the door open and stepped in. Bran was right behind her and was about to say something, but stopped when he came through.

The room was a small, square space that looked as if it had once been a ragtag office of some sort. There was an old air conditioner in the dusty window, humming a little louder than it should have. On the floor was an assortment of things: dishes, newspapers, a bed that was in worse shape than his own, and a desk that was warped. The walls were lined with cobbled-together shelves, and on the shelves were rows of record players.

Sewey had an old record player, which he used when he was practicing his saxophone, thankfully a rare event. But Astara obviously had been collecting the old things for years, some of them dusty with their horns broken or missing, others polished and cleaned so they might even be worth something as antiques. There were about a dozen of them, and the shelf below was littered with spare parts, while the table had another phonograph and some tools. There were old vinyl records lying out of their cases all over the floor.

"Do you like music?" Astara asked when he didn't follow her through the door.

"I don't listen to much, no," Bran replied. Truthfully, what little music was brought into the house were Sewey's old favorites or whatever was on Radio Dunce, usually songs like "No Home for Gnomes" or "Off with the Pointed Red Hat (And Their Heads Too)."

"Well, hang around me long enough, you'll start liking it," Astara assured him as she moved toward the table. As she went, she turned her hand, and from across the room the needle on the record player hopped onto the vinyl. There was a squeak, and a slow rock rhythm started quietly. Bran studied the room further, cases of vinyls strewn about on the floor and tacked to the walls, cassettes in heaping piles on the table, even a few scratched CDs, though these were hung up by string and reflected light as they spun slowly. He saw only a few things resembling music from the recent decade.

"You like old music?" he asked as the sounds softly filled the room. Astara shrugged.

"No, not just that. But the old stuff seems timeless," she said. "It doesn't disappear or get forgotten, like everything else these days."

By the tone of her voice, Bran felt she wasn't only talking about the music. The sounds wafted in the air, and Astara brushed some things off the table.

"Where did you live before here?" Bran said.

"The streets," she replied.

"Homeless?"

"A runaway is closer to it," she said. "Couldn't live at the Crouch's anymore."

"Were they your family?" he asked. She shook her head.

"No, just the owners," she said. "They had the orphanage back in Crandon."

"You don't know your family either?" Bran said.

"I don't. I've got nothing," she replied simply, shaking her head. "Well, almost nothing. I have this."

She turned the black band around her wrist. It was plain and thick, something that couldn't have been worth more than a sib. But as she turned it, he noticed something stamped darkly against the black: a strange, crooked marking in the middle, written in silver. It almost appeared to be a jagged letter S, but before he could look closer, she turned and hid it again.

"It's worthless," Astara said. "That's why they didn't take

it from me. Probably the first letter of my last name, but who knows? It might not even be from my parents. But it's all I have. And I can't go back to Crandon to look for any records at the Crouch's...not since I ran away."

"What did they do to you there?" Bran asked.

"Whatever they wanted to," she replied grimly. "It was on the bad side of town: the bad side of *Crandon.* They locked me in a closet for three straight days once. I nearly went mad, and I wrote on the walls like a lunatic. That just got me in more trouble." She nodded with the memory. "The bruises always healed, but I will *never* forget that place."

"You couldn't get any help from the police?" Bran said.

"Listen," she said sharply. "Crandon is the definition of lawlessness. The police are *worse* than the thieves. That's the role the owners filled: thieves. When they found out I could do magic, they had this plan for me to open the safe of the bank down the street."

"How did they teach you to do that?" Bran said. "If the Mages Council found out—"

"They brought in a witch," Astara stopped him. "Unregistered, nothing to do with the Council. A mage for hire, and not usually for good. She wasn't a Netora, though she had access to books to teach me what they needed."

"Were they caught?" Bran said. Astara shook her head.

"No, because it never happened," Astara said. "I was only six years old, but in that place you know to be wary, and I overheard their plans to kill and bury me after the robbery, cover up the evidence. So I got help from the cook to escape on trains going north, to Gordontown, where one of her cousins would pick me up." She sighed. "But I never made it. My ticket money ran out, right at the stop in Dunce." She looked down. "And that's how I saw your mother being killed."

Bran forced himself not to flinch at her words. She gestured toward the table and chairs.

"Want to sit down?" she offered. She sat across from him and leaned back, looking away. The sounds of the record filled the air; the volume almost magnified by the silence between them as Astara gathered her words.

"Like I said, when I came to Dunce I had nowhere to stay," Astara said. "I had to stay hidden until I could find *someone* to help me. I didn't want to get caught and sent back to Crandon." She looked up and met his gaze. "That night I didn't have anywhere to go, so I hid in an alley on the outskirts of town, trying to sleep between some crates to keep warm. Then the car came."

By the look that came into Astara's eyes, Bran could see the memory still scared her.

"The car sat for a while, and I was still—no, I was trembling, but quiet." Astara said. "Then I saw your mother get out, with you in her arms. Then everything happened very quickly."

She shook her head. "Your mother put you in the trunk, and then a woman came from nowhere, so fast I hadn't even seen her. She threw your mother to the ground, pulled the trunk open...but you were gone."

She had sent me to the bank vault, Bran realized. He bit his lip, a sudden anger going through him upon hearing how the woman had treated his mother.

Astara took a deep breath. "I couldn't move, I couldn't do

anything. The woman asked your mother where she had sent you, and when your mother wouldn't tell her, she aimed the pistol...and shot her."

Bran drew a sharp breath, almost hearing the shot ring out in the back of his mind.

She wanted me for Baslyn, he thought, almost feeling as if Baslyn was there with him in the room. The woman must have been working with Joris. The pieces of the puzzle were beginning to fall into place in his mind. He realized that the woman was probably one of those who had escaped the police in Farfield.

"I thought I would scream, Bran," Astara said. "But I didn't. I managed to hold it in. The woman left her there, and the moment I saw that it was safe, I ran to her. She was still barely alive, probably using magic to do it, but she was dying, and she didn't want to hold on."

Bran stared at the window across the room.

"She tried to talk to me," Astara went on. "That's when she told me about her crime."

He sat up straighter. "The Farfield Curse?"

"That's when she said it," Astara replied. "I didn't understand her. I might have been forced to grow up fast, but I was still very young. But her words burned into my mind so deeply I could never forget them, and now all these years later, I know what she was talking about."

Astara looked over Bran's shoulder, behind him at the wall, remembering something from the deep recesses of her mind.

"She told me about a crime..." Astara said. "She spoke of something that she had created years ago with a man named

Baslyn, something about the Farfield Curse. She said that everyone was keeping it a secret, that no one was supposed to know about it because it was so terrible. But she told me there was more to it, Bran." Astara met his eyes again. It look painful for her to say it. "She said it started in the summer, many years ago. No one knew why it happened or what caused it—this gathering of people in the desert. Nearly three thousand men, women, and children, all to one spot. They were called there, no one knew how or why, and then—" She snapped her fingers. "—they were gone. And no one has heard from them since."

"But how?" Bran stammered. "They had friends and families and jobs! How would the government have explained it?"

"Earthquake," Astara said. "They said it opened up and closed them in afterward. Some said evil spirits, or a horde of trolls. But I know the truth." She took a deep breath. "I know...because your mother told me *she* had done it."

The deepest part of Bran seemed to quiver thinking of it. Just imagining the magic for such a thing was incomprehensible, though he knew from where it had come...the power of the Dormaysan that Adi had spoken of.

"She told me it took her magic to do it," Astara said. "She told me it was part of a plot by a man more evil than she had anticipated."

Baslyn... Bran thought. *What had he been planning?*

"Was that the Farfield Curse, then?" he asked her.

"No, not all of it," Astara shook her head. "This was before it, part of it: whatever she did, whatever she was going to do...she needed those souls. She needed those lives, those *people.*"

Bran felt terror deep inside of him, an impending doom

or premonition of something nightmarish that was going to happen.

Astara shook her head. "Like I said, I didn't understand, but now I know why she said it all. I was the last person she could tell her secret to. That was when she gave me the necklace, and made me swear I would give it to you if I ever found you, and that I would tell you the truth." Astara paused for a moment. "After I promised...she died."

Bran couldn't say a word. He felt angry and drained at the same time, a mixture of fear and emptiness inside his soul.

"Maybe she could have kept herself alive, Bran," Astara whispered. "But she knew her time was up. So she let it go." Fright was in Astara's eyes, even then, as she spoke. "But I was six years old, I didn't know what to do. So I ran off, looking for anyone who could help me." She shook her head. "There was only one store with a light on, and that was a bookstore."

"Highland's Books?" Bran said, and she nodded.

"Mr. Highland was working late here, for some reason," she said. "I pounded on the door until he came, and took him to her. By then, the police were there because of the gunshots. They found something with her name, and since there was no one to claim the body, Mr. Highland did."

Astara took a deep breath. "When no one showed up, Mr. Highland paid for a coffin and buried her on a small piece of land he owned. He didn't let me go but showed me where the grave was later on, and he let me have a room in the store, and when I got older, let me work in his shop."

"I guess there still are good people in the world," Bran remarked.

"I thought that too," she said. "Even when I went and told him I was a mage, and why I had run away—even after that, he still didn't turn me in. It might have been part of the reason he began work with the Mages Underground. Afterward, I didn't dare tell him the full story, but he got out of me that Emry had a son. He knew that if you were still alive, finding out about her death would ruin you, so one night we emptied the police file and burned the contents."

Astara slid her hand across the table, touching his arm softly.

"Bran, your mother *was* a good person," she said. "A good person...just caught in a bad past."

Bran pulled his arm away, feeling a strange, saddened anger with everything around him.

"I wish I was back there," he said under his breath. "I would have killed anyone who tried to hurt her."

"Bran, that woman didn't hesitate to kill your mother," Astara said. "She wouldn't have hesitated to kill you, either."

"She didn't *want* to kill me," Bran hissed. "If I die, everything is in vain. They want me *alive.*"

Astara didn't seem to understand, and she brushed the hair out of her face. He didn't turn to meet her eyes, but he could feel they were on him.

"What do you mean?" she asked him softly. Bran took a deep breath, but he knew it was already too late to keep it from her any longer.

"There is more to this than even *you* know," he said. "There are men right here, in Dunce, looking for me right now. That's why all this is happening. That's why I came into this very shop, and found that file."

He opened his eyes. "Somehow, Baslyn is *still* here, Astara. He is following me, day and night, in my dreams, with magic. He speaks to me, haunts me."

Bran slid his fingers through his hair. "I don't know if I'm going mad from this or if he is there, watching me somehow with magic. If he is dead, how is it he haunts me? If he is alive, how can no one else see him?"

Astara let her hands fall to the table and sat back, and Bran stood bitterly, walking to the window and looking out. He didn't know what else to say to her, for he had no answers on how to get out of the mess that he had fallen into.

They were both silent for a long while. He couldn't even open his mouth to speak; he didn't know what to say anymore. It seemed as if suddenly everything was hopeless again, and even with all she had told him, he was further into the mystery than before.

"How old are you?" he broke the silence, not turning.

"What?" she asked, confusion in her voice.

"How old are you?"

"Fourteen," she replied slowly.

"Same as me," he said. He pressed his forehead against the glass.

"Strange thing is, I can't remember any of my past," Bran said, trying to keep himself talking. "My mother must have cleaned my memory out."

He shifted. "I can't even remember her face."

He could feel her eyes on him, watching his reflection.

"I know that's terrible," he said, searching for words to say. "I can't even remember anything about this person I call my mother. Sometimes when I'm awake at night, I wonder about her. What did she look like, you know? What color were her eyes? Why'd all this happen?" He stopped. "You don't know... or maybe you do know how it feels to lose something that's so important to you, even when you've never had it, you miss it like your life is dependent on it."

Bran took a deep breath, and it felt like there was a deep, hard pressure on his chest.

"But I just can't bring myself to hate her for everything she's done," he said. "You know why? Because I love her, this mother I never knew, who did all these terrible things, who left me behind...and I guess..." He paused again. "I guess you might feel like I do too, because you've been through it all, mistreated by everyone. Maybe that's why you care enough to do all this, and tell me the truth, and keep your promises when you very well could just forget them."

He looked at her, and he was very moved to see that there was a soft tear going down her cheek. He could see by looking into her eyes that there was something there, behind them. He wasn't sure, but it looked like she really cared.

"I only wish I knew what was going on," Bran whispered, and he turned back to the window. He felt worse inside, knowing some of the answers but unable to piece them all together.

But even as he peered out the windows, he saw Baslyn's face in the crowds: looking up from a newspaper, then vanishing; his reflection in a window across the street, gazing at Bran, then disappearing as soon as Bran focused on it. He felt Baslyn watching him constantly from afar, haunting him no matter which way he turned his gaze.

There was deep, dark magic, and Bran felt as if he was getting nowhere, for he hadn't any idea what powers Baslyn had weaved over him. Everything seemed to connect with that: as long as Baslyn was there, haunting his every move, Bran felt he would never be free.

He realized that the only person who knew enough about magic to tell him any answers would be Adi. As much as he didn't want to, he knew he had to go back to her, and if not tell her the truth, at least try to make amends with her for running out.

"I've got to go," Bran said. He looked up at Astara. She was still sitting there.

"Where?" she asked.

"Go figure this out," he said, turning for the door.

"Do you think you'll be all right, Bran?" she asked him, standing.

"I don't think that matters anymore," Bran replied. Astara stayed there as he moved for the door, leaving her behind with the soft music droning in the background. He wished almost that Astara would come, but she didn't, and inside Bran knew it was better that way.

Chapter 25

Lopsis Volgitix

Bran left the alley and crossed the street, knowing that Adi should be at the TBD by that time, and he could hopefully get her away, maybe to talk in the café across the street. When he opened the door, however, Sewey was sitting at Adi's desk, spinning in circles in her chair.

"Oh," Sewey yawned, turning his neck as his chair went on spinning. "There you are. You missed breakfast."

Bran ignored him and looked about, but didn't see Adi anywhere. "Where's Adi?"

"Humph," was all Sewey would say. Everything was very quiet in the bank except for the soft creaking of the chair as he spun around and around, kicking the floor.

"Well, where is she?" Bran insisted.

"Who do you think I am?" Sewey snorted irritably. "I'm a banker, not an information broker! Jolly rot, she called in and said she's just going to work late this evening. Says she's got an appointment to see her uncle in the local jail."

"Her uncle?" Bran asked, startled. "I didn't know Adi had an uncle in Dunce."

"Never met him," Sewey yawned in a bored tone. "She sees him often, though. Usually after the city catches a gnome, I've noticed."

Bran looked up with slight alarm.

"Probably to comfort him, that's all," Sewey went on, oblivious. "I mean, he *is* in the same jail as a *gnome,* and those gnomes do break out *so* very often."

Bran nodded quickly. Sewey spun around a few more times.

"Funny thing is," Sewey said after a while, "the gnomes always seem to break out the *same* day Adi goes to visit her uncle. Every time."

"Maybe she's...scaring them off," Bran said lamely.

"I suppose so," Sewey said, yawning another time.

Bran knew it was a ploy by Adi. She might even be back at her house by then, depending on how long it took her at the jail. So he told Sewey he was leaving, though Sewey was hardly paying any attention at all.

It was hard to lose that strange feeling of being watched, even as Bran took his bike and started off. He didn't see any black vans as he pulled out, and the farther he got from Third Street, the further away the feeling felt, until it faded into nothing. He didn't like it, but he couldn't think of that now. He was too preoccupied with finding a way to Adi's house.

What if she asks me about last night? he wondered frantically. He knew he couldn't tell her. Even with as much as he trusted her, he knew that telling her would only bring more danger, but he also knew he had to find some answers: answers about how Baslyn was appearing to him. If anyone had the answers, it would be Adi.

When he finally found her house, he noticed instantly that her car wasn't parked in front. He told himself it might be in the garage, and it put his mind at rest, if only a little. He started up to the door and gave a soft knock.

The door had a sharp, deep sound to it. It was quiet for some time behind the door without any movement to be heard, and even though Bran tried to peek through the curtains on the windows, they were so thick he couldn't see in. Suddenly he remembered that Polland couldn't go out and he must be inside the house somewhere, so without thinking he knocked a few more times.

"Polland!" Bran said in a hoarse whisper. "It's me, Bran. Let me in."

There was no reply from beyond for some time, then he heard a sudden shifting of the bolts. He heard another click, and another, and then the handle turned and the door swung open, revealing the inside of Adi's house, but no one at the door to greet him.

"Step through," a muffled voice said. Bran couldn't see where the voice was coming from.

"Now!" the voice hissed. "*Before someone sees.*"

Bran hurriedly obeyed, and the moment he stepped inside the door slammed shut behind him. He spun around, and there was Polland, standing on a stool behind the door, with a huge revolver in one hand and a flowery watering can in the other.

"You fool!" he hissed. "What's going through your head, coming in the middle of the day!"

"I'm sorry, I didn't even think about it," Bran apologized.

"Of course you didn't think!" Polland grumbled loudly, hitting his head with his fist a few times. "Because if you would have thought," he jumped off the stool, "you would have kept at home and covered your head with a pillow!"

"I'm very sorry," Bran said, and he really meant it.

"Oh, just lock the door," Polland huffed. "I was just watering my plants, and now that you're here you might as well watch my back for me."

"So Adi really is at the jailhouse?" Bran said.

"Shush!" Polland said. "We got a report at four in the morning: Mrs. Tuskett's husband didn't return from his Sevvenyears sneak-in last night. The informant said she was distraught."

"You think Adi will get them out?" Bran said.

"She already did," Polland said. "Called me earlier: luckily he's fluent and she didn't need me. But I doubt she'll be coming home until later. She's working late tonight to make up for it." His face turned grim. "She does that when she's upset, sometimes works clear through the night and just stays until the next morning. It's her way of dealing with things."

"Is it because of me?" Bran whispered.

Polland looked downward, and Bran didn't need a reply. He felt terrible for all the trouble he had caused for her. Polland finally gave a shrug and kicked the stool into a closet, tossing the revolver somewhere in the back.

"It's a toy," he told Bran. "The gun, I mean. Goodness knows I need it with all the burglars in this town, breaking in at any odd time of the day. You're not the first strange noise at my front door."

"I hope I didn't scare you," Bran said. "I was just coming to, you know, apologize."

Polland took a deep breath and closed the closet door. "Aye, right you are." He turned to Bran. "Adi was pretty upset, you should know. She was so worried, and the lamp in her room was on all night. I don't think she slept a wink, and probably won't tonight either."

Polland's words only made Bran feel worse. However, Polland finally shrugged.

"But when she comes home I'll tell her you stopped by," he said. "I don't think either of us really blames you, do we? It's hard enough for us to hear it, and how much more so for you?"

Polland started toward the stairs with the watering can still in his fist. Bran followed him up, but instead of going for Adi's office, Polland moved for another door on the other side.

In an instant, Bran knew the room had to be Polland's. Hardly a square inch of it was empty of something green: from the floor to the walls, pots and pans filled with dirt and leafy things sticking in every direction. There were trays of sprouts and foliage across the bed, the floor covered with clay jars, tiny trees, and vines growing up sticks in the corners. There were many open windows that viewed the backyard and thus couldn't be seen well from outside, with even more plants on the sills and in wire boxes. The room was filled with the smell of outside air.

"An Archon, no doubt about it," Bran said.

"How can I resist?" Polland said. "This cold and heartless city of Dunce doesn't bear any resemblance to my homeland, so at least my room's a safe haven for me."

"Do you ever get to see your hometown?" Bran asked.

Something passed over Polland's face, like the memory of something sad, but he shrugged it off quickly.

"I don't think I shall ever visit it again," he said wistfully. "These are all I need from there."

Polland nodded toward the long box of plants he was

watering. Bran stepped closer, and instantly he noticed there was something odd about them. Where the flower petals should have been, there were instead mouths, with white teeth and tongues that licked up any droplet of water Polland spilled on its lips as he poured. There were no eyes or even a face, just lips, and the end of them narrowed into a thin stalk in the pot of dirt, just like a flower.

"They're native to my homeland," Polland said, gesturing toward the teeth. "It gets to be quite a chore when you've got fifteen carnivorous Lopsis Volgitix whose teeth need regular cleaning, all while they're trying to chew your arm off."

The Lopsis Volgitix swallowed the water and licked its lips again as Polland moved on to the next one, pouring some water into its mouth and tossing pieces of meat to the others. The other mouths waited anxiously with their teeth apart, licking their lips and stretching toward Polland.

"Careful, now," he warned. "You trip and fall into this box, and you're flower food."

One tried to nip at his arm, but Polland dodged it and stuffed some meat down its gullet. Bran had a hard time looking away, but his eyes caught something on Polland's dresser: a line of photographs of short people in different places. All of them wore tall, conical red hats.

"Those are my family," Polland said, gesturing toward them. "The two together are my parents. Then my older brother Sol, and then younger brother Franklin, Fillip, then sister Nell."

Polland's parents were standing close together on a hill so the photographer could see the famous Claudius Bell clock tower behind them. Sol had a goofy smile and was looking away, while Franklin was busy with a shovel and Fillip was looking up and grinning at a small crow perched on the top of his hat. Nell was in a garden holding a large carrot half as big as she was, and surrounding her were three blank-eyed gnome statuettes.

"What are the statues for?" Bran asked, pointing to them. Polland glanced over.

"Those are signals," he explained. "Gnomes travel a lot, and some kind people put fake statues of gnomes in their gardens as a sign of goodwill, meaning we can pull up a bit of food in return for some magic put over the garden."

He shrugged. "Others leave gnome statues around the house or in a window, so we know who will let us take lodging for the night. Even outside Dunce, it's hard to tell who's on our side."

"Your own network of supporters," Bran said, and Polland nodded in agreement, tossing more food to the flowers. As Polland slid about, Bran couldn't help but stare at his pointed red hat. Polland must have noticed because he chuckled, and Bran looked away quickly.

"No bother," Polland said. "I'm quite used to it. Look here—"

First he glanced about, then leaned forward and slipped his cap off, much to the surprise of Bran. As he had said before, he was indeed bald on the top of his head, though Bran never would have guessed it with his hat on, as he had a ring of very natural hair going around the sides.

"I thought you couldn't take it off," Bran said, confused. Polland looked back at him, and all of a sudden he seemed much shorter, as if a quarter of his size had been knocked off.

"Oh...well, see," he stammered. "*I've* got to get over such things. In case of emergencies, like police blowing through the door. Can't let them see me with it on, can I?"

Polland, though, looked wistfully at the cap in his hands. He glanced at Bran, then back at his hat, and he blushed. He reached behind him and picked up a small washrag and set it on his head.

"*Well...*" Polland stammered, adjusting the washrag under Bran's amused stare, "it *is* bothersome going stark hatless among company...even yours."

Polland held his hat out at arm's length, sizing it up, and he turned it so that the point was facing away from him, and closed one eye, testing the tip of it. He held it out.

"There you go," Polland said, and Bran reached out and touched the surface of the hat. It had the feeling of fur and was very soft under his fingers, but had hardly any string to it at all, like very soft, thin fuzz. It was perfectly red in all parts. Bran turned it over and looked inside of the hat, and saw that it had a hidden form that narrowed inward so it didn't slip on Polland's head, and a golden tag sewn tightly to the side with black lettering that read:

Handcrafted by the *Hatcrafters Duvalle Company*
Material composed of:
10% Reddinn™
10% Spirit
80% Love

"Perfect perfection," Polland said, pouring more water. "Ten percent Reddinn, that's awful spiffy. It's what makes it fire- and waterproof! Spirit always keeps your head in the right place. And eighty percent love? Tops it off like icing on a cake."

Polland chuckled, and Bran forced himself to laugh with him, though the feeling within him was cold. Polland seemed to notice it instantly, because his merriness faded quickly.

"Something's on your mind, isn't it?" Polland said. Bran nodded slowly. Polland put his hat back in place and sighed.

"It's your mother again?" Polland seemed to be able to read Bran's face.

"Tell me more about her," Bran said, starting abruptly but gathering up his courage as he spoke. "Her magic, I mean. Doesn't anyone know how it happened?"

Polland did not answer him for a bit, so that Bran almost thought he might not reply. Bran knew the question had been unexpected, but then he realized that it was probably far the opposite, and Polland had known it was coming and had been avoiding it. After a few more moments, Polland finally shifted the can upward, leaving two of the mouths stretching for more.

"There are legends," he said bluntly. "Few, but they do exist, for I have read them. However, any truth to them would be shrouded in ages of mystery."

"But please tell me," Bran insisted. "It's really all I have."

Polland tilted the watering can forward again and sighed."I have read some that tell of powers like your mother's, of Dormaysan, the darkest and most evil," Polland said. "They say hers is only possible through great and terrible magic used to bestow the powers, magic that probably neither you nor I will ever know of. It takes that magic, but most of all, a choice: one to sacrifice all traces of good magic within her soul."

"But if it's true, and she was unable to do good magic," Bran said, "how was it then that she sent me to the bank vault?"

Polland stared out the window, thinking. The watering can went on running into an all-too-obliging mouth.

"That is a hard question," he finally said. "Research is scarce. But all powers must stay in balance. One cannot bear a magic essence of two halves evil and one half good at the same time: three halves do not make one whole. So for such magic to work, the powers of good must be disconnected and removed somehow and placed somewhere else, like transplanting a heart, so that the evil could replace it. Perhaps if this goodness were kept, as impossible as such may be: maybe, she might be able to do a small bit of good, connecting with what she was before."

Polland shook his head. "But those are deep and mysterious magics, far from the knowledge that I hold."

"But," Bran said, "if my mother also held the powers of the Drimra, could she not have saved a piece of herself in that way, to come back?"

Bran, though thinking of his mother, felt as if his real question was not of her spirit, but of the spirit of Baslyn that haunted him. Polland did not respond, but checked that every mouth had gotten some water. The flowers were standing straight and tall, lips closed and formed into slightly wicked, though content, smiles. He set the can aside.

"Follow me," he said. They crossed the hall into the sitting room, and though the fireplace was out, warm light fell across the books from the windows. As the bookshelf was many times his size, Polland drummed his fingers on the ledge and examined the titles.

"Hmm," he said. "Where is that one with biographies?"

About three columns down, a book on the high shelf slid out, as if pushed by invisible hands. Polland muttered his thanks and hoisted himself onto the countertop, hopping to grab the book. He sat on the edge, paging through, and Bran slid next to him, reading over his shoulder.

"Here he is," Polland said, finding something about halfway through. On the page to the left was a pencil sketch of a man's face, shaven cleanly and with thinning hair. He appeared to be a bit bookish, and his gaze did not entirely look forward, as if he was wary of something.

"This man's name was Karl Yultz," Polland said. "A mage from a century ago. Not many know who he is, though the Drimra look to him as one of the greatest of their missiv."

Polland ran his finger down the biography on the page to the right. The border of both pages was a line of black, and Bran saw from the bunches of pages that they were divided by colored sections. This was a section of biographies for the Drimra.

"Karl had an obsession with death," Polland said lowly. "The mysteries of it, the powers that it held over all creatures, magic and non-magic alike. Death holds the greatest authority over all, the power to end the life of whomever it chooses. Karl devoted his life to the study of how to change it, to manipulate it."

Polland's face went grave. "But death is not a plaything to be toyed with. The realms in which Karl entered were vastly illegal, the powers too great and destructive."

Polland pointed his finger to a section halfway down the page, which read:

Karl Yultz devised, with years of research, a powerful Drimra magic which would allow him to separate his spirit from his material body: to place it elsewhere, into a host, so that in keeping it preserved and separate, the body, while missing its soul, would not age or decay, until both were brought together again; thus giving him the ability to outlive centuries if he desired.

However, that which happened to the spirit, would affect the body as well: and also, that which affected the body would affect the spirit, due to their deep and vast connection, thus meriting the need for his followers hide his soulless, undecaying corpse in a tomb or crypt, keeping it safe from destruction.

Upon discovery, the Mages Council tried and sentenced Karl Yultz for Severe Magic Abuse.

"It *has* been done," Polland said. "It is one of the gravest secrets of the Drimra, such that when one dies nowadays, they are always cremated, so their lives pass naturally."

"But what if a dark mage uses the magic?" Bran asked. "There must be a way to stop it."

"Destroy the object their souls are connected to," Polland said. "'Burn the haunted house,' that's the way they put it. Burn it all so there is nothing left. Fire is the only real way to end the life of a Drimra whose body still has life to live."

Destroy it... Bran thought. For Baslyn to haunt him, something had to be carrying the spirit, something that if Bran found it, he might be able to be rid of it.

But what? he thought, as Polland quietly slid the book back onto the shelf.

Chapter 26
The Good-Bye

Bran was still quiet when he got back to Bolton Road. As he came inside, Rosie rushed past.

"Quick, it's Formal Dinner Night!" she said in a hurry.

"Should we all hide?" he asked.

"No, silly!" Mabel huffed from across the room. "Clean! Disinfect! This house is a dustbin!"

Baldretta was calmly gluttonizing herself with a sack of goodies on the couch. Balder was nowhere to be found, which meant he was most likely in the same place he was ninety-eight percent of the daylight hours. Mabel flew up the stairs as if she was never to be seen again. Luckily, that left Bran and Rosie alone to pick up the house.

Evening came, and the sun began to set, and the street was covered in yellow light when Sewey got home. Rosie was in a rush to get the food made on time, and the platters started to pile up on the table in the kitchen. She finished the main course and got to work with the recipe for Rosie's Famous Whipped Cream Pie. It was a favorite, and Sewey always got double by taking Mabel's uneaten share. Bran washed the pots as Rosie finished with them, and Balder was at the kitchen table, gazing with delight at the dishes.

"Look at all that food!" he said, licking his lips.

"Don't touch any of it!" Mabel squealed. "They're all special!"

She grabbed a scroll off the counter and, drawing the ribbon, let it spill to the floor. She started to check the things off.

"What's that?" Sewey asked, coming in.

"The food to prepare," Mabel hissed. "It's a photocopy of the menu from the Demark's Formal Dinner Night. Everything's completely organic, and not a bite was tested on ferrets."

"Hmmm..." Sewey said. "This Formal Dinner Night may not be so bad after all."

He elbowed Balder. "Who needs Pig-Out Week when you can have Formal Dinner Night?"

They cackled. Sewey went upstairs to change. Rosie curled Baldretta's hair and doused her with hair spray, snapping two earrings onto the bottom of her ears. Mabel dragged Balder upstairs, kicking and screaming, and got him all dressed up also, and ordered that Bran find a suit. He stood in front of the mirror with Sewey and Balder, adjusting their ties in the reflection.

Once the Wilomases were seated and munching away, he and Rosie escaped downstairs to the kitchen to eat, and Rosie surprised him with an entire pan of her Famous Whipped Cream Pie.

"I made an extra one," she said, smiling at him. "We can have it all to ourselves!"

Bran looked at her. Something was very different about the way she was acting. She seemed to glide toward the counter when she got their food, and she set it out on the table, making sure everything was just right. He tried to take his eyes off her, but his gaze wouldn't break free.

She handed him his plate, and then made her own and sat down to eat across from him. She reached for her cup of water and almost spilled it, and Bran noticed that her hands were shaking slightly, and she tried to laugh it off, but he knew something was on her mind.

"Do you like the chicken?" she asked him. "I hope I made it right."

It was delicious, and Rosie had also given him some warm, creamy mashed potatoes and a bit of corn and some steaming gravy to go over the top. The room was quiet, so peaceful that it felt odd, as if Baslyn had been stifled out of the room, and all of the pain and worries that were on Bran's shoulders seemed to fall away. He thought about Adi and wondered if she had gotten home yet, and he wondered about himself, and what was going to happen to him. Very quickly he began to worry about Rosie, and Bartley, and what would happen when she got married and left the house. The idea seemed so foreign that it almost felt like he had made it all up. Would he ever get to eat downstairs in the quiet with her again?

"It's good, isn't it?" Rosie said, and he nodded. He caught her gaze, but she looked away quickly. He saw that there was something in her smile, something behind it she wasn't telling.

"Bran…" she began, but she cut herself off. She looked down at the floor for a moment and stopped eating, and Bran looked at her. But her words just wouldn't come out, and there was a pain that appeared behind her eyes, mixed in with whatever joy and gladness was there.

"What is it?" he asked, putting his fork down.

"Oh, nothing…" She went back to her food, but he could tell

her mind wasn't on it, because all she did was cut her meat up until it was nothing but tiny shreds.

"Bran..." she started again, and her shoulders fell, and she put her fork and knife aside, and looked straight at him.

"Bartley and I are leaving tomorrow, before everyone gets up," she said bluntly. Bran was startled by her words. It felt as if Rosie had just driven a train straight into him.

"Tomorrow?" he whispered. Rosie nodded.

"I've got to get out of here without the Wilomases knowing, or else they'll do something awful to Bartley," she said. "And I can't let them know I'm leaving, because they'll do something awful to me. And I can't let them know we're getting married, because then they'll throw a fit and cause an outcry through the whole town and find some way to ruin it!"

All of a sudden, Rosie started to cry. He had never seen her cry before, not a single time in his life: not through all the rejections at the newspapers, not through all the troubles the Wilomases had made her go through, not through anything. She had always stood strong, but there in front of him, she was crying, and she leaned forward and put her head into her hands, and he could hear her sobbing softly. It pained him to watch her.

"I don't know what to do!" she said. "I think...I'm going to call it off and not get married!"

Bran looked down, feeling as if everything around him had disappeared, and all the problems he had and all the things that were happening to him were absolutely nothing. Slowly, he got to his feet and walked around the table, and he put his arm over her shoulder and held her. She leaned against him, and slowly she stopped crying, until only a few tears came from her eyes. Bran could see she was being torn in two pieces: the Rosie who wanted to stay, and the Rosie who wanted to go.

"How about we go outside," he said softly. "Maybe the sunset will make you feel better."

Rosie nodded, and they left the house. There was just a sliver of the sun down the road, mostly blocked by the house that was on the end. The sun was very wide, however, and threw beams all over the thin clouds, making a spectacular horizon of pinks and blues. Rosie wrung her hands, and Bran looked for a place to sit, but he couldn't find any.

"Over here's fine," Rosie said, going to the edge of the sidewalk where the curb met the road, and she sat down on the edge, and Bran moved next to her. His suit was stiff, but he didn't care, and Rosie stared off to the south, away from the house, not even looking at the sunset, completely immersed in her own thoughts. There was a distant sound, far away, of someone turning on a water hose, and a car horn going off; the sounds almost seemed to soothe the air.

"It *is* strange, Bran," she said, in a soft voice. "How could I want something so much, but want something else just as much also, so that I don't know which way to go?"

Bran picked some grass off the ground. He twirled it in his hands, letting it fall into the wind.

"I guess in times like that," he told her, "the only thing to do is pick one and not look back."

Rosie didn't say anything to him, but just went on staring in the distance, her mind wandering. A cool wind blew on them, but the road was still.

"But I *can't* just choose one," Rosie said with distress. "I can't just go on and change my life, and never look back on the way it was before. I can't just...just move on, when everything has been so much the same for all these years." She fidgeted with her hands. "It's almost as if it *can't* change, it *won't* change; it feels like it should just go on all the way into the future, and never be different, just because..." She sighed softly. "Just because that's the way it's *always* been, and I've been happy."

Bran nodded at her. "But things do change, every day."

Rosie's expression turned grim as she thought.

"I suppose some times are like that," she said. "Whether we like it or not, life just seems to slip through our fingers, and before we know it, the people we knew are different, they've grown up and changed..."

She looked toward the pink clouds on the horizon. Bran's eyes wandered to Rosie's face, and then away again. Her words seemed to go straight to his heart. His eyes began to trace the tiny rocks in the gravel.

"But I hate to watch things change," she said softly. "Sometimes it hits me, and I look around and I wonder... where am I? How did I get here?" She looked up. "It seems like only a day ago I was...I was your age, Bran, and I didn't have to worry about working, or driving, or getting married. Then I stop and I look around and all of a sudden I'm here, thirty-nine years old, and everyone and everything's different."

"But you have to remember," Bran said thoughtfully, "that's not the only thing that changes. I guess we do too, and just don't notice."

Rosie nodded slowly. "But how am I supposed to get married? It'll change everything—every part of who I am, who I've always been!"

Bran looked up at the sky and was quiet for a while. The wind rustled a plastic bag down the street, a quiet scraping in his ears, letting her words settle between them.

"Seems to me," he finally said. "I remember a certain wise person telling me about heroes."

She closed her eyes softly, and a thin smile crossed her face.

"She told me a hero is a person who can be in the depths of despair, with nowhere left to turn," Bran went on. "And they still don't give up."

He turned. "You're not going to give up, are you Rosie?"

She didn't reply, swimming instead in her thoughts and his words. He swallowed hard and gazed in the same direction as she was, and they sat there unmoving, until Rosie suddenly reached out and put her arm around Bran, and hugged him tightly.

"This sunset is so beautiful, I don't think I'll ever forget it, Bran," she said, and she turned and looked at him straight, and he looked at her, and she hugged him again.

"And don't worry, I won't ever forget you either," she said. "Even if that Bartley takes me all the way to the end of the world, Bolton Road will always be my home."

She held him tightly, and even though she was smiling and laughed a bit, he could feel tears going down her cheek.

❋ ❋ ❋

When the sun had finally set and the street was covered in darkness, Sewey called Rosie inside from the window.

"Want to come in?" Rosie asked Bran as she stood. He shook his head.

"I just want to stay here a little longer," he said. She looked a bit saddened, but finally she drew toward the house and left him alone. He sat there, staring into the darkness, until the streetlamp far down the street finally flickered on, casting a dim light that didn't reach him. The moon was high above in the sky, and lights from a few of the houses illuminated the street.

"It is a cold night to be outside," a voice said next to Bran. He did not jerk to turn around, as if a strange familiarity had come over him.

"What do you want, Baslyn," Bran said, looking over his shoulder from where the voice had come. He saw the figure, bent over in the shadow next to the tall tree in the yard, not a few feet away from where Bran was sitting. His face was barely perceivable, though his eyes seemed to reflect the light as his gaze held with Bran.

"You know what it is that I seek," Baslyn said, his voice cool, as if waiting for Bran to surrender to his demands.

"I don't even know what you want," Bran hissed, looking away with contempt. "I don't even know if you're real."

"Am I not real before you?" Baslyn asked.

"I don't know what *is* real anymore," Bran said. He tried to ignore Baslyn standing there, like a shadowy presence that was neither physical nor a simple wandering of his mind. Baslyn's chill seemed to radiate toward Bran, the coldness of death that nipped at his skin. Bran wished that Baslyn would simply fade away like an old nightmare, but Baslyn stood there, waiting.

"Why haunt me?" Bran finally said. "I have done nothing to you. I have nothing that you own, nothing as your host." He shook his head. "I will never help you with the Curse, to bring it back or whatever it is that you want. So you can leave me, and tell your men and Shambles to leave too. I don't want any part in your plotting and magic. I just want to be left alone."

Baslyn did not respond, but Bran was too far in his bitterness to even feel afraid of anything then. It was as if Rosie's words had cast a numbness over him, so that Baslyn did not frighten him, even as he stood so close.

"Then it is an apology I owe to you," Baslyn finally said, though his voice held no remorse. "For I cannot grant what it is you wish. I am bound to you just as you are to me."

"I am not bound to you," Bran hissed, turning to him. "Whatever you want with the Farfield Curse is over."

"Not yet," Baslyn said, his voice still holding the edge of calm control. "When you return me to life, you will have the powers I need to finish the Curse, just as your mother left it."

"And how will you make me?" Bran hissed, his voice staying low. "I think you will find a new person to haunt when you realize I'm not listening to you anymore."

Bran arose angrily, passing Baslyn without so much as an inch between them as he went toward the house. Baslyn did not turn, though Bran heard him give a small, regretful laugh.

"So blind, as always," Baslyn said. "Yet again, I have laid the truth before you, and still you cannot see things as they are."

"I see enough," Bran said over his shoulder.

"And I see enough as well," Baslyn replied. "How is it then

that I see all you see, and hear all you hear, and always seem to be around the next corner?"

Bran stopped, a reaction he could not hide when he heard Baslyn's words.

"You're beginning to see it now," Baslyn said. "How is it that I follow you, and you alone? How is it that you are the only one who sees me and hears my voice?"

"You are lying," Bran said, not turning, not wanting to face Baslyn again.

"Why would I lie?" Baslyn said from behind him. "You know the truth. The host for my spirit lies within *your own self.*"

The words startled Bran even as he realized what Baslyn was saying, the sheer terror of such magic being done upon him. It was almost as if he couldn't believe it, couldn't hold with the thought it something like it—Baslyn's spirit being a part of him.

"So unfortunate." Baslyn lifted his head. "I was sure that if our project was discovered, I would be killed; I knew too much to be kept alive. That's why I had prepared it within you before, as a safeguard, waiting for me to give up my first life." He laughed. "And who could convict you, who would even suspect? My spirit would live on, trapped within you, until the moment when I would emerge with new life."

"I don't believe it," Bran said, trying to deny Baslyn's words, turning on him to search his face for any lie, but finding none.

"You had better start believing," Baslyn replied sharply. "You are as bound to this as I am."

The realization of the truth in Baslyn's words came at Bran like one final, powerful blow being dealt. It was as if Baslyn had just placed him one move away from checkmate, with absolutely no alternatives of escape.

"That's why your men are so careful," Bran realized. "That's why they waited so long, for my magic to awaken: for you to come back. If something happens to me, you will die as well."

"And you finally have come to realize it," Baslyn said, his voice like the hiss of a snake. "But there are many things other than death to convince you." A thin smile appeared on his face. "And though I am bound to your being, invisible to others, I see and feel things no mortal can see or feel—" He looked away. "—even those happening across the city."

Bran stared at him. Questions raced through his mind: *What could he mean by that?*

The corners of Baslyn's lips moved an inch, as if suddenly, he had seen something he liked very much. He turned his head and looked into Bran's eyes again.

"What are you doing?" Bran asked, but Baslyn would say nothing. Fear scraped up Bran's back like claws coming to rest on his shoulders. "Tell me what is happening!" he demanded, but Baslyn only shook his head.

"Where are the black vans?" Baslyn asked.

The question was sudden, and Bran blinked, unable to think of a reply. It was one he had not expected. He tried not to move, but couldn't keep himself from glancing down the street: there was no van guarding it anymore. And he couldn't remember seeing one even earlier, all day. A dire feeling passed over Bran's skin.

"Where are they? Why were they not following you today?" Baslyn asked again.

"I—I don't know," Bran stammered.

Baslyn smiled. "They *were* following you, Bran," he said. "All day, everywhere. Every step you took, every turn you made. They were behind you, watching, always following." Baslyn lifted his head. "My time for freedom has just come closer," he said, and then he was gone.

Chapter 27

The Escape of Rosie Tuttle

Midnight came, and the house was finally quiet.

Sewey snored, and Rosie poked one eye open. He gave another, so she slid out of bed and started for the kitchen. Bartley was already wheeling himself up with the dumbwaiter. It was such a tight fit, he looked partially flattened.

"You get the taxi," she whispered after helping him out, and then went to her room to pack.

A while later, she checked the alarm clock beside her bed. Half past one. She stuffed the clock into her bag and rushed around the room, picking up things and trying to make as little noise as possible. She went to the list on her desk. Everything was checked except one final thing.

"*As you walk out,*" she read, "*do not forget the envelope. This is IMPORTANT.*"

She crossed her arms. "There he goes, ordering me about. I get away from one Mr. Wilomas only to get married to another."

She heard the sound of a car coming outside.

"There's my cab!" she said, trying to contain her excitement as she closed the window. She grabbed her bags and the envelope, and was just switching off the lamp when she noticed one last thing, sitting on the dresser. She dropped her bags and rushed to it: a single photograph in a tiny frame. The picture was of her and Bran, standing together. They had taken it on Bran's birthday the year before.

For a moment she stopped and completely forgot about the car and Bartley. She picked up the photograph and turned it so she could see it straight. Something caught in her throat, but she forced herself to keep her chin high.

"Come now, Rosie," she said. "It's no time for sad thoughts."

She turned and tried to stuff it into her bags, but try as she could, it just wouldn't fit.

"Oh, rot," she said to herself. She swiftly covered her mouth.

"Goodness, fifteen years and Sewey finally rubs off on me!" she said with shock. She zipped her bags back up with effort.

"I guess I'll just have to carry it," she said, tucking it into her pocket. She looked up at her room. It seemed so empty without her things. She shook her head sadly.

"This was a good room," she nodded. "I wonder what strange and interesting people will inhabit it one day."

And with that, she turned, keeping her head high, and started out the door. Her shoes were silent as she went down the stairs. When she got to the bottom, she turned and looked back up, all the way to the top, getting one last look at the place she had called home for so many years. Then she remembered the envelope.

"You," she said, dropping it on the couch, "go here."

She chuckled just a little bit.

"And how I wish I could be here when Sewey finds you," she said to it, and then she turned and marched for the door. But she stopped.

"Wait a minute..." She slowly set her bags down and looked back at the stairs. She bit her lip.

"This is no time to be leaving things undone," she said, and she started back up with slow, intent steps. When she got to the top, she moved for Bran's ladder and looked up. It was awfully high. But she grabbed the sides of the ladder anyway, hoisting herself up. One step after the other she pulled, until her head went into the attic, and she finally crawled over the edge, her face red with exertion. She wiped her brow and spotted Bran's bed by the window. He was sleeping.

"Now's no time to wake him," she said, pulling herself to her feet and slowly walking toward the bed, the boards creaking under her steps. She came to the edge, looking about the room where he had lived for so long, and she looked down at Bran sleeping there. She felt something swelling up inside of her. She was leaving him.

"One day," she whispered, "you will have your very own room, with a new bed and pillows."

She nodded, but she felt her lip trembling. As she stood there, a bit of wind must have rustled through the hole in the window, for the papers on Bran's desk moved slightly. It caused her to turn and look at the rows of drawings tacked to the board next to his bed, and her eyes presently fell on the one that was sitting in the middle of his desk. When she saw it, she drew closer.

It was fresh and unfinished, the pencil sitting next to it as if Bran had intended to complete it in the morning or had stopped abruptly in the middle of his work. The words written on the paper were what brought Rosie to look closer, and what brought tears to her eyes.

TO
BARTLEY AND ROSIE
ON YOUR WEDDING DAY

The letter B was large, just like on all her letters from Bartley, with what looked to be dim markings of flames on its edges that Bran had tried to erase. Below the words was a penciled silhouette of two people holding hands, and around the page, the sketching of an unfinished border. It was more beautiful to Rosie than any priceless painting in the world.

"And one day, you shall have the best drawing paper money can buy," she said, though her voice was choked so much they hardly came out. Quietly, she reached into her pocket, and pulled the photograph of her and Bran out; and with one last look at it, she set it on Bran's desk, taking the drawing and holding it close. She leaned over to kiss him on the cheek.

"There, that's good-bye for now," she whispered, and a tear started to fall from her other eye, but she wiped it away and started for the ladder, holding the paper. She stopped once, looked back at Bran, and then disappeared into the darkness.

If she had stayed a second more, she would have seen a tear go down the side of Bran's face, though he didn't move until the room was silent again. And she was gone.

Bran opened his eyes—awake, as he had been minutes earlier when he had heard Rosie coming up the ladder. He heard the cab pulling from the house. He hadn't slept any, and probably wouldn't sleep at all that night.

He sat up, wiping the edges of his eyes. He couldn't be that way. He tried to tell himself that she was happy, that she would come back sometime, but nothing could ease the pain away. The air in the house seemed to whisper to him, making him wish that Rosie would come back and he would hear her voice in the doorway or cooking downstairs or bringing in the newspaper.

But nothing happened. All was silent. The house felt dead.

He looked toward his desk, where Rosie had taken the drawing he had been making for them. In its place, he saw the silver frame of a small photograph, and slowly he reached for it.

He remembered when the photo had been taken. She had preoccupied the Wilomases with a special dinner party at the Mayor's Palace and had brought Bran out for ice cream on his birthday. It was the most anyone had done for him, as simple as it was, but it was something a mother would have done, if Bran had one. And Rosie had been more a mother to him than anyone else...until the time had come for her to leave.

Bran looked at the photograph again, and, unable to hold the tears in any longer, he fell to his knees next to the bed, clutching the picture. In a rage, he pulled at the magic inside of him, suddenly and viciously. He reached and tore his pillow into pieces, feeling magic coursing through his arms. He grabbed another and tore it also, sending shreds over the bed and onto the floor. His eyes fell onto the photograph next, and he reached to break it also. But the moment his hand touched it he saw Rosie's face in it again, smiling back at him, and immediately his anger was brought to nothing, and he fell against the bed and cried against the side.

He felt a cold hand on his shoulder, and didn't need to look up to know who it was.

"There, there," he heard Baslyn's voice, comforting him, the iciness of his fingertips like a sting against his skin. Bran went silent, feeling Baslyn near him, sitting on the edge of the bed.

"Why have you done this?" Bran hissed, not looking up. Baslyn was silent. "My mother's gone," Bran said. "Now Rosie's gone. And you have cursed me."

"I have not cursed you," Baslyn said. "Your curse comes from your own mother."

Baslyn stroked his shoulder, a chilling touch that Bran could not bring himself to push away.

"Every day, I grow stronger," Baslyn said. "And every day, you grow weaker." He turned to walk away, and as he moved, his form left no reflection in the mirror over Bran's dresser. He stopped in the doorway and turned slightly to look back at Bran.

"It's like Polland said," Baslyn whispered. "There are only two ways to get rid of me: either you return my spirit to my body, or you must die and take me with you."

Bran clenched his teeth together. "I'm going to Adi. She'll find a way to get you out."

Baslyn gave a small, evil smile, knowingly, as if he could see the turmoil within Bran.

"Why don't you answer that first," Baslyn said, nodding his head toward Bran. And in that same moment, Bran heard a sudden buzzing sound. It took him by surprise, so that he jerked upward, looking about, and he saw a soft light coming from the top of his dresser. He rushed to his feet, and saw in an instant that it was Joris's cell phone, the screen all lit up. It was shaking; someone was calling.

Bran looked back up, but Baslyn was gone. The screen on the phone flashed again insistently, and Bran finally grabbed it, shakily flipping it open and putting it to his ear.

"H-hello?" he asked, his voice cracking. There was silence on the other end, almost as if whoever was calling had hung up. He could hear something humming lowly in the background.

"Hello, Bran," a voice said. "I see you made it back from the tavern?"

"Joris," Bran hissed, instantly recognizing the voice of the man who was searching for him.

"Bran," Joris said with fake surprise. "I do believe you have something of mine in your hand."

"What do you want?" Bran demanded, tightening his jaw and keeping his voice to a whisper. He was on his guard. He slid down next to the bed, pressing his back against the side.

"What do I want?" Joris said. "All I want is my phone back, and for you to bring it to me."

"I don't think so," Bran whispered, reaching to hang up the line.

"Oh you won't?" Joris stopped him, and the catch behind his voice caused Bran to stop.

"But your friend was so insistent," Joris said. "She very much wants you to come over and see me face-to-face again."

Bran's grip on the cell phone tightened. "What, who is it? Who do you have?"

His palms were sweating against the cell phone, the side of his face hot from pressing it against his ear. Joris was quiet for a few seconds, moving somewhere.

"Let's have her invite you herself," Joris said. Bran heard the phone slide next to someone.

"H-hello, Bran," came a voice. Bran closed his eyes.

"Astara?" he whispered, but before she could reply, he heard the phone pulled away.

"You led us on quite a chase this morning," Joris said, his voice lined with evil. "But it is easy to follow one when they go to a bookstore."

Bran clenched his free hand into a fist. How could he have been so stupid?

"If you *dare* hurt her…" he said through his teeth.

"I won't do anything," Joris said. "Though my men are getting a little restless." His voice lowered to a deep, menacing whisper. "I wouldn't take all night getting here, or else they might do something we would both regret."

Chapter 28

The Garage

The streets were cold. Bran wore the necklace, but it was cold also, as if the life that had once been in it had left. He gripped the handlebars of his bicycle as he went, the road dimly lit by streetlamps. The world felt dead around him.

Joris's directions were clear: he gave Bran a route across town, into a district of warehouses and garages. The sun was beginning to rise over the horizon—the early morning of Wednesday, April eighteenth. Few cars were about at that time. It was daunting to be in that part of the city, looking at the broken windows and graffiti. It left him cold.

He stopped his bike away from the street Joris had directed, and stole across the rest of the way on foot. Silence was his ally, and the shadows helped to hide him. He knew Joris would have the men watching and listening for him; he couldn't afford to be caught before he got into the building. Every extra second he had was to his advantage.

He quietly came around a corner and saw a tall building with garage doors. They were closed, but there was an open door between them. The windows on most sides of it were busted, and the building was made of thick, undecorated concrete. He knew it was where Joris was waiting.

"What a cheery place," Bran muttered, studying it from across the street. Suddenly, he saw something: a side door. It wasn't much more than an opening, but it gave him an idea.

"Just go through the front," Bran said, remembering Joris's instructions. Did Joris really think he was that foolish? Just let himself be taken? Bran had come too far to give them the upper hand. He had nothing left in Dunce anyway. Astara had already been through enough for him. He was going to find some way to get her out, if it took everything he had to do it.

He came quietly around to the side door, watchful for anyone who might try to spot him. He couldn't sense anyone watching, even as he pressed himself against the side. There was graffiti painted all around the opening, strange symbols and names. It was foreboding, but Bran wasn't going to let his fear get the best of him. Everything beyond was pitch black.

But as he stood in the doorway, he could hear voices. They were in there, so he stepped into the dark. The rising sun was on the other side of the building and left no light to pierce the hall. Bran took a few steps, his hand out in front of him, the sounds getting louder the farther he went. After a few steps, he glanced back, and the outside seemed to be at the end of a long tunnel. He slid his fingers across the dusty wall, feeling his way down the dark passage. The walls were rough, though he couldn't see them. When his foot hit something, he stopped.

Stairs, he realized. The stairway went a few steps and then turned to the right, and he followed it again, winding upward. There was a soft glow that came upon his face the higher he got, and when he came to the last steps, he saw a lone light bulb, yellow and dusty, covered by a metal cage to protect it from thieves. Below it was a thick door, and beyond it, Bran could hear voices.

He pressed his ear against the edges of the frame. Everything around him was yellow from the light; the bulb was buzzing softly, but Bran could still perceive voices through the metal door. He couldn't make out anything they were saying, but he knew who they were. Bran reached for the handle, turning it slowly and pulling the door open an inch.

He was at one end of a gigantic balcony that went around the perimeter of the warehouse. There was metal railing against the edge and stairs at both ends, with doors lining the sides. Dim light shone from windows and a gigantic skylight high above Bran. He stepped out slowly, careful not to make a sound. The balcony was high above the garage, and as Bran came within a few steps of the edge, he saw two black vans far below, and the men standing around.

Bran could hear them whispering below, their voices echoing up and down the chamber. For a moment he was frozen, but then he crept to the edge, leaning against the metal railing for balance. They were all there, talking to each other: Joris and two rough men, one with brown hair and the other with black, and both of the bald men standing close behind, stiff and unmoving in long, dark coats. The vans were parked away from each other, facing toward the garage doors. Bran crouched down so they couldn't see, and underneath him, sitting in a chair, was Astara.

Her hands were held behind her back with thick strips of masking tape, wound tightly around her wrists. She couldn't move, and Joris was bent toward her, anger on his face.

"I won't tell you any more," Astara was saying to Joris, her face set and her voice echoing.

"Why was Bran at the bookstore, then?" Joris snapped.

"Haven't you gotten yourself in enough trouble as it is, kidnapping me," Astara said.

"You're the one who's about to be in trouble," Joris said. "You are beginning to try my patience, and that is something one does not trifle with."

"Are you going to kill me?" Astara returned defiantly.

Joris didn't let it perturb him. "I've killed people for less," he said. "Some of them, never found again. Others, found—though those who found them wish they had not."

Both of the bald men shuffled their feet, shuffling to look about. Bran pushed from the edge, holding his breath—*had they seen him?*

"What's the matter?" Joris asked. Neither of the men spoke.

"I don't hear anything," Joris said. "Marcus: check on Shambles."

The man with black hair moved for the van. Bran stiffened, pushing down with his hands against the balcony railing. He couldn't see through the van windows because he was so high, but Marcus nodded back that Shambles was still there.

Then Bran heard a sound—a low noise coming from below his hand. He looked down and saw a large bolt, holding the balcony railing down. It was old and had come loose, bending out from him pushing against the rail. He quickly pushed away, but by then, it was too late.

There was a loud pop that filled the room, the balcony railing cracking forward suddenly, bolts breaking and hitting the walls. The metal gave a wrenching break and snapped, a loud squeal of metal erupting in the garage as the supports jerked and gave away, tumbling down toward the garage below. Bran gasped, but then he saw something that seemed to make time stop: Astara was trapped right below where the railing was going to fall.

"Astara!" Bran shouted, and he heard her scream. Bran leapt to the edge. He saw the metal falling, as if in slow motion, going straight down toward her.

His breath nearly stopped. But instantly, he felt it leap within him—magic, jumping to his fingertips. He didn't even have a chance to think about it, not a moment to make sure he was doing it right. He saw the metal falling, and he seized the power, and in a split second, he threw it in front of the railing like a cushion between it and Astara. He felt a sudden rush, pushing him, jerking him, as something came from all corners of the room, flying at his command. He felt it moving, and then it was over.

In a second, all sound was silenced.

He looked down, over the edge. Astara was there, gasping for breath, her eyes wide with fright, but far below, hovering above her head, was the metal, barely an inch before it would have hit her. Bran's hand was out, pointed toward her, holding the railing there with magic, and with clenched teeth, he drew his hand aside, and the metal clattered to the floor away from her.

Bran's eyes were wide, his breath quick. As he looked down, his eyes met with those of the men, all of them looking back up at him with shock. They were all frozen in place.

"It's Bran," he heard Joris mutter.

Astara looked back up at Bran, neither of them able to say a word. Suddenly, Joris's eyes narrowed on him.

"So the infamous Bran Hambric finally arrives," he shouted up, stepping back to see better. "I knew you would come. You're too heroic to resist trying to save her." He shook his head. "If I'd have known you'd be stupid enough to try and sneak in, I'd have greeted you at the door."

"Well, I'm here now," Bran hissed. "You can let her go."

"Do you take me for a fool, Bran?" Joris said. "This girl is obviously of some importance to you. After all, you've risked your life coming here with plans to save her, no doubt." Joris shook his head. "A pity."

He waved his hand, ushering the bald men forward.

"Just take him," he said, gesturing, and the bald men stepped from behind him, their coats sweeping the floor. Bran tensed up, but Joris raised a hand.

"I wouldn't move if I were you," he said. He pointed to Astara. Bran heard a click, and his gaze darted to the two men with pistols, aiming their guns at her.

"We might need you alive, but she is another matter," Joris finished. The bald men stepped past, drawing out thin wands: deep, dark black and reflective, each with a fiery red gem on the back. Bran stiffened, and the moment he did, it was as if something broke free inside him again.

Suddenly, he could see it all, as if he had a million eyes, watching the room from all angles. He could see the tiny pieces of glass, shattered in from a window; a sliver of wood lying behind the van from a broken crate; the glass skylights on the ceiling high above them…even the bullets inside the pistols, loaded and ready to kill Astara. He could see it all, feel it all, as if magic had taken over his senses, and he was in every place at once. In a split second, he had it all together again, and it was so sudden of a realization that a thin smile appeared on his face before he could hide it.

"Look at the wand," commanded Joris, and Bran's gaze shifted to the bald man instantly. His wand was leveled at him.

"No magic tricks, boy," Joris said in a low, evil voice.

Bran narrowed his eyes at him. "What sort of tricks do you have in mind?" he said.

"Do as I say," Joris ordered. Bran looked at the wand, though inside his mind was working in overdrive, seeing everything around him. "You will move for the stairs to your left." Joris glanced at the metal stairs going down to the garage floor from the balcony. "You will come to the first step, and stop."

Bran didn't move. The bald man stretched his wand out farther.

"The stairs," Joris ordered, and Bran slowly obeyed. As he came to the first step, his mind grabbed at things, reaching across the room, feeling the walls and the floor.

"Start down the steps, one at a time," Joris said. Bran looked at him.

"Don't try my patience," Joris warned, and Bran did as he said, taking them one by one. The wand stayed trained on his heart, never lowering for a second. The second bald man stood next to the first, unmoving, watching Bran coldly like a machine. Bran kept moving, the floor getting closer, until he accidentally stepped on the edge of a step and stumbled forward. Joris stiffened, and the bald man pushed his wand out farther.

"Stop there!" Joris ordered, and Bran regained his balance against the wall and was still.

"Take the next step and stop," Joris said, and Bran moved slowly.

"Next step," he said, and Bran took it, closer to the floor, keeping his gaze on the wand. He glanced to Astara, with Craig and Joris standing a few paces from her with their guns pointed in her direction, and Joris watching him on the stairs very closely. The bald man raised his wand.

"Do not move your eyes from the tip of the wand, or he will burn them into your skull," Joris warned strongly. Bran glanced at Marcus and Craig. He could feel they knew the extent of his powers all too well, and though they tried to disguise it, he could see fear glimmering in their eyes…fear of *him.*

"Next step," Joris commanded, and Bran moved down another. Three more to go before he touched the ground. His mind began a silent countdown, the magic at his grasp like an all-too-familiar sword, his mind connected to things in a thousand places in the room like invisible ropes coming from him, waiting to be sprung.

"Next step," Joris said, and Bran took it, his eyes not leaving the wand.

"Next," he said, and Bran stepped downward. He could hear Astara's breathing echoing in the garage, as if she could feel something about to happen. There was one step left.

"Now step to the floor," Joris said. "And do not let your eyes—"

But it was too late. The instant Bran's foot touched the floor, he was ready, and it happened.

He glanced at the roof.

In a second, he pulled it with his mind, wrenching at every crack in the skylights above them. There was a sudden sound, a deafening smash that filled the garage like an earthquake breaking out. Everyone jumped, turning their heads up for a split second, and Bran didn't waste it.

He leapt against the wall, under the shadow of the balcony, as he heard a shattering noise above his head, and the giant windows high above them crumbled. Every piece started to fall, a million jagged shards plunging down like knives toward the men below.

"Look out!" Joris roared, the men diving for cover as the shattering sound drowned out his voice. And then, Bran noticed with horror that Astara was still in the middle of the room.

It was as if time had stopped. She was juggling against the tape that held her. He saw it split across, broken with her magic the instant the men were distracted. But Bran could see the glass, coming down above her, inches away from her flesh, falling faster than she could move.

He almost shouted, but he couldn't. He heard her scream, but in that moment, he moved, throwing his hands out in front of him, and with it every ounce of magic he could muster, shoving a wall of anything he could place between her and the wall of glass raining down.

She screamed and fell. In that second, he saw the glass striking the floor softly at first, and then in a sudden storm, breaking like raindrops into tiny fragments...but he held the magic.

His hands were shaking, but he could see Astara, lying with her back to the floor, completely still. Her eyes were open. Above her, directly where his outstretched hand was pointing, was a shimmering sheet of air, so thin that Bran could barely see it save for the glass shards bouncing off. The glass continued to fall, and Bran held the magic, and Astara didn't move, strips of torn tape still stuck to her wrist. He felt a piece of glass bounce from the floor and scrape across his skin. He winced, but didn't move. He saw the glass embedding itself into the roof of the van, striking into the concrete floor.

And then, it was finished.

The only sound in the room was that of the rushing sheet over Astara. Bran held the magic a second longer, and then let it go, the sound of it disappearing and leaving them all in silence.

And scattered across the floor, like millions and millions of tiny diamonds, were shards of glass, glimmering in the light from the open ceiling. Bran couldn't move. He looked up. Across the room, separated from him by the glass, were the men.

They all looked back, aghast: some of them fearful, some of them disbelieving. Astara rose to her feet slowly, surrounded on all sides by glass, like a river trapping her on an island.

Everyone was silent.

Bran glanced to his shoulder, where the glass had struck him and a thin line of blood was gathering down his arm. He wiped it away, and looked back to the men.

"I asked you," he said, "what sort of tricks do you have in mind?"

"Enough from you!" Marcus muttered under his breath, and before anyone could stop him, he raised his pistol and shot at Bran in rage. Bran didn't even have time to notice the bullet before the magic made him move, the powers already around it.

He raised his hand and swept it to the side as if brushing something out of his face, slinging the bullet into the left headlight of the closest black van. The light shattered, and Bran glanced to the van quickly. His gaze penetrated the front window, to the back of the van: glowing there were the eyes of a creature he had hoped never to see again. It was Shambles, staring back out at him—trembling, it seemed, with fear, though strangely held there and not moving.

"Put that away!" Joris hissed, striking Marcus's arm, before turning to Bran. "There is no point in fighting any longer."

Bran didn't move.

"You're outnumbered five to one," Joris said, sweeping his hands around from across the river of glass. They were at a stalemate, neither daring to make a move. Joris stared at Bran, and Bran stared back, his gaze not wavering. Finally, Joris looked away.

"Well, if it must come down to this," Joris said, "we still have one card higher than you, and that is this girl here."

Joris waved his hand, and Craig and Joris raised their pistols. But instead of fear, there was anger in Astara's eyes.

"You can't kill me," she said, and their heads turned to her.

"What did you say?" Joris asked her. She tore the last shred of tape off her wrist, tossing it aside and sliding her black wristband down.

"You can't kill me," she said, her voice stronger. Joris narrowed his eyes at her.

"We most certainly can, from two *different* angles," he hissed.

Astara glanced at Bran, and his eyes widened.

What are you doing? he screamed at her in his mind, but she only shook her head and looked back at the men.

"I said you can't kill me," she said, and Joris spun back to her.

"I am quite tired of your mouth," he hissed. "One more word and that is the end of you."

Astara opened her hands. "*I'm waiting.*"

Joris nearly erupted with rage. He jerked his hand out.

"Kill her then!" he shouted. Marcus and Craig looked at her and hesitated.

There was no fear in her eyes, even with the guns leveled at her.

"Shoot her, now!" Joris yelled again, and both men fired. Bran didn't have a second to think, a second to pull at the magic, before both bullets were gone, flying toward her.

But suddenly, there was a rush of movement, something flying from across the room—an explosion of wooden shards, as the bullets were slammed aside by the impact of a wooden crate hitting them full force. The crate flew across the room, colliding with the wall and taking both bullets with it. The crate exploded into dust and wood, spilling all over the ground. The eyes on both of the men widened.

"She's a mage too!" Marcus gasped. Craig shot again, the sound bursting in Bran's ears. Astara was faster, though, her arm a blur of motion in a circle, and the bullet clattered into the wall beside her. Craig shot again, but she was ready for him and held her hand up. The flash of the bullet was stopped one inch from her palm and hovered right in front of her. She looked at it, then to Craig. He was sweating. She struck the bullet out of the air with her hand, like she was swatting a fly out of her face. Bran was taken aback at what he had seen her do.

"That was impressive," they heard Joris say, and both spun to face him again. "I must commend you both. You're well versed in magic."

"Thank you," Bran said, keeping his voice steady and cold, though inside he was in awe at what he had seen Astara do.

"However," Joris lifted a finger. "You have yet to see any displays of magic on our side."

He waved his hand, and both of the bald men stepped forward from behind him. Bran felt something inch its way under his skin, a fearful part of him becoming unsure.

"You may be able to stop a bullet," Joris said. "Or two bullets, or ten bullets. But you are no match for trained mages—" He smiled, staring at Bran. "—and you know it."

Bran tried not to let his gaze falter, but he felt that it was in his eyes, and Joris had seen it. Bran held his ground, not moving back.

"I have two mages who will do my bidding," Joris said. "When you play with fire, someone's bound to get hurt."

Both of the bald men leveled their wands at Astara. She froze, looking from one to the other. Joris turned to Marcus and took something from him, and then turned back to Bran.

"So, Bran, you've got a choice to make." Joris held up what was in his hands. It was a pair of handcuffs, with a small box attached to the side of it. Bran recognized them instantly: *magecuffs.* The same that the police used to keep people from doing magic.

"You can put out both your wrists and get in the van," Joris said. "Or you can have your wrists forced in front of you and your eyes burned out of their sockets to keep you submissive." Joris shrugged slightly. "You choose."

He narrowed his eyes.

"And please choose fast," he said. "Or else we'll have to load your unconscious body into a crate in the back of the van."

Instantly, an idea leapt into Bran's mind that he had not thought of before. It was so abrupt, it sent a chill down his spine, and so unexpected, it made his thoughts of escape a thousand times louder again.

Chapter 29

Inside the Black Van

Bran stood there, staring at Joris and his men from across the garage. None of them moved.

"Your choice," Joris said, holding the handcuffs out farther. Bran took a deep breath. He stared at them—but in the same moment sent his mind toward the van. In an instant he could feel it, his fingertips brushing against the metal, as if he could wrap his hands around its form.

"Choose, now," Joris said, louder.

Bran's mind was so wrapped in what he was doing, Joris sounded only like an echo. Bran pushed at the magic, forcing more out like a rope, wrapping it around the van, feeling it, moving inward. His mind touched the van and its workings, and suddenly he could feel down into the deepest parts of it.

"Bran!" Joris shouted, and the sudden sound gave Bran a start, and he looked back to Joris. Their eyes met for a moment, and Joris took a step backward.

"I'm through with this," Joris shouted. "He's doing magic—take him!"

Both of the men jumped forward, but it was too late. There was a flash of motion, and the headlights on the van burst on. A screech of tires came roaring in their direction. Joris fell away as the van came hurtling toward him, and Craig and Marcus jumped, but the edge of the van clipped them, throwing them into the wall.

Bran felt his inner senses scream out, and he dove against the wall as well. A sudden flash of heat shot by him. He gasped and covered his face with his shoulder, and felt it burn the back of his sleeve. He saw the bald man, his wand outstretched, and the end of the wand begin to glow, brighter, and another flaming arrow of fire came hurtling toward him.

He didn't have a chance to pull for magic, and dove out of the way, fire leaving a burnt circle on the wall. The bald man shot again, and Bran moved; another came, and Bran lifted his hand, bringing the magic between him and the fire and deflecting it back. The bald man saw it and leapt out of the way, and it hit the wall where he had been standing a second before.

Bran saw a flash out of the corner of his eye, as the second bald man shot a beam at Astara. Bran couldn't get his magic there in time, but she was ready, and the shards of the crate she had slammed into the wall came hurtling across the room again, piecing themselves in front of her like a wall in a split second. The beam of fire slammed into it with such force she was almost pushed off her feet, but she held it, until the bald man released the magic, and the pieces of wood fell to the floor, burning and filling the room with thick smoke. Bran coughed as the smoke began to rise, gathering high above them and going out the destroyed skylights.

"Get behind the van!" Bran shouted to Astara, coughing. They started to run, keeping to the path the van had made through the river of glass.

"Stop them!" Joris shouted, pulling himself from the floor, his hands bloodied from the glass on the concrete. Both of the bald men lifted their wands, fire launching like cannonballs toward Bran and Astara. Bran dodged it, and the ball went past him; Astara wasn't ready and she tripped, her palms slamming into the metal. Bran was next to her in an instant, and he pulled her around to the other side, using the van as a shield between them and the men.

"Are you all right?" he gasped. She nodded quickly. Bran heard a shot ring out and something slam into the wall behind him. He heard Joris start shouting and the men run across the room, kicking the glass shards. The room smelled of blood and sweat and fire mixed together.

"We can't hold them all off," Bran gasped. "You've got to get into the van!"

"How will that help?" Astara hissed at him. Bran looked through the windows of the van and could see the men coming toward them.

"I don't have time to think about it," Bran said, and he reached forward and jerked the door open. Luckily, it was unlocked, and she jumped in. Bran leapt in after her into the driver's seat and slammed the door behind him, searching the control panel on the door. It was filled with too many buttons, and he didn't have any idea which one to press.

"How do you do the locks?" Bran shouted urgently.

Astara reached across him and pounded all the buttons at once, and he heard the locks click.

"What do we do now?" she said. Bran looked about the van for anything that might help them. It was filled with bags of equipment, all tightly closed. He saw a gun lying on the bench in the back, and the men through the window, running toward them. Suddenly, he noticed keys in the ignition.

Oh, no, Bran thought. *Don't even think about it.*

But he heard the men shouting, closer; and he looked over his shoulder and made up his mind. He lunged forward and turned the keys, and the engine roared to a start.

"Bran!" Astara gasped. "You're not actually going to *drive* the van!"

"I think I am," Bran said under his breath, still not sure of what he was doing but reaching forward to shift the gears anyway. He pulled it into drive but slipped down too far to the next gear and had to pull it back up again.

"Get out of there!" Craig shouted, running to the side window. Bran blocked him out, trying to remember how he had seen other people drive.

"It's in gear," he said out loud, checking. "Brakes off…"

"Get out of that van!" Craig yelled, and he seized the door handle. It was locked, but Bran heard it click from the inside, and it made him jump and slam his foot down on the pedals. The van flew forward and threw him in his seat.

He spun the wheel and found himself going toward the men. They leapt out of his way as he tried to slam on the brakes, but pushed on the gas instead. Astara shouted as they ran over a pile of wood, nearly throwing Bran from his seat as he struggled to make the van go straight.

"Turn the wheel!" Astara screamed, and Bran jerked it about the other way.

"Watch out for the doors!" Astara shouted, trying to hold onto her seat as Bran went hurtling toward the garage doors.

"That's where I'm *trying* to go!" Bran yelled over her. He pushed on the pedal, holding his arms against the steering wheel as the garage doors sped closer and closer, nearing impact…

"Hold on tight!" Bran said loudly, and he tightened his teeth together, the sound of the engine roaring in his ears like jets, and he slammed into the doors.

The impact hit him hard, but he saw the doors explode out in front of him. The pieces went flying outward, some of them into the road and other parts hurtling over the top of the van. Bran didn't stop to look back, spinning the wheels around as the van shot off onto the street, filling the road with noise.

"Watch out for the building!" Astara screamed.

He skidded onto the curb and came onto the sidewalk and fell back onto the street again. He heard a roar behind them and looked over his shoulder—the second van had just erupted from the garage, its front window broken.

"Speed up, Bran!" Astara shouted, and Bran spun back around and slammed on the gas. The engine gave a loud noise, and the van lurched forward, with Bran struggling to keep it in the road. He swerved around the corner and nearly hit a streetlight.

I'll never complain about Sewey's driving again, he breathed to himself, his palms becoming sweaty as he gripped the steering wheel. The van gave a lurch as he ran onto the curb, but he held on as tight as he could. He slammed into some boxes on the edge of the street, sending them flying as he sped past, and Astara turned and looked out the back window.

"They're gaining on us, Bran!" she yelled over the engine.

Bran tightened his teeth together. "I have *no* idea what I'm doing," he muttered to himself, pressing on the gas again. He saw a turn and took it. There were tall buildings all around, cars parked on the side of the road.

Great, Bran thought. *Obstacles.*

He didn't dare slow down but tried to navigate between the cars on the side of the road. He saw a glimpse of something in his rearview mirror, but he knew that he didn't have time to hesitate for a second or they would be lost. He swerved to miss another car and turned a corner.

"Do you have any idea where to stop?" Astara asked him. "They're gaining on us big time!"

Bran glanced at the rearview mirror again. The van seemed to be right up next to them. He winced. They were pulling up next to them, slowly but surely.

"The moment we stop they've got us," Bran said. Suddenly, there was an enormous clash behind them, and the steering wheel was nearly pulled from his hand. He felt an impact in the back of the van and nearly lost control.

"They're running into the side of us!" Astara yelled. There was a sudden gunshot, and the taillight of the van exploded, glass going everywhere across the street. Bran felt the van collide with them again, pushing them farther against the side of the road. He pulled the steering wheel, fighting back, and he felt them hit again. He sped faster, moving in front, and suddenly the van behind them swerved to the left and off onto a side street, out of view.

"We lost them!" Bran shouted, excitement rushing up over him. He checked every mirror—they were gone. He let off the gas pedal and looked over his shoulder, still trying to slow the van.

"They're going to catch up with us ahead," Astara said quickly, turning around to face the front. Her voice was low. Bran glanced in her direction.

"Quick, turn off onto this street," she said quickly. Bran eased into the turn.

"And your turn signal's on," she whispered. Bran glanced at the levers and hit one of them, and the clicking noise stopped.

"Thanks," Bran said, searching the roadway ahead. He entered onto a street with a few cars, pressing on the brake so he wouldn't attract any attention. He was coming up to an intersection and immediately recognized where he was.

"The bank is right up here," he said aloud. "We'll drop the van off at the corner, I'll call Sewey and get the police over here."

"But we'll both go to jail!" Astara protested, turning toward him. "If they find out we're mages, we're done for!"

"No, *you* won't be," Bran said. "You're going back and acting like this never happened."

"What?" Astara said. "I can't just go back to the bookstore. What if they follow me there?"

"Where else are you supposed to go?" Bran said, gripping the wheel as he came to a crossing.

All of a sudden, there was a screech of tires to Bran's left. He turned, but it was too late, as the second black van came lurching out from the darkness of the intersection and slammed into the side of them full force.

Bran's neck was snapped around, and he felt a jolt of pain go through his shoulders. Suddenly, the world around him began to spin. The van went flying through the air before it slammed into something: a light post on the street corner. He heard Astara scream, and then the engine of the van give a loud burst and died out.

He shouted, but in a split second it was over, and he was no longer on the road, the van having skidded to the side with the impact. The hit had been light but Bran was in pain, and the inside of the van was immediately engulfed in darkness.

"Astara!" Bran shouted. She grabbed his hand and he saw her there—she was all right.

"Quick, get out!" he yelled, and she kicked her door open and fell onto the sidewalk, pulling him with her. Bran scraped his elbows against the concrete as he fell. The area was bathed in the brightness from the second van's headlights. He heard the men shouting and jumping out but didn't waste a second, pulling Astara to her feet and running from the crash.

A bullet burst against a building next to Bran, spraying pieces of brick. They were on Third Street. The place was cold and abandoned, and the businesses weren't even open yet. Bran heard more shouting behind him, and jerked Astara across the street. He was running as fast as he could, the men coming around the van. He was nearly out of breath, his lungs pounding. The door to the bank was getting closer with each step, and he dove toward it.

"Hurry!" he shouted, grabbing the handle. He didn't even think if it might be locked before he was slamming into it, and both he and Astara fell through the door. He slammed it shut behind him, turning both locks as quickly as he could. Instantly the sounds of the street outside were drowned out. He bent over, gasping for air.

"We're safe," he said between breaths. But then he heard a sound.

It was a gasp, from across the room. His heart almost stopped.

He looked up, and there was Adi, standing behind the desk, pale and lit by a single lamp. She was staring at them, her face filled with shock.

"Bran?" she gasped. He only stared back, feeling the blood run from his face. He opened his mouth to speak, but nothing would come out.

"What's happened?" Adi gasped, but the moment the words left her mouth, the entire front of the bank exploded.

Chapter 30

Fire and Books

Everything seemed to happen in slow motion. Bran could feel the flame coming at his back; he could see it reflected in Adi's eyes. He could sense it behind him, and in a split second, as the bricks and wood and metal blew inward toward him, he leapt to the side, hitting Astara, both of them falling to the ground.

He heard it going over him, rushing like a train over his head. He could feel the dust; he saw Adi falling. He saw the windows blown away as the front wall of the building on both sides of the doors exploded into flames, and behind the explosion, he could see the shadows of two men, stepping toward the openings they had just created.

Before Bran could react, he felt rough arms seize hold of him, slamming him against the wall. Astara was pushed next to him, then Adi, all three of them lined up.

Joris held Bran, pressing his lips against his ear. "Thought you could get away, did you?"

He tightened his fingers around Bran's arms, like claws that threatened to tear his flesh. "No one escapes: not your mother, not Clarence, and not you either."

"But I'm the one you need alive," Bran said through clenched teeth.

"We'll see how close we can get with you as well," Joris said. He turned to Craig and Marcus, holding Adi and Astara against the wall with their pistols drawn.

"We're going back to the bookstore, across the street," he hissed. "There'll be police crawling all over this bank in five minutes."

Bran was pushed toward the doors. The doorway was there, its frame still intact, but on both sides, where the windows had once been, there was nothing but bent pieces of the frame of the building, parts still smoldering from the fire. Bricks hung loosely at the sides, glass broken in everywhere, and dust and shrapnel thrown through the walls and onto the sidewalk. Both sides were left to nothing but gaping holes. Adi coughed as Craig wrenched her around to follow.

"Wait, please," she said. "If you want the bank's money, I'll get it for you."

"I'm afraid you're mistaken," Joris hissed. "I don't need more money. I need this boy."

Suddenly, Adi jumped away from Craig, jerking something out before they could react. She held it out in front of her, brandishing it, and Bran saw that it was her wand. But in the same instant, before she could even call a single magic, both of the bald men reacted, their wands out and leveled with her. It caught her by surprise, and she froze. Joris jerked Bran closer.

"What is this?" he hissed at her. Adi's eyes were wide, her wand shaking. "You drop that or they'll kill you, mage," Joris said through clenched teeth.

Adi hesitated, looking at Bran, and what she held in her eyes made his heart wish he was anywhere else but there. She was terrified for her life.

"Put it down, Adi," Bran finally said. "He's right."

She swallowed hard, debating, but finally she dropped the wand. Instantly, Joris took it.

"Put her in magecuffs," he ordered Craig. "That will keep her silent until we get across."

Adi didn't fight them, even as Craig slid the handcuffs over her wrist. He spun a dial on them, and she didn't make a sound, but in a second, all strength seemed to fade from her face. She stumbled, unable to stand, and Craig caught her, holding her tightly as they stepped out.

They crossed the street, but there were no cars. Part of Bran wished the police would show up or someone would see, but he knew none of the shops were open that early and the police wouldn't arrive in time. They were pushed down the alley until they reached the bookstore. The door opened when Joris pushed on it. Bran guessed it was still unlocked from when the men had kidnapped Astara.

There was a small lamp in the middle of the floor, which Joris turned on, and it cast light in a circle about them. Bran was forced to stand, and Astara was shoved across from him. Craig pushed Adi into a chair and wound the handcuffs around it so she couldn't move. The others stood guard with guns and wands, keeping them from any method of escape.

Joris spun to Bran and held his hand out. Bran stood there, not sure what to do. Joris insisted.

"Come on, you're here now," he said. "Hand me the phone."

Bran reached in his pocket and fumbled with it, holding it out. Joris smiled and reached to take it, but with a sudden spin of motion, he grabbed Bran's wrist and jerked him forward. Bran was pulled from his feet, his arm was twisted behind his back, pain shooting through his nerves like a thousand needles puncturing him at once.

Joris pushed him forward, throwing him to the floor against a crate. Bran didn't have a chance to catch his balance before his face hit the floor, his arm scraping against the side of a box. He coughed and hit his head, and he felt blood running from his nose. He spun around, trying to stand but falling against the stack of crates. He touched his face and got blood on his fingers.

"So we're all here now, aren't we?" Joris said. The lamplight threw shadows under his eyes. "We are all gathered here today," Joris began, "because one boy decided to cause trouble."

"Just take me and let them go," Bran said. "You have what you want with me."

Joris turned to him. "These two have caused enough trouble for me already." He looked at Astara. "You with your knowledge—" He turned to Adi. "—and you for having this wand. I don't like mages getting involved in things. It gets complicated."

"Listen," Adi said, her voice weak. "Neither of these children have done anything wrong. If you want a mage, I'm the one you need."

"Oh, no," Joris said. "It is him that we need." He pointed the wand at Bran. "That's the boy who is behind all of this."

"But why do you need him?" Adi asked, her words almost slurring in weakness. Bran looked down, not meeting Joris's eyes. He felt as if Adi was watching him, looking for answers.

"This boy," Joris pointed with the wand, "is Bran Hambric, surviving heir of Emry Hambric—the boy who was taken and hidden by his mother, hoping to keep him from us." He nodded. "Inside of Bran is something we need, something your MIPs could not find."

He looked at Bran. "Inside Bran is the *spirit of Baslyn.*"

Bran's gaze met with Adi's, but then he looked down, unable to hold it.

"You are lying," Adi said to Joris weakly. "Baslyn is dead."

"You know of Baslyn?" Joris turned to her. "Clearly more has gotten out than we thought."

"It doesn't matter what I know," Adi replied. But Joris slowly stepped closer, until his shadow fell over her. She looked up at him weakly, unable to move as he stared down at her.

"Actually," he said in a deathly voice, "I think it means everything."

Polland jerked awake in bed, sweating. He looked about the room for intruders, his senses immediately alert.

"Who's there?" he called, reaching into the shadows and curling his fingers around the gnarly edges of his dark, wooden wand. He drew it closer, almost the size of a small knife to him, a tiny green gem on the back end wrapped in root-like twists. *Something was not right.* He could feel it.

He climbed out of bed, taking his wand with him; he drew the tip of it closer to his lips.

"*Silmali felami iensida,*" he whispered, blowing on the

end, and instantly, a small light like a candle flared up within it, illuminating the floor and the plants in a circle around him.

"Working late, is she?" he said. But it had been too long for her to be gone. Something was not right for her to have never come home—something more than what he had thought.

He went through every room in the house, shining his light into every corner. No sign of Adi. He stopped his search at the bottom of the stairs and slid to sit at the bottom. He blew on his wand again, and instantly the light went out.

"Where are you?" he asked, though he knew no answer would come. He was so worried he didn't know what to do. Something deep inside of him felt sick, as if there was something deeply wrong going on, and Adi was at the center of it. He looked through the high windows and closed his eyes, thinking. He murmured a few prayers into the air, trying to calm his soul as he sat there, and when he had finished, he lifted his head and knew what he was supposed to do.

"Enough of this waiting," he said. "If Adi's in trouble, I might as well get into some myself."

He struck off for the garage and threw the door open. It was mostly empty with coverings over the windows so no one could see in. There were a few boxes to the side, and sitting in the middle of the floor was a car, the one they saved for emergencies. It was smooth and small but still much too large for him to drive. He took a deep breath.

"I'll just have to wear my driving stilts," he said. He opened a cabinet and pulled them out: long, narrow sticks with little shoes on the end to make him taller. He strapped them onto his feet and teetered his way to the car, stacking old phone books onto the driver seat before hopping in. He set his wand in the seat next to him.

"I have a feeling I'll be needing you very soon," he said grimly as he pulled out.

Joris stepped away, and Bran sat up straighter, following him with his eyes.

"Wait," Bran said quickly. "What are you doing?"

Joris looked at him. "We're taking *you* with us."

Craig pulled Bran roughly to his feet, forcing his hands behind his back. Bran fought his arms free, but Joris lifted a finger and pointed at Astara.

"She's the first to go if you fight us," he said, and Bran stopped and let Craig slip the magecuffs onto his wrists. He tightened them until Bran winced as they bit into his skin, and he felt the weight of the black box on the side, though Craig didn't switch it on.

"What are you going to do with us?" Astara demanded, standing up. The bald man grabbed her shoulder, forcing her down roughly. Joris looked at her and thought for a moment.

"We'll be taking you along to make sure Bran stays reasonable," he said. "And with both of you, we'll get to the border gate and leave this city for Farfield."

Joris kicked the lamp and it shattered, putting the light out. He stopped in the doorway, and Bran looked at Adi, still handcuffed to the chair. There was no strength left in her eyes.

"You," Joris said to her, "are too dangerous to keep alive."

Bran opened his mouth to speak, but Craig grabbed hold of his shoulder to stop him. He was pushed next to Astara in the open doorway. Joris stared at Adi for a few moments, then nodded.

"I think it best to kill you now," he said, with so little emotion it seemed almost as if it was more of a chore than anything else to him. "Then burn this place so there is nothing left."

"No!" Bran said. "She's not part of this!"

He struggled, but one of the men slammed him against the wall, knocking the breath out of him as the other gave Joris his pistol.

"Sedate those two and take them out," Joris said. Astara fought them and screamed, and the room erupted into mayhem. Bran fought against the handcuffs, grabbing for magic to pull the gun as he fought their hold. But he was already too late, as Craig lunged at him, wrestling him against the wall for the dial on the magecuffs, and in his other hand was a rod with two prongs, energy crackling between them. He touched it to Bran's skin, and instantly Bran felt energy shoot through him, coursing down his spine and through his nerves, carried all across his body. He went limp, hitting the wall.

He looked back and tried to speak, but nothing would come out. Adi had bowed her head, closing her eyes, as if she had been ready for it, had known the last moments had come. The men pushed Bran toward the door as Joris lifted his gun, striking Adi across the head with it, so that she went completely limp. Then he pulled the trigger, and a single shot rang out.

The sound echoed in the cloud that was drifting over Bran's consciousness, the men dragging him away, struggling to hold Astara down as Craig pressed the prongs to her arm, and she also went limp. Joris had already turned his back before Adi slumped over.

"Burn this bookstore," Bran heard Joris say, and as his vision faded, he saw the bald men lift their wands from the doorway, and orange flames spew from the tips toward the crates of books. And that was when all around him went black.

As Polland drew closer to Third Street, he instantly knew that something was wrong. From blocks away, he could see flashing lights of police cars. He felt his face go pale when he saw it.

"Adi..." he gasped. He turned the car a street before the bank, getting ready to park it. This street was abandoned, but he could hear the sirens. He hurriedly hid the stilts in the backseat.

"I'll take the alley," he whispered to himself. "Watch from across the street."

He swept a coat over himself. He reached to take off his cap, but hesitated.

"Come on Polland, you're over such things..." he told himself. But he couldn't help looking up and down the street to make sure no one was looking, and then he slid his hat off and threw the hood of the jacket over his head, just in case.

"I'm just a short man, taking a walk," he said aloud. He shuddered and started toward the alley, but then he heard a sound and his shoes scratched to a stop. A van was coming in his direction. He lowered his head and pressed against the bricks, and in a second he began to shrink instinctively, his skin hardening as he did like mud washing over him and drying. He became stone, almost invisible then as a van burst from the darkness of the alley next to him—and when he shriveled back to his regular form, he saw it turning at the end of the street. *A black van.*

His eyes followed it. He could smell smoke. Something was not right.

He checked the street—no one was coming. Spinning, he dashed into the alley, following what he smelled and going deep into where the van had emerged from.

"I'm coming, Adi," he told himself desperately, praying deep within him she was still alive. He could feel her, a deep connection. He was getting closer. Smoke drifted in the air, and as he ran down the alley he could hear it crackling and burning, steadily getting closer. He began to run when all of a sudden his senses wrenched him around. He stopped—it was a door.

"What?" he asked into the darkness. His senses as a gnome were much stronger than that of others: he could smell the smoke, and as he stretched his fingers out, he could feel heat radiating from that direction. He gritted his teeth and ran into the door, and was immediately thrown backward off his feet. He hit the ground and the air was knocked out of him. *Locked!*

"No door will stop me!" he challenged, and he grabbed his wand from his coat and lifted it, and instantly the ground next to him crumbled as two giant roots spewed out like hands with a hundred fingers each, the sound of them cracking through the dirt like strings being ripped.

"*Seeizu!*" Polland ordered, pointing, and instantly the brown roots flew past him, grasping the frame of the door and growing into it with tiny pieces of ivy. Polland tightened his jaw, mustering all the strength he had in his mind.

"*Reemovu!*" he said, and the roots leapt back, ripping the entire door from the frame. It gave a loud crack as the hinges split, and as the door fell, a burst of smoke poured out from behind it. Polland leapt to the entrance, and the roots slid back as if dead, leaving the door buried halfway. The bookstore was filled with thick smoke, so much that even Polland had to bend over to catch his breath. Flames lit up the room, burning crates like columns of fire.

"Adi!" he called, his face burning in the heat. "Where are you?"

There were several crates gathered around in a circle, burning, some toppled over. He started for them, waving his wand as he did.

"*Bimea wirate!*" he ordered, and instantly water sprayed from the tip of his wand like a strong hose, rushing over the fires and calming the flames as he ran. He coughed, and when he came around the corner, he almost stumbled. There was Adi, bound to the chair, blood on her forehead. She was unconscious…or dead. He couldn't tell.

"Adi!" he gasped. He fell next to the chair, trying to revive her. She was limp.

"What evil was this?" he said, his eyes going wide. He felt a deep anger rise within him. His eyes stung with the smoke and heat. Something fell next to him, and he covered his face with his shoulder, shouting as fiery ash fell around him and burned his skin.

"Come on Adi, stay alive!" he pleaded—though even as he pushed her, she drew no breath.

Sewey woke up with a strange feeling in his bones.

"Great rot!" He jumped out of bed and tore through the house, looking up and down for Bran and Rosie, calling out their names. He lifted every couch in the house and even checked in the bushes. They were nowhere to be found. He made so much racket that Mabel and the children woke up, and they all gathered at the bottom of the stairs in their pajamas.

"*Gone!*" Sewey said, wringing his hands. "I checked the kitchen, the basement, even the grandfather clock! Bran and Rosie are *gone!*"

He looked up the stairs again. All of a sudden, the house seemed very hollow, as if their voices were echoing in an empty chamber. Balder and Baldretta looked at each other.

"Well, we can't just stand here!" Sewey burst. "Now that they're gone, who's going to cook breakfast? Who's going to feed the cat? Who's going to iron my clothes and get the mail and set the table and wash the dishes and—"

"My goodness!" Mabel gasped. "You can't expect *us* to do those things!"

"It'd kill us!" Balder squealed.

Sewey gulped and put his hand on his forehead. He felt sweat forming there just thinking of all the chores in the house.

Come on Sewey, he thought. *All you have to do is get to work, and you're free...*

All of a sudden, his eyes caught something sitting on the couch.

"Oh?" he said into the air, and he stepped forward in a great bound and caught it up.

"Hmmb?" Baldretta asked, wobbling over to him.

"This, Baldretta," Sewey replied, "is an envelope."

"Open it! Open it!" Balder demanded. Sewey carefully tore the edge and shook the envelope over his hand. Two thin slips of paper fell out neatly into his palm. He squinted.

"*To my dear brother…*" he read, narrowing his eyes with rage. "*Bartley…basement…dumbwaiter…Rosie…eloping…this week!*"

Gradually, as the story came out, his voice became more and more of a painful, pathetic moan. "Great rot! Bartley and Rosie are secretly getting married!"

He was about to fall into a dreadful fit, when he saw something at the bottom of the letter.

"*P.S. I had planned to give this to you when you learned how to handle money correctly, but I had also hoped to give it to you before the end of time.*"

Sewey narrowed his eyes on the paper.

"*P.P.S. Don't spend it all in one day,*" Sewey read. "What do you suppose he means by that?"

"Maybe the other paper!" Balder said, and Sewey took it out. He almost fainted on the spot.

"Great Moby!" he shouted. "It's a check for exactly *half of the inheritance!*"

Mabel shouted and Balder screamed, and Sewey leapt in the air and kissed the check.

"We're absolutely *positively* rich!" he burst. He danced in a circle, waving the check in the air like a madman.

"Oh, goody, goody!" Balder squealed. "Megamus Maximus, here I come!"

"Oh, goody, goody!" Mabel screamed. "I'll *own* the medicine companies!"

"Oh, goody, goody!" Sewey cried. "I've got a whole week of parades *and* an elephant!"

Baldretta sat on the floor, throwing her hands in the air in exasperation. And as the three Wilomases danced around in a circle, one might have heard the mountain of bills in the dining room give a great sigh, as they would once again go unpaid.

Part IV

Chapter 31
Into the City

Bran found himself falling in and out of consciousness, his thoughts fleeting and disconnected. It made him feel sick inside, and even when he tried to gather his senses and think of escape, they rushed from him, taunting him until he forgot everything.

He found himself awakened once, when the van came to a stop in an unfamiliar part of Dunce. Everything was hazy to him. His back was to the last row of seats in the van, his eyes facing out the windows on the back doors. He heard Joris talking, then rolling his window up. Bran could barely move, but for a moment he thought he saw something familiar, speeding in his direction down the dark road behind the van. It looked like Adi's car.

"Adi," he whispered, though hardly anything came out of his throat, and as soon as he said it, the van began to move again, leaving the border gates of Dunce behind.

He didn't know how many hours passed before he awoke again, every muscle still aching. The first thing he noticed was that his necklace was gone; the men must have taken it. He fell back against the seat and looked at Astara. She was still unconscious, lying against the side of the van, the lights from outside playing against her face as the van rushed along the road. They were passing through the middle of a thick city, black storm clouds making midday seem almost like night, the streets lit by the headlights of cars and the lamps overhead. There were tall buildings all around, higher than any in Dunce, glowing with lights in the windows and down the sides, towering over them so high that on some, Bran couldn't see the top. The roads were empty except for a few cars and buses. Everything was very different from Dunce.

"Where are we?" Bran asked softly. Marcus heard him and turned to look.

"Welcome to the big city," he replied lowly. "We're in Farfield."

"Farfield," Bran said with alarm. He could remember Adi telling him of it: the plotting of the Farfield Curse that his mother had been a part of, the raid on the dark mages in the same city. It was seared into his memory. This was where his mother had committed her crimes.

Bran watched the buildings as they passed, the van turning down another street. Every building seemed to glow with different colored lights, blues against black and gray. The van drew closer to the hub of the city, slowing at one building jutting into the air and blocking the view of the sky.

"What's that?" Bran asked. Marcus glanced at him, but didn't answer for a moment.

"That's where we're staying," Marcus finally replied. "The famous Farfield Tower."

Bran sat up straighter to see. The building had rich, black marble sides at the bottom, windows and a set of glass doors glowing from the gigantic sprawling lobby. He could see many people inside, eating at tables and booths. He saw the tops of red felt hats as well as the heads of people in formal attire, though the gnomes appeared to have been seated a distance from the humans. The windows above ground level were tinted so darkly they almost appeared to be of mirror-like stone, and a piercing blue light shone up the sides, causing the building to appear even more imposing from the ground.

"Banks, restaurants, malls," Marcus went on. "That's all at the bottom and underground. Upward are hundreds of hotel rooms and office complexes."

"How can you afford this?" Bran asked.

Marcus shrugged. "It's Joris's money," he said simply. The van slid across a few lanes toward the building, down a street and into the alley beside the skyscraper. Immediately, they were thrown into the building's shadow as they moved out of the lights, and Joris parked away from the corner.

"Get ready to leave," Joris said. He was about to continue, but then he stopped, and his gaze shifted to look over Bran's shoulder.

Instantly, Joris went very still. Bran turned his head and saw what Joris was looking at: a black car with tinted windows crossing the street they had just taken. There was a painted device on the door, like the head of an eagle leaning forward, made of simple dark blue lines. Below the eagle were the words Magic Investigational Police. After it had passed, a second one like it followed. All eyes were on the street until both had disappeared.

"What do we do?" Craig asked lowly, his voice holding an edge of anxiety.

Joris hesitated. "You," he pointed to Craig, "watch Bran. And you," he pointed to Marcus, "watch the girl. We'll take them in quietly through the left elevator."

"What if they're waiting for us?" Craig voiced into the air.

"They're just on patrol," Joris assured them. Bran let his breath out slowly as he listened to them moving equipment, briefcases clicking shut as they packed. Every few minutes, he saw Joris look up, checking the windows, watchful for anything. They weren't taking any chances.

Stay calm, Bran told himself. He would need all of his wits to get them out of this—if anything, to get Astara out alive. He glanced in her direction. Her eyes were still closed.

"Wake up," he whispered. He nudged her lightly, and she slowly blinked her eyes open. "Be quiet. We're here," he said in a low voice, and she sat up straighter and looked out.

"Where are we?" she asked.

"Farfield," Bran said, glancing at the men.

Astara shook her head, trying to clear it.

"They took us all the way?" she said with disbelief. Before Bran could say anything else, Craig pulled the back doors open and cold air flooded in. He felt the wind nip at his skin.

"Out, both of you," Craig ordered. Bran moved first, his feet unsteady on the hard concrete. He tried to balance himself, but his legs were weak from being in the van, and he tripped forward. He was unable to break his fall, and slammed straight into Craig.

The man shouted, stumbling backward and hitting a parking meter. Bran stumbled into him, but Craig lashed out, throwing Bran to the concrete. His shoulder hit, and he gasped with pain.

Astara broke away and rushed to Bran, but Craig seized hold of her. In a flash, she slammed into him with her shoulders, so suddenly that he was taken by surprise. He fell and shouted, recoiling and bashing the side of his hand into her face. She fell to the pavement next to Bran.

"Stop!" Bran shouted, trying to sit up, but Craig was already moving to kick her on the ground. At that moment, Joris came rushing around the van.

"Craig!" he hissed, and they froze. Joris looked at him wide-eyed.

"Are you out of your mind?!" he hissed. "Get them up, before someone sees!"

Marcus caught hold of Astara's arm, dragging her to her feet. Craig was in obvious pain, but he took hold of Bran's arm, clenching it so tightly it burned Bran's skin. Joris looked at Craig, then Astara, but there was no pity in his eyes for her bleeding cheek.

"There won't be any of this inside," he said sharply. One of the bald men and Shambles left with the van for the parking garage, and Bran could see the side where the metal was damaged from the crash in Dunce. The rest of them followed Joris to a door. He slid a key card in the lock, and they shuffled into an enormous, empty ballroom, tables all about with chairs resting in perfect alignment, and place mats and floral arrangements ready. There was an empty stage on the far end, but the place was dark, the only lights coming from small lamps attached to the walls, reflecting off the darkened chandelier. The rich red and gold carpet masked their footsteps as they crossed the room unhindered and came to another door.

"Take those off them," Joris said.

Bran felt his arms go free.

"No sudden moves, either of you," Joris warned sternly. He swiped his key card again, lights flooding in from the hallway when the door swung open. Bran blinked in the sudden brightness, but they continued without pause. He could hear the babbling sounds of people nearby, and the carpet ended and was replaced with marble. He managed a glance and saw that the lobby faced the front of the building, the ceiling towering above his head and glass doors facing the streets outside. There were people moving about, some of them glancing at him, but only for a moment.

As they rounded the corner, Bran saw doors for eight elevators, four on each side, with two separate doors for fire stairways. Bran didn't even have a chance to turn before the elevator doors had slid shut with them inside. It was smooth and quiet, and Bran felt himself being brought higher, the elevator speeding up as it went.

When it finally came to a stop, the doors slid apart, and everything behind them was shrouded in darkness. Gone were the lights from downstairs; instead, they had come to a dark, wide hall, with empty walls and a thick door on the far end. The air in the room was different than below—a processed, hotel air. Joris moved for the door across the room, sliding his key card across the panel like a knife, and the handle gave a click.

He pulled it open, and Bran was forced through.

The room was somewhat circular, with an indention in the floor that went down a step. There were no lights on, but Bran could almost make out every detail, for the walls on either side were lined with clear glass that reflected lights from the city below. Bran couldn't help glancing out, and when he did, he saw that they were high above the streets, the city like the design of a map.

In front of the windows were tables, and on them were piles of things: notepads, books, newspapers, videotapes. Nearly a dozen computer screens were flashing and making soft sounds. He saw a laptop like Adi's, the program on the screen split up into four windows, and in the windows were views from different security cameras.

His eyes caught movement at the far end of the room, next to a set of doors. Almost as if she had appeared out of thin air, Bran saw a woman.

He turned quickly. She had been watching him. She was tall and looked to be in her early thirties at most. Her skin was pale, and she had piercing, cobalt blue eyes, her hair long and black with a streak of white going down the side, almost as if all the color had been dispelled from one lock of it. She wore dark clothing and was beautiful in a way—a dark way. Bran's eyes darted away from her face, and they caught on something that was tucked in her belt: a smooth, black wand with a diamond tip that glittered and threw colors.

"This," Joris hissed to him, "is Elspeth."

Bran looked back and couldn't tear his eyes from her. She was staring at him with a cold gaze, so powerful that anyone would tremble under it: unmoving and solid, so thick that he could not break it. It seemed to burn at his eyes, holding him fast, until he was so lost he couldn't pull away.

"*Just like your mother,*" she spat in anger. Bran jerked his eyes away, trying to hold himself together.

"I can feel it in you," she said. "So arrogant, yet so weak..."

"And yet it took six people to bring me here?" Bran said, and the instant his words were out Craig wrenched his arms back, so hard that Bran winced with pain.

"It's only right to escort the carrier of our master's spirit," Elspeth said, watching the pain on Bran's face closely, her words unfaltering. "Those men and myself are all that is left of our great society, save for a few others who are hardly significant, hiding in fear for their lives."

"You were lucky to have escaped." Bran said, spitting his words out.

"So you know then?" she said with some curiosity in her voice.

Bran stood up straighter. "I know everything now," he said.

"Well then," she said, "you probably know it was my shot that killed your mother."

Bran felt a sudden fury leap into him, but Craig squeezed tighter on his arm so he was kept from moving away. He clenched his jaw in rage, wishing that he could reach for magic then, but knowing that if he did, they would not hesitate to hurt Astara in return.

"It was good to see her dead after all those years," Elspeth said, taking a deep breath, as if recalling a fond memory. "I always hated her."

Craig held Bran still, and Bran tightened his fingers into fists; but in an instant, he forced himself to release them. Elspeth watched him with interest, and then switched her gaze to Astara.

"And who is this?" she asked. Joris stepped forward.

"The hostage," he said. Astara did not flinch under Elspeth's gaze. Shambles whimpered in the corner, hiding in the darkness, so much that Bran had hardly noticed he had joined them.

"And you?" Elspeth said, turning. Shambles pushed against the wall, his eyes wide with fear. Suddenly he fell down, curling on the floor, hiding his face from her. Bran could hear him breathing and choking, a rasping sound... the same sound he had heard on the roof, nights before. Bran saw something on Shambles's wrist—a bracelet with a green stone. The rock was glowing slightly, and Shambles hissed with pain, tearing at it, as if it was burning him.

"Pleassse!" Shambles pleaded.

Elspeth shifted her gaze from him, and he went limp.

"We shall do this quickly," she said, starting across the room. She stopped in front of the door on the left and pulled it open. Behind it wasn't another room, as Bran had expected, but another door, thick and gray. It made him think of the door to the vault at the bank, and it was very much set apart from the rich furnishings around him. On the right side of the door was a small screen, and below it, a keyboard. The screen flashed the words Enter Password.

Elspeth typed a long string of keys, and when she finished, Joris stepped forward and typed another password in. There was a rush of air, as if the pressure of the room inside had changed. The door gave a pop, and Elspeth pulled it open. Bran felt cold air rushing out. A sudden white light flashed into his eyes, pouring from the room beyond. He tried to shield his face, but Craig held his arm tight. The air was so strong it stung.

Bran felt himself being pushed forward. Beyond the door was chilling, as if they had come to a refrigerator, and his breath came out as a thick mist. Elspeth moved in front, blocking Bran's view, and he almost tripped down a step as the floor lowered a few inches from the room before.

Elspeth stepped to the side, and for a moment Bran was blinded by a thick white light. It poured from the ceiling and seemed to fall onto the middle of the small room like a waterfall. He squinted, just barely able to see. But as he stepped inside, suddenly he recognized it.

Everything was white, like a sterile plastic that held no life within. The walls, the floor, the ceiling—all of it shaped like a small, round shell of a room. As he looked over it, Bran knew where he had seen it: the same room as when he had first put the necklace on. The same place he had seen the corpse, awakening and falling, the same place he had seen for barely an instant.

And as Bran looked up, his gaze moved to the one object in the center of the room: it was a bed, and in the bed was a body.

Baslyn's corpse was dressed in the same black robes Bran had seen so many times. His hands were at his sides with his palms turned upward, his eyelids closed with dark circles around them, his flesh completely preserved. His face seemed to be tortured even though he was limp—a strange face that Bran couldn't draw his gaze from. There was a cowl drawn over the top of his head. Though Bran had seen him so many times already, staring at his corpse sent a chill down his back in a way even the coldness of the room could not.

"Here is the body of Baslyn," Elspeth said in a loud voice, and Bran's head turned upward to look at her. She was staring straight at him, the light from the ceiling against the top of her head.

The room went still. Everyone stared at Bran, waiting for him.

"But one is not made of body alone," Elspeth said, looking from Bran to the others. "His soul must reside within him to make him whole. One cannot survive without the other."

She looked back to Bran. "One cannot *live* without the other."

Bran swallowed hard, and he felt as if his hands were beginning to tremble. He looked from her to the body, and then back to her.

"And in this child," she said, her gaze unwavering. "Many years ago, Baslyn hid his spirit...so that if one day, he might die in body, his spirit would live on..."

She looked upward. "...to one day return."

All of a sudden, she lifted her right hand and gestured toward Craig. Bran stiffened, but he felt the rough arms of the man release from his sides. In a moment, he was free, and his mind snapped before he could react. He felt the magic jumping up, so quickly that it seemed to burst, and in a split second he made his move.

He spun around and raised his palm outward to Marcus, slamming the magic into his body full force. Marcus didn't have a chance to react. His body lifted from the ground, hurtling through the air into the wall behind him.

"Run, Astara!" Bran shouted, hearing the pistol clatter to the floor.

She dove to the side, and Bran didn't hesitate a second, reaching his hand toward the gun, pulling it toward him; but the second his mind touched it, a hand seized it up.

"Don't move!" Elspeth shouted, and he froze, his hand still out. And as suddenly as it had begun, all chaos ceased.

She was on the other side of the bed, Astara in front of her and standing painfully still—for in Elspeth's hand was the pistol, and its end was touching the side of Astara's head. Astara's eyes were wide. Elspeth's other hand tightened around the side of her head like claws.

"If you move," Elspeth said, "I pull this trigger, and she dies."

She pushed the pistol closer, deeper, and Astara's head was forced to the side with the pressure on her skull. Elspeth's fingers made indentions in Astara's cheek. Bran felt his hand wavering in front of him, shaking as he looked at Astara. In a second, his mind released, caressing the bullet inside the pistol, feeling it. Could he stop it? Would he risk it? Astara met his gaze. There was fear behind her eyes, and it dug into Bran's heart. She was afraid to die. Very slowly, Elspeth's finger tightened on the trigger.

"All right," Bran finally said, dropping his hand to his side. "Don't kill her."

Elspeth smiled. "You *are* just like your mother."

She gestured toward the bed with her head, "Now touch his hand, and it will all be over."

Bran looked at the body on the bed. It filled his entire being with dread, fear, horror…every terrible feeling at once. He felt as if he was being pushed from it by a magnet, repelling him; but at the same time, another part of him being pulled closer, almost sliding him off his feet in its direction.

"Touch your hand to his," Elspeth demanded, her tone hardening.

Bran hesitated, unable to move. Elspeth let out an impatient sigh, and she glanced at Marcus. He came forward, and with the back of his hand, slapped Astara across her face, so that she screamed in pain.

"No!" Bran said, but when he moved toward her, Craig blocked the way, a cruel smile on his lips. Elspeth wrenched Astara's arms back further, holding them apart.

"Touch his hand," she hissed. Astara pleaded with her eyes, trying to tell Bran not to do it.

"*Touch Baslyn's hand,*" Elspeth spoke again, and Bran felt as if her voice was just an echo.

"Bran, don't do it!" Astara screamed all of a sudden, struggling to get free. But Elspeth only pulled her closer, pressing her hand over her mouth. She screamed and fought, but Bran could do nothing. He pushed against Craig, but the man only stood there like a wall.

"*Now,*" Elspeth commanded him, the pistol in her hand not falling for an instant.

Astara only fought all the more, her arms held tight; Joris and the bald men stood to the side, emotionless. Elspeth looked to Marcus again, and he hit Astara across her face a second time.

"Wait!" Bran shouted, trying to get past Craig. But the man only stood there, pushing Bran back, laughing brutally as he did. Joris looked at Bran, his teeth tight together, and there were tears of pain in Astara's eyes as blood ran down the edges of her lips. She was crying, and Elspeth pressed the gun to her head even harder, digging it into her skull.

"Please, don't hurt her anymore," Bran said, his voice breaking. "I'll do it."

Bran couldn't bear to look at Astara any longer, and Craig pushed him toward the bed. His hands shook as he turned toward Baslyn's body, fighting the dread within him. He looked down into Baslyn's face, so dead and empty. Every part of Bran's soul cried out, screaming to make him leave. As he looked at Baslyn's corpse, he felt as if something he had swallowed was trying to be free, rushing around inside of him to get out. He closed his eyes for a moment, and when he opened them, his hand trembled, shaking as it moved slowly to Baslyn's palm... hesitantly, the seconds ticking by like decades...

His hand came closer and closer, until it was right above Baslyn's own—his skin bathed in the whiteness of the light above.

"Do it," Elspeth said in a whisper.

And he did.

And the moment his skin touched with Baslyn's, he felt a rush inside.

Chapter 32

The Spirit Awakens

It jerked from him, pulling and quickening all at once—electrifying, as if something was born inside of him, a weight flying from his shoulders. And in that same second, Baslyn's hand jumped and grabbed Bran's in his own.

Bran gasped, and he heard Baslyn gasp also, pulling the air in deep. He clutched Bran's fingers tightly, squeezing so hard that Bran felt his bones grinding against one another. Bran bent over with pain, and suddenly, Baslyn's eyes opened.

"Baslyn!" Elspeth said in a startled breath. Bran looked at Baslyn and saw his face: his eyes open, his skin white...but now, alive.

All of a sudden, Baslyn shoved Bran away. Bran fell backward, hitting the cold floor, and in an instant, Baslyn's shadow was over him. Bran looked up and saw his face, blocking the light.

"You deserve to die, Bran," Baslyn said with a sudden fury, looking as if he was about to lash out at Bran with rage.

"I have done nothing but defend myself," Bran said.

"You have done nothing at all," Baslyn spat, "except cause trouble since the moment I allowed your mother to bring you into this world."

"I kept you alive," Bran said. "Isn't that enough?"

"You kept me a *prisoner,*" Baslyn hissed and he took a step forward.

Bran fought the urge to edge away as Baslyn came closer, his shadow falling over him—a powerful, real shadow.

"If it wasn't for you," Baslyn said. "I would have had no reason to hide."

He turned his back on Bran, his shadow sweeping over the floor.

"Elspeth, Joris." Baslyn nodded at each of them and then turned to the other two men.

"Craig and Marcus," he said. "I see you have stayed behind with me."

He turned again, toward the door, where Shambles was lurking in the darkness. The moment Baslyn's eyes met with his, Shambles began to tremble.

"Shambles," Baslyn said, "you've finally come to see me."

Shambles trembled, and Baslyn nodded. "If it wasn't for you, they never would have found the boy, and for that you deserve a reward."

He glanced at Elspeth, and she jerked her wand out, slinging it across, almost as if to hit Shambles from far away. In the same instant, Shambles was knocked from his feet, and his head hit the wall with a sickening thud.

"Look: your magic is just as good as when I left you," Baslyn said to Elspeth. Blood dripped from the side of Shambles's head. Baslyn began to walk away as if Bran didn't even exist.

"Baslyn!" Bran said, and he stopped. He turned slowly but only stared at Bran.

"Should she punish you as well?" he asked, spitting the words out. Bran clenched his teeth.

"You've lost," Baslyn said, opening his hands. "It is the end. They brought you here, just like I said from the beginning."

He leaned forward, close to Bran, lowering his voice.

"It's *over,*" he said. He held his gaze, then gestured to Elspeth.

"We're keeping the two of them," he said.

"We have a warded room," she replied in a low voice.

"You're a step ahead of me then," Baslyn said. "Put them inside and we'll see if they can think of a way to escape."

Craig took Bran's arm, and he didn't fight, watching as Baslyn and Elspeth stepped through the door, and he heard Shambles weeping on the floor.

Bran and Astara were escorted to the main room and to the door on the right. With a sudden movement, Craig shoved Bran forward. He tripped and fell onto the carpet of the room, and Marcus pushed Astara in beside him.

"We'll check to see your progress later tonight," Craig said with a sneer. "Try the windows first—we're at the top of the highest building in Farfield, and it's a long drop."

He laughed, slamming the door. Bran let his breath out. He felt tired all of a sudden, as if all his strength had finally left him, and he could fight no more.

"Bran?" he heard Astara's voice in the darkness. He searched the floor, sliding his hands across the carpet until he found hers. He grasped them tightly and pulled her closer.

"Are you all right?" he asked, unable to see her in the dark.

"I'm still here," she said, her voice low and close to his ear. He heard her voice crack.

"I tried, Bran," she whispered, her voice breaking again. "I really did."

"No, it's over now," Bran said, comforting her. "It's not your fault."

She shook her head. "No, Bran, back at the bookstore," she said. "I tried to use magic, to catch the bullet before it hit Adi. I had it for a second, but I think I was too late."

There was such deep sadness in her voice that Bran felt a sting through his heart. He moved next to her and pressed his back against the wall, and they were silent, letting the darkness drown them out. It was very cold, and Bran shivered. He felt Astara trembling next to him, though he couldn't tell if it was because of the cold or the fear he knew she was hiding.

"I thought I could get to you and help you escape," Bran said. "I guess I couldn't. Maybe if I had been more careful, they wouldn't have followed me to the bookstore in the first place."

The darkness took over again, and slowly, Bran began to make out shapes in the room. He could see a large table beside a dresser against the wall, and the door to a closet. He saw a window that had thick curtains covering it, and he stood and moved for it.

He slid the curtains aside and looked down. He had to take a step backward at the sudden sight below. As his eyes fell upon the people and the cars, like little toys down below, he began to feel dizzy. All the buildings were lit with bright windows. He let the curtains fall again. His entire being felt so tired…

"Astara, why did you even care at all?" he asked abruptly. He turned from the window, sitting down next to her. "You could have left me alone to solve this by myself a long time ago—or never even helped me in the first place."

She was silent for a while. He knew she was troubled, fearful for her life and on the brink of despair.

"I guess I knew you needed me," she said simply.

Bran took a deep breath, because he knew it was the truth. He never would have made it that far without her.

"We've got to keep going," he whispered. She closed her eyes, and to him it almost seemed that Astara, for the first time since he had met her, had lost all hope. It pained him to see her that way, and he felt powerless because he had no means to comfort her.

As he leaned against the wall, unable to say much more, he slowly began to hear faint noises vibrating behind him, so that in the dead silence of the room he thought he could almost make out voices. He turned slightly, craning his neck to the source of the sound, feeling the rough plaster of the wall with his fingertips as he listened.

"Do you hear that?" he whispered.

Astara nodded quickly. Bran pressed his ear to the wall, and Astara did the same, sliding softly to find the best place, their breath slowing so they could hear better. For a few moments Bran didn't hear much, but he finally found a part of the wall that seemed to be less muffled, so that when he pressed against it, he could just barely make out what they were saying in the next room.

"Over here," Bran said, and Astara slid closer, pressing her ear to the spot beside him. Bran concentrated hard on the sounds, trying to make words from them.

"I don't care about you," Joris was saying, anger in his voice. "I don't care about the boy or any of this. I've held up my end of the deal, and now I want my investment back."

"Your investment is irrevocable," Baslyn hissed. "There is no refund to the amount you have put into the Project. Farfield is not yet complete."

Joris seemed to be mulling over this, for he did not speak for a few moments.

"I *tire* of Farfield," Joris said strongly. "Where has it gotten us? Where has it gotten *me?*" He let an angered breath out. Have you no concept of the life I could have had if I had never once fallen for your scheme?"

"You entered the deal willingly," Baslyn said, his voice plain and controlled. "You entered it with the risks. You entered it with the chance of benefits."

"I see no reason not to kill the boy now and leave this place," Joris hissed. Bran's eyes met with Astara's, a clear look of panic crossing both of their faces at Joris's words.

"You know the powers he holds," Joris continued. "You know them just as well as I do. Why risk a second time when he could be another Emry?"

The room beyond was left to such clear, angry quiet that Bran almost felt that they were finished talking. Baslyn said nothing in return, his silence seeming to anger Joris more.

"My promised benefits have yet to be reaped," Joris finally hissed. "We made a deal—"

"The deal has changed, Joris," Baslyn cut him off. The room

was again abandoned to silence, as Joris seemed to think over Baslyn's words.

"We will see," Joris said, his voice low enough that Bran almost didn't catch it, and then he heard the door of the other room opening roughly. Bran and Astara pushed from the wall.

"What are we going to do, Bran?" Astara asked.

"I don't think there is much we can do," Bran said, as he heard the door from behind the wall close with a darkly resounding thud.

Nearly an hour passed in silence before their door was flung open.

Bran and Astara looked up, squinting in the light from the doorway. It was Craig.

"Come with me, Bran," he commanded.

Bran arose, and Craig locked the door again. Bran saw Marcus at a desk, a briefcase open beside him. He loaded some equipment into it and started for the elevator. Craig came to the next door over and pulled it open, gesturing inside.

"He's waiting," Craig said, and Bran mustered up his strength and stepped through. The door closed behind him, and the light disappeared. Bran was left in deep darkness, but as he looked around, his breath was taken away.

On the far half of the room, the walls were lined with glass windows, with hardly a space between them. Bran could see over the edge of the building, all across the city, the lights sprawling below. It was a dazzling sight in the darkness, the room dimly lit by the reflection. Outside the windows in front was a concrete ledge long enough for a helicopter to land, and high above, through the glass, he could see the shape of the moon. It was a crescent, just like his necklace, though seconds later black clouds drew over it again, choking its light away.

In front of the windows was a desk, the top of it shining like a dark mirror. Bran swallowed hard when he saw Baslyn's hand on the side of the chair behind it, the back turned to him.

"Come in, Bran," he heard Baslyn's voice say. "Sit down."

Bran hesitated but knew it was too late to fight now. With slow steps, he crossed the room and came to one of the chairs. He forced himself to sit across from Baslyn.

The chair turned after a few moments of silence, and Baslyn looked at him closely. Bran tore his eyes from the face, not willing to look at him any longer.

"Can you not look at me without feeling remorse?" Baslyn asked, catching Bran by surprise.

"It is a horrible face," Bran clenched his teeth. "You are the reason for all that happened."

"And what do you believe happened?" Baslyn asked him.

"Everything," Bran said, not hesitating for a moment as the anger welled up within him. "My mother's death. Astara, Adi, me—*all of it.*" He slammed his fist on the desk with anger. He looked away, even though he could feel his eyes upon him. There was silence between them, and neither of them moved, until Baslyn reached to the side for a smooth glass cup and poured some clear water into it.

"Would you care for anything to drink?" he asked.

Bran kept silent.

"I don't believe you've had anything to drink for a long while," Baslyn said. "In fact, you haven't slept for a long while as well." He poured the water. "Nor have you done much of anything, except *run* from everything."

"I haven't run from anything," Bran said, looking up. "I have looked for answers to questions that have haunted me all my life."

"And you were surprised," Baslyn said, "when you found that *I* was the answer."

Bran looked down.

"Are you sure you don't want anything?" Baslyn asked again. Bran finally reached for the cup, drinking it down furiously as his thirst overtook him. He set it down, and Baslyn filled it again, and Bran drank it until it was empty. When he had finished, Baslyn smiled contentedly. They were silent for a long while, Baslyn watching him closely. It made Bran feel uncomfortable, but he tried to ignore it, knowing that Baslyn was trying to break him.

"You *are* much like your mother, you know," Baslyn started, and Bran's gaze met with his.

"You want to save the world, to make up for crimes you didn't commit." Baslyn leaned forward. "You want to be the hero—to right *her* wrongs."

Baslyn's words had been unexpected, because inside, Bran knew they were true.

"I wonder," Baslyn said, "if you've ever seen what your mother looked like?"

Bran's heart skipped a beat. Without thinking, he leaned

forward, eager to hear more. Baslyn caught the movement, and Bran forced himself back again.

"I-it doesn't matter," Bran said, trying to act as if he didn't care, but it was too late.

"Oh, but it does," Baslyn insisted. "You thirst for it. It eats at you every day."

Bran tried to show nothing through his face, but he knew he couldn't hide it.

"When I first saw her, I could hardly believe that someone such as her could be so intelligent," Baslyn went on. "She was so young at the time…"

Baslyn moved his hand, and it distracted Bran's gaze. Very swiftly, Baslyn slid something across the table: it was a solid white wand all the way to the tip, cold and reflective like glassy snow, and on the back end of it was a long, jagged blue crystal, shaped almost like a knife There was something ancient about it. Wrapped around the sharp crystal were molded shapes of two solid white tigers, their mouths open as if attacking each other, holding the crystal between their fangs. Baslyn gently touched the tip to the side of the cup, and it gave a small ring.

"I remember Emry's face clearly," Baslyn said.

All of a sudden, something began to shimmer inside the stillness of the glass. It was an image, a picture…but not just any picture. It was a face.

Chapter 33

The Farfield Curse

The face was of a woman. She looked both hard and soft at the same time, like a young person who had been forced to be an adult. She had long, black hair and traces of makeup around her eyes. Her skin was slightly pale, though not like Baslyn's; it made her look alive before Bran's eyes, almost as if he could reach forward and touch her. She was beautiful, with a slight smile on her lips—the type of person he could go on looking at for hours. She had a way of capturing his eyes and holding them, where he couldn't break his gaze for a moment, even with Baslyn watching him. There was a thin white streak through her hair, long and complete. Her expression was so confident that it radiated from her face, as if she had the power to do anything she wished to anyone. And as Bran looked into her eyes, he saw that they looked exactly like his own, so similar they instantly told him who this woman was.

My mother.

Suddenly, Baslyn pulled the wand from the glass, and the image shriveled up.

Bran jumped. "Bring it back!" he demanded.

"I shall not," Baslyn said calmly.

"Put it back!" Bran shouted, jumping to his feet in rage. Baslyn put his fingers together, very still, and he looked up at Bran through the edges of his eyelids.

"I am a Drimra," he said. "Illian magic in my wand is limited. I will not waste it on you."

"You are evil," Bran spat.

"Am I so evil I refuse drink to my prisoners?" Baslyn asked.

"You do it only to keep me alive," Bran hissed. "You need me."

"And do I?"

"Yes. You know the powers I have. You know I can do what my mother did."

Baslyn was silent.

Bran looked away, closing his eyes and remembering the face. "But I won't," he said. "Her magic was held to darkness, but I am free from the curse. I am not held to do only evil."

Baslyn nodded slowly in contemplation. "Your mother was held by a curse—and with it, she created a curse."

He began to slide his wand toward the glass again, and Bran quickly turned to look. *Was he going to show her again?* He leaned forward with anticipation, and he heard the glass ring again as the wand touched it. An image shimmered, deep in the water, and came into view—but instead of his mother's face, he saw something else.

In the middle of the glass was the image of a long room, the view moving across it slowly. It was a warehouse, so long and far in all directions that Bran couldn't see the end. But what he saw inside was chilling.

There were rows upon rows of white cots, filling the entire floor of the warehouse and stacked one upon the other in towers up to the ceiling. At first, Bran couldn't see well enough to discern what the cots held, but as soon as his eyes focused on them, he saw that there were people in them, still and motionless, as if dead. But the people in these beds were not what he had expected, for lying one to each cot were thousands and thousands of bald men.

They looked exactly the same as the two bald men Bran had already seen with Joris, their eyes closed and their arms by their sides. Their skin was pale and their faces expressionless, each one exactly the same as the one before.

"Behold," Baslyn said. "*The Farfield Curse.*"

Bran looked at him with wide eyes, the glow from the colors still playing upon his face.

"This," Baslyn said, "is the terrible thing which Adi could not tell you of, the terrible thing which *I* created. It is an army, hidden so far and so deep, the Council still hasn't found it."

Baslyn looked at the glass. "Those were the bodies—my part of the Curse, or as we preferred to call it, the *Project.* But it's deeper than just an army. Your mother added the second part."

The image in the glass shimmered. Now it showed another room, lit overhead by florescent lights. In this room, lining the walls, were rows of glass cages, stacked on both sides of the room. They were large enough for a person to stand up or lay down in, seven columns going down the hall and three rows up, so that they almost touched the ceiling.

Inside the cages were creatures, their bodies deformed and destroyed. They were all behind glass, one to a cage, some sleeping, some clawing at the walls, others seeming dead or eating like dogs from food dropped on the floor. Each creature was different, their clothing in tatters. They were thin, bones sticking out from their flesh. Some had large eyes, others had skin so loose it barely fit their skeletons.

Bran struggled to look away but couldn't tear his eyes from the glass, even as the image began to change, to move across the cages, to display the hideous creatures. It came to one, its skin white and its eyes deep gray with no pupils. The creature turned its head slowly, staring back at him, its teeth jagged and a hungry look on its twisted face, as if it wanted to consume Bran's flesh. The image shimmered and moved again, to the next cage.

Inside was a creature he felt he had seen before: it looked almost exactly like Shambles. Its skin sagged and its eyes were large and green, with fingernails like claws and a scarred face, but instead of having dark skin like Shambles, this creature's skin was gray, and it threw itself against the inside of the cage, screaming. Bran could hear no sound, but the shout seemed to leap into his soul, echoing in him. He jerked his gaze away.

"Don't show me anymore!" he said, struggling to catch his breath. He felt sweat on his forehead and his hands trembling.

"You must look," Baslyn said. "It is the work of your own mother."

"No," Bran said, trying to turn away, to deny it.

"You wanted the truth," Baslyn said, "so I am giving it to you. We brought these people in for her, kidnapped them right off the streets. All had to be mages. She finally got everything right: any mage in our way was instantly drained of their powers and made to feed my army. And thus we have come to the next part of the Curse: the spirits she called to the desert."

Bran remembered with a start what Astara had told him: what his mother had said as she died. The people in the desert, the gathering that had disappeared...

"She needed them to give my army intelligence, to shape them to be complete," Baslyn said. "She needed their minds, so she created the Curse, trapped the souls, and held them for my use."

Baslyn shrugged slightly.

"So I would form the bodies, and she would take one of the spirits and give it a mind. And then she would use one of the mages behind the glass to feed the body *magic.*"

Bran took a quick breath, trying to block Baslyn's words out.

"And that is it," Baslyn said. "An army of fully functional mages at my bidding, ready to bring down the Mages Council. But there was more."

Baslyn smiled slightly. "In the process of feeding magic to my armies, sadly it would drain the mages day after day, until there was nothing left but a pitiful skeleton of a body in a glass cage, feeding my armies with their power from far away. Thus, any mage who even tried to fight us would soon make my army more powerful. Once they were cursed, there would be no breaking free—and no mages left to oppose me."

"The secret..." Bran realized. "The Council kept it secret so people wouldn't turn on them."

"Every non-mage would certainly wish to destroy everything magic if they heard something like this was possible," Baslyn said. "They'd kill every mage in sight to keep themselves safe."

"But why was my mother in any of this?" Bran asked.

Baslyn stared deep into his eyes. "Like you," he finally said, "she also wanted to save the world, to make up for crimes she did not commit. She joined me because she wanted to change the Council. Adi would not tell you. No one would. But now, as always, I will tell you the truth." He slid his fingers across the table. "I wasn't always a criminal, as they might have led you to believe. In fact, I was rather well-known—a researcher, commissioned by the Council. I specialized in old documents and languages from magic history." His face turned slightly in grim memory. "When you get to be a famous mage—and a Drimra at that—you start to be invited to Council events. It was then that I came to realize just who I was working for." He shook his head. "A bunch of greedy, pleasure-seeking bureaucrats who hardly followed all the laws they made and were ready to assassinate anyone who crossed them."

"I don't believe it," Bran said.

"It doesn't matter," Baslyn hissed, turning on him with a sudden anger in his eyes. "It's true. Even your mother realized it, and thought she could change it. And that was our plan. We were so close. We could have taken the Council by storm, changed it into something better, but—" Baslyn lifted his head. "*—you* were born."

Bran could feel an underlying anger in Baslyn's words.

"Your mother changed after that," Baslyn said. "She wasn't the same, lost interest in the Project—practically threw away all the power we had worked so hard to get her."

He hit the desk, but with that, he caught himself, as if realizing that he had spoken too much. "Somehow the police found out," Baslyn went on. "It was mere days before our Project would be set. Your mother escaped, as did some of the others, and thus we are here, every piece still hidden in secret, still as alive as it was before, with only one thing standing in my way."

His eyes met with Bran's. "The power of Dormaysan."

He looked over Bran slowly. "As your friend Adi said, your mother's powers are within you now. Shouldn't it be right for you to follow her path, to finish the job for her?" He smiled slightly. "Maybe it would make her proud of you."

Bran could hardly believe the words he was hearing. He was smart enough to know what Baslyn was asking of him. He wanted him to be like his mother, to take her place and help him bring the Farfield Curse back.

Baslyn took a sip from the glass.

"But…I'm not a Dormaysan," Bran said slowly. "Adi said I'm free from the curse."

Baslyn turned his gaze away, as if he had heard something repulsive.

"It doesn't make any difference to me or your mother," Baslyn said. "If you're free from the curse, then so be it, but the powers are still alive within you."

"But I won't do it." Bran said strongly.

"Maybe you should think before you make your decision." Baslyn hissed.

"I've already thought," Bran hissed back. "I will not be a part of something that kidnaps people and locks them in cages to make an army to overrun the Council."

"So you would make the same mistake your mother did?" Baslyn asked. "Let your heart get in the way of what you should do—get in the way of what's right?"

"But it's *not* right," Bran said. "You killed people to make the Farfield Curse."

"It all ends up right in the end," Baslyn said. "A few must be sacrificed for the good of all."

Bran shook his head. "I don't care what happens or what my mother did. My loyalty is to those who are my friends, and their loyalty is to the Mages Council."

Baslyn slammed his fists onto the desk.

It made Bran jump, and Baslyn leapt to his feet, seething with anger.

"*The Mages Council!*" Baslyn burst. "What if I told you that the Mages Council has lied to everyone, even Adi, and they did *not* destroy the Project, but kept it, and hid it for their own use if ever they should need it?" He hit the desk again. "And what if I told you that I once followed the Mages Council, and was *used* by them in secret? And once they were through with me, my name was erased, and my research destroyed..." He bent closer. "What if I told you that someone very close to you is part of all of this, and that the research of the Farfield Curse itself was *started* by your accursed Mages Council?"

Bran hardly knew what to say, shocked at Baslyn's fury. Bran could do nothing but stare back at him, until finally Baslyn turned away.

"Believe what you wish," Baslyn said angrily. "But you're too smart of a boy to hide it from yourself. The Mages Council is but a fantasy, and all the good people who serve under it are nothing more than well-meaning pawns..."

He curled his fingers into fists. "...each doing what they think is right, but combined, working for an evil they struggle so hard to fight off."

"That can't be true," Bran said. "The Mages Council works for good."

"Do they?" Baslyn shot back. It took Bran by surprise how quickly he had responded.

"Do they really seem to work for good?" Baslyn asked again. "It seems to me your city still doesn't allow mages, gnomes are still being killed, and the world is at its deepest point of unrest." He raised his chin. "Seems like there's a slow, unseen war going on, Bran—a war between what is right, and what many mistakenly believe is right. How can you be sure that *you* are on the right side? How are you so sure *you* are not being deceived?" He lowered his voice even further, "It's a war, brewing and stirring right underneath our feet, ready to break at the slightest tipping of the scales. Can't you feel it?"

His voice sounded ominous, and what terrified Bran most was that Baslyn's voice seemed to hold no lie.

What does he know? Bran wondered.

"But you are just a child," Baslyn said, sliding away. "You do not realize how short life is."

He dropped his voice. "And you are not as valuable to me as you might believe."

With that, Baslyn reached for an intercom button on his desk.

"Bring her in," he said, and Bran heard the door open behind him. He stiffened and heard Astara struggling in the doorway. Marcus escorted her in, and Craig caught Bran by the shoulder. Baslyn arose, and Bran was roughly shoved to the other side where Baslyn had been sitting. He was forced down into a hard chair, and he felt another slammed to the back of his. He looked over his shoulder, and he saw Astara being pushed into it, her back to him.

"What's going on?" she whispered to Bran, as Joris stepped into the room. His face was grave though he said no words, and in his hands were two pairs of magecuffs.

"This," Baslyn said, "is called *creative disposal.*"

Joris clicked magecuffs over their wrists, binding them to the chairs though he didn't yet turn the power on.

"It's actually quite simple," Baslyn replied. "It's much like killing two birds with one stone. See, with all the time I have been kept here, we are sure to leave tracks behind, through which the police might find us."

Marcus had begun to carry in a set of small black boxes. He set them around the room, one near the corner, the next halfway, the next beside the desk, until he had gone all the way around and out into the hall. Baslyn watched him, then turned back to Bran.

"And, since you have refused every offer I have presented you," he went on, "you leave me with no choice but to cover up the tracks I may have left with *you* as well."

"You're going to kill us then," Astara said.

"It's war." Baslyn shrugged. "Some people die."

Marcus connected wires between the boxes. Baslyn gestured at them. "These boxes contain powerful explosives, not enough to bring the building down but quite sufficient to destroy this room and both of you, no matter how strong your powers are."

Bran pulled against the handcuffs, but they were tight and

unmoving, and his arms were pinned behind his back. Craig handed Baslyn his pistol and a remote.

"This is what will happen." Baslyn said. "First, I shall kill each of you myself. Then, I will press this remote."

He pointed to a larger box, to which the others were connected. "Once the button is pressed, there will be forty seconds for me to take the stairs down, and while everyone below is panicking, we will escape the city." He turned. "And this floor will be destroyed, leaving nothing behind to track us by."

His words were smooth, icy. Gone was the anger Bran had seen on his face; there was no emotion at all. Baslyn was through with him, and he was just finishing the job.

Baslyn looked to Joris. "Go ahead and turn them on. Then I will finish here."

Joris nodded, and he leaned toward the magecuffs. Bran heard a click as they were switched on, but for some reason, he felt no different than before. It was oddly disturbing, so much that when he lifted his wrists to turn them, the handcuffs almost felt as if they weighed less than he remembered from the van, though he dared not test it by pulling for magic. With one last glance in Bran's direction, Joris turned for the elevators.

When Bran heard the elevator doors slide together, the room seemed to become empty. He felt sweat beginning to form on his forehead as Baslyn stepped toward his desk.

"Look," Baslyn said, taking something out of a drawer. "I almost forgot: Adi's wand."

He dropped it to the floor. "How sad," he said with fake regret. "In the fire, her wand might never be found."

Bran felt anger boiling up inside. Baslyn began adjusting things on the pistol, and Bran forced himself to be very still, trying to clear his mind. He searched for any way to escape, any idea that might free them. He heard the clash of thunder, and rain began to beat down outside the windows on the stone porch.

"You know Bran, I am sorry it has to end this way," Baslyn said. "I had expected you to do things differently than your mother—to finish what she started." He shook his head. "So many questions left unanswered for you, so many things you have not yet discovered about yourself."

"I know enough," Bran said, trying to hold on to his courage, even when he heard the pistol clicking. He felt Astara's hands next to his, behind his back; they were cold and trembling. Baslyn seemed to be considering something, still clutching the pistol.

"I suppose there's one thing you should know before I kill you," he said. He lifted his chin.

"The reason Clarence never came to get you," he said, "is because Clarence is *Shambles.*"

Bran stiffened in the chair. *No. It couldn't be.*

But even as he denied it, he knew. He could remember Shambles on the roof, he could hear his voice in the back of his head, saying his mother's name—it came back to him in a rush. He could remember the horrible images of the creatures, locked in the cages.

"Yes," Baslyn hissed. "Clarence was his name, before he lost his mind, before we made him a host for the Project. It was your mother's idea to save his life. I thought we should have killed him early on, but for some reason she would hear none of it." He shook his head. "I don't know why she did it. All that was left was a maddened, torn scrap of a creature, completely out of his mind and hardly anything but a skeleton. She called him by his name, Clarence; Joris called him by the state his mind was left in." He gave a small, wicked laugh. "It was Shambles's idea of repayment to swear to save her life one day in return. A pity, since he never made it to Dunce—not even in time to see her die."

Bran pulled against the magecuffs, his arms shaking because his fists were held so tightly.

"When Emry ran," Baslyn went on, "Clarence disappeared as well, though Elspeth tells me Joris caught him. And not even his loyalty could stand up to their questioning."

"The bracelet," Bran remembered, trying to stall for time. "She held him prisoner with it!"

"More a pawn than a prisoner," Baslyn said. "The bracelet wasn't created by us. Your own mother made it for him as a gift. He wore it as a symbol of his promise to her. Elspeth only had to change its powers to speak within his mind."

Baslyn nodded. "Of course Elspeth could not leave to look for you. Every MIP in the world is looking for her. And though Shambles denied it for years, he knew where to look." Baslyn met Bran's gaze. "He wasn't the only one who knew where you were, either. Someone else did, and he knew the house."

All of a sudden, Bran saw something out of the corner of his eye: movement, outside of the doors. It was more of a shadow, sliding across the floor, so dark and quick that he barely noticed it. He heard a click and shifted his gaze back to Baslyn. He was readying the pistol.

"And since your mother couldn't, *I* shall free Clarence from his promise," Baslyn said. "Because once you are gone, there will be no more Hambrics for him to serve."

He began to lift the pistol, and Bran held his breath. He could see the end of it, aimed in his direction. The room seemed to go still, the silence invading Bran's mind as he looked at the gun, the bullet that was about to end his life. Bran stared into the blackness of the barrel.

"Good-bye, Bran," he heard Baslyn say, and Bran saw his finger move toward the trigger.

But all of a sudden, there was a sound at the door.

Chapter 34

The Battle on Farfield Tower

Baslyn spun around when he heard the scrape.

"What?" he hissed, his voice dripping with rage. "Why aren't you with the others?"

Bran saw someone in the doorway, crouched over and tense. For a moment, the figure met Bran's gaze, and Bran looked back, unable to say anything.

It was Shambles.

As Shambles looked at him, Bran saw something different in his eyes than what he had seen before. Behind them was something Bran hadn't expected—determination, as if his mind had been clouded, and in an instant had cleared, listening to the words that Baslyn had spoken. And suddenly, Shambles turned to Baslyn. There was a small knife in the creature's hand.

"Bassslyn..." he hissed, and in a flash of motion, he leapt.

Shambles's body slammed into Baslyn full force, taking him by surprise, knocking him to the floor. Bran heard Baslyn gasping, the sound of his fist slamming into Shambles's skin.

"Bran!" he heard Astara hiss. He tried to turn.

"Look," she said, "the magecuffs aren't working!"

"What?" he gasped, lifting his wrists, hearing Shambles and

Baslyn struggling on the floor. He pulled them against the chair but couldn't come free.

"Bran, they aren't *working,*" Astara said quickly. "I think they're missing their battery cells!"

Bran glanced toward Baslyn, but he could not see beyond the desk. He heard the struggle, Baslyn cursing at Shambles as they fought for control. Bran heard Baslyn attempting magic but Shambles bit him, breaking his concentration and causing Baslyn to shout in pain.

Bran bit his lip, fearing what pain would come if Astara was wrong, though knowing it was their only chance. He grabbed for the magic, and he was shocked to feel it come to his fingers, so that with hardly a thought he pulled at the handcuffs which bound his wrists, and he heard the metal ripping behind him. He gasped, and he heard the handcuffs clatter to the floor as Astara also ripped hers apart. The moment Bran was free, he leapt up.

"Bran!" Astara gasped, but he didn't have a second to react. He felt someone grab him, and suddenly he was facing Baslyn. Bran lost his balance, and Baslyn threw him forward with fury. Bran's back hit the windows, glass shattering behind him as his body broke through and outside.

Freezing air and rain slammed into him as he fell against the cold stone of the outcropping. He hit his head on it, blinking, the breath knocked out of him. He could hear cars and sirens, rain and thunder at once. He blinked his eyes open and squinted in the rain. Over him was the night sky, and all around him, shards of glass. The moon was gone, covered by black clouds.

In a second, Baslyn was over him, kicking Bran, pushing him backward, knocking the breath out of him once more. Bran winced with pain, but he was too dizzy to move. He had come to the edge of the porch, and for a moment he could see over, all the way to the streets and cars below. Everything shone in dazzling lights.

"Trying to escape?" Baslyn said, shouting to be heard over the wind. Rain drenched him, and crimson blood fell down the side of his white face. "No one can protect you now. Everyone you hate has defeated you." He laughed, an evil sound. "Who was it that came when you were lost in the rain? Who came to comfort you when Rosie left?" He stepped forward. "Was that not I?"

Bran didn't have the strength to respond. He saw Astara, framed in the broken windows. He was so weak he could hardly keep his eyes focused on her.

"How can you go on fighting when the world is against you, and everything you ever dreamed of is gone?" Baslyn said, spitting his words at Bran like knives. "How can you fall, weak and powerless, and still fight me?" His voice lowered and he stepped forward, until his feet were inches from Bran's flesh.

"How can you face your death," Baslyn said, "and still say you are right?"

Bran was silent. He could only lie there, still and trembling.

"Sit up," Baslyn hissed. Bran didn't move.

"*Sit up,*" Baslyn commanded again through his teeth, his voice harder, and Bran forced himself to move, to meet Baslyn's eyes. The rain poured down, soaking his clothes and his skin, washing across his face. Bran had to tilt his head back just to look up at Baslyn's face, so filled with evil it seemed to be made of it. Baslyn narrowed his eyes.

"Look at you," Baslyn said, raising his voice. "You have *failed.*"

He flung something at Bran, and it clattered across the stone, striking his leg. A quick flash of lightning through the blackened sky glimmered across its surface. It was his mother's necklace.

"Look at what it represents," Baslyn said. "Your mother's goodness, given up into a simple necklace, like those before her. And for what?"

Bran didn't have the will to fight Baslyn any longer. He slid his fingers forward and took the necklace into his hands. Baslyn sneered.

"She gave it up for powers that made her great." Baslyn said. "She cared for the powers more than anything else in the world. She was willing to ***kill*** for them."

As Bran touched the necklace and lifted it up, there was no feeling in it. It was dead against his fingers, like a candle that had melted its life away. Baslyn gave a small laugh. Bran was unable to move, staring down at the necklace, letting Baslyn's words bite at his soul.

"You always wanted to be like her," Baslyn said. "And so you are. Both of you failed."

Then, as if by grace, the skies above Bran stirred. The rain continued to fall, drenching every inch of him. But the clouds broke, so that almost instantly, the light of the moon came free of its bonds, whiteness falling upon the top of Farfield Tower.

For a moment, Bran saw nothing. But the next instant, something flared up before him, in his hands, like nothing he had seen before. The necklace was glowing, so much that in the same second, it threw light all across the roof, and they were blinded by it, causing Baslyn to cringe.

The pendant on the end of the string had leapt into a fiery white and silver. It was as if he held the very moon in his hands, glowing in his face, the warmth of it coursing through his palms, down his arms, and through his skin. And seared into the necklace with a fiery white, almost as if in a silent message, was the name.

Hambric.

Bran stared at it. In a moment he wasn't looking at the name anymore, but deep into its silvery surface, into its reflection, in which he saw someone looking at him. At first he was startled, for beyond the surface were the eyes of his mother, the same from the picture Baslyn had showed him. But the next second, he realized it wasn't his mother's eyes at all. It was his own reflection staring back.

Something seemed to move within him, the stirring of a memory. In a moment, he was no longer on the roof. He was back in Dunce, at the thirteenth house on Bolton Road, just like it had always been, before everything had happened.

He could smell it, feel it, almost instantly. He could hear the sound of the front door opening, of feet on the steps, of the wind through the crack in his bedroom window. As he looked on the necklace, he was suddenly back in the house he had called home for so long, never knowing his past, never knowing of magic or secrets. He felt as if it had all only been a moment ago, and his life had never changed.

And then he could hear something else familiar, playing in the back of his mind: a voice he had heard so many times, speaking to him, her words echoing in the back of his head.

"*But what type of person* are *you going to be, Bran?*" he

could hear Rosie say, her voice as clear as if she was next to him.

"Are you going to be ordinary like everyone else?" she said, and he could almost feel her voice like a presence against his skin.

"Will you just give up when things get hard? Let them force you to forget who you are? Or will you find the courage to make the choice—and be a hero?"

With those final words, it was as if a torch dipped in oil had caught flame within his soul, lighting him inside once more. The world that had stopped around him came back in a rush—the rain on his shoulders, the glow of the necklace, the rumble of the lightning—and again, Baslyn was before him.

"You're wrong, Baslyn," Bran managed to whisper, shaking though energy came back to his muscles. Baslyn's eyes opened wide. Bran stopped, and in a second, everything dawned on him.

"This necklace represents what she gave up," Bran realized, speaking louder. "It is what she wished she could have had back: the curse she wished she could have undone!"

Baslyn was held in place, though Bran could see he could not deny it. Something came behind Baslyn's eyes, so slight it was nearly impossible to see—an edge of panic. Bran lifted the necklace.

"My mother left this to remind me of who I am," he said. "This necklace is the echo of what goodness she once had, what she wished she could take back, but couldn't."

He lowered his voice. "In the end she gave up the Curse, and all her power, and all her life, and everything you offered her—" He narrowed his eyes on Baslyn, "—because she loved *me* more."

"Bran, look out!" Astara shouted from the window. Baslyn had readied his wand, and in a blur of motion, he swung it upward, launching a flash of blackness toward Bran. It came out like a net, a screaming sound like that of hundred snakes hissing, but Bran was ready, and he fell to the ground, rolling to the side. The blackness screamed in Bran's ear as it flew over, like the cry of death, a stench that immediately threatened to suffocate him.

Bran slid across the roof, falling again as the blackness came toward him like a ghostly specter, death in a cloud. He lifted his hands, throwing magic before him, shoving the shadow away. He hit it full force, and it flew outward like a thin silk blanket, folding in the middle, its scream deafening.

"Bran!" Astara shouted, and he spun. She was standing in the window, and in her hand was Adi's wand. She threw it toward him, and he didn't hesitate, holding his hand out, calling it, and it shot into his grip.

The moment it slid into his hand, it was as if he had extended his arm far beyond his reach, as if his abilities were suddenly heightened. It was like the powering up of a weapon in his palm, a stretching of every skill he had, further and more powerful than before. His didn't have a chance to hesitate in it. His senses called to him, and he followed their bidding, slinging the wand in front of him and letting the magic flow across his skin and into the wand.

Magic surged forward and a burst leapt in front of him. It came out as a giant blue wall, almost transparent like a shield of energy, the same as he had done before in the park. It appeared not a moment too soon, as a blast of magic like a blackened hand leapt from Baslyn's wand, nearly knocking Bran off his feet with sheer force. Bran held the shield, the fingers of the blackness stretching toward his heart to rip the life from him, the power of it causing sweat to run down Bran's forehead as he held it.

He shoved Baslyn's magic away, and it broke, the streak of it flying like a cloth through the sky. Baslyn paused, considering his next move, beginning to walk to the side. Bran kept up with him, keeping across the roof. There was no hiding the exertion on Baslyn's face from the magic.

"You don't stand a chance against a master of mortality." Baslyn hissed. "I should have killed you when you were a child."

"You would have killed yourself," Bran said. "If it wasn't for me, you'd already be dead."

Bran took another step, and Baslyn followed, wand at the ready, just like Bran's. Neither of them dared to reach for magic, slowly contemplating each other's weakness. Bran clutched the wand in his right hand, and in his left he held the necklace, almost feeling strength from it. He saw Astara out of the corner of his eye, poised and ready for the first chance she got. He didn't look up at her for fear that Baslyn would notice, but he instantly knew what she was going to do.

Bran started to walk faster, making Baslyn move with his back to Astara.

"You won't make it from here alive," Baslyn said.

"I might as well try," Bran said, not breaking his gaze, his every thought bent upon what he was doing. His mouth was dry, his fingers sweating against the wand. One more step. He saw Astara standing there, waiting for the right moment.

Then she yanked her hand back toward her, as if pulling on a rope, and Baslyn's foot was swept out from under him. He fell to the roof, but as he did, he slung his wand backward, rolling over. Astara hadn't been ready for it, and she screamed, her body picked up from the ground and slammed into the wall. She crumpled, but Bran didn't have a second to turn to her; he saw Baslyn fall and didn't waste his chance.

In a sudden motion, Bran swept his hands apart, pulling at every bit of magic he could grasp, sending it at Baslyn before he could get to his feet. It was so much Bran couldn't hold onto it, and the moment he let it loose, he felt it burst. Baslyn tried to stand, but the blast was too powerful—an invisible wave that threw him into the wall, the roof shaking underneath them.

Baslyn struggled to rise, but Bran dashed forward and snapped Adi's wand down, straight at Baslyn below him. Bran was breathing hard, magic flowing through his skin so freely his senses were ready for anything, but he stopped, seeing Baslyn there before him. It was as if everything had happened in that very instant, and it was just then that he realized where he was.

"Oh, Bran," Baslyn choked. He looked up, pain in his eyes but a dark smile on the edges of his lips. He was trying to crawl back, to gain his balance, shaken from his fall.

"Your first murder?" Baslyn said, his words tinged with fake regret.

Bran faltered, holding the wand still but hesitating with the final magic as he realized what he was about to do.

"My second death," Baslyn coughed, "and it's the first murder for you to commit."

Bran felt something icy sliding across his skin, as if in the rush of what was happening, he had lost what he was doing. Baslyn managed to smile.

"Don't worry," Baslyn whispered, "Even your mother found it hard at first..." Baslyn's gaze shifted downward. "...but the second murder will be easier."

Suddenly, Bran saw something flash in the corner of his eyes, a stab of light. In a second, his senses screamed to him; he jumped, sliding back, but it was already too late. Baslyn pushed up with a shout, bringing the end of his wand up and driving the jagged gem into Bran's side.

Bran choked, and in a second, everything stopped.

Bran's head was down, his eyes wide, the glimmer from the icy tip of Baslyn's wand on his face. Baslyn's head was inches from Bran's, his teeth together in fury and hate; and as Bran looked down, choking as he did, he saw the knife end of Baslyn's wand had pierced through his shirt, and staining its glowing surface was a soft line of red blood.

Bran stammered, unable to say anything, pain wracking his entire body and radiating from the wand. Time became so slow he could hear his own heartbeat in his ears. Baslyn seethed, holding the blade, steadying himself and ready to drive it further.

"It's the end," Baslyn hissed. "Just as I foretold."

All had stopped. Bran's eyes moved over Baslyn's shoulder, where he saw Astara beginning to stir from the rooftop.

"Die, Bran," Baslyn whispered close to his ear, "and with you, the last of the Hambrics."

Baslyn's hand moved to the end of the wand, his palm against it, to drive it through into Bran's heart, his teeth clenched together in furious hate. The world around Bran stopped as he saw Astara slowly coming to. They would both die here.

Then, as if his mind had found a tiny, last drop of strength hidden deep within him, he felt something rising through his hands, as if magic were comforting his final moments. There was hardly an inch of it, but it was sudden and quick, and it was all he needed.

Bran looked to Baslyn, just as he clenched his teeth to drive the wand further. And then Bran lifted his hand, and with it, gripped the end of the wand.

"Not yet," Bran said with all the voice he could muster, and he felt his fingers tighten against the metal of Baslyn's wand, and his mind seize magic once more.

It happened in a flash: the rush, the power that came to him, just as before, just as with Adi's wand. It was as if a gate had been broken, the connection of Bran's magic through Baslyn's wand, coursing from where the knife edge pierced through his skin. It carried like a current through the wand, connecting to Baslyn's hands solidly gripping the other end.

"*Eclectri…firinge…*" Bran gasped, hardly able to breathe, using the first and only defense that came to him, the magic he had done at Adi's house. But it was enough.

It came as a sudden burst, for though Bran was weakened by the pain from the wound, the connection was strong through him, the powers coursing out before Baslyn had a chance to block it. And even more powerful than the magic had been before, the blue lightning crackled like a thousand headlights, bursting forth like flame, splitting and diving across the metal, striking Baslyn fully in the chest.

Baslyn cried out as the beam struck against his body, crackling through it like electricity. His hands gripped the wand, fighting to regain the power, to launch it back at Bran, but it was already too late. Baslyn screamed as the energy crawled up his body, gathering around him, swirling through his skin, moving faster, growing louder. The noise grew stronger and stronger, screaming like a jet, burning as Bran felt the blade still underneath his skin.

And then, Baslyn cried out once more, and something within him released with a giant roar. It came out in a wave, colored in blacks and purples, rushing in all directions from the center of the wand. The force of it threw Bran and Baslyn apart, the blade flying from the cut in Bran's chest, his fingers scraping across the rooftop as the power pushed at him like a tempest.

Bran shouted, though he couldn't hear his own voice over the sound of the rushing power. He dug his fingers into the thin roof ledge, but they did nothing against the onslaught, and he felt his knees go over the edge, and he shouted as he felt himself begin to fall…

Suddenly, a hand caught with his.

He looked up. It was Astara.

"Hold on, Bran!" she shouted. She pulled at his arm, his body hitting against the rooftop, a splash of rainwater going around him as his fingers touched with the solid stone again. And in a moment, all was still.

Chapter 35

Clarence

The rain beat against Bran's back as he fell onto the roof, struggling to breathe, and Astara fell next to him, holding him up. He felt his hand become wet with his own blood. But he was alive, and in the grip of his other hand, he felt the necklace. The way he held it caused the side to catch the moonlight once more. The name Hambric glowed with such brilliance it was a spotlight, a beam into the night that seemed to spell victory.

"You almost died!" Astara said, and she held him tightly, and he didn't let go. Water from the rain fell into his eyes, and he saw the body of Baslyn, lying motionless, all power gone. His wand was lying next to him, and he did not move.

"Is he dead?" Bran said, rising weakly to his feet. He looked down at Baslyn's body. Blood was gathering next to it on the rooftop. Bran could only stare at it and hold the wound in his chest, bloodying his shirt, but the cut of it never deep enough to kill him.

"Shambles saved us..." Astara gasped.

"Shambles!" Bran said in a low voice, and he dashed for the broken window. Astara was a step behind him, and Bran saw Shambles's body in the middle of the office floor. For a moment,

Bran thought he was dead, but when he came in, Shambles moved his arm.

"You're still alive!" Bran burst, rushing to his side. Blood stained Shambles's skin, and as Bran moved him, his eyes looked blank and empty, just a hint of life left behind them.

"Hambric..." Shambles hissed in a low voice, rasping with what little strength he had left. Bran tried to lift him, but as he looked into his eyes, he saw that Shambles had been weeping.

"I have failed..." Shambles whispered. Bran stopped, aghast. He looked at Shambles's twisted face, and all of a sudden, every bit of fear that Bran had once had for Shambles disappeared, and in that same instant was replaced with shame for every inch of his tortured body and mind. It came as a rush upon Bran as he realized it, looking at Shambles crying into his hands.

"No, Shambles," Bran said, his voice filled with disbelief. "You came back to save us."

Slowly Shambles looked into Bran's eyes, and Bran saw they were glimmering with tears. Bran touched Shambles's shoulder to help him up, his skin like sandpaper.

"We've got to leave before Elspeth and the men come back," Bran pleaded. But Shambles only shook his head, and he nodded forward, almost as if he wasn't going to speak. But then, slowly, he reached into the folds of his rags, and he pulled his closed fist out.

"Look," he hissed, opening his shaking hand. Inside was the note with Bran's name, just the same as before, with the tear along the bottom and the handwriting from his mother.

"You still have it," Bran said with shock, and Shambles nodded, then he reached into his rags again, and pulled something else out. It was the second slip of paper, from Mr. Swinehic. Bran looked at both of them, and opened his mouth to speak, but stopped, for Shambles had slipped his hand away once more. Very slowly, he pulled what was in his hand toward the first two slips of paper, trembling as he did, and Bran looked at what he was holding.

It was another scrap of paper, crinkled and dirty, with writing. As Shambles moved it toward the others, Bran realized what it was. It was the third piece of the note.

"It wasss with me, and it tore when we fell at the houssse..." Shambles hissed slowly, showing Bran the bottom pieces. Bran looked close at it, the pieces together like a small puzzle in Shambles's hand. And he read the page, all three parts now put together.

Bran Hambric, born June 17
To: Clarence
Meet me at midnight in Dunce to pick up Bran. Since I cannot save him, you must do it for me; and in return your promise will have been kept, for saving the life of a Hambric I value more than my own.

Emry Hambric

And above the last name of his mother was scrawled the simple shape of a moon, the same shape of his necklace as if it was part of her signature.

"Ssshe gave it to me," Shambles said. "It was her promissse, if I would protect you."

He pointed to the pieces. "Ssshe wrote the letter, then tore my name off the top after, just in cassse they read it. And when you ran into me, it ripped the sssecond piece in half."

Shambles bent forward. "And when ssshe left you, she mussst have written your name on the piece, becaussse it was all ssshe had."

Shambles shook his head, coughing.

Bran saw something on his wrist: the bracelet with the green stone, still glowing, silently torturing Shambles's mind.

"Quick, the knife!" Bran said, and Astara grabbed it from the floor. With one slice, Bran tore the bracelet from his wrist. Shambles took a sudden breath, and in a second the cloud behind his eyes seemed to subside. His gaze slowly came to focus, and it rested upon something in Bran's fist. Shambles reached toward it.

"The necklace..." Shambles said, and he touched it. The second his finger rubbed against it, Bran saw something come into his eyes, as if finally he had awakened from a long sleep.

"It was hersss," Shambles said, "before ssshe left."

Shambles caressed the edges of it, his rough fingers brushing against the soft beauty of the pendant, his broken and cracked claws sliding against the smooth surface. The muscles on his shoulders tightened, and strength seemed to return to his soul.

"Let usss leave thisss place," Shambles hissed.

But suddenly, a shadow fell on them all. Bran looked up to the windows, and outlined in the light of the moon was the shape of a man. Bran and Astara froze.

"A Drimra is not easily killed," he heard Baslyn choke. Baslyn moved his hand, and in an instant, Bran saw what he was holding. He didn't have a chance to move before he heard a click, and then a beep from each of the explosives. Baslyn dropped the remote.

"Forty seconds," Baslyn seethed. "No one goes through that door.

Shambles was suddenly stumbling to his feet. Baslyn clenched his teeth when he saw him, but in his weakness lost his balance, falling to the floor as pain overtook his body. He fumbled with the pistol, but before Bran could react, Astara jerked Adi's wand out. Baslyn let out a shot, but Astara swung the wand to the side, the bullet torn in half and slamming into a shelf of glass cups, shattering them everywhere. They dove behind the desk, and Bran heard the timer beep.

"How do we get out of here?" Bran shouted, hearing another shot over their heads.

"The stairsss!" Shambles hissed, grabbing their arms and lunging toward the door. Baslyn picked himself up, shooting as they came from behind the desk, but too weak to aim. He stumbled forward to catch them, and the timer gave a beep: *twenty seconds!*

They burst through the doors, running toward the hall on the end. It was open, and Bran heard Baslyn behind them in an instant. He shot again, spraying plaster from the wall.

"Thisss way!" Shambles coughed, his voice filled with pain he could not mask as his steps became weaker. He stopped in the final doorway and pushed Bran forward, but Bran refused to leave him, pulling on Shamble's arm.

"The door's just ahead, hurry!" Bran shouted.

The creature struggled again to push him forward, but Bran managed to pull Shambles so that he leaned on his shoulder, and he could drag his weakening steps closer to the fire escape. He heard Baslyn behind them but could not look back.

He heard another shot, but only pulled harder on Shambles, drawing closer to the exit, with Astara helping on the other side. The creature was heavy and weak, but they struggled on. The timer beeped again, and finally he could see the door.

"Almost there!" Bran said. Seeing the door in sight seemed to give Shambles a burst of strength, because he was on his feet again, no longer using Bran as a support, but dragging him forward, faster, as the countdown reached ten seconds. They slammed into the wall beside it, and Shambles grabbed the handle, wrenching the metal door open.

"Quick!" he hissed, and before they could do anything, he pushed Astara through and Bran behind her. Shambles's move was so sudden Bran didn't have a chance to catch his balance, and he stumbled and fell as his feet hit the concrete steps, sliding and hitting his head at the bottom. He spun, dazed but ready to run down the steps, but when he looked up, Shambles was still standing in the doorway.

"Come on!" Bran shouted. But Shambles only stared at him silently.

Bran stopped.

He saw Baslyn, coming behind Shambles; he saw the rage, the hate in Baslyn's eyes, ready to kill them, ready to stop them from escaping, as the seconds on the timer counted down...

And suddenly, Bran knew what was happening.

"Don't do it," he whispered, but Shambles took a deep breath, and with one last, pained look, the creature smiled, with tears clouding his eyes and his form framed in the doorway. And then Shambles spun, slammed the door shut, and held it closed so Baslyn could not get through.

"Shambles!" Bran shouted, but in the same instant, the timer reached zero.

He opened his mouth, but nothing came out. All at once, the explosives went off, and Astara pulled him down the steps as a burst of fire erupted above them.

Joris was standing next to the van in front of Farfield Tower when suddenly there was a shattering explosion that shook the ground beneath his feet. He placed his hand against the van for balance, screams coming from people and alarms going off. He looked up and saw flames blasting out the windows on the top floor, shrapnel flying through the air.

"The deal *has* changed, Baslyn," Joris said lowly, and in his hands, he clutched battery cells for two pairs of magecuffs. Elspeth saw it, though showed no remorse.

"So he was a fool after all," she said.

Then, Joris heard something hit the ground, and he turned and saw that one of the bald men had fallen to the pavement. His face had gone a deathly white. The second bald man collapsed next to the first, the blood seeming to drain from his skin.

"Baslyn is dead," Elspeth said to Joris. "Shambles died with him."

"And so it ends," Joris said, taking a step away.

The bald men were motionless, their eyes staring straight into the night sky. As Joris stared, it was as if decay invaded the bodies, so that the bald men suddenly began to crumble, until their bones were all that were left…and within a minute, nothing but their coats and wands. Elspeth lifted her gaze, her face showing no emotion.

"It's not over yet," she said.

She turned for the van.

"We are leaving this place," she said. "There has been a change of plans."

He heard her slam the door to the van but couldn't bring himself to leave yet, and so he stood there, staring at the fires and watching them burn.

As Astara pulled Bran down the stairs, everything seemed to be a blur around him. He felt his feet moving down the steps, hitting against each one, the small bulbs over his head lighting the way as they rushed down each floor. He was breathing heavily, his mind clouded, and when they came to another level, Astara pulled him around the corner and down the next flight, until they finally came to the bottom and a thick metal door.

They burst through and stumbled into a crowd of people running by. Bran heard screams and shouts all around him. He fell against the wall, trying to catch his breath, holding the wound in his side. Police pushed past them into the stairway they had just come through.

"The whole top floor is gone!" someone shouted, rushing by. There were men and women all dressed up, looking very frightened, and police running through the front doors.

"Was anyone on that floor?" Bran heard a woman shout. She had a badge and was looking through the crowds of people. A police officer pulled on the woman's arm.

"Anyone who was on that floor is dead now," he said to her.

In an instant, Bran felt as if a final weight had been taken from his shoulders, and he was just noticing it for the first time. He felt as if he had lost something very close to him, something he had held to all his life, though removing it was like taking a thorn from his heart. It was as if the final imprint of Baslyn on his soul had been wiped away forever.

"Shambles..." Astara said, and her voice was filled with remorse. At first, he didn't know what to say. There were so many mixed emotions in his heart: so much joy, and yet, so much pain.

"He kept his promise," Bran finally said. "And now, he's finally free."

The word seemed to ring in Bran's ears: *free.* That was how he felt. That was the strange, elusive feeling that he suddenly recognized. For as he stood there, looking at Astara, he realized that somehow they had both survived. And now, Baslyn was gone.

Astara suddenly jumped forward and put her arms around his neck, holding him tightly. They had both come out alive, as impossible as it had seemed to be earlier. He held her, unable to do anything else. More firefighters pushed past, and Bran stared straight ahead to the glass doors of the building, his gaze going through the reflection of the room and outside.

He managed to catch a glimpse of a black van before it pulled away from the building. But the second it was gone, he saw the doors parting as someone stepped through. He gasped.

"Adi..." he whispered. She stepped through with her eyes wildly surveying the frenzied crowd, Polland just a step behind her with his wand already out. Adi's face was filled with fright, bruised and messy and beaten, but the moment she laid eyes on Bran, her gaze locked with his.

Bran just stood there. Everything around them seemed to fade at once. He could do nothing but stare at her from across the room. He saw the disbelief written on her face.

"You're alive," he whispered, and as Adi looked at him, he saw her smile with relief, and it was then he realized that it was all over.

Chapter 36

The Grave of Emry Hambric

Two days passed before Bran got the call from Adi, though he just barely managed to convince Sewey to drive him.

"My poor bank!" Sewey was still moaning. "All from those blasted gnome burglars. I should be there, not driving you anywhere!"

"Come on Sewey, I found your pocket watch," Bran said. "You at least owe me one drive."

"Hmmm..." Sewey said. Bran had even polished it after picking it up from Adi's house.

"Leaves me wondering exactly *how* it disappeared in the first place..." Sewey mused, but in the end he started for the Schweezer. Bran smiled; he, Polland, and the cotch were the only ones who knew the truth.

They drove across town, and when Bran saw Helter Lane and Jackston Road coming up, he reached for the string around his neck. He could feel the necklace under his shirt, touching his skin, and still felt where Baslyn had struck him with the wand. The cut had already almost healed, leaving hardly any mark behind, almost like a symbol of Baslyn's power fading away.

"Park there," he said, pointing ahead at a car sitting on the side of the road.

"Well, look at that!" Sewey said. "That car looks just like Adi's, but she's been on vacation."

His brow furrowed. "And what rot! She didn't even ask before leaving!"

At just that moment, Adi opened the door of the car and stepped out. She had done well in covering the bruises from Joris's gun, but simply seeing her nearly sent Sewey into fits.

"Great goodness…it *is* Adi!" he gasped. He was watching her so intently he nearly ran into her car. Bran slid out and saw Astara pulling a lumpy package from Adi's backseat. He had to keep from smiling at its obvious shape of Polland hardened into stone and wrapped in paper.

"Adi Copplestone!" Sewey straightened his suit. "It is most unprofessional to take leave from work without first informing those who are in charge—namely *me.* For uncountable days I've slaved to find what twelve times twenty is, and I didn't have an assistant to figure it out for me!"

Adi merely stood there, looking at him with a smile on her face. She offered no explanation, but then she reached out, took his hand, and gave it a good, strong shake.

"Two hundred and forty, Mr. Wilomas," she said. "And a very good Banker's Assistant Holiday to you as well."

She then lifted Sewey's hand, and in it she placed a single, used bullet shell.

"I brought you a souvenir," she told him, with a glance at Astara. When the fires at the bookstore had been put out, and they had gone to salvage Astara's things, they had found it on the floor next to where Adi had been: the bullet stopped by Astara, saving Adi's life.

Sewey blinked at the bullet, aghast with wide eyes. "Banker's Assistant Holiday?"

He was thoroughly startled. Finally he spluttered, coughed, and spun on his heels.

"Bah!" he said to Bran, and he climbed into the car and closed the door, and just sat there. Bran was still, but Astara came to him.

"Come on, Bran," she said, and he followed her. It was warm and quiet, and as Bran walked, he heard the leaves crackling underneath his feet. When they were deep in the woods, Astara unwrapped Polland, who came tumbling out and was back to normal in a flash, coughing for breath. He brushed himself off and hastily drew the hood of his jacket over the top of his hatless head. He was being extra careful that day.

"You look so much shorter without your…" Bran said, intentionally letting his voice trail off.

"*Harumph,*" Polland huffed. The whole forest smelled alive: so different from last time. When they reached the headstone, he bent in front of it and read the words to himself. Sunlight shone through a crack in the trees, casting shadows on the etchings. Everything was still.

"I'm ready," he said, and Astara handed him a small garden shovel. Bran dug a hole a few inches deep in front of the stone, then took the three parts of his mother's letter from his pocket.

"*…and in return your promise will have been kept, for saving the life of a Hambric I value more than my own,*" Bran read the end, coming to his mother's name at the bottom.

"You kept your promise, Shambles," Bran whispered.

Polland handed him a pen. Very slowly, Bran moved it across the bottom of the page, signing his name next to his mother's. When he finished, he paused, and as an afterthought, he moved the pen again, adding the small shape of a moon right above his name, just as his mother had done. Then he folded the three pieces up, dropped them into the hole, and quietly covered them up.

"It is finished," Bran said quietly, and Adi put her arm around his shoulders.

"You are very brave," she said, holding him tightly. "Your mother loved you enough to leave the Farfield Curse unfinished, and anyone who can love so much to risk her own life could never have been evil to the end."

"No, she couldn't have," Bran said. He touched the necklace. It felt warm again, as if the part of his mother that had been good was there to comfort his soul. He had told them everything—the only ones who knew the truth of his past, and what had happened with Baslyn.

"We've got a surprise for you," Adi said. Polland held out a package. Bran looked at it, then to Polland, taken aback. Polland insisted, so Bran took it.

"Well, open it!" Polland burst, and Bran tore it apart. Under the paper was a painting.

It was in most startling colors Bran had ever seen. In the picture was the chair, and Polland was sitting in it, his feet pushed against the armrests, and in front of him was the fireplace, the glow from it playing on his features. Behind him was the window, rain pouring outside and the cotch nailed to the wall beside it. Sitting next to Polland's chair was Bran. It was so real, he knew instantly what it was—a picture of when he had first come to Adi's house, the night when he had learned the truth about his past. He reached forward to touch it, and when he brushed his fingers against the chair, he could feel the softness of it, just as if he was there again.

"It's the Friendship Gift," Bran whispered. "Just like you promised."

Polland nodded proudly, and Bran looked up at him, then Adi, then Astara, unable to say a word. It was a Friendship Gift—and they were his friends.

Before he could thank them or say anything else, he heard a loud crunching sound, and they all froze. All of a sudden, Sewey tore through the brush, stumbling into the clearing.

"Bran!" he burst with exasperation. "Whatever is taking so—"

All of a sudden, his eyes fell on Polland, and he stopped with his mouth open.

"A beard?" Sewey said, blinking. "You look rather *small*..."

No one said a word. Bran looked to Adi, unsure of what to do.

"In fact," Sewey went on, narrowing his eyes, "one might even confuse you with a *gnome!*"

"What nerve!" Polland burst.

Sewey jumped with a terrified expression. "Eek!" he gasped, curling away. "It speaks!"

"Of course I speak!" Polland said, crossing his arms. "And what an assertion!" He hesitated, but then threw the hood of the jacket off to expose the top of his head. "Look there!" he said. "No hat!"

"Goodness, you're right!" Sewey said with horror. "That's the baldest head I've ever seen!"

Polland went red, and Sewey spluttered.

"In all my life, I have *never* seen a balder head!" Sewey gasped. "My goodness, two hundred and forty apologies about the gnome business, small, bald sir!"

"Apology accepted," Polland said, and he hesitated, but then reached his hand out.

"My *name* is Polland," he said, and Sewey looked at the hand, stretched up in his face. He twisted his mouth around curiously, but finally reached out and shook it.

"Mr. Wilomas," Sewey said, giving it a good strong shake, and Bran realized that Sewey had broken his rule: he had shaken hands with a gnome, without even knowing it. They all looked at each other, and suddenly started laughing simply because they couldn't hold it in. For the first time in a long while, Bran's soul was happy once more.

Sewey twisted his face up, looking at them as if they were insane.

"Well then," he said. "Now that this ridiculous trip is over, it's time to go home."

Bran told everyone good-bye, and as the car drove off, he saw his friends waving back at him.

When he and Sewey arrived home, the sun had cast a golden glow all across Bolton Road. Mabel and the children were out shopping. Needless to say, there was no Megamus Maximus and no elephant, though Mabel had a great deal of new medicine bottles, and cabinets lining the walls to store them. Sewey made a beeline for his office. Bran went up to the attic and hung the Friendship Gift over his bed; it looked as if it had been meant for that place all the time, right next to the picture of him and Rosie.

"Good thing it's all over," Bran said to himself, sitting on his bed. Fatigue from all that had happened was finally beginning to set in. He was looking forward to some much-needed rest.

He was settling down when suddenly Sewey shouted for him to come downstairs—so he did, as much as it irked him. When he got to the landing, he was shocked to see that Sewey had changed clothes. Now, he was dressed up in camouflage pants and a vest, with a dark hat on his head and a fishing pole with no string in his hand.

"What the rot are you doing upstairs?" Sewey griped. "We have serious business to attend to."

"More?" Bran said with dismay. "Haven't we had enough of that?"

"Hardly," Sewey nodded solemnly. "I've realized that since Rosie's gone, and I've got my inheritance, and gnome burglars are burning the bank down, there's only one thing left to do."

He tapped the pole on the floor. "We're are off gnome-hunting before my fortnight is over."

Bran couldn't think of anything to say. Sewey still didn't get it.

"But wait," Sewey said, narrowing his eyes with a sudden, puzzled expression. "You don't think they've skipped town, do you?"

Bran was aghast, but then, a smile crossed his face as he looked at Sewey's ridiculous costume. He didn't say anything, but simply turned around and went back up to his room, leaving a very befuddled Sewey Wilomas behind.

Epilogue

The judge pounded his gavel, and Mr. Rat awoke from his sleep. He looked about groggily. Everyone in the courtroom was staring at him, and the judge cleared his throat.

"As I was saying!" the judge barked. "You have been charged with multiple counts of attempt to sell magic objects, as well as indecency in public: namely, your attempt to sell these magic papers at our city's own Twoo's Day celebration! And you have pled not guilty." He gave a snort. "Now that the city's prosecutors have spent the last eight hours proving your ultimate guilt, we will give you five minutes to convince us otherwise, or hopefully confess so we can get to our dinners."

The judge picked up a plastic bag that was next to him, in which were two pens and a stack of papers. He sniffed them and then held the bag out with disgust.

"You can start by explaining where you got these hideous, blasphemous objects!" the judge said, and he quickly handed them to an officer. He reached for some disinfectant and washed his hands with it, then graced the air with some Mage-Be-Gone spray. That finished, he looked down at Mr. Rat with strong eyes—so deeply that Mr. Rat felt as if he might melt under them.

"Well?" the judge growled. "We're *waiting*..."

Mr. Rat gulped and looked about the room, his shackles and chains rattling as he moved. All around him were faces, and each held stony contempt. They practically wanted to eat him alive.

"Please officers, judge, jury!" Mr. Rat began, trembling. "I found those in someone's house!"

The judge choked. "You mean you *took* these items from the house of *another* Duncelander?"

Mr. Rat's head bobbed up and down. "That I did! Came to the house, slipped through the doggy door, took some silverware, then I heard a noise...so I ran upstairs."

"What sort of noise?" the judge asked.

"A...a noise like a very tiny man, walking down the hall," Mr. Rat stammered.

"Like a gnome?" the judge pressed.

Mr. Rat's head bobbed again. "Right it was, sir!" he said. He put his hands out. "So I run up the stairs, see, down the hall, through the door, into the office," he said quickly. "I was scared for me life, I was, and I tried hiding behind the desk."

"Desk?" the judge said.

Mr. Rat nodded. "I was leaning against the wall," he said, "and all of a sudden, it gave a lurch! The bookshelf moved, so I pulled, and there it was: a door to a stairway!"

"Stairway?" the judge echoed.

"Right, sir," Mr. Rat said. "So I runs into the room beyond, then I hears the noise, the little man, coming behind me. So I says to meself, 'I can't break into this house for nothing!' so I took some papers off the desk, and some pens next to it, and slid out the window by the drainpipe."

The judge stared at him. Mr. Rat stared back.

"You...did all this," the judge said, blinking, "and then you slid down the drainpipe?"

"Yes, sir, that's what," Mr. Rat assured him. "'Twas not till later when I was addin' how much the two forks and spoon I'd taken from the kitchen was worth that I found what the papers did."

"Hmm..." the judge said. "So *you* didn't make the papers magic?"

"No, sir, I didn't!" Mr. Rat said assuredly. "But I know, I knows for sure who it was. Sure as day, I always know who owns the house before I break in."

"And who, pray tell," the judge waved his fingers, "did this house of the magic papers belong to?"

Mr. Rat swallowed. He looked about the room, and he could feel them all leaning forward, waiting to hear what he was about to say.

"It was..." he began, and he swallowed again. "It was *Adi Copplestone's* house!"

All of a sudden, the entire room burst out in a roar of laughter. The police, the audience, even Mr. Rat's own lawyer. The judge was laughing so hard, he started to pound his fist on the desk.

"That's the best one I've heard in years!" The judge chuckled. "Adi Copplestone! The most respectable woman in all of Dunce, a *mage!*" He took a deep breath. "Obviously, *you* are not a mage, but simply stupid: and in return for this rotten comedy, I hereby sentence you to a fortnight of community service, scrubbing the walls of the Dunce Sewer System!" He beat his gavel on the desk like a drum. "It is so ordered!" he said, and he stumbled away as the crowd continued to laugh.

Mr. Rat trembled and shook. Two officers approached him and something was shoved into his hands. He jerked his gaze down to see what they had given him.

In one hand was a bucket of soapy water. In the other, a sponge.

"Oh, no..." he moaned, but the officers gave a tug on his arm, and Mr. Rat was hauled from the courtroom.

hambric

Acknowledgments

In writing this book, many people have helped tremendously, and without each of them it would never have been possible.

Dad: still the Great Idea Giver.

Mom: for forcing me to write one page a week when I was nine, in spite of my protests.

Jaden, Maddi, Blaise, and Avery: for being the first to read any of it, and for not disowning me when I took Mrs. Tubtom out.

Carol Teltschick-Fall: for actually suffering through editing my first drafts, again and again and again.

Brendan Forsling: for ripping my story to bits so we could sew it back together without any holes.

Sarah Brown, Catherine and Anna Biewer, Mr. and Mrs. Forsling, and everyone else who read the endless stream of drafts.

Rachul Gensburg, Becka Grapsy, and Lauren Suero: for being my pro-bono publicists, and my brains after one a.m.

Michael Gaudet: for helping polish my grungy rock of a story into something shiny.

Lyron Bennett: for believing in a new teenage writer and the story I had to tell.

Daniel Ehrenhaft and the Sourcebooks team: for all your hard work and dedication to making this book the best it could be.

And last but certainly not least, thanks to my agent, Richard Curtis: for making my dreams a reality.

About the Author

Kaleb Nation

On the third night of the third month of 2003, fourteen-year-old Kaleb Nation suddenly imagined a boy and a banker on a roof, waiting for a burglar to come. From that original idea was born the story of Bran Hambric, a novel that would take most of Kaleb's teenage years to write.

Aside from writing, Kaleb is a blogger and a former radio host. He turned twenty in 2008 and currently lives in Texas.

Visit Kaleb online at www.kalebnation.com.

About the Illustrator

Brandon Dorman

Brandon currently lives near Mt. Rainier with his wonderful wife, Emily, and their two boys. He loves to eat nachos, string cheese, and once ate a pig's eyeball. Since graduating from Brigham Young University-Idaho in 2005, Brandon has created over 400 illustrations for books and magazines. Please visit him at www.brandondorman.com.

VISIT
WWW.BRANHAMBRIC.COM
FOR CONTESTS, VIDEOS, DOWNLOADS,
AND MORE!
BRAN HAMBRIC
THE FARFIELD CURSE
"BRIMS WITH MYSTERY, MAGIC, AND FUN."
—D.J. MACHALE
KALEB NATION